KILLIGREW AND THE INCORRIGIBLES

Also by Jonathan Lunn

Killigrew R.N.
Killigrew and the Golden Dragon

KILLIGREW AND THE INCORRIGIBLES

Jonathan Lunn

headline

First published in Great Britain in 2002
by HEADLINE BOOK PUBLISHING

10 9 8 7 6 5 4 3 2 1

Cataloguing in Publication Data is available
from the British Library

ISBN 0 7472 7440 1

Typeset by Letterpart Ltd
Reigate, Surrey

Printed and bound in Great Britain by
Mackays of Chatham plc, Chatham, Kent

HEADLINE BOOK PUBLISHING
A division of Hodder Headline
338 Euston Road
London NW1 3BH

www.headline.co.uk
www.hodderheadline.com

For James Hale

ACKNOWLEDGEMENTS

I should like to round up the usual suspects who are guilty of aiding and abetting me in writing this book, namely: James Hale (fence), Sarah Keen and Yvonne Holland (accessories after the fact), and last but by no means least Alastair Wilson, for his patience in correcting my technical errors, from the obscure to the embarrassingly basic (once again, if you find any mistakes, I guarantee it's because I occasionally took liberties with strict historical accuracy for dramatic effect, rather than because he failed to set me straight).

I should also like to thank the following for providing inspiration: J. M. Barrie, Walter Brennan, Charles Dickens, Sidney Greenstreet, Robert Hughes, Thomas Keneally, Jan Lawrence, Granville Allen Mawer, Herman Melville, Liam Neeson, Diana Rigg, Jack Rosenthal, Dorothy Shineberg, Kevin Spacey and Donald Thomas.

Prologue

Norfolk Island, 1850

'Wyatt's out,' Solomon Lissak announced, joining his messmates at one of the tables in the lumber-yard, where the convicts ate their meals.

Robert Murdoch looked up from his bowl of salt beef and cornmeal. 'You're sure?' he asked, his face pale.

'Heard it from Speeler.' Lissak was somewhere in his sixties, an old lag with grizzled hair and precious few teeth left.

'Gammon,' snorted James Vickers. 'Wyatt's dead.'

'Says who?'

'Says Dick the Crow,' asserted Vickers. 'Anyhow, there's no way anyone could survive a week in the water pit, not even Ned Wyatt. Not after two hundred on the triangles. I heard he was half croaked when they put him in. If he's coming out, they're dragging him out dew-beaters first.'

'We'll see,' Lissak said dubiously, waiting for his turn with the cutlery.

There were nearly a thousand men at the tables in the lumber-yard, all of them dressed in the black and yellow 'magpie' fatigues of 'incorrigibles' – men who had proved themselves beyond redemption by repeatedly reoffending even after they had been transported to the Australias. For this they had been further sent to Norfolk Island, the most notorious penal colony in the world. During the day they were put to work at various tasks, labouring in the fields or building the new gaol. At noon they had one hour off for dinner, when they were herded into the lumber-yard and issued with one mess-kit – knife, fork, spoon and pannikin – between six men, forcing them to eat in rotation or use their fingers.

Black-uniformed guards armed with carbines patrolled the walls that surrounded the lumber-yard, keeping an eye out for trouble. When Lissak had first arrived on Norfolk Island six years earlier, the lumber-yard had been the domain of The Ring, and even the

1

guards had been afraid to enter it. A warder that treated a member of The Ring too brutally might be murdered; The Ring had plenty of members who preferred to guarantee themselves the death penalty by killing a warder than go on living in the hell of Norfolk Island, in spite of the few comforts membership could secure.

But things had changed in the three and a half years since John Price had taken over as commandant. When Major Childs had been in charge, The Ring had operated openly, so that the settlement had only been able to run with the tacit consent of the ringleader, Jacky-Jacky Westwood, as much commandant of the island as Childs had ever been. But things had got out of hand. The convicts mutinied and Price replaced Childs as commandant, punishing the ringleaders ruthlessly. The Ring had, to all intents and purposes, been crushed.

A few months later Ned Wyatt had arrived on the island, and slowly and surely started building his own ring. He had never raised it to the scale it had operated on under Childs – Price would never have allowed that – but Wyatt was cleverer than Jacky-Jacky had been and he worked more subtly. In some ways, his Ring was more dangerous than Jacky-Jacky's had ever been.

Solomon Lissak had never been a member. As a cracksman, he had only ever worked with a partner, never in a gang, and he had always loathed violence – to him, it was the mark of an amateur. You found a partner you could trust – trust with your life – and stuck with him through thick and thin. He had only once made the mistake of working with a gang; that was how he had got lagged in the first place. But he knew better than to cross The Ring, so he kept his head down, his mouth shut, and stayed out of trouble. That was the only way to stay alive on Norfolk Island. And the only way to stay sane was to dream of escape.

No, he told himself. *Not dream – plan*. Fools dreamed; those that wanted to get anywhere in life planned. And Lissak wanted to get off Norfolk Island. He was an old man now, with perhaps not many years left in him, but he wanted to be free again before he died. In the past he had escaped from just about every penal colony the Australias had to offer, but the police always seemed to catch up with him.

And Norfolk Island, by the very virtue of the fact it was an island, was a horse of another colour. He had a hundred and one plans for breaking out of the prisoners' barracks and getting on board a whaler, but how to stay undetected as a stowaway until the ship touched land again, perhaps weeks later? It could not be impossible – the word 'impossible' had no meaning in Lissak's vocabulary – but it would be very, very difficult.

So he drove himself mad by trying to stay sane with plans of escape; but in a place like Norfolk Island, madness had its uses. Wyatt was as mad as a hatter, and people feared him for it. Lunatics were unpredictable, and unpredictable people were frightening. That was why Lissak had cultivated a little insanity of his own. Or perhaps he had always been a little mad. Back in London, his young partner had always said he was crazy. 'As crazy as a fox,' Lissak had replied proudly.

'Foxes are cunning, not crazy.'

'Ain't I cunning too?' Lissak had demanded, and his young protégé had been forced to concede the point.

A startled exclamation from Vickers broke Lissak out of his reverie. 'Jesus Christ!'

Lissak looked up and saw the convict staring towards the entrance to the lumber-yard. He followed Vickers' gaze, and as he did so an awed hush fell on the convicts gathered there.

Ned Wyatt was being escorted into the lumber-yard by two guards. They flanked him on either side, but as soon as he was across the threshold he shrugged off their arms and took a couple of tottering steps forward. He was in his mid-thirties, haggard and emaciated like all the other convicts, but toughened by years of hard labour. His hair was flaming red, and a greasy beard only partially covered a powder-burn on his right cheek. He had the palest grey eyes Lissak had ever seen, the irises so light it was hard to tell where they ended and the white of his eyes began.

Wyatt wore thirty-six-pound irons – as if those could keep him out of trouble – and brand-new fatigues. Presumably the clothes he had been wearing when he had been put into the water pit a week earlier were no longer fit to be worn, not even by one of the forgotten incorrigibles of Norfolk Island.

The water pit was just that – an oubliette waist-deep in brackish water in which convicts were lowered for days on end as a punishment. The theory was that a man in the water pit could not sleep for fear of drowning, but Lissak – who had so far managed to steer clear of it – had heard that there was a way you could wedge yourself into one corner to remain upright as you slept. As far as the commandant's punishment log – for the consumption of the comptroller-general of convicts in Hobart Town – was concerned, the water pit was no longer in use, but there were many ways of punishing convicts which were not officially in use yet were still common enough on Norfolk Island – and to these the latest commandant had added a few ideas of his own.

An awed silence hung over the lumber-yard as Wyatt stood there, swaying on his feet. He looked as if he might collapse at any moment, but then he lifted his head to reveal a triumphant expression on his face, and raised two clenched fists in a victorious gesture.

3

A roar of approbation went up from the other convicts, and then they began to stamp their feet, hammer their cutlery against the tables, or bang mugs against mess-kits, making a tremendous din.

'Stop that!' roared the superintendent, struggling to make himself heard above the pounding. 'Stop that noise at once, d'you hear? Stop it, I say!' He ordered one of the guards to take the names of every man present, but he might as well have saved his breath. On Norfolk Island even the slightest infraction of the rules could be punished by a 'scroby': an agonising thirty-six lashes of the cat-o'-nine-tails. But when so many men were openly defying the superintendent it was impossible to punish them all. Every day John Price thought of new ways to crush their spirit, but once again Ned Wyatt had proved to them that sometimes the human spirit could be unbreakable. The commandant and the convict had been on a collision course from the moment Wyatt had arrived on Norfolk Island, and even with all the warders, guards and the soldiers of the garrison at Price's disposal, Lissak was not convinced that the commandant was fated to win.

The pounding only died down when Wyatt crossed to where Lissak and the others sat and joined them at the table, and even then it did so slowly. Without waiting to be offered, Wyatt took the pannikin and spoon from Murdoch and proceeded to shovel corn-meal into his mouth while the other five members of the mess stared at him in astonishment. Only when he had polished off the last of the food, without regard for anyone who might still be waiting their turn to eat, did he look up at them.

'What's the matter, lads? Aren't you pleased to see me?'

'Course we are, Ned!' said Vickers, and there was general hand-clasping and back-slapping in which Lissak reluctantly joined. Known as 'Buzzing Bob' because he had been a pickpocket – called a 'buzz-cove' in thieves' cant – Murdoch remained where he sat, ashen-faced.

This was not lost on Wyatt. 'What's the matter, Bob?' he asked, grinning. 'You look like you've seen a ghost!'

'I . . . We'd heard you were dead!' stammered Murdoch.

'I wouldn't give that bastard Price the satisfaction!' sneered Wyatt.

'Any idea who peached on you, Ned?' asked Vickers.

Wyatt shrugged. 'One of Price's dogs, trying to avoid a scroby.'

One of the many ways Price maintained order on Norfolk Island was by maintaining a network of spies and informers, known amongst the convicts as his 'dogs'. Any dog who failed to keep Price supplied with information received a flogging, so they often made things up, getting innocent inmates punished rather than suffering a

4

scroby themselves. But it was a brave dog that had trumped up a charge against Ned Wyatt.

'We'll find him,' said Murdoch. 'Ain't that right, lads?' The others murmured their assent.

'Don't bother,' said Wyatt. 'Whoever it was, he ain't worth it.'

This prompted some raised eyebrows around the table. Ned Wyatt was not known for his forgiving nature.

'Don't you lads get it? That's exactly what Pricey wants us to do. Breed suspicion amongst us, keep us at one another's throats. Well, I'm damned if I'll play his bloody game.'

'But supposing whoever it was betrays our plans next time we try to make our lucky?' asked Vickers.

'You got an escape plan, Fingers?' asked Wyatt.

Vickers was known as 'Jemmy Fingers', not because he was light-fingered – in fact the crime he had been transported for was rape – but because he had a peculiar habit of sucking his fingers. Now he shook his head and sucked an index finger.

'We'll worry about that when the time comes, then. Whoever peached on me, I know none of you lads did it. If we keep our next plan to ourselves, there's no way anyone can betray us. Right, Bob?'

'Right, Ned,' stammered Murdoch.

Wyatt grinned. 'No need to look so scared, Bob. The past few days in the water pit gave me a lot of time to do some thinking. If you're afraid I'm still bearing a grudge over that fight we had about the baccy, forget it. I have. If we're all going to stay alive long enough to get out of here, we're going to have to stick together. These other bastards may cheer when they see me walking after a week in the water pit, but there's plenty of Price's dogs amongst 'em who'd sell their own mothers for a fadge. From now on it's just the four of us.' He held out his hand to Murdoch. 'Pals?'

Murdoch hesitated before taking Wyatt's hand. Lissak could not blame him: even after that heart-warming speech, he would not have put it past Wyatt to pin Murdoch's hand to the table with one hand while driving a knife into it with the other. But Wyatt just clasped Murdoch's hand – admittedly making him gasp with the strength of his grip – and clapped him on the shoulder. 'That's more like it.'

The bell rang then, signifying the end of the dinner hour, and the convicts had their irons inspected for signs of tampering before being escorted back to their assigned tasks. Lissak and his mess-mates did not have far to walk: that day they were assigned to the limekilns, on the sea-wall overlooking Sydney Bay. In the lagoon, the gaol-gang – three dozen of the worst convicts on the island – worked waist-deep in the wet quarry, under the supervision of a detachment of soldiers from the garrison, who watched them from the pier that jutted out into the lagoon. The breakers boomed monotonously against the reef, and beyond the wide blue Tasman Sea stretched some nine hundred miles to the east coast of Australia.

The coral quarried from the lagoon was put in the kilns and burned down to provide quicklime for the cement used for building the new gaol being constructed to replace the old one, where the gaol-gang were held at night. The latest load of lime had been cooked a week ago, and only now had it cooled sufficiently to be slaked in water. Lissak and his messmates were put to work raking the stones and ashes out from the side holes in the kilns. It was dangerous work, and they had to be careful of the clouds of dust that were kicked up: the quicklime burned, and if it got in your eyes it would blind you permanently.

They had been working for about half an hour when Wyatt turned to one of the two warders supervising them. 'Can I have a word, Mr Lang?'

Had any other inmate on Norfolk Island asked to 'have a word' with one of the warders when he was supposed to be working in silence, he would probably have earned himself a scroby for his impertinence. But Wyatt was not just any convict. The last warder who had marked him down for a flogging had been found dead a week later, expertly garrotted. Wyatt had had a cast-iron alibi, of course. Nowadays when Wyatt asked to 'have a word', warders generally listened.

Wyatt put down his shovel and crossed to speak to the two warders in a low voice. Judging from the expressions on their faces, they did not like what he had to say, but they nodded and turned away, disappearing around the side of the kilns.

'Where are they going?' Murdoch asked as Wyatt returned to join the others.

'I told 'em to take a break, smoke their pipes,' explained Wyatt, rubbing the powder-burn on his cheek with the heel of his palm. 'So we won't be disturbed for the next five minutes.'

Murdoch stared at him, and then turned to run. But Vickers had already stepped up behind him and held him fast. Powerless to move in his fellow convict's grip, Murdoch started to scream for help.

He was quickly silenced by a punch from Wyatt, and his head dropped down. 'Shut up!' Wyatt grabbed a fistful of Murdoch's hair and pulled his head back to look into his eyes. 'You stupid bugger. You know what hurts the most? It's the way you insult my intelligence. Did you really think I wouldn't find out you were the dog who peached on me to Pricey?'

Wyatt kicked Murdoch's legs out from beneath him, and Vickers

6

released him in the same instant so that the pickpocket crashed to the ground, cracking his head on the flagstones.

'Don't worry, Bob,' said Wyatt. 'I ain't going to croak you. Let's face it, dying is a release from this hell, and after that scroby you got me I don't feel like doing you any favours. But I can't let you go on spying for Price, can I?' Wyatt picked up his shovel once more, and scooped up some of the quicklime. 'Hold him, Fingers.'

Murdoch was dazed, but not so much that he could not realise what Wyatt intended. He tried to get up, but Vickers crouched over him and held his head down. His teeth bared in a savage grin, Wyatt deliberately tipped the quicklime from the shovel over Murdoch's eyes.

The agonised shriek that issued from Murdoch's lips sent a shudder down Lissak's spine. Vickers stood up and backed away, leaving the blinded pickpocket to thrash about, his body convulsing in agony. He tried to rub the quicklime out of his eyes; in his agony he had forgotten that only worked it in deeper. The only thing that might possibly have saved his sight then was to wash the lime out of his eyes with water. There were barrels of the stuff standing by for slaking the lime, but neither Lissak nor any of his messmates dared to risk Wyatt's wrath.

'It's a pity we couldn't see eye to eye,' said Wyatt. Vickers giggled hysterically.

Lissak felt sick.

The two guards came back at a run. When they saw Murdoch writhing on the ground and realised what Wyatt had done, they blanched.

'Jesus, Wyatt!' gasped one. 'You said you was just going to rough him up a bit. You never said nothing about—'

'Buzzing Bob's had a little accident,' Wyatt said with a smile. 'Ain't that right, lads?'

No one argued.

Murdoch had exhausted his breath now and his screams had died to a sobbing, the pain of his eyes doubtless diminished by the destruction of so many nerve-endings. Nevertheless, his earlier cries had been loud enough to have attracted the attention of the man who broke off one of his frequent rides about the settlement to come galloping up to the limekilns on his horse.

About six feet tall, bull-necked and bow-legged, his face burned brick red by the sub-tropical sun, he wore tight pantaloons and an old-fashioned bobtail coat, with a neckerchief of black silk tied sailor-style across his broad shoulders. Two six-barrelled revolving 'pepperbox' pistols were tucked in a broad-buckled leather belt six inches across. A small straw hat with a blue ribbon was balanced on top of his oiled, sandy hair, looking ludicrous above his large bullet-head.

7

Dressed in this eccentric manner, John Giles Price was a familiar figure to all the convicts on Norfolk Island. He jumped down from the saddle and faced both convicts and guards challengingly.

'What happened?'

'Bob had an accident,' offered Vickers.

'I wasn't asking you,' snapped Price. 'Take that man's name, Mr Lang. Thirty-six lashes. Now tell me what happened.'

'It's like he said, Mr Price,' said Lang. 'Murdoch had an accident.'

'We saw the whole thing,' added the other guard, and Lang nodded.

Price shook his head in disgust. 'I'll see you two later.' He crouched over Murdoch, holding him still. 'Who did this to you, lad?'

'Me eyes!' sobbed Murdoch. 'I'm blinded! Oh God, me eyes!'

Price slapped him, then grabbed him by the front of his jacket and shook him vigorously. 'Blow on who faked this, Bob.' Despite his aristocratic birth, Price was fluent in thieves' cant. Where he had learned it was anyone's guess, but it added to the impression that it was impossible to keep anything from him.

'It was Wyatt, wasn't it?' Price persisted as two more guards came running up to investigate the commotion. 'You don't have to voker anything: just nod. Tell me it was Wyatt, and I'll put him on the triangles and bung him such a scroby no one will ever need fear him again, granny me?'

'Accident,' Murdoch sobbed in a weak voice. 'It were an accident, I swear it!'

Price threw him down with an expression of disgust. 'Take him to the hospital lock-up,' he ordered two of the guards. Then he rounded on Wyatt. 'You don't waste time, I'll say that much for you.'

The convict regarded Price with contempt, but said nothing.

'You needn't smile, Wyatt. You might frighten your fellow inmates – you may even scare some of my men – but you don't frighten me. You think you're a regular pebble, eh? Well, I've broken iron men before now. Don't think you're any different. I'll break you, Wyatt. I'll break you like you were made of china. By the time I've finished with you, you'll lick my arse and like it. You'll beg me to kill you. But I'm not going to let you off as easily as that.' He turned to the guards. 'Put him back in the water pit. A few hours in there should soften his skin up nicely for his next flogging. Three hundred lashes.'

'Three hundred!' sneered Wyatt. 'Not worth taking my coat off for.'

'Five hundred, then. I'll take the flashness out of you, my joker! Take him away.'

8

As the guards led Wyatt away, Lissak shook his head. Three hundred lashes would have killed any normal man. Five hundred should have taken care of most of the toughest 'pebbles' amongst the inmates. But if Price thought it would break Ned Wyatt, he had another think coming.

I

The Good Samaritan

Lieutenant Kit Killigrew was awoken by someone knocking on the door to his cabin. He was sprawled on the bunk, his shirt drenched with sweat. It was evening: no light came through the tiny porthole.

Still half asleep, wakened from a nightmare, Killigrew slithered over the board at the side of the bunk, opened the locker below and took one of a brace of six-barrelled 'pepperbox' revolving pistols from its mahogany case. Crouching on the floor, he levelled the pistol at the door with a trembling hand.

'Who is it?'

'Strachan,' returned the sloop's assistant surgeon. 'May I come in?'

'One moment!' Awake now, realising that he had been dreaming of events that had happened over a year ago, Killigrew returned the pepperbox to its case, closed the locker, and stood up. He struck a match, applied the flame to the stub of a candle, and glanced around the cabin. A bottle of Irish whiskey, three-quarters empty, stood on the fold-down desk. He corked it and thrust it down the side of the mattress on the bunk, then checked his appearance in the mirror. He brushed his tousled black hair as best he could, but there was nothing he could do about the bags beneath his bloodshot brown eyes, and as for his unshaven jaw, well . . . that was one of the perils of having a swarthy complexion.

'Come in.'

The door opened and Strachan entered. He tried to peer over Killigrew's shoulder as if looking for evidence of the lieutenant's drinking – since the lieutenant was an inch shy of six feet in height, almost a head taller than the assistant surgeon, he was on a hiding to nothing – before he met Killigrew's gaze with the china-blue eyes that blinked owlishly behind his wire-framed spectacles.

'Is everything all right, Killigrew?'

'Of course. Why shouldn't it be?'

11

Strachan shrugged. 'I was just asking.'

'What can I do for you?'

'I'm just going ashore, to go to the theatre. I wondered if you wanted to come.'

Killigrew shook his head. 'No, thank you. I thought I'd get an early night.'

'It'll do you some good to go out for an evening. You spend far too many of your off-duty hours cooped up in this cabin. It's no' healthy.'

The lieutenant smiled wanly. 'Is that your medical opinion, Mr Strachan?'

'It's a piece of advice from a friend. Damn it, Killigrew. You've got to snap out of this . . . this *lethargy*. Come on. There's a production of *The Merchant of Venice* on at the Theatre Royal. You like Shakespeare, don't you?'

Killigrew sighed. 'I'll need to get permission from the Old Man.'

'He's already given—' began Strachan. He broke off and bit his lip.

The lieutenant nodded slowly as realisation dawned. 'Was it his suggestion you drag me out of my cabin?' he asked quietly.

'I was going to ask you anyhow,' Strachan replied defensively. 'It's not as if we've never gone to the theatre before. I seem to recall we used to go all the time, before . . .'

'Before Hong Kong, you mean?'

Strachan nodded. 'Look, if the Old Man told me to drag you along, I'm sure he did it with the best intentions. He's worried about you, Killigrew. We all are. These past few months . . . ye canna deny you've been off the fang.'

'Off the what?'

Strachan blushed. Usually there was little trace of his native Perthshire in his accent, but occasionally he would betray his origins with a Scottish turn of phrase. 'Out of sorts.'

Killigrew picked up the fob-watch that lay on his desk and glanced at the face. 'I haven't eaten yet.' Now he was just making excuses.

'The curtain doesn't go up until eight. We can dine at a chop-house ashore. Westlake tells me there's a place on Campbell Street where they do a first-rate toad-in-the-hole.'

'Very well,' Killigrew said wearily. It was all one to him if he could forget for a couple of hours by losing himself in a Shakespearean drama or by drinking himself into oblivion. 'Give me a quarter of an hour to get changed and I'll meet you up on deck.'

Strachan withdrew. Killigrew stripped off his sweat-soaked shirt, shaved, and scrubbed his face and hands at the washstand. He put on a clean shirt, waistcoat and his undress navy-blue frock coat.

12

Admiralty regulations demanded that any naval officer going ashore should wear his cocked hat, but the Admiralty was on the other side of the world, and Killigrew would feel self-conscious wearing a cocked hat in a chop-house, so he put on his peaked cap instead. He made his way up on deck.

It was eighteen months since the *Tisiphone* had set out from Portsmouth, stopping off at the ports and colonies of the British Empire to 'show the flag'. Eight score feet from stem to stern and thirty-two feet in the beam, the brig-rigged paddle-sloop was a relatively small ship, intended for inshore work rather than fleet actions. A single black funnel rose between her two masts, and her armament consisted of two thirty-two-pounders abaft the paddle-boxes and a sixty-eight-pounder pivot gun on the forecastle. Beneath her prow the figurehead – a representation of the snake-haired scourge of the damned after which she had been named – glowered over the dark waters where the lights from Hobart Town glittered in the night.

Only the men of the anchor watch were on deck; most of the starboard watch had been given permission for a run ashore, and were presumably engaged in their own pursuit of debauchery. Strachan was waiting, and the boatswain had ordered the ship's dinghy to be lowered to take the two officers ashore.

There were dozens of ships crammed in the harbour that evening: whaling ships for the most part, but there was a convict brig recently arrived from England in company with a couple of ship-loads of free emigrants, a sandalwood trader returned from a successful voyage to Shanghai via the New Hebrides, and a rakish, flush-decked topsail schooner of about a hundred and fifty tons. The last of these, the *Wanderer*, was said to belong to a millionaire who owned half of New South Wales; the fact that his yacht flew the white ensign – a privilege reserved amongst civilian vessels for members of the Royal Yacht Squadron – indicated that he was certainly a man of some influence, whoever he might be.

The dinghy's crew rowed the officers across to the quayside and left them there. Killigrew looked at the buildings on the waterfront. Some fine Georgian brownstone warehouses lined Salamanca Place off to their left, while Murray Street ahead of them was flanked by the customhouse and a large hotel. The streets were bustling, even at that time of night: shabby-genteel sheep farmers celebrating successful sales and purchases at the stockyard, whalers in oilskins making the most of a run ashore by staggering from tavern to whorehouse and back again, and prostitutes of every class, in last year's fashions from Paris, cruising for trade.

'Which way is Campbell Street?' asked Strachan.

'I've no idea. Let's ask.'

Killigrew was looking for someone who might be a native of the town – and it seemed to be a toss-up between a prostitute cruising for trade and a chain-gang of convicts in yellow fatigues decorated with broadcloth arrows, being escorted back to their barracks for the night – when a black lurched out of the crowd towards them, clutching his right arm in his left hand. Killigrew stepped aside to let the weaving black pass, but the man collapsed on the boardwalk outside the customhouse.

The other passers-by gave him a wide berth: just another Aborigine drunk on the streets of Hobart Town. It was fifteen years since the British had – with the kind of good intentions that paved the road to Hell for others – shipped the last of the Van Diemen's Land Aborigines to die on Flinders Island. But there were still one or two Aborigines on the streets of Hobart Town, and it was nothing unusual to see one fall down drunk in the gutter.

Killigrew was worldly-wise enough to know that when a man collapsed on the street right in front of him, it might very well be a diversion for an attempt to rob him. He glanced about them to make sure there were no unsavoury characters – something of which there was no shortage in Van Diemen's Land – loitering with intent in his immediate vicinity.

'We'd better see if we can help him,' he told Strachan. A man of radical political notions, Killigrew was keenly aware that as an officer of Her Majesty's Royal Navy, he was one of the bulwarks of the Empire that had allowed the Aborigines to die out. So it was a vague, liberal sense of guilt which motivated him; that and a healthy dose of good old-fashioned Christian charity – the kind that did good works for their own sake rather than to trump the neighbours in a holier-than-thou spirit. If he was a cynic, it was only because he had seen too many of the romantic ideals he cherished crushed underfoot by a cruel world.

A fellow humanitarian, Strachan did not need Killigrew's prompting to go to the black's aid, and he crouched to examine him. The unconscious black wore bell-bottomed trousers and a striped guernsey under a monkey jacket. Like most sailors he was bare-footed. But the quality of his clothes, while not exactly top-drawer, was certainly good enough to suggest he was not one of those impoverished Aboriginals one usually saw falling down drunk in the streets of Hobart Town and Sydney.

Strachan indicated the blood that soaked the black sailor's sleeve. 'Have you got a knife I can borrow?'

Killigrew handed Strachan his clasp knife and the assistant surgeon cut away the cloth. The lieutenant drew his breath in sharply when he saw a splinter of bone protruding from the sailor's forearm.

14

'A compound fracture,' Strachan said matter-of-factly. 'I don't think he did this falling down.'

'Can you do anything for him?'

'Aye. But first we have to get him off the street.'

'All right.' Killigrew glanced about and saw the Harbour View Hotel on the other side of the street. 'In there. You take his feet.'

'Mind his arm.'

As the two of them lifted the unconscious man between them, Killigrew saw another sailor hurry round the corner of the custom house. An American Indian, to judge from his copper-toned skin, aquiline nose and long, raven-black hair – probably from one of the Yankee whaling ships anchored in Sullivan's Cove. The sailor came to an abrupt halt when he saw the two naval officers carrying the unconscious man. Their eyes locked – Killigrew wondered if this was the man who had broken his burden's arm – and then the Indian turned and hurried back the way he had come.

'Jings!' gasped Strachan. He had his back to the custom house and had not seen the American Indian sailor. Killigrew did not want to worry him by mentioning it. 'He weighs a ton!'

They carried the unconscious man across to the hotel where the arrival of two naval officers carrying an unconscious black man caused something of a furore in the entrance hall. Killigrew forestalled any objections by using the crisp tones of command he usually reserved for the deck of the *Tisiphone*. He snapped his fingers – no easy feat in kid gloves – at a couple of flunkeys.

'You and you – carry this fellow up to a bedroom.' Although Killigrew belonged to the Upper Ten Thousand of Society, he probably ranked about nine thousand, nine hundred and ninety-ninth, and could hardly afford a room at the Harbour View Hotel on a naval lieutenant's income; but he would worry about that later.

The flunkeys gawped at him. One of them crossed to the open door behind the reception desk and called through it, 'Mr Palgrave?'

An officious-looking fellow with slickly oiled hair stepped into the doorway, and regarded the flunkey who had summoned him disdainfully before turning his attention to the unconscious man at Killigrew's feet. 'What on earth is going on here? This is a respectable hotel! Get that deuced jacky out of here at once!'

'This man is in urgent need of medical attention,' snapped Strachan.

'What's going on here?' demanded a new voice.

Everyone turned as a prosperous-looking gentleman descended the grandiose staircase. He was in his late fifties or early sixties, a splendid set of snow-white whiskers linking his sideburns via his upper lip as if to make amends for the shiny dome of his balding head. His girth was equally opulent, with a large gold watch chain stretched across the front of the white satin waistcoat beneath an exquisitely tailored brown kerseymere tailcoat. He held a fat cigar in one kid-gloved hand, and Killigrew was enough of a connoisseur of fine tobacco to know a Havana when he smelled it.

The oily hotelier converted from a disdainful snob into a fawning, obsequious minion at once. 'I do apologise for this, Mr Thorpe. I'll have these fellows removed from here at once.' He did not specify whether he was talking about the unconscious black or the two upstart naval officers.

'Indeed you shall. You'll have him removed to one of your finest rooms; and see to it that he gets the best medical attention Hobart Town has to offer. I'm sure I don't need to tell you that money is no object.'

The hotelier's jaw started to drop, but he recovered himself before it reached its fullest extent. 'Of course, Mr Thorpe. Right away.' He turned to the two flunkeys. 'You heard Mr Thorpe. See to it at once!'

'Handle him like china.' As the flunkeys lifted the injured man between them, Thorpe dropped a shiny crown piece into the pocket of one of them.

'Yes, *sir*!' Ministering angels of mercy could not have borne the injured man up the stairs more tenderly. Strachan went up after them, and Killigrew was about to follow, but the mysterious philanthropist laid an ebony cane across his chest to stop him.

'Wait one moment, sir. I crave your indulgence. That was a deuced Christian thing you and your companion did, bringing that poor fellow in here. I should like to shake you by the hand, sir.'

Killigrew had no objections. Beneath the kid gloves, Mr Thorpe's grip was firm and confident; a little too firm for Killigrew's liking, but it would have been churlish to massage his fingers afterwards, except by clasping his hands behind his back and doing so discreetly.

'We only did what any charitable Christian soul would have done, sir,' he replied, embarrassed by the praise.

'I wish I could agree with you, sir. But sadly, Christian charity is clearly in short supply in Hobart Town these days. I wonder if it would have occurred to me to stop and help that poor fellow had I come across him in the street? Had the Good Lord presented me with such a test, I fear I should have been found sadly wanting, without your shining example to show me the way. You shame us all, sir, you shame us all. I should be honoured to be acquainted with your name, young man.'

'Killigrew, sir. Lieutenant Christopher Killigrew, HMS *Tisiphone*.

16

And my friend is Mr Strachan, our assistant surgeon.'

'Thorpe's the name, sir. Thaddeus Thorpe. Tell me, Mr Killigrew, have you and your friend dined yet this evening?'

'No, sir. As it happens, we were just about to stop at a chop-house on our way to the theatre when we encountered that poor fellow and—'

'Chop-house be damned! Tonight you dine here at the Harbour View Hotel.' Thorpe turned to the hotelier. 'This young man and his companion dine at my expense. Treat him well, Palgrave.'

'Yes, sir.'

'Really, sir, there's no need,' protested Killigrew. 'We only did our duty.'

Thorpe was not having any of it. 'Poppycock, sir, poppycock. Enjoy your meal. I should be delighted to join you myself, but I've been invited to dine with Sir William Denison, and it doesn't do to turn down an invitation from the Lieutenant-Governor. Perhaps some other evening?'

'Only if you allow me to return the courtesy of extending an invitation to you to dine in the wardroom on board the *Tisiphone*, sir. It's not Rules, but our cook does tolerably well for us as long as we're in harbour and there's fresh meat and vegetables to be had; and we've a fair stock of wines on board.'

'I shall be delighted, sir. My card.' Thorpe presented him with a piece of pasteboard, before calling for his hat and cloak. 'Enjoy your repast, Mr Killigrew. I can heartily recommend the turkey *poults piqués et bardés*.' As soon as a flunkey had handed Thorpe his silk top hat, the gentleman raised it to Killigrew before placing it on his head. 'Good evening, sir.' Thorpe swept from the hotel in a swirl of evening cloak.

Killigrew glanced down at the card he was holding:

> Thaddeus Thorpe, Merchant
> c/o Thorpe & Co.
> Thorpetown
> New Hebrides

The lieutenant shrugged and tucked the card inside his jacket before turning back to the hotelier. 'Will sir require to freshen up before he dines?' Even after Thorpe had gone, the hotelier remained obsequiously polite, perhaps fearing that a report of a poor service might get back to the merchant's ears.

Killigrew shook his head. 'I'm due back on board my ship in an hour, which doesn't allow me enough time to give what I'm sure would be an excellent meal the attention it deserves.' It was a white lie: Killigrew did not want to give offence to Thorpe, but at the same time he did not feel comfortable accepting a free meal from a man about whom he knew nothing. 'Which room was the injured man taken to?'

'Room 107, sir.'

'Thank you.' Killigrew tripped lightly up the stairs to the room. The door was unlocked and he went in to find that the black had been laid on one of the beds where Strachan was attending him.

'Can you do anything for him?'

'Not without my medicine chest. You stay here with him while I send a flunkey to fetch a doctor. Then I'll head back to the *Tisiphone* to see if I can persuade Westlake to come and attend to him.'

The black revived a little shortly after Strachan had gone and tried to get up, but Killigrew gently pushed him back down.

'Rest easy, my bucko. A doctor's on the way. Savvy English?'

'Yes, sir. I speak English.' Albeit with an American accent. 'Thank you.'

'Least we could do,' said Killigrew. 'Anyhow, don't thank me; thank Mr Thaddeus Thorpe.'

'Thaddeus Thorpe?' Clearly the name meant no more to the injured man than it did to Killigrew.

'Your benefactor.' Killigrew gestured around the opulently appointed room. 'He's the one paying for all this, not I.'

'Why?'

Killigrew shrugged. 'Christian charity.'

'Father Geddie teach me all about Christian charity. One-time I believe in it,' the man added bitterly.

'Well, perhaps tonight's experience will renew your faith in human nature.'

The man glanced at his broken arm, and grimaced bitterly.

The lieutenant sat down in a chair and lit a cheroot with a match. 'The name's Killigrew, by the by. Kit Killigrew. What's yours?'

'They call me Johnny Blubbermouth.'

'Not your real name, I'm sure.'

The man shook his head. 'On my island I am called Wadrokal.' He sighed as if he wished he were there now.

'Your island?'

'Aneiteium, in Vanuatu. The islands you call the New Hebrides.'

'Ah, so you're a Polynesian negro. Didn't think you looked like a VDL Aboriginal, somehow. How did you come to break your arm like that, anyhow?'

Wadrokal turned his head away. 'It does not matter.'

'Perhaps I should rephrase the question. Who broke your arm?'

Even as Killigrew spoke, the door opened and three men entered. 'I did,' said one. He was a young man, not yet eighteen, tall and

18

gangly, but he carried himself with a self-assurance beyond his years. He regarded Killigrew with cool grey eyes, a faint sneer playing on his lips.

Killigrew recognised one of the men who flanked him as the American Indian he had seen earlier when he had found Wadrokal in the street. The other was European, dark-haired and olive-complexioned. Both were dressed as sailors and had the kind of broad shoulders one got from a lifetime of pulling at oars and pushing at capstan bars.

The lieutenant stood up. 'And you are?'

'Peleg Starbuck,' returned the young man. He spoke with the distinctive nasal twang of a New Englander, and could only be an officer of one of the many whaling ships that crowded Sullivan's Cove. 'You?'

'Lieutenant Christopher Killigrew, HMS *Tisiphone*.'

Starbuck nodded thoughtfully. 'I'm obliged to you, Mr Killigrew.' His tone of voice suggested anything but obligation. He indicated Wadrokal. 'This kanaka is a deserter from our ship. We'll take care of him from now.' He turned to the two sailors. 'Vasques, Squanto: bring him.'

As the two sailors moved towards the bed, Wadrokal cringed away from them.

Killigrew quickly interposed himself. 'I beg your pardon, have I misconstrued the situation in some way? I thought you said just now that you were the one who broke this poor fellow's arm.'

Starbuck nodded. 'That's right. What of it?'

'I've never been to the United States, Mr Starbuck, so I don't know how you Yankees do things there. But Van Diemen's Land happens to be a British colony, and we have laws here. I can assure you that the law takes a dim view of breaking people's limbs.'

'He's not a person, he's a kanaka. *My* kanaka.'

'Slavery's another thing we happen to have a law against. I'd like to think that one day the Americas will catch up with the rest of the world in that respect.'

'Who said anything about slavery? This kanaka happens to be a contract labourer. Stand aside, Mr Killigrew. You're starting to bore me.'

'Sorry to be a hotel-room lawyer, but if you think I'm going to stand by and let you take this man after you've freely confessed to seriously injuring him—'

'Do you like walking, Mr Killigrew?'

'Walking?'

Starbuck nodded. 'Because right now you've got a choice between walking out that door, or never walking again. Which is it to be?'

19

'If you think I'm going to be intimidated by your threats—'

'I'm not in the business of making threats. Vasques, Squanto: get rid of this jackass.'

A brass belaying pin slid out of Vasques' sleeve and into his hand. He swung it at Killigrew's head, but the lieutenant ducked and punched him in the stomach. Vasques doubled up, but even as Killigrew turned to face Squanto, the Indian drove a fist into one of his kidneys. Pain exploded in his side and he staggered. A hand smashed his head against the wall. The room spun, and Killigrew's legs crumpled beneath him. Another blow landed against his ribs – a vicious kick, perhaps; he was too stunned by the sudden onslaught to be sure – and the room became dim.

'Want me to kill him, Mr Starbuck?'

'No. Just throw him out of the window.'

Squanto lifted the unresisting Killigrew under the armpits and Vasques had recovered enough to seize his ankles. By the time the full import of Starbuck's instructions had hit Killigrew, the two sailors were swinging him between them and any attempt on his part to struggle was useless. On the count of three, they threw him out of the window without the courtesy of opening it first.

'Roll up, roll up! Find the lady!'

Ordinary Seaman Seth Endicott glanced across to the crowd that had gathered around a man who had set out a folding table in the street in front of one of the waterfront taverns in Hobart Town. 'What's going on over there?'

'Just a little game of three-card monte,' Able Seaman Wes Molineaux told him. 'Save your money – it's rigged.'

The two seamen from the *Tisiphone* presented an unlikely pair: Endicott, a tall, lean Liverpudlian with lank fair hair and an eye for the ladies; and Molineaux, a broad-shouldered man with a shaven head and a gold ring through one ear. There was no shortage of seamen who wore earrings in an effort to look piratical, but Molineaux was one of the few who could carry it off.

Despite Molineaux's warning, the two of them shouldered their way through the crowd to watch the broadsman cheat anyone foolish enough to think he could beat the house at 'find the lady'. Inevitably, there was no shortage of takers. Some people never learned. The broadsman laid three cards face-up on his table: two jacks, and the queen of spades.

'I'll have a go,' said a heavily built man with one of his front teeth missing. 'How much is it?'

'Anything over a tanner, cully,' said the broadsman. 'You pays your money and you takes your choice.'

The man put a sixpence piece on the table, and the broadsman flipped the cards over and moved them around one another. 'Round and round and round she goes; where she ends up, nobody knows. Which one, cully?'

The man pointed to a card. The broadsman flipped it over and revealed the queen of spades. 'You win,' he said, giving the man back his sixpence and paying him a shilling on top. 'Who's next?'

'I thought you said it was rigged?' Endicott murmured to Molineaux.

'That cove was a plant, to gammon flats like you. The next one will lose: you watch and see.'

Another man stepped forward and quickly proved that Molineaux did indeed have the gift of foresight: the second man went away disappointed.

'Who's next?' asked the broadsman. 'Who else wants to try their luck?'

'Come on,' said Molineaux, turning away. 'Let's catch up with the others.'

'How about you, cully?' the broadsman called after him. 'All you've got to do is find the black lady. Should come naturally to you, Sambo!'

Molineaux froze.

Endicott groaned. 'Come on, Wes. Leave it. He ain't worth it.'

The black seaman turned back. 'Give me a deaner, Seth.'

'You ain't going to lose it, are you?'

'I'll triple your money. Watch this.' Molineaux stepped up to the table. 'Find de black lady, you say?' His London accent was gone, replaced by the patter of a comic 'darky' from a Marryat novel. 'Why, dat sure do look easy to me, sho'nuff. I'se gwine to win me some money, oh yassur, lawdy!' He put Endicott's shilling on the table.

The broadsman grinned as he shuffled the cards around. He was thinking this was going to be like taking candy from a baby. 'The swiftness of the hand deceives the eye. Find the lady, my friend.'

Molineaux indicated a card. 'Dat one, mas'er. I'se sure dat's de one, yassur, lawdy indeedy!'

The broadsman flipped over the card without bothering to glance down at its face. 'Sorry, Sambo. You lose.' A sharp intake of breath from the crowd made him look down. 'What the hell . . .?'

'Dat's t'ree shillin's you owes me, mas'er.'

'No!' protested the broadsman. 'It can't be! You cheated, you black bastard.'

'What you mean, I cheated? You tole me to find de lady, and I'se gone done found her, mas'er. I won fair and square, sho'nuff.' He reached for the money, but the broadsman snatched it away.

'You bloody cheated! And I'll tell you how I know: the queen of spades was up my sleeve the whole time,' he declared triumphantly. He looked up his sleeve, found the card gone, and then blanched when he realised what he had said.

Molineaux caught him by the lapels and butted him on the bridge of the nose. As the broadsman went down with blood jetting from his nostrils, the broad-shouldered plant tried to grab Molineaux. The seaman twisted out of his grip, and then punched him in the stomach, once, twice, and then delivered a right cross to the point of his jaw. The plant staggered and sprawled on the cobbles.

Molineaux crouched over the dazed broadsman and helped himself to three shillings and a tanner from his pocket. 'Let me give you a piece of advice, cully: never gammon a gammoning cove.' He stood up and kicked the broadsman in the ribs. 'And that's for calling me "Sambo", you dumb, good-for-nothing, pasty-faced piece of white trash.'

The crowd cheered and applauded. Molineaux bowed theatrically, and then tossed the sixpence to the man who had first been rooked, before handing Endicott two of the shillings. 'There's your deaner; and there's a return on your investment.' The other shilling he slipped in his own pocket. 'That's my commission.'

When Killigrew came to, he was lying amidst a pile of broken crates in the alley behind the hotel. He could not remember much about the fall from the first-floor window, but he was pretty sure the crates had been intact before he hit them. It was difficult to say whether the crates had broken his fall or made it worse: it was impossible to imagine more pain than he was already in, and he was no stranger to physical discomfort.

At last the sea of general agony that swamped him became focused in specific areas: his ankle, his shoulder, his ribs, his elbow. The worst was a throbbing pain in his temple that threatened to rob him of consciousness once more, and when he raised a hand to examine the bump he found the side of his head was sticky with blood. The least of his pains came from his leg: surprisingly, because when he glanced down he saw a large shard of glass he had fallen on had sliced through the kerseymere of his pantaloons and embedded itself in his thigh.

Hissing at the pain, he eased himself into a sitting position and plucked the glass from his thigh with a wince. The blood flowed freely, until he took out his linen handkerchief and bound it over the wound. He tried to stand up, but a smashed crate had somehow wrapped itself around his leg and when he pulled it away he saw he had put the knee through his pantaloons and grazed the skin beneath. But the real suffering started when he tried to put his weight on his other leg. It felt as though he had sprained his ankle, and he hobbled about the alley in a desperate effort to keep his balance.

Yet despite the multitude of his injuries, it was clear that none of them was immediately life threatening. After leaning against the wall of the alley to retch drily, his throbbing head had cleared enough for him to remember how he had come to be thrown out of the window in the first place – and to think what he intended to do about it.

He hobbled out of the alley, his teeth gritted against the pain that shot through his ankle every time he tried to put weight on it. His only plan was to stagger back into the hotel and send a flunkey to fetch a constable, before returning to the saloon bar for medicinal purposes. But as he rounded the corner at the front of the hotel, he was just in time to see Starbuck, Vasques and Squanto emerge from the front door, the American Indian dragging Wadrokal by the ankles behind him, heedless of the man's broken arm bouncing against the cobbles. The pain would have been unbearable, if Wadrokal had not already fainted. Either that, or the three whalermen had silenced him, either temporarily or permanently.

Seeing Wadrokal subjected to such ill usage gave Killigrew a feeling of tight rage in his stomach. He had often been warned that his explosive temper was going to be the death of him, but he was in no mood to curb it now.

'Hi! You!'

Starbuck stopped and turned. Seeing Killigrew – and the state he was in – the youth laughed out loud. 'Oh, dear. You are a glutton for punishment, aren't you?'

Killigrew hobbled across to where they stood. 'I want a word with you,' he snarled.

Starbuck arched an amused eyebrow. 'A word? I'll give you much more than that, my friend.' He turned to the European sailor. 'Vasques? *Now* you can kill him.'

'My pleasure.' Vasques produced his belaying pin once more and advanced on Killigrew. He swung the pin at the lieutenant's head.

Killigrew blocked the blow with an upraised forearm, then caught Vasques by the wrist, spun him around, pushed him aside and tripped him up. The sailor sprawled on his back on the cobbles and Killigrew stamped on his crotch.

Squanto dropped Wadrokal's ankles, drew a large knife from his belt and came at Killigrew. He slashed at the lieutenant's chest. Killigrew jumped back, but then his ankle gave up on him and he fell to the ground with a gasp. Squanto kicked him in the side, and then reached down with his left hand to grab a fistful of the lieutenant's shirtfront, lifting him up off the ground all the better to slash at his throat with the knife.

Killigrew caught him by the wrist with his left hand and smashed his right fist into the sailor's jaw. Squanto's head was snapped round, and he let go of Killigrew's shirt. The lieutenant dropped back to the cobbles, and lashed out at one of Squanto's kneecaps with the sole of one boot. The sailor went down with a scream.

Killigrew rolled on to his front and pushed himself to his feet. A large crowd of onlookers had gathered and stood in a circle to watch, keeping a safe distance. Ignoring them, Killigrew retrieved Squanto's knife and advanced on Starbuck, dragging his right leg behind him.

Starbuck continued to regard him with amusement. 'A knife,' he sneered. 'I'm shaking in my shoes.'

Killigrew's ungainly advance was slow enough to give Starbuck plenty of time to unbutton his frock coat, pull out a revolving pistol and level it at the lieutenant's head.

Killigrew froze. It was not the first time someone had drawn a gun on him. He had seen active service in the Levant and in China, and had faced slavers on the Guinea Coast and pirates in Borneo and the China Seas. He had faced death enough times for his own reaction to be familiar by now: that frisson of excitement that coursed through his veins like a drug, heightening his senses and tensing every nerve-ending in his body.

But not tonight. Tonight, he realised with a shock, he just did not care. Let Starbuck pull the trigger and kill him. It made no difference to Killigrew. In many ways he would have welcomed death, and if dying in a street brawl were a comedown for a decorated naval officer, at least it would not carry the disgrace of suicide.

Then he realised he *did* care; he *wanted* Starbuck to pull that trigger.

The young man obliged.

Killigrew flinched as the sound of the shot filled his ears, and he felt the wind of the bullet as it soughed past his head.

'Jesus!' gasped a man in the crowd behind Killigrew. 'I . . . I've been shot!'

'Goddamnit!' Starbuck muttered irritably. He pulled back the hammer of the revolver with the thumb and forefinger of his left hand and took aim again.

Letting himself get killed was one thing, but it was not in Killigrew's nature to stand by and let innocent people get hurt. He threw the knife.

It spun through the air, turning end over end, and buried itself in the young man's throat. Starbuck clapped a hand to the wound, gurgling horribly, and went down with blood gouting from his neck. A woman screamed.

24

Killigrew hobbled to where the young man lay in a pool of blood and crouched over him. Starbuck was still alive, but the life was pumping out of him, and even if the best surgeon in the world had been present there was nothing he could have done for him.

The lieutenant shook his head sadly. 'You stupid bastard,' he murmured softly, his face twisted with contempt. 'You poor, stupid bastard.' He hated Starbuck then: hated him for the way he had treated Wadrokal, hated him for forcing Killigrew to kill him, but most of all he hated him for being a rotten shot.

Someone laid a hand on Killigrew's shoulder and the lieutenant looked up to see a pair of burly constables standing over him. 'Better come with us, sir,' said one.

Killigrew nodded and rose to his feet.

II

Trying Times

'You've got quite a reputation, haven't you, Mr Killigrew?' asked
the coroner.

'Sir?' Although this was by no means his first appearance in a
court of law, Killigrew was having difficulty concentrating; not least
because of the man who sat in the gallery, glaring at him with
murder in his eyes. Dressed in a double-breasted black frock coat
and a glazed hat, he was an unprepossessing individual: neither tall
nor short, fat nor thin, young nor old, it was difficult from looking
at him to pick out any one physical feature that would aid future
recognition. Then he unfolded his arms, and Killigrew saw that in
place of his left hand he wore a steel hook on the stump of his arm.

'Awarded the Humane Society's silver medal when you were
eleven years old, for crawling down the shaft of a collapsed tin
mine to take food and water to some trapped miners. Received the
Royal Navy's General Service Medal for taking part in the Syrian
campaign . . .' The coroner looked up from his notes. 'That was ten
years ago. How old are you, Mr Killigrew?'

'Twenty-five, sir.'

'So you'd've been fifteen when you were at the bombardment of
Acre?'

'Just turned sixteen, sir.'

'Hm.' The coroner referred to his notes once more. 'Received the
China War Medal in 1842 and you attracted favourable notice for
your services in suppressing slavery on the Guinea Coast . . .'

Killigrew squirmed. He had done his duty over the years, it was
true, but the coroner's litany was making some of the younger ladies
in the court look at him as if he was some kind of hero. Not that he
did not enjoy the company of young ladies, but all too often he got
the uncomfortable feeling they expected him to be something he
was not.

The senior naval officer in Van Diemen's Land, Captain Erskine of HMS *Havannah*, had assured him – after bawling him out for getting into a brawl in the first place – that the inquest was purely a formality. Violent scenes such as the one that had taken place on Murray Street three nights ago were commonplace in rough and ready Hobart Town, however much the more genteel inhabitants of the colony might deplore it. This was perhaps something to be expected in a colony were free settlers had only lately started to outnumber the convicts and ticket-of-leave men.

For a naval officer to be involved in one was something of a novelty, which explained why the gallery was packed out. But there were plenty of witnesses who had already testified to the effect that Killigrew had acted in self-defence, so why the coroner felt it necessary to establish the lieutenant was a young man of good character was beyond him.

The coroner disabused him of this notion with his next statement, however. 'And in London three years ago you were found guilty of manslaughter. "The Pall Mall childkiller", I believe you were called in the papers. And you were court-martialled and dismissed the service.'

Killigrew grimaced. 'That was a . . . misunderstanding.' He did not want to go into details. 'I was subsequently declared innocent of all charges, and reinstated to my former rank.'

'I'm aware of that, Mr Killigrew. Then there's this matter in Hong Kong last year . . .'

'The conspiracy I helped to uncover?'

'No, Mr Killigrew. I was referring to the sinking of a clipper; and the death of a young lady.'

The lieutenant clenched his fists. 'An informal enquiry cleared me of all culpability, your honour.'

'Nevertheless, Mr Killigrew, it seems to me that people do have the unfortunate habit of dying by violent means in your presence. I wonder if you can account for that?'

Killigrew gritted his teeth. 'Just lucky, I guess.'

The coroner banged his gavel against the bench before him. 'Mr Killigrew! I will not tolerate flippant remarks in my court! This inquest may have been brought forward to accommodate Commander Robertson's request that his ship be allowed to sail on Thursday with its second lieutenant on board, but if you persist in provoking me I shall have no hesitation in having you locked up for contempt of court until after the *Tisiphone* has sailed. Do I make myself clear?'

'Yes, sir.'

'Good.' The coroner took a deep breath before continuing. 'And now we come to the incident of Friday the twelfth of April, in the year of our Lord eighteen hundred and fifty. We have already heard that four members of the crew of the United States' whaling ship *Lucy Ann* were seen leaving the Harbour View Hotel. Two of them were carrying a third between them. You were then seen emerging from the alley at the rear of the premises. Perhaps you'd like to tell the gentlemen of the jury in your own words what happened next?'

'I attempted to carry out an arrest.'

'Did you inform them you were an officer of Her Majesty's navy?'

'I was in uniform, I'd've thought it was pretty obvious—'

'Answer the question, yes or no?'

'No, sir.'

'Hm. I assume that as an officer who has carried out several arrests in the course of his duties you are aware that even felons have rights? You must therefore be aware that for an arrest to carry legal weight, the suspect must be informed that he is under arrest. Did you inform these men that such was your intention?'

'There wasn't time. They turned to attack me and—'

'Yes or no, Mr Killigrew?'

'No, sir.'

'Hm! Then what happened?'

'I was successful in rendering two of the men *hors de combat*.'

'*Hors de combat!* A very pretty phrase. By that I take it you mean you broke the jaw of one and crippled the other for life by smashing his kneecap?'

'Yes, sir.'

'Does the phrase "reasonable force" mean anything to you, Mr Killigrew?'

'Yes, sir.'

'Is it your considered opinion – and I advise you to think most carefully before your answer – is it your considered opinion that you used "reasonable force" on the night of Friday the twelfth?'

Killigrew indicated the crutch he was leaning on for support. 'The gentlemen in question had just thrown me out of a first-floor window . . .'

'Yes or no, Mr Killigrew?'

'Yes, sir. I have some experience of handling violent situations. I judged that the three men I was dealing with were of a violent and ruthless disposition and needed to be dealt with accordingly.'

' "Some experience of handling violent situations." I see. If I may interrupt your narrative briefly, perhaps I can ask you about your feelings on the subject of slavery?'

'My feelings on the subject of slavery are a matter of record, sir. I think my actions on the Guinea Coast speak for themselves.'

'Oh, they do indeed, Mr Killigrew. Volumes. So it would be fair to say you are passionately opposed to slavery?'

'It's contrary to the laws of both God and the British Empire, sir.'

'So when you saw these three men attempting to recapture a deserter from their ship, you automatically assumed they were slavers and acted accordingly.'

'Yes, sir.'

'And it never occurred to you to stop and enquire the details further? To find out that the coloured man known as Johnny Blubbermouth was in fact an indentured labourer, and that Mr Starbuck had every right to apprehend him?'

'You can call it indentured labour if you wish, sir. It's still slavery.'

'I beg to differ, Mr Killigrew. There are no laws in the British Empire against the employment of indentured labour. And the captain of the *Lucy Ann* had a contract signed by Mr Blubbermouth.'

'His real name was Wadrokal, sir. And any fool can draw a cross and write "Johnny Blubbermouth, his mark" beneath it.'

'Duly signed and witnessed.'

'By other members of the *Lucy Ann*'s crew?'

'Nevertheless, the document was legally binding. But let us return to the night of the twelfth. Having rendered Mr Vasques and Mr . . . ah . . . Squanto *"hors de combat"*, as you so poetically put it, what did you do next?'

'I attempted to arrest Mr Starbuck.'

'And what did he do?'

'He presented a revolving pistol at me.'

'Did that surprise you?'

'Sir?'

'You attacked two of his companions, seriously injuring one and crippling another, and then you advanced on him holding a knife. Were you surprised that he then drew a revolver?'

'It surprised me when he took a shot at me.'

'So you killed him.'

'In self-defence. And in defence of others. His shot might have missed me, but as we've already heard, it injured a man in the crowd. Mr Starbuck clearly had every intention of firing a second shot.'

'So you killed him. You, an experienced naval officer of thirteen years' service – a man who, by your own admission, has "some experience of handling violent situations" – killed a young man of sixteen.'

'He was old enough to pull a trigger, sir,' Killigrew said tightly.

'And there was no way a man with your "experience of handling violent situations" could have disarmed him without killing him? You could not conceive a less fatal manner of resolving the situation? There was no way you could perhaps have thrown the knife so that it dashed the pistol from his fist, perhaps?'

'I'm a naval officer, sir, not a circus performer.' That won Killigrew a chuckle from some of the people in the gallery, but the coroner scowled.

'Perhaps you could have thrown the knife at his leg?'

'I could have done, but then he would still have been capable of squeezing off a shot. He had already wounded one onlooker. I felt it was my duty to prevent any further injuries. There might even have been a fatality.'

'There *was* a fatality, Mr Killigrew: the unfortunate Mr Starbuck.'

'Someone who didn't deserve to die, I mean,' said Killigrew. As soon as the words were past his lips, he realised he had made a mistake.

The coroner's eyebrows shot up. ' "Someone who didn't deserve to die"! Mr Killigrew, are you telling me you took it upon yourself to act as judge, jury and executioner over this young man?'

'No, sir. What I meant to say was, I did not want any other innocent bystanders to get hurt.'

'I see. Very good, Mr Killigrew. I think we've heard enough. Please stand down. Well, I don't think we need waste further time on this matter. The facts of the case speak for themselves, and in the light of the evidence given by the other witnesses, I have no choice but to find that Mr Christopher Killigrew acted in self-defence and therefore I shall not be bringing an indictment against him . . .'

Out of the corner of his eye, Killigrew saw the hook-handed man get up and leave the gallery.

'However, I do feel it incumbent upon me to reprimand him publicly for excessive use of force,' continued the coroner. 'I find it appalling that an experienced naval officer should, in the first instance, provoke a street brawl and then, in the course of that brawl, put himself in a situation where he felt he had no choice but to deprive a fellow human being – a young man of sixteen – of his life. It is a shameful indictment of the standard to which the young officers of the Royal Navy have sunk, and it is my most sincere hope – aye, and recommendation – that Mr Killigrew's superiors discipline him most severely. This inquest is now closed.'

Killigrew was glad to emerge from the stuffy atmosphere of the court-house. Commander Robertson was waiting for him outside. A burly man somewhere in his forties, the commander was notorious for his gruffness. Someone had once accused him of not having a good word to say for any of the men under his command, prompting him to retort that he could think of plenty of good words for some of them. The *Tisiphone*'s ratings called him 'Tommy Pipes' because his stentorian tones could easily drown out the shouts of boatswain's mates to whom that nickname was usually given. But such was Robertson's temper that it was when he lowered his voice you knew you had to watch yourself: it was the ominous calm before the storm.

Today the commander was in a thunderous mood, but for once Killigrew was not the object of his wrath. 'That coroner was a damnable disgrace! He acted more like the counsel for the prosecution at a trial than a coroner at an inquest . . .'

'Mr Killigrew?'

They both turned to see the hook-handed man who had been sitting in the gallery.

'Yes?' said Killigrew.

'I thought I'd take the liberty of introducing myself,' the man said cheerfully. He spoke with the nasal twang of a New Englander. 'I'm Quested. Captain Barzillai Quested, master of the *Lucy Ann*. Peleg Starbuck was one of my crew. He was also my nephew.'

Killigrew was not quite sure what to say. He had killed plenty of men in his time, but this was the first time he had ever had to confront a grieving relative of one of his victims. Not that Quested seemed to be grieving much. For a man who had lost a nephew only three days earlier, his smile was frighteningly broad. 'I don't suppose it's much consolation, Captain Quested, but all I can say is I'm truly sorry . . .'

'No, you're not.' Quested's smile did not falter for an instant. 'How many men have you killed, Mr Killigrew? Ten? Twenty? What's one more to a man like you?'

'If there's anything I can do . . .'

'Anything you can do? Can you give me back my nephew?'

'Captain Quested, please try to understand. Your nephew gave me no choice—'

'And you gave him no chance. I'll tell you what you can do, Mr Killigrew. This isn't a request for a favour, though. It's a piece of advice. Remember me.' Quested tapped him on the chest with the curve of his hook. 'Because I'll remember you.'

'I hope that isn't a threat, Captain Quested,' growled Robertson. 'In the British Empire we take a very dim view of threatening behaviour.'

'Oh, of course. Unless it's soldiers and sailors like you bullying foreigners. That's acceptable, isn't it?' Quested turned back to Killigrew. 'One day we'll meet again,' he hissed softly. 'One day soon, I hope. And we won't be in the British Empire when it happens.' He turned abruptly on his heel and marched away.

'Damned impertinent fellow!' spluttered Robertson. 'You know, for a few seconds there I was feeling sorry for his loss?'

'If anyone got Peleg Starbuck killed, it was him,' Killigrew said bitterly. 'As captain of the *Lucy Ann*, he must've been the one who kidnapped Wadrokal. And he was probably the one that put the gun in his nephew's hand.' The two of them started to walk back to Sullivan's Cove, Killigrew leaning on his crutch to preserve his twisted ankle. 'By the way, sir, did you find out what happened to Wadrokal?'

'Forget about it, Second. It's over. The matter is closed.'

Killigrew stopped abruptly, and stared at the commander. Robertson halted and turned to face him.

'He was handed back to that fellow Quested, wasn't he?'

'You heard what the coroner said: an indentured labourer. I'm sorry for it, but there it is. The law is the law, Second.'

'Then the law is an ass, sir.' They resumed walking. 'Let me go aboard the *Lucy Ann* tonight, sir. If Quested's using slave labour, I'll soon find proof.'

'You'll do no such thing! The *Lucy Ann* is an American vessel. Do you want to provoke an international incident?'

'The *Lucy Ann* may be an American vessel, sir, but she's moored in British territorial waters. We have every right to search her.'

'Not without a warrant.'

' "Reasonable suspicion", sir. If I find slaves aboard, it will prove I had grounds for—'

'You're not thinking, Second. If you find slaves aboard, don't you think Quested will have indentured contracts for every one of them, the same as he did for Wadrokal? Listen, Killigrew, I've seen other officers act the way you've been behaving these past few months. They're perfectly good officers – a little foolhardy, perhaps, but what young officer worth his salt isn't? Then something happens to them. A prize court judgement goes against them. They get passed over for promotion by men with less experience but more "interest" at the Admiralty. They see a comrade killed in action, or – ' Robertson looked away, but gave Killigrew a sidelong glance – 'a sweetheart. Something snaps inside them. They decide they're fighting a losing battle, and then they stop trying. They become slovenly. They take to drink. They become careless. They start taking foolish risks.

'What I'm trying to say, Killigrew, is that if you want to get yourself killed, I have absolutely no objection. But kindly have the decency to do it on your own time, and not the navy's. If you've decided the game isn't worth the candle, then you're no good to me as an officer any more. But there are ninety-nine men in the *Tisiphone*'s crew beside yourself; men who count on you, and if you should imperil any one of their lives through your reckless behaviour, I will personally keelhaul you and have you strung up from the yard-arm. Right now you're a powder keg looking for a spark. I don't want to be around you when you go off; and I don't want any of my men to be around when it happens, either. Hoist in?'

'Aye, aye, sir. Lecture over?'

'Damn your eyes, Killigrew! If you're too mutton-headed to realise when your friends are trying to help you, then by God you don't deserve their help!'

They reached Sullivan's Cove where Robertson's gig waited for them at the wharf. Once the two officers were seated in the stern sheets, the gig's crew rowed them back to the *Tisiphone*. Killigrew cast a curious glance at the whaling ships tied up at Kelly's Wharf and wondered which one was the *Lucy Ann*.

'By the way, did you know Mr Thorpe sent a letter of recommendation to Sir William Denison as a character witness before the inquest?' asked Robertson. 'How is it you come to know Thaddeus Thorpe, of all people, anyhow?'

'I only met him on Friday night. Why? Have you heard of him?'

'Heard of him? Of course I've heard of him. You would have, too, if you'd crawled out of that whiskey bottle you've crawled into. He's only one of the most celebrated men in Hobart Town. Or perhaps I should say "infamous". That's his yacht over there.' Robertson pointed to where the *Wanderer* was moored.

'He's a member of the Royal Yacht Squadron?' mused Killigrew.

'And one of the richest men in the Australias; although where he gets his money from is anyone's guess. Since he arrived in Van Diemen's Land eight years ago he's invested in half a dozen doomed trading ventures: sheep farming, whaling, contract labour.'

'Contract labour?'

'I know what you're thinking, Second. It's already been investigated. Accusations of slavery have been made, but HMS *Havannah* visited his trading station in the New Hebrides the year before last and gave him a clean bill of health.' Robertson chuckled. 'He calls the place "Thorpetown". They say he runs it like his own personal fiefdom, lording it over the natives. Even prints his own damned currency for his employees.'

'A modest sort of a fellow, then.'

'Boat ahoy!' the marine sentry on duty at the *Tisiphone*'s entry port challenged as the gig drew near.

'*Tisiphone!*' returned the coxswain. The gig reached the sloop's side and Robertson was piped back on board by one of the boatswain's mates. Killigrew followed him up on deck, making his obeisance to the quarterdeck by tipping his cocked hat as he climbed up through the entry port.

'Better let Mr Westlake take a look at that leg of yours, Second,' said Robertson, who apparently did not have a very high opinion of the surgeons of Hobart Town.

'My leg's fine, sir.'

34

'We'll let Westlake be the judge of that, hm? Go on, down to the sick-berth with you.'

Killigrew made his way down the forward hatch, to where the sick-berth was located in the bows of the sloop. There was no sign of the surgeon, but his assistant was there, heating up a flask of chemicals over a spirit lamp. Aside from being a skilled apothecary who was well on the way to qualifying as a surgeon under Westlake's tutelage, Strachan was a scientific polymath who could put a Latin name to any fauna or flora known to man. He had joined the navy because of the opportunities it afforded him to study the world's natural history at first hand. Robertson turned a blind eye to the amount of time Strachan spent on his scientific investigations, provided they did not interfere with his duties as the *Tisiphone*'s assistant surgeon. The Admiralty was all in favour of scientific investigation, and if Strachan turned out to be the next Sir Joseph Banks then it would not do Robertson's reputation any harm.

He glanced at the lieutenant as he entered. 'I'll be with you in two shakes of a cat's whisker,' he promised.

Killigrew nodded. 'What is that?'

'A compound of acetic acid, saturated solution of gallic acid and crystallised silver nitrate. I'm experimenting with the standard formula for photographic paper to try to reduce exposure times.' As a keen botanist, amongst other things, Strachan often took calotypes of some of the exotic plants he encountered on his travels; as a zoologist, he also wanted to do the same for wildlife, but the thirty seconds' exposure required made it almost impossible to take photographic portraits of animals.

'I wish I hadn't asked.' As intrigued as Killigrew was by the possibilities of the new process of photography, as soon as Strachan started to talk about chemicals he might as well have been speaking a foreign language.

Killigrew's joshing was like water off a duck's back to Strachan, who was used to it by now. 'How did the inquest go?' he asked.

'Just capital. The coroner accused me of excessive use of force and the youth's uncle made a thinly veiled threat to kill me.'

'You're as adept as ever at making friends, I see. You cannot blame yourself, Killigrew. You had to kill the lad. You had no choice.'

'Didn't I?'

Strachan looked up from his chemicals to stare at Killigrew in surprise. 'You told me yourself: if you hadn't killed him, he'd've killed you for certain. Or is that not how it happened?'

'That's the way it happened,' the lieutenant assured him.

'Then what choice did you have, other than to stand there and let him kill you?'

Killigrew just looked at him.

The scene in the try-works was Stygian as the crew of the *Lucy Ann* worked through the night to finish trying out the blubber of the whale they had caught. A couple of lanterns tried to cast their weak, flickering light across the interior of the barn-like building on Kelly's Wharf, but they were no match for the hellish glow of the furnaces beneath the massive copper try-pots set in a brick framework.

Like most whaling ships, the *Lucy Ann* had its own try-works on board, set in a shallow, water-filled cistern called the 'goose-pen' abaft the fore hold. But fire and whale oil made for a dangerous mix on board a ship at sea, and when he caught a whale close enough to one of the many land-based try-works Captain Quested preferred to do his trying-out ashore.

A good-sized sperm whale would yield about a hundred barrels of whale oil, and even working continuously in six-hour shifts it took two days to try out that much oil. The blubber, flensed from the carcass of the whale with flensing knives – two-foot blades on six-foot shafts, more like poleaxes than conventional knives – was cut into strips and put in the mincing tub. After being chopped up even more finely, the blubber was put in the try-pots and rendered down into whale oil. The fibrous fritters that floated to the surface of the bubbling pots were scooped off with a long-handled ladle and thrown in the furnaces, which burned even more fiercely. Then the tryed-out oil was drained into the cooling cauldron. Once the oil was cool enough, it was poured into casks that were then left to stand for a day until they were properly cool.

A wooden platform stood over the try-pots, from which the blubber could be tipped into the boilers, and it was from this vantage point that Captain Quested surveyed his men as they worked.

The *Lucy Ann*'s chief mate, Mr Macy, entered the try-works and climbed the rickety steps to the platform where Quested stood. 'Fallon's outside, sir.'

'Fallon? What does he want? I thought he said there was to be no further contact between us before we meet at Norfolk Island?'

'Says he wants a word.'

Quested thought for a moment. 'Very well. Bring him in.'

Macy went outside again and returned with a young man with a Vandyke beard, elegantly dressed in a bottle-green frock coat over a fancy embroidered waistcoat and fashionably checked trousers. He wore a stovepipe hat with a rakishly curled brim at a jaunty angle on his head and carried an ebony cane in one hand. The other hand held a handkerchief to his nose and mouth.

36

Macy conducted Fallon to the platform where Quested stood. 'Are you sure you weren't followed here?' demanded Quested.

'Quite sure.' Fallon spoke with a soft Irish brogue. 'I learned everything there is to know about giving informers the slip when I was in Ireland, believe me. Do you think we could continue this conversation outside?' He gestured helplessly with the gold head of his cane. 'The stench . . .'

'That's the smell of money, Mr Fallon. Hard-earned money. Whaling may strike a gentleman such as yourself as a filthy, stinking trade, but it's the trade that puts oil in the lamps in your home, whalebone in the corsets of your sweetheart and ambergris in the scent you're so fond of.'

'The most pungent toilet water in the world could not be competing with this stench, even if I'd doused myself in a bucket of the stuff!'

Quested chuckled. 'I'm sure you didn't come here to discuss perfumes, Mr Fallon.'

The Irishman shook his head. 'I heard about your nephew, Mr Starbuck. I came to offer my condolences. I'm sorry.'

'There's only one man who should be sorry: Lieutenant Christopher Killigrew.'

'Yes. I hear you confronted him outside the Criminal Courts this morning?'

'What of it?'

'Are you sure that was wise? What did you say to him?'

'That's between me and Killigrew.'

'No, Captain Quested. The *Lucy Ann* is my charter now. Your business happens to be my business.'

'The man shot my nephew, Mr Fallon, and they let him off scot-free. Was I supposed to say nothing?'

'Damn it, man! You shouldn't have drawn attention to yourself that way!'

'That wasn't drawing attention to myself, Fallon. Now, if I'd followed my instincts and gunned him down on the steps of the Criminal Courts like the dog he is, *that* would have drawn attention to me. He won't walk away next time we meet. And don't tell me there won't be a next time, because—'

'Oh, there'll be a next time, all right,' interrupted Fallon. 'I think I can just about guarantee that. For your information, Captain Quested, Killigrew just happens to be the second lieutenant of Her Majesty's steam-sloop *Tisiphone* – the ship that's taking me to Norfolk Island!'

'The *Tisiphone*! I thought you said you'd be travelling out on a convict brig?'

'I did. But it seems the usual convict brig is too short-handed at present, what with half the male population of Van Diemen's Land heading off to California for the gold rush. The *Tisiphone*'s bound for the Fijis, so they're dropping me off on the way.'

'And if the *Tisiphone*'s still there when we arrive?'

'She's a steamer. She'll be long gone by the time you get there with the *Lucy Ann.*'

'You'd better be right,' said Quested. 'I'd like to run into this Mr Killigrew again; but another time, another place. I still say you should sail to Norfolk Island on the *Lucy Ann.*'

'And how am I to get ashore? While you were bandying words with this fellow Killigrew in the streets, I was speaking to an old lag who'd done time on Norfolk Island. There are two landing places there: Sydney Bay on the south side of the island, and Cascades Bay on the north. Sydney Bay is out of the question: it's right under the noses of the garrison at the main settlement of Kingston. Cascades is three miles away and unguarded, but there's a reason for that: the only way ashore is by a big wooden derrick they have on the cliff-top. If a boat crew wants to come ashore, they have to lower a rope from a derrick and winch them up, boat and all.'

'And the derrick can only be operated from the top of the cliff,' concluded Quested. 'They must use specially strengthened boats. Try to winch one of my whaleboats up with the crew still in her, and she'd snap like a twig.'

'Then you'd better see to it that you reinforce one of your boats on the voyage out to Norfolk Island.'

'When does the *Tisiphone* sail?'

'Thursday.'

'Then I'd better sail tomorrow, on the dawn tide. The Westerlies are fairly steady at this time of year; we should reach Norfolk Island Thursday week. We'll stand off the coast, out of sight below the horizon during the day, and come in closer to the island during the night. Make sure you take your bull's-eye: if we get your signal, I'll send a boat ashore, so be ready to winch her up.'

'There'll be three of us to carry off the island.'

'Three? I thought it was just you and—'

'I'll be needing a guide when I get to the island. The old lag I spoke to last night recommended one of the convicts: the commandant's butler.'

'Can you trust him?'

'I doubt it. But I think he'll help us if it means he gets a chance to escape from the island.'

'Oh-kay, three of you it is. But I'm only staying there for a week, so if you don't show by the night of Wednesday the first of May, I'm leaving you to rot on that island with your buddy.'

'We'll be there,' Fallon promised him. 'Just make sure that—'

38

He was interrupted by an ear-splitting scream that was shrill enough to be audible over the hissing of the try-pots and the roaring of the fires in the furnaces. 'What the devil's that?'

'My deserter. After he ran away, that naval officer found him and tried to put him up at the Harbour View Hotel. Johnny Blubbermouth was only out of our sight for a few minutes, but it was enough time to blow the gaff on our plans.'

'Mary, Mother of God! If he talked . . .'

'If he talked, the plan's off,' Quested told him calmly.

'How can we be sure he didn't?'

'Gog and Magog are just finding that out now.'

'Gog and Magog?'

'Two of my men. Come on, I'll introduce you to them.'

Grinning, Quested motioned for Fallon to follow him off the platform. They descended the stairs and Quested led the way to an office at the back of the try-works. Thanks to the stench of the burning blubber, Fallon looked green about the gills as it was, but the sight that greeted his eyes as they entered the office drained what little colour remained in his face.

A black man was sprawled on his back on the floor while one of the biggest men Fallon had ever seen stood over him. Only a couple of inches shy of seven feet in height, unlike most unnaturally tall men this one was not gangly but well-built; husky, even. His ugly, ill-formed face was in sharp contrast to his muscular physique: his wide mouth was like a clumsy slash across his face, and two piggy eyes glinted beneath his gnarled brow. It seemed impossible to believe that one such human behemoth could have sprung from the womb of any woman; but the man's identical twin stood on the other side of the room, leaning his back against the wall with his brawny arms folded while waiting for his turn to inflict punishment on the squirming black.

'Meet Peter and Paul Lawless,' said Quested. 'Also known as Gog and Magog.'

The man standing over the black nodded a silent acknowledgement at Fallon, and then placed a massive foot squarely on the compound fracture in his victim's arm. The black screamed in agony.

When the screams died away into a whimper, Quested turned to the fourth man already in the room, a muscular Polynesian in Western clothing. He was probably a big man himself, but the Lawless twins dwarfed him.

'This is Mr Fallon, the gentleman who's chartered our ship for our forthcoming voyage,' said Quested. 'Mr Fallon, meet Simon Utumate, my specksnyder.'

'Specksnyder?' echoed Fallon.

39

Utumate shook the Irishman by the hand. 'Chief harpooner,' he explained.

'Has he told you anything yet, Utumate?' asked Quested.

The Polynesian grinned. 'I don't think he got around to telling anyone anything.'

'Thinking isn't good enough, Utumate. We need to know for sure, or the whole deal is off.' Quested turned to the twin standing over Wadrokal. 'Stand back, Magog.'

The whaling skipper crouched over Wadrokal and seized a fistful of his hair, pulling his head back cruelly. 'It doesn't have to be like this, Johnny,' he said, almost tenderly. 'Just tell me what you told Killigrew, and the pain stops now.'

'I tell him nothing, Cap'n Quested!' sobbed Wadrokal. 'I swear it! I only wanted to escape from the *Lucy Ann*.'

'Not a word about our little voyage to Norfolk Island? You're sure?'

'I tell him nothing!'

'If you told him, it would be better to tell me now. I shan't lie to you and say I won't be angry – you know me better than that – but I'll be more angry if I find out you've lied to me. Do you understand? We're going to put you back on board the *Lucy Ann* now; but if it turns out you've lied to us and the Royal Navy is waiting for us when we get to Norfolk Island, the pain begins again. And I'll make it last the rest of your life, and that's going to be a long, long time. Do you believe me?'

Wadrokal nodded.

'Now, before I tell Gog and Magog to put you back on board the *Lucy Ann*, are you quite sure there's nothing you want to say to me?'

'I tell him nothing, sir. I swear it, as God is my witness.'

Smiling, Quested straightened. 'That's more like it. Gog, Magog, you know what to do.'

The two giants lifted Wadrokal effortlessly between them and carried him out of the office.

Fallon was ashen. 'Jesus, Quested! Did you have to torture him?'

'Would you rather you went aboard the *Tisiphone* the day after tomorrow and found the crew were waiting to take you to Norfolk Island, not as a visitor but as a permanent resident? It's no wonder your little rebellion was such a fiasco. You people have no stomach for what it takes to succeed in this world.'

Quested and Fallon emerged from the office to see Gog and Magog carrying Wadrokal up the steps to the platform overlooking the try-pots. The black screamed and struggled furiously when he realised what his fate was to be.

'Sweet Jesus, no!' Fallon started to run across the floor after them, but at a signal from Quested two of the sailors working in the try-works intercepted him and held him fast between them.

'Sorry, Johnny!' Quested called to where Gog and Magog held Wadrokal between them on the platform. 'But if I let you live I've got no guarantee you won't go running off to the lime-juicers anyway.'

'For Christ's sake, Quested!' pleaded Fallon. 'You said you were going to let him live . . . you were going to put him back on the *Lucy Ann*.'

Quested scowled at him peevishly. 'Well, *of course* I said that. You think he'd've told me the truth if he'd thought I was going to kill him anyway?'

On the platform, Gog and Magog grabbed an arm and a leg each and started to swing Wadrokal between them.

'Please, Cap'n Quested!' screamed the black. 'I'll tell no one, I swear!'

'You're darned tooting.' Quested nodded to the twins, and they hurled the screaming Wadrokal headfirst into one of the try-pots. The black's legs thrashed spasmodically for a second or two, and then became lifeless.

Fallon staggered over to a dark corner of the try-works to be violently sick on the floor.

Quested chuckled to himself. 'Like I said, no stomach for this kind of work.'

Fallon wiped his mouth with a handkerchief. 'Maybe you had to kill him, maybe you didn't,' he snarled. 'But you didn't have to kill him like that.'

'That was for your benefit as much as his, Mr Fallon.' Quested tapped the Irishman on the chest with his hook. 'The remaining five thousand dollars waiting for me when we get to 'Frisco, just as we agreed; otherwise you'll end up the same way.'

Refusing to be cowed, Fallon glanced down at Quested's hook. 'You know you can get perfectly good prosthetic hands, Captain?'

Quested grinned. 'This is scarier.'

Fallon shook his head. 'You're a bloody lunatic!'

The captain nodded. 'Bear that in mind, Mr Fallon, and you and I shall get along famously.'

As Fallon staggered out of the try-works, the *Lucy Ann*'s second mate, Zecheas Forgan, entered. He glanced with amusement at the ashen-faced Irishman as he passed, and then turned to Quested. 'Fallon?'

Quested nodded.

'What was he looking so sick about?'

'I reckon the smell must've made him feel queasy.'

Forgan glanced at the feet protruding from one of the try-pots. 'Uh-huh. Wadrokal?'

41

'Oil for the lamps of China, Mr Forgan.'

The second mate grinned. 'You sure are one *loco* sonuvagun, Cap'n.' Although he spoke with the accent of South Carolina, like many veterans of the Mexican War, Forgan's speech was laced with Spanish.

'Did you have any luck finding replacements for Vasques and Squanto?'

'*Nada*, Cap'n. I tried, but hands are hard to come by. These days everyone seems to be more interested in going to . . .'

'California?'

Forgan nodded. 'Maybe when we get to 'Frisco we should try prospecting ourselves.'

'Forget it. Most of the seams will be worked out by the time we get there. And with so many men heading to California, there'll be fewer whalers working the South Seas. Supply goes down, the price goes up.' He patted a cask. 'This is liquid gold, Mr Forgan. With any luck we might catch a couple of fish on our way to California; Fallon's agreed we can stop to chase any whales if we spy a fall on the way.'

'It'll be hard to catch any fish when we're four hands short. We'll only be able to put three of the boats into the water at a time.'

'We can put in at Aneiteium or Thorpetown on our way to 'Frisco. We'll need to touch somewhere for fresh water and fruit, and you can usually pick up a beachcomber or two at those sandalwood trading stations. They'll jump at the chance when they hear we're bound for California. Now, let's look lively: we sail on the dawn tide, and we've got a lot of work to do before then.'

In the try-pot above them, Wadrokal's feet slid slowly out of view.

III

'Who the Devil is Devin Cusack?'

'Excuse me, I wonder if you'd be so good as to tell me which one of those boats is HMS *Tisiphone*?' On the quayside at Sullivan's Cove, Mrs Cafferty addressed a man working in a flory boat. She was well aware that the vessels she was referring to were ships, but is always amused her to see nautical gentlemen get in a froth when they heard their beloved vessels referred to as 'boats'.

The boatman snatched his cap off his head. 'Uh . . . that one, your ladyship.' He pointed to a paddle-ship with two masts and a funnel rising between them. At about a hundred and sixty feet from stem to stern, it was not much of a warship, but it was still the largest vessel in the anchorage.

'I'm a "ma'am", not a "ladyship", but thank you anyhow. I wonder if you could take me out to it?'

'It?'

'The boat, man, the boat.'

'Oh! You mean the *Tisiphone*. Begging your ladyship's pardon, but she's a ship, not a boat; and ships are called "she", not "it".'

'Thank you for the lecture; here's one in return: since I was referring to the *ship* in the dative case, the correct particle of the preposition would be "her", not "she".' That would teach him not to argue semantics with a governess. 'But frankly I consider this whole business of referring to ships as if they were women as a ridiculous affectation.' She reached into the pocket of her skirt and produced a sixpence. 'Could you take me out to her?'

'Of course, ma'am! Step down.'

'My trunk.' She gestured behind her.

'Of course, ma'am.' He climbed the stone steps to the quayside and blanched when he saw her trunk.

'It is rather heavy,' she admitted as he braced himself. 'Perhaps I should give you a hand?'

'No, no, ma'am. I can manage.'

'Really, you'll hurt yourself if you try to lift it by yourself.'

'It's all right, ma'am. I'm as strong as an ox. Besides, a fine lady shouldn't have to go lifting heavy things.'

'Why not?'

'Well, it's . . . it ain't ladylike.'

'Nonsense. It's a commonly accepted fact that physical exercise is beneficial for health and wellbeing for men. Why should the female constitution be affected any differently? If you must insist on lifting that by yourself, might I suggest you lift with your knees rather than your back? Otherwise you'll give yourself a hernia.'

'Thanks, ma'am, but before I were a boatman I were a porter, and I think I know a thing or two about— Oh, Gawd!'

'There now, you see? You've gone and injured yourself.'

'Call a doctor . . .' the man moaned weakly.

'I'm sure they'll have a surgeon on board the *Tisiphone*.'

'Can't . . . row . . .'

'Well, how difficult can it be?' She lifted the trunk, carried it down to the boat, and then came back for the boatman, laying him gently in the stern sheets. Then she cast off the painter and sat down on one of the thwarts amidships, pushing off with one oar.

The boatman tried feebly to stop her. 'Please, ma'am, you don't know what you're doing. It takes years of practice to learn how to row. If you sink us, you'll sink me livelihood. 'Swelp me, I'll starve. What if you lose the oars? We'll be adrift . . .'

'Wouldn't that be terrible? We might drift all the way to the other side of the harbour before we were rescued. That might not be for . . . ooh, minutes.' She fitted the oars in the rowlocks and started to row across to the *Tisiphone*. It was awkward at first – she had never rowed a boat before – but she picked it up in a matter of seconds and before she knew it, she was propelling the boat across to the sloop at the rate of knots. 'How am I doing?'

In the stern sheets, the boatman groaned piteously.

When she judged they must be getting near to the *Tisiphone*, she glanced over her shoulder to make sure the bow was aimed at the accommodation ladder suspended below the entry port. There was quite a crowd lining the sides to gape open-mouthed at the spectacle of a young lady rowing a boat. If the petty officers did not berate the seamen for neglecting their duties, it was because they were gaping alongside them. Mrs Cafferty gave them all a friendly wave, and rowed the last few yards to the accommodation ladder.

A fellow in a scarlet tunic – he looked more like a soldier than a sailor, what did they call them, marines? – challenged her. 'B . . . b . . . boat ahoy!'

'Ship ahoy,' she called back. 'Permission to come on board?'

The marine looked confused. 'You're supposed to say "Aye, aye!"'

if you're a distinguished visitor – or "No, no" if you're not.'

'Then modesty demands I should respond: No, no. May I come on board?'

An officer joined the marine at the entry port. 'Well, I, uh . . . I don't see why not, Miss . . .?'

'Cafferty. *Mrs* Cafferty.' She tied the rope to a wooden post and tripped lightly up the steps. After rowing the boat across the harbour, she was flushed and breathless when she set foot on deck, and quite exhilarated. 'Are you Commander Robertson?' she asked the officer.

'No, I'm Hartcliffe.' He bowed, and offered her his hand, obviously expecting her to curtsy, but she just shook it. He looked even more confused. 'I'm, er . . . well, I'm the first lieutenant, ma'am.'

'Delighted to meet you, Mr Hartcliffe.'

'Actually, it's . . . er . . . *Lord* Hartcliffe. But everyone just calls me "Hartcliffe".'

'As you will. Do you have a surgeon who could take a look at the boatman? He seems to have injured himself lifting my trunk.'

Hartcliffe peered down at the man who still lay supine in the bottom of the boat, and then snapped his fingers at a couple of seamen. 'Yorath! O'Houlihan! Lift that fellow out of the boat and carry him down to the sick-berth. Mr Cavan, perhaps you'd be so good as to inform Mr Westlake that he has a patient.'

'Aye, aye, sir.' A fair-haired youth, barely seventeen – presumably a midshipman – hurried below. As the two ratings Hartcliffe had addressed hurried to help the boatman up the side ladder, Mrs Cafferty became aware of two other seamen, a blond man and a negro, staring at her. The blond sailor was combing his lank hair in a predatory manner.

The negro nudged him. 'Forget it, Seth. Above your station, shipmate.'

'And above yours?' Seth replied in a Liverpudlian accent.

'Now I didn't say that.' The negro licked a fingertip and smoothed down his eyebrows. 'It ain't so much a question of *class* as of *style*. And you ain't got none.'

'Perhaps when you two gentlemen have finished preening yourselves, you'd be good enough to bring my trunk on board,' called Mrs Cafferty.

The two seamen looked embarrassed and confused. Hartcliffe quickly intervened. 'Pardon me, ma'am. Did you ask to have your trunk on board?'

'I'm so sorry, should I have asked through you?'

'Er . . . it's not that . . . that is to say, it's not *just* that . . . but . . . well, this *is* a ship of war. There seems to be some misunderstanding.'

'Then this should explain things.' She drew the letter Sir William Denison had given her from one of the voluminous pockets of her skirt and proffered it to Hartcliffe. 'Would you give this to your captain?'

'Of course, ma'am. Perhaps you'd like to come below out of the sun?'

'Thank you.'

He gestured for her to precede him down the after hatch. 'After you, ma'am. You may find it easier to go down backwards . . .'

'Thank you, but I'm sure I can manage.'

'Mind your head, ma'am.'

She waited for him at the bottom of the companion ladder, and he led her round a corner and down a passageway. Another marine sentry stood on duty outside a door at the end of the passage. 'A Mrs Cafferty to see the captain, Hawthorne,' said Hartcliffe.

'Yes, sir.' The marine crashed the stock of his musket against the deck. 'Lord Hartcliffe and Mrs Cafferty to see the cap'n!'

'Who the blazes is Mrs Cafferty?' a voice from the other side of the door boomed back.

Hartcliffe smiled awkwardly. Mrs Cafferty returned his smile, squeezed past the astonished marine and opened the door. In the day room within, she found three officers standing around a table, poring over a chart of the Tasman Sea.

'I am,' she said sweetly.

'Mrs Cafferty, sir,' said Hartcliffe, following her in. 'She brought this letter from Sir William Denison.' He held out the envelope to one of the officers, a burly figure in his mid-forties: Commander Robertson, she presumed. He took the letter from Hartcliffe and tore it open. Wordlessly, he read it through – twice, she guessed – and then folded it.

'Well, gentlemen, it seems we are to make a stop at Norfolk Island on our way to the Fijis,' he said with evident distaste. 'We're instructed to land Mrs Cafferty and two gentlemen there.'

'Norfolk Island?' said Hartcliffe. 'That's a penal settlement, isn't it?'

Robertson nodded. 'It seems that Mrs Cafferty here has been offered a position on the island as governess to the commandant's children, pending approval following an interview with the parents.'

'They're shipping you all the way out to Norfolk Island just so you can be interviewed by the parents?' the youngest of the four officers present asked Mrs Cafferty in surprise. He was a tall, lean man roughly the same age as herself, with bruises all over his bronzed face.

'That's where the children are.'

46

'There are children on Norfolk Island?' Hartcliffe exclaimed in astonishment.

'Why shouldn't there be?' asked Mrs Cafferty.

'Oh, no reason I can think of,' the young man with the bruised face said airily. 'Except that from what I hear Norfolk Island is the most brutal establishment in the Crown's penal settlements, reserved for the "incorrigibles": the most persistent and vicious reoffenders amongst the transportees of the Australias. Hardly a suitable environment to raise children.'

'Mr Price lives on the island with his entire family: his wife and five children, three boys and two girls,' explained Mrs Cafferty. 'Mrs Price has been delicate ever since she lost her sixth child, so Mr Price feels she needs a governess to help her raise the remaining children. All of the servants on Norfolk Island are convicts, but he thought it would be best to advertise the position elsewhere.'

'Were there many applicants?'

'I believe I was the only one.'

'You astonish me.'

'Irony does not become you, sir.'

'Oh?' The officer looked disappointed. 'I thought I was rather good at it.' He offered her his hand. 'Lieutenant Christopher I. Killigrew, at your service, ma'am.' He introduced himself in the American fashion, including his middle initial without making any attempt to account for it.

'What does the "I" stand for?' she asked drily. ' "Impertinent"?'

Her retort left him at a loss for words, although he seemed more amused than put out to find himself in such a situation.

'Obviously Mary Wollstonecraft was accurate in her assessment of naval officers,' Mrs Cafferty said.

'Mary Wollstonecraft?' echoed Hartcliffe.

'Mary Shelley's mother,' said Killigrew. 'The author of *A Vindication of the Rights of Woman*. What was it she said? Something about us being "positively indolent"? Being confined to the society of our own sex, we "acquire a fondness for humour and mischievous tricks"?'

Mrs Cafferty was startled to have any man quote Wollstonecraft at her, let alone a naval officer, but she quickly recovered herself. ' "But Mind is equally out of the question, whether they indulge the horse-laugh or the polite simper." '

'Oh, I prefer a horse-laugh to a polite simper any day of the week,' Killigrew assured her.

It was left to Hartcliffe to complete the introductions. 'Commander Robertson, our captain . . .'

Robertson grunted.

'. . . And Mr Yelverton, our master.'

47

'I thought the master of a ship *was* the captain?' said Mrs Cafferty.

'Not on navy vessels, ma'am,' said Yelverton. A beefy-faced man in his late forties or early fifties, the master spoke with a hint of a Norfolk accent. 'I'm the officer responsible for navigation, that's all.'

'Mr Yelverton does himself an injustice, ma'am,' said Hartcliffe. 'As the *Tisiphone*'s master, he may not be the most senior officer on board after the captain, but I hardly think any of us would deny he's the most important.' He turned to Robertson. 'Who are the other two passengers, sir?'

'Mr Nairn – the assistant comptroller-general of convicts – and some Yankee journalist who's been given permission to inspect the conditions in the settlement. We'll have to double up to make room. Mrs Cafferty can have your cabin, Second; you can sling a hammock in with Hartcliffe. Westlake will have to move in with Vellacott so Mr Nairn and this Yankee can share a cabin.'

Killigrew took hold of a crutch which had been propped against the table and wedged it under his right armpit. 'I'll start moving my things so you can move in at once, ma'am. If you'll excuse me, sir?' He hobbled out of the day room.

Mrs Cafferty took her leave of Robertson, Hartcliffe and Yelverton and followed the second lieutenant. 'Mr Killigrew – forgive me for asking – but what happened to your face?'

'Hm? Oh, I was defenestrated a few nights ago.'

'Defenestrated? Oh, you mean . . . oh! You're the fellow who was thrown out of that window at the Harbour View Hotel.'

Killigrew blushed. 'You heard about that?'

'My dear Mr Killigrew, let me assure you that everyone has heard about that. You are to be congratulated, sir. You are the talk of the town.'

'Capital!' he said brightly; her mocking tone seemed to cheer him up. 'I've wanted to be the talk of the town ever since I was a boy.'

'Do you often find yourself cast through windows?'

'Not as often as you might expect.' He opened a door to their right and motioned for her to precede him through it. 'The ward-room. This is where we dine.' He led her across to one of the doors that opened off the far side of the room. 'And this is my cabin, where you'll be accommodated.'

She surveyed the cramped cabin: a bunk, a washstand, a fold-down desk beneath some shelves weighed down with a motley miscellany of books. The latest novels of Dickens and Currer Bell vied for space with Latin poetry, historical romances by Dumas, philosophical works in English and French, and Edward Lear's *A*

48

Book of Nonsense. The cabin was plain and functional, but she had stayed in worse. 'Cosy,' she remarked.

'Sorry it's such a mess,' he said, quickly moving so his body blocked her view of the bottle of whiskey on the desk. Behind his back he opened the drawer and slid it out of sight. She pretended not to have noticed. 'Of course I'll clear my stuff out of here, and there will be clean sheets on the bunk.'

She glanced at the mess on the desk: some paperwork Killigrew had been working on, a peacock feather with a double-eye, and a small, framed calotype of a darkly pretty young woman. 'Your sweetheart?'

'One-time,' he said curtly.

'But still you hold the torch of love for her. What happened? Did she break off the engagement?' she asked archly. 'Leave you standing at the altar?'

'She was murdered.' He tried to sound dismissive.

She had always hated going through life being terrified of saying the wrong thing, so she had never worried about it. As a policy it had worked fine, but now, of course, the inevitable had happened and she had well and truly put her foot in her mouth. 'I'm sorry,' she whispered.

He shrugged. 'You weren't to know.'

Fortunately, the awkward moment was ended by the voice of the marine sentry on the deck above them: 'Boat ahoy!'

'Aye, aye!' came the reply.

Killigrew stood on tiptoe to peer out of the porthole. 'Ah-ha! It looks as though your fellow travellers have arrived. I'd better go up on deck to greet them.'

She followed him up on deck and they emerged from the hatch to find Hartcliffe and a bespectacled young officer greeting two gentlemen. One of them was a small, brisk, fastidiously neat man with a businesslike manner.

'Ah, Mrs Cafferty,' said Hartcliffe. 'May I introduce Mr Nairn, the assistant comptroller-general of convicts?'

'Mrs Cafferty and I have already met,' said Nairn, beaming as he shook Mrs Cafferty's hand. 'So, you didn't have second thoughts, ma'am?'

'My mind is quite made up, Mr Nairn. I'm determined to see this through.'

'Good for you, ma'am. Don't worry, I'm sure you'll be fine.' He gestured to his companion, who touched the gold head of his ebony cane to the rakishly curled brim of his top hat. 'Mrs Cafferty, gentlemen: may I present Mr Malachi Fallon, a reporter for *The Irish-American*?'

'*The Irish-American*?' queried Killigrew.

49

'A political newspaper published in New York,' explained Fallon, tipping his hat.

'Mr Fallon writes articles about how beastly we British are to our Irish subjects,' Nairn explained enthusiastically, as if he heartily approved.

Fallon smiled. 'There's no need to tell our readers how beastly the British are to the Irish, Mr Nairn. Most of them emigrated to New York when the famine was at its worst, as I did myself.'

'Now that's hardly fair,' protested Killigrew. 'The famine was an act of God. I'm the last person in the world to speak in defence of the British government, but you can hardly—'

'The last person in the world to speak in defence of the British government?' Fallon echoed with an amused smile. 'Forgive me for saying so, but that seems like a peculiar sentiment for a British naval officer to be expressing.'

'One can love one's country without caring for the poltroons who call themselves the government of the hour, Mr Fallon,' retorted Killigrew. 'At any rate, one can hardly blame them for what happened. When they realised the extent of the suffering in Ireland, they did try to alleviate the situation.'

'Too little too late, Mr Killigrew; and no consolation to the hundreds of thousands of men, women and children who died in terrible agony.'

'If I could turn the clock back, Mr Fallon—' Killigrew said tightly.

'But you can't, can you?'

'In Killigrew's defence, I should point out that he was very active in raising money for Irish famine relief,' said the bespectacled young officer who had been on deck with Hartcliffe. 'He squeezed a hundred pounds out of my guv'nor; how he managed that I'll— Yeow!' The officer hopped up and down, clutching his foot.

'Sorry, Strachan,' said Killigrew. 'My crutch slipped.'

Mrs Cafferty gave the lieutenant a curious look before turning to Fallon. 'If you are so keen on Irish politics, may I ask what interest you have in penal institutions? Is penal reform another of your editorial lines?'

'In a manner of speaking. It so happens that Devin Cusack is a prisoner on Norfolk Island.'

'Who's Devin Cusack?' asked Strachan.

Everyone on deck turned to stare at him incredulously. He might as well have asked who Queen Victoria was. 'Who's Devin Cusack?' echoed Killigrew. 'The Battle of Boulagh? The Widow Cormack's cabbage patch?'

Strachan blinked at him.

'Don't you *read* the newspapers?'

'No.'

'What, not *ever*?'

'Not unless you count *The Lancet* and *Curtis' Botanical Journal*. Killigrew, in light of the fact I'm not interested in finance, politics, foreign intelligence, what the Queen's been up to, buying a carriage or looking for a position as a servant, I can't think of a singularly more futile pursuit than reading the newspapers. Now will you please tell me: who the devil is Devin Cusack?'

'Who the devil indeed! Devin Cusack is a rebel and a traitor who can count himself fortunate that the government saw fit to commute his sentence of death by being hanged, drawn and quartered to one of transportation for life.'

'I beg to differ, sir,' said Fallon. 'Devin Cusack is one of the leading lights of the Young Ireland movement, a man who courageously risked his life for the repeal of the Act of Union between Great Britain and Ireland, along with William Smith O'Brien and the others in the rebellion at Ballingarry.'

'I'm sorry, I'm still none the wiser,' said Strachan. 'Mrs Cafferty, since you appear to combine an Irish name with an English accent, I wonder if I might turn to you for an unbiased explanation?'

She smiled. 'I'll certainly do my best. Along with William Smith O'Brien, Devin Cusack is one of the leaders of the Young Ireland movement, dedicated to repealing the Act of Union.' Ever since the Act of Union of 1800, the Irish Parliament had been abolished and Ireland ruled from Westminster by the British Parliament. Ireland returned its own MPs to Westminster, but they formed a minority in the House of Commons, which meant that unless one of the British political parties at Westminster supported the Irish, they could never get any laws passed in their favour.

'Two years ago, when the famine was at its height, they gave up on the political process,' explained Mrs Cafferty. 'Or rather, attempted to continue it by other means, as Herr von Clausewitz would have put it. In fine, they publicly declared their willingness to take up arms against the British government. When the government heard this, they suspended the law of *habeas corpus* to allow them to arrest the Young Irelanders without a charge and to hold them indefinitely. The Young Irelanders felt they were left with no choice but to start a rebellion. They marched around Tipperary trying to raise an army. When they reached the town of Ballingarry they had a small force of just over a hundred men and women, a few of them armed with muskets or pikes. While they were there, they learned that a large force of policemen was marching to meet them. They built a barricade across the main street of the town, and when the police saw it they beat a hasty retreat to a large house a short distance from the town. The rebels pursued them and besieged the house.

'While O'Brien was trying to parley with the policemen, fighting broke out. I don't know which side opened fire first, although I dare say at least two gentlemen present have their own opinions. In any event, two men were killed – both of them rebels – but after a couple of hours the rebels realised they could not capture the house and they melted away when they received reports of an even larger body of policemen approaching the town. Smith O'Brien and the other leaders were arrested trying to flee the country. They were tried for treason and sentenced to death. Those, at least, are the facts as I understand them.' Mrs Cafferty glanced challengingly at Killigrew and Fallon. 'Would either of you care to dispute them?'

They shook their heads, quailing like naughty children before a . . . well, a governess.

'None of which explains what Devin Cusack is doing in a place like Norfolk Island,' said Hartcliffe. 'I thought only hardened criminals were sent there? Even the British government accepts that O'Brien and the other rebels were political prisoners.'

'I can explain that,' said Nairn. 'When O'Brien, Cusack and the other rebels arrived here in Hobart Town last year, I went on board their ship to meet them. Acting under instructions from Sir William, I offered them a chance to live in relative comfort. They were to be kept separate but, as long as they gave their word of honour that they would make no attempt to escape, they were to be allowed to live normal lives and to move about freely within the respective districts to which they had been confined. After debating the offer amongst themselves, they all decided to give their parole: all except William Smith O'Brien and Devin Cusack.

'O'Brien was sent to live under guard in a cottage of his own on Maria Island and remains there to this day; Cusack was sent to the Salt Water River penal station. Not having given his parole, of course, Mr Cusack felt under no moral obligation to stay, and so in spite of the extensive security precautions put in place he contrived to depart within two weeks of his arrival. He only got two miles before he was picked up by the local yeomanry, of course, but it was felt that in order to forestall any further such harebrained attempts to abscond it would be wisest to remove him posthaste to a location from which there would be no possible chance of escape . . .'

'Norfolk Island,' concluded Killigrew.

'The Isle of Mis'ry,' put in Fallon. 'Where Satan never sleeps.'

Nairn smiled. He seemed to find Fallon's attitude amusing. 'Mr Fallon is under the impression that Mr Cusack is being held in general circulation and is being subjected to the same indignities and punishments as the other inmates of Norfolk Island. Indeed, he wrote a number of inflammatory articles in *The Irish-American* to that effect earlier this year. These articles were brought to the attention of the British consul in New York and a rather heated correspondence between the two of them ensued in the pages of *The Irish-American*. Finally the consul invited Mr Fallon to go to Norfolk Island to see for himself that Mr Cusack, far from being held in durance vile, has a cottage to himself on the north side of the island and lives in not inconsiderable comfort. For a prisoner, that is.'

Fallon smiled like the cat that swallowed the canary. 'I don't believe the consul imagined for a moment that I would call his bluff.'

They went down to the wardroom where they made small talk over a pot of tea while they waited for the cabins to be prepared. At last her cabin was ready, and Mrs Cafferty entered it, carefully closed the door behind her, and heaved a sigh of relief.

She unpacked enough things from her trunk to see her through the voyage. Then she took a small double-barrelled 'turnover' pistol from amongst her undergarments and slipped it into one of the pockets of her skirt.

IV

Passage to Purgatory

'You may order Mr Muir to stop the engines and let the fire die out, Mr Killigrew,' Robertson said once the *Tisiphone* had cleared soundings. 'And I believe we shall unrig paddles.' Removing the paddles from the wheels reduced drag, but it was a dirty and difficult task, usually reserved for any defaulters.

'Aye, aye, sir.' Killigrew passed the word on to Midshipman Cavan, who hurried below to inform the chief engineer, and Robertson turned to the master.

'Lay me a course for Norfolk Island, Mr Yelverton.'

'Aye, aye, sir. We should be able to fetch it on a course of north-east.'

'Very good. All plain sail, Second, course north-east.'

The sloop had weighed anchor and steamed out of Sullivan's Cove on the dot of noon. Now she had emerged from the Derwent Estuary and crossed Storm Bay to the open sea beyond. Robertson went below, and Hartcliffe came on deck shortly before four o'clock to take over from Killigrew as officer of the watch.

Supported by his crutch, Killigrew hobbled down to the log room to update the ship's log with the sailings of the afternoon watch, and then he was his own man; until the end of the first dog watch, at any rate.

He entered the wardroom on his way to his cabin. Mrs Cafferty and Fallon were there, making polite small talk over another pot of tea. Their presence reminded Killigrew that he had to go to Hartcliffe's cabin now, to which Private Hawthorne had already moved all his things.

As soon as he entered the wardroom, Fallon rose to his feet. 'Settling in nicely?' Killigrew asked him, propping the crutch in one corner.

Fallon seemed distracted by the question. 'What? Yes, thank you. Mr Killigrew, why have the engines stopped?'

'Don't concern yourself: it's nothing to worry about. We're proceeding under sail. We've only got enough coal in the bunkers for two weeks' steaming, so we like to reserve it for emergencies, difficult manoeuvres or navigating busy waterways when the wind's against us.'

'You mean, we're going to *sail* all the way to Norfolk Island? How long will it take us?'

'Less than two weeks. We've got the Westerlies behind us; we should reach the island early next month.'

'Next month! If I'd known it was going to take so long, I'd . . . Is there no way you can persuade Captain Robertson to proceed under steam?'

Killigrew smiled. 'I'd rather not try, if it's all the same with you; he doesn't care for extravagance. Why? What's the hurry?'

'Oh, no hurry, no hurry,' Fallon said quickly. He paced up and down a couple of times, and then stepped out of the wardroom without another word.

'Well! I don't imagine anyone's ever been in a hurry to get to Norfolk Island before.' To preserve his right ankle, Killigrew hopped rather than walked across to the sideboard. Mrs Cafferty struggled to suppress a giggle, prompting him to smile.

'It's all right, do feel free to laugh.'

'I'm sorry.'

'No need to apologise. I must present a pretty comical sight, mustn't I? Twisted ankle.' He poured himself a glass of whiskey from one of the decanters. 'Can I offer you a drink, ma'am?'

'It's a little early in the day for me.'

'Sun's well over the foreyard.'

'I never drink before six o'clock in the evening.'

'As you will. Chin-chin!' He drained the whiskey in one, poured himself a second, and then sat down at the far end of the table from her so as not to crowd her. A copy of the *Hobart Town Daily Courier* lay on the table and he picked it up, leafing through to the gossip columns; not that they made much sense to an outsider, but it was that or the shipping intelligence.

He found he could not concentrate on the print, however: he was conscious of Mrs Cafferty's gaze burning through the paper. He lowered the paper and found that she was indeed staring at him.

'What is it?' he challenged.

'Why didn't you want Mr Strachan to tell me about your charitable work, Mr Killigrew?'

He blushed. 'Not the sort of thing a fellow talks about, is it? I know plenty of would-be philanthropists who wear their charity work like laurels; but I've always felt that if one is going to do good work, one should do it for its own sake, not to win the praise and admiration of your peers. Besides, I wouldn't want you to get the wrong idea about me. I don't really care a jot about the starving Irish, you know. I only do charity work because it means I get to spend time with Baroness Burdett-Coutts.'

Mrs Cafferty placed her elbows on the table, intertwined her fingers and rested her chin on the backs of her hands. 'And why would you want to do a thing like that?'

'The wealthiest, most beautiful unmarried heiress in the world . . . I can't imagine, can you?'

She laughed. 'What am I to make of you, Mr Killigrew? You despise the Irish rebels, and yet raise money for Irish famine relief – and then try to laugh it off as an infatuation with Baroness Burdett-Coutts. You have a passing familiarity with the works of Mary Wollstonecraft, and yet you become the talk of Hobart Town by engaging in street brawls. You laugh everything off as a joke, and yet you're the unhappiest man I've ever met.'

'What makes you say that? No, wait, let me guess: you've been speaking to Mr Strachan, haven't you? I suppose you asked about that calotype in my cabin and he mentioned that business in Hong Kong?'

She nodded. 'I'm sorry, I'm sure it's none of my business.'

'You're right, it is none of your business.' He said it without malice. 'Have a care, ma'am. I fear Mr Strachan is endeavouring to play cupid between us.'

'Would you like that?'

'No, thank you. You seem like a lovely woman, but cupid's arrows have already wreaked enough havoc in my life, thank you very much. In two weeks' time you'll be taking up your new position on Norfolk Island, and I'll be sailing on to the Fijis – to be eaten by cannibals, with any luck.'

'Do you really want to be eaten by cannibals?'

'As long as they remember to drink white wine with white meat. I couldn't think of anything more ignominious than being washed down with a glass of claret.'

'Now I know what your middle initial stands for: Idiotic.'

'That's me: "Idiotic" is my middle name. Now, what about you? You're a mass of contradictions yourself, if you don't mind my saying so. A free-thinking woman who seems willing to subject herself to the real penal servitude of being a governess . . .'

'Financial necessity, Mr Killigrew. Ever since Captain Cafferty died, I've had to make ends meet as best I can.'

'I'm sorry. Now I'm the one who's prying.'

'It's all right, it was a long time ago. More than eight years now. I was very young when we married.'

57

'Captain . . .' mused Killigrew. 'You don't strike me as a naval officer's wife.'

She shook her head. 'Army. Forty-Fourth Regiment of Foot.'

He raised his glass. 'Here's to the Little Fighting Fours,' he said, and then put two and two together. 'Where did he die?' he asked quietly. 'Gandamack?'

She shook her head. 'It was before that, on the third day of the retreat from Kabul, when the Ghilzais started sniping at us from amongst the rocks.'

'Christ! You mean you were there with him? With Lady Sale and the others?'

She nodded. 'He died in my arms. I suppose that must sound terribly melodramatic to you, but that's the way it happened. It was not the way it happens in the theatre, however. Sean was in a great deal of pain . . .' She looked down.

'It's all right. You don't have to go on. It's really none of my business.'

She looked up at him, her eyes bright but dry. 'There's not much more to tell. I was still holding on to his body, with the rest of the army marching past all around us, the women and children dying on all sides, when the Ghilzai horsemen appeared out of nowhere and carried me off. It all happened so suddenly, I was terrified. I didn't know what I thought was going to happen . . .' She smiled. 'No. I knew exactly what I thought would happen. But it didn't. The Ghilzais handed me over to Akbar Khan, the leader of the Afghans. The next day I was joined by Lady Sale and the married officers with their wives and children; Khan had taken them under his protection. At least, that's what he called it, but we were hostages really. But we were always treated honourably. Well, the rest you probably know.'

Killigrew nodded. He had been in Singapore, on his way to the Opium War, when he had heard of the destruction of General Elphinstone's Army of the Indus in the Khyber Pass. Only two men had survived: Dr Bryden and Harry Flashman, the Hector of Afghanistan. But the news that Lady Sale and the other captives were safe and sound had come months later, after the Treaty of Nanking had concluded the war with China. The hostages had spent three months at Akbar Khan's fortress at Budeeabad – during which time the fortress was struck by an earthquake – before a sally from Jallalabad led by General Sale had inflicted a defeat on the Afghans, forcing Khan to move his hostages deeper into Afghanistan. They had been force-marched through the mountains of the Hindu Kush for weeks, until they had reached Bameean, where they had been rescued by General Sale more than eight months after their initial capture. As honourably as the Afghans might have treated their prisoners, it must have been a terrifying ordeal for a young woman who could not have been a day over eighteen.

'When I got back to Calcutta I learned that my brother Francis had died; I was alone in the world. But I had no wish to become a self-pitying wretch, dependent on the charity of others, so I left India and got a job as a governess to the children of an American family in upstate New York. I worked there for five years, until the youngest of their children was old enough to go to school. That was when I saw Mr Price's advertisement in the *Seneca Falls County Courier*.'

'Mr Price certainly seems to have advertised widely in his search for a governess.'

'Apparently his advertisements in the Australian press did not meet with much of a response.'

'If it isn't prying, might I ask why you would want to accept a position as a governess on Norfolk Island?'

'I'm in need of a position; Mr Price's children are in need of a governess. And the remuneration is generous.'

'Even so . . . the world's most notorious penal settlement?'

She lowered her gaze. 'I've seen brutality, Mr Killigrew. It would be dishonest of me to claim that it does not frighten me, but at least I have some idea of what to expect. In that respect, I feel I am well qualified. And as I said just now, other applicants were few and far between. If I did not do the job, who would?' She raised her eyes to meet his once more. 'Does that sound foolish to you?'

He considered the point for a moment, and then shook his head. 'No. No, I know exactly what you mean.'

'There you have it, Second.' On the quarterdeck of the *Tisiphone*, Commander Robertson gestured the island they now approached from the south-west. 'Her Majesty's penal settlement of Norfolk Island. Nowhere in the world exists a greater concatenation of villainy, roguery and malevolence,' he remarked to his second lieutenant.

Killigrew smiled faintly. 'Outside of the Reform Club, sir,' he could not resist adding.

Robertson glowered at him. 'Spare me your feeble attempts at humour, Second. Mr Cavan, be so good as to go below and inform our passengers that we will shortly be dropping anchor in Sydney Bay.'

'Aye, aye, sir.' Midshipman Cavan saluted smartly and went below.

The two-week voyage from Hobart Town had been leisurely. The gash in Killigrew's thigh had healed sufficiently for Strachan to remove the stitches; the bruises on his face were scarcely visible, and he was getting around without the crutch, hardly limping at all.

They had seen little of Fallon or Nairn during the voyage; the assistant comptroller-general of convicts had been laid low by seasickness, while the journalist only emerged from the cabin they shared to eat or to demand the latest estimate of when they would be arriving at Norfolk Island. The slowness of the *Tisiphone*'s progress seemed to drive him to distraction: Killigrew could only assume that Fallon was an impatient man, for his reassurance that Cusack would still be there when they arrived did nothing to alleviate Fallon's mood.

But if Fallon was a queer fish, the voyage had had its compensations in the form of Mrs Cafferty. Killigrew had spent most of his off-watch hours talking to her, which had helped the time to pass all the more swiftly. She had overcome her initial hostility to him when they had discovered they shared the same radical politics. She was a lively and intelligent conversationalist, and not afraid to contradict him and speak her own mind on the few things they did not agree on. He could not remember enjoying anyone's company so much since . . . well, since Hong Kong. Not that he had the same depth of feeling for her that he had done for the young woman he had lost; but there was no denying he was going to miss her when they left her at Norfolk Island.

And now they were off the coast already.

Robertson surveyed the island briefly through the telescope before handing it to Killigrew. A volcanic plug rising up out of the northern fringe of the Tasman Sea, Norfolk Island was about five miles long and three miles wide, according to the chart. For most of its coastline, sheer black cliffs laced with streaks of red rose three hundred feet out of the sea, where breakers boomed constantly over a ring of reefs. Here and there strands of flax covered the cliffs densely, while elsewhere dark pinnacles of basalt rose up. On top of these forbidding defences was a rolling landscape of verdant meadows and spiring pine trees, a veritable paradise according to its discoverer, Captain James Cook.

The *Tisiphone* exchanged signals with the signal station on Point Ross, on the south side of the island. Having established that the convicts had not mutinied – something had happened several times in the past, with bloody consequences – and that the island was still under the garrison's control, Robertson complied with their instructions and dropped anchor in Sydney Bay, opposite Kingston, the main settlement on the island.

Beyond the reef, Killigrew could see a lagoon – a crescent of white sand, half-built stone pier with a boat-house nearby, some buildings of white stone with red roofs clustered around a green with a flagstaff on it. To the right of those stood three compounds surrounded by high stone walls, the central one enclosing a three-storey building that looked like a barracks. Behind these, about half a mile inland, there was another strand of buildings – a mixture of houses and barracks. All of these were hemmed in on three sides by steep hills, and on the fourth by the sea.

The paddle-sloop hove to and dropped anchor outside the reef. 'Boat coming out, sir,' warned a lookout.

Robertson had a look through the telescope and handed it to Killigrew. 'What do you make of it, Second?'

Killigrew looked for himself. It was a whaleboat, nearly thirty feet long, crewed by eight men wearing cork lifejackets over their chequered 'magpie' fatigues. Two black-uniformed guards armed with carbines supervised the oarsmen.

An eleventh figure sat in the bows and waved to the men on the sloop's deck. He looked to be about six feet tall, bull-necked and bow-legged, his face burned brick red by the sub-tropical sun. He wore tight pantaloons and an old-fashioned bobtail coat, with a neckerchief of black silk tied sailor-style across his broad shoulders. Looking ludicrous on top of his large, bullet-head, a small straw hat with a blue ribbon was balanced on top of his oiled, sandy hair.

'Boat ahoy!' the marine sentry challenged from the entry port.

'Don't shoot!' called the oddly dressed individual in the boat.

'Identify yourself, mister!' growled Robertson.

'John Giles Price, civil commandant of Norfolk Island. Permission to come aboard?'

'Permission granted.'

The whaleboat bumped against the *Tisiphone*'s side, immediately below the entry port, and Price leaped for the side-ladder, climbing athletically up on deck. He looked distinctly green about the gills as he pressed a wadded linen handkerchief to his lips, before inserting a monocle in front of one of his cold, grey eyes and using it to survey the men on the quarterdeck. Finally he turned back to Robertson. 'Have I the honour of addressing the captain of this vessel?'

Robertson inclined his head. 'Commander Robertson at your service, Mr Price.' The two of them shook hands. Killigrew knew from experience that Robertson had the kind of firm grip that could leave your fingers numb – the commander was not showing off, he simply did not know his own strength – but even he winced at Price's grasp.

'. . . And this is my second lieutenant, Mr Killigrew.'

Price turned his gaze on the lieutenant. 'No relation of Rear Admiral Killigrew?'

'His grandson.'

Price nodded. 'I remember you. Weren't you the little boy who

61

climbed down that collapsed tin mine to take food to the men trapped inside, until they could be dug free?'

Killigrew grimaced, embarrassed. 'I was very young and very foolish. At the time I thought it was just a big adventure.'

Price smiled. 'I met your grandfather several times. He and my father were good friends.' He did not need to tell Killigrew that his father was Sir Rose Price of Trengwainton, a baronet of the Cornish aristocracy. When Killigrew had been a boy, he had overheard many conversations about what a young tearaway John Price had grown up to be, and how he was bound to come to a bad end unless he mended his ways. Price had been packed off to the colonies only a few months before Killigrew had joined the navy, at such short notice that everyone suspected some sort of scandal, although if there had been one, his father had covered it up very effectively indeed.

Price gazed about the *Tisiphone*'s deck. 'So, you joined the navy, eh? We often wondered if you'd follow in the family tradition.'

'I think we all knew that you'd end up in a place like this, one way or another,' Killigrew replied with a smile.

Price stared at Killigrew in shocked disbelief, and then roared with laughter. 'It's good to see you've got a sense of humour at last!' he said, and turned to Robertson.

'The rear admiral often used to complain to my father that his grandson was as mournful as an undertaker's mute, and forever with his head stuck in some damned book!'

'I think you'll find he's changed considerably since then,' Robertson said drily.

The three passengers had come on deck now. Price recognised Nairn at once, acknowledging him with a smile. 'Mr Nairn. This is an unexpected pleasure.' His eyes widened and he smiled with delight when he saw Mrs Cafferty. 'And may I be permitted to make the acquaintance of this enchanting creature?'

'But of course,' said Nairn. 'Mrs Cafferty, this is Mr John Giles Price, commandant of Norfolk Island. Mr Price, may I present Mrs Philippa Cafferty, with whom I believe you have corresponded?'

Price took Mrs Cafferty's hand and kissed it. 'Forgive me, madam. I should have known, but I was not expecting someone quite so . . . youthful.'

'I'm older than I look,' she assured him with a smile. 'I have six years' experience of working as a governess to a large family . . .'

'I received Mr Stanton's letter of recommendation in the last mail packet,' said Price. 'He speaks most highly of your abilities as a governess. Rest assured, ma'am, your competence is not in doubt. I know of no reason why I should not employ you at once; but perhaps first we ought to go ashore so you can meet Mrs Price and the children. Got to let the little woman have her say, eh?' he added with a wink at Nairn. 'And before you commit yourself, you should have an opportunity to meet the little desperadoes.'

'There is one other matter which requires our attention before we go ashore,' said Nairn. 'This is Mr Malachi Fallon of the New York press.'

'My friends call me "Panama",' explained Fallon, transferring his cane to his left hand so he could shake Price's hand with his right.

'Do they indeed, Mr Fallon?' said Price.

Fallon was not put out by the implied snub, merely smiling with amusement.

Price turned to Nairn. 'This has something to do with Cusack, doesn't it?'

'Mr Fallon writes for *The Irish-American,* a newspaper notorious for its pro-repeal editorials,' explained Nairn. He smiled thinly. 'To read some of its articles, one might be forgiven for thinking that Mr Cusack was kept in general circulation with the other convicts on this island.'

'You'll have to admit it's understandable, gentlemen,' said Fallon. 'I don't mean to give offence, Mr Price, but Norfolk Island does have something of a . . . well, shall we say a . . . reputation?'

'No offence taken, Mr Fallon,' Price replied, unconcerned. 'This is a penal settlement, not a spa town. The desperadoes in my care are here for the benefit of the rest of society, not for their own.'

'And when you talk of such desperadoes, do you include Devin Cusack?'

'Let me make one thing absolutely clear to you, Mr Fallon. As far as I'm concerned, Mr Cusack is a traitor and a rebel, and if it were up to me I'd have him put in the gaol-gang, working in the wet quarry alongside the toughest villains on Norfolk Island. However, my instructions from the comptroller-general are quite specific: Mr Cusack is a political prisoner and is to be treated as such. He has a cottage to himself on the north coast of the island where he lives in considerably more comfort than the average Irish immigrant in New York, I'll warrant.' Price turned to Nairn. 'Might I have a word with you *in camera,* sir?'

'By all means. If you gentlemen will excuse us . . .?' Nairn and Price walked over to the taffrail to have a low confabulation.

While they waited, Fallon produced a couple of cigars and offered one to Killigrew, who shook his head: he was supposed to be on duty. Fallon shrugged, returned one cigar to an inside pocket, snapped the end off the other and lit it.

Killigrew watched Price and Nairn. The commandant did most of the talking, and his expression and gestures made it clear he was not happy about something; but the assistant comptroller-general had the last word.

The two of them walked back to where the others waited. 'Mr Price has generously given permission for you to interview Mr Cusack,' Nairn told Fallon.

'I'm glad to hear it.'

'Under certain conditions,' added Nairn. 'First, you are not permitted to roam freely on the island. Wherever you do go, you will be accompanied by a constable appointed by Mr Price. Mr Price is to be kept informed of your whereabouts at all times. Second, you may not talk to any of the convicts other than Devin Cusack – except where necessary in dealing with those convict-constables who by virtue of their "trusty" status you may have cause to address from time to time. You will be permitted to talk to Cusack and to ask him any questions you may have, but only in the presence of Mr Price. You may make notes of your conversation with Cusack, but Mr Price will require to censor those notes if he feels that anything within them compromises the demands of security within the settlement. You may not pass Mr Cusack any notes, nor may you give him any gifts, money, tobacco-products or other objects.'

'That all seems perfectly reasonable,' said Fallon.

'Thirdly, you will be required to sign a waiver.'

'A waiver?'

'Accepting responsibility in the event of any . . . shall we say, unpleasantness?' Price smiled nastily. 'I keep a firm grip on these scoundrels, Mr Fallon, but they're as cunning as they are vicious. There have been no mutinies since I took over as commandant and discipline has never been stronger, but I would be lying if I were to give you any guarantees.'

'I understand that your family lives with you on the island, your wife and children,' remarked Fallon. 'That many of the officers of the garrison also have wives and children living with them. Have they signed such a waiver?'

'These are Mr Price's terms and conditions,' said Nairn. 'He has the last word.'

'Do you not have authority over him?'

'The Convict Department employs Mr Price because it has confidence in his ability to control the convicts here and run this establishment. The responsibility for all that happens here lies with him. I should need good reason before I overrule him in any matter relating to the security of the island.'

Fallon blew smoke in Price's face. 'Where do I sign?'

Nairn turned to Robertson. 'Commander, perhaps your clerk would be good enough to assist us in drawing up the necessary documentation?'

'But of course.'

Robertson guided Nairn, Price and Fallon down to his day room. They re-emerged fifteen minutes later, all parties seemingly satisfied with the conclusion of negotiations.

'We'll be staying at Norfolk Island for two nights,' the commander told his two lieutenants. 'Apparently the officers of the garrison are holding a ball at the civilian hospital tomorrow night, and Mr Price has cordially invited the senior officers of the *Tisiphone* to attend. Tonight we'll be dining at Government House.'

'I do hope you'll join us, Mrs Cafferty,' said Price. 'I'm well aware that most governesses find themselves in an awkward position in an alien household, being neither servants nor family members. For as long as you're on Norfolk Island, I'd be grateful if you'd think of yourself as one of the family.'

'Thank you. I only hope I can prove myself worthy of the honour you extend to me.'

'Be so good as to inform the other wardroom officers about dinner tonight, Second,' said Robertson. 'Full dress.'

'You might like to wear your undress uniforms until you're ashore, and then change into your number-one rigs,' said Price. 'The passage through the reef can be a mite rough at times.'

V

The Isle of Mis'ry

The oarsmen bent furiously over their oars and propelled the whaleboat into the boiling maelstrom. They had to cross the reef with the breaker, or else the hidden rocks would rip the bottom out of the boat. The next wave hit them astern, drenching Killigrew and the other officers in the stern sheets, and the boat was lifted on the breaker. It was desperate work for a few seconds. The oarsmen struggled to find purchase with their oars in the foaming waters while the swirling cross-rips appeared to spin the boat this way and that. Then, just when it seemed the boat must surely be capsized, they were through; gliding forwards over the calm, clear waters of an aquamarine lagoon. Glancing over the side, Killigrew could see red snappers darting amongst the coral at least two fathoms down, the water was so clear.

'A mite rough, did he say?' grumbled Strachan.

'Buck up, man,' said Killigrew, unperturbed. 'The sun will soon dry us out. Besides, I'll lay odds you're the first ever palaeontologist to visit Norfolk Island. Perhaps you'll find some interesting fossils while we're here.'

'Don't be ridiculous,' snorted Strachan, trying to dry the lenses of his spectacles with a linen handkerchief that was scarcely less sodden than the rest of him. 'For fossils you need a sedimentary geological structure. Any fool can see that this island is predominantly igneous.'

'But of course,' Killigrew said with a wry grimace.

The first whaleboat had already reached the jetty and the crew held it steady while Price, Nairn, Fallon, Robertson and Mrs Cafferty climbed out. Then the convict crew of the first boat rowed it into the surf before carrying it up to the boat-house on the beach beyond, while Price and the others waited for the second boat on the jetty.

A detachment of a dozen soldiers in scarlet tunics stood on the jetty, watching over three-dozen convicts who worked up to their waists in the water alongside. The men of the work-party were mostly white, but there were enough men of other races to remind them that Norfolk Island's inmates came from all over the British Empire: a Chinese with a pigtail, a turbaned Sikh, a Maori with a tattooed face. The whaleboat bumped against the jetty on the far side and one of the oarsmen jumped out and tied up the painter.

Once they were all safely on dry land, Price was about to stride towards the foot of the jetty but Fallon paused to watch the men working in the wet quarry. 'Thirteen guards standing watch over three dozen men,' he remarked. 'That's rather a high proportion, isn't it, Mr Price?'

'That's another reason why there've been no mutinies since I took over as commandant, Mr Fallon,' Price responded with evident self-satisfaction. 'Because I take no chances. Those men belong to the gaol-gang. That's why we have soldiers from the garrison to watch them, rather than the usual warders and convict-overseers. The men who are sent to Norfolk Island are the worst scum of the Empire; the men assigned to the gaol-gang are the scum of the scum. I put them to work here, on the wet quarry, cutting coral from the reef to burn in the limekilns ashore. Iron men, they're called. Give 'em three hundred lashes on the triangles and they won't so much as whimper, though you can see their ribs.' If Killigrew had not known better, he would have guessed that Price was proud of the convicts' stoicism.

'Three hundred lashes?' said Mrs Cafferty. 'That's a little harsh, isn't it? My husband was careful to make sure I never had to witness a flogging with my own eyes, but I've seen what fifty lashes can do to a man's back. Three hundred . . .'

'This is a harsh place, ma'am,' said Price. 'I shan't try to pretend otherwise. You should know what you will be letting yourself in for if you accept my offer of a job as governess to my children. Oh, you'll be safe here – on that I give you my word of honour. But only because I know how best to handle the likes of this scum.' He indicated the men working on the wet quarry.

'Three hundred lashes!' exclaimed Robertson. 'Good God! We shouldn't be punishing men like that, we should be recruiting them into the navy!'

'You wouldn't want them,' said Price, and pointed to one of the men working in the water alongside the jetty. 'See him? That's Edmund Wyatt, also known as Flummut Ned. Wyatt! Come here, you dog!'

Wyatt scowled and stopped what he was doing to wade across to the jetty. He moved slowly; more slowly than the resistance of the water could account for.

'Climb out,' Price told him. 'I want these fine gentlemen and the lady to see what a real desperado looks like!'

Wyatt placed his palms on the surface of the jetty and tried to heave himself out of the water, scrabbling against the stonework with one leg while letting the other hang straight down. He seemed to be struggling, his brick-red face turning redder with the effort, but at last he got his backside on the pier and turned to grab the chain fettered to his right leg. When he pulled up the chain, Killigrew saw why he had moved so slowly through the water, and why it had taken him such an effort to climb out: a thirty-six-pound iron shot was bolted to the other end of the chain.

He dropped the shot on to the pier, stood up, and straightened. Killigrew could not help noticing that one of the soldiers kept his musket constantly trained on the convict, following his every move.

'Tell the lady and these gentlemen what you were transported for, Ned,' ordered Price.

Wyatt hawked and spat on the ground, dangerously close to one of Price's boots. 'Bit-faking.'

'You're too modest, Ned.' Price turned to his guests to explain. 'Ned here was one of the most notorious coiners the London underworld has ever known. That may not sound like much of a crime to you, but believe me, it's big business. The police inspector who brought Wyatt to heel reckoned he and his gang had flooded the British economy with thousands of pounds' worth of false coins. And don't try to tell me it's a crime without a victim: the production of false coins on that scale debases the currency and can do severe damage to the economy. Not that that would worry a vicious brute like Wyatt. Isn't that right, Ned? You're quite the pebble, aren't you?'

Wyatt shrugged.

'When the police raided the house in Shoreditch where he was running his coining operation, he and his gang put up a fight,' explained Price. 'Four policemen had to be hospitalised: one had an arm and three ribs broken from being struck with a crowbar, another had concussion and a suspected fractured skull from being hit by an iron saucepan. A third had his hand badly burned when one of the coiners threw molten metal at them, while the fourth was blinded in one eye and scarred for life when someone dashed the acid they used for electroplating in his face. The only reason no one was hanged for that was because Wyatt and his pals had a good lawyer, and none of the policemen could remember who had done what to whom in the mêlée.'

'They deserved it,' said Wyatt. 'They were peelers.'

'What about the sailors who died in that mutiny on the convict ship you were lagged on? Did they deserve it?'

Wyatt looked insouciantly at each of the naval officers present, until at last his eyes came to rest on Killigrew. The two of them looked one another up and down. 'There's only one thing I hate worse than peelers,' he drawled. 'And that's laggers.'

Price chuckled. 'You'd better believe it, Mr Killigrew. Ned here would kill you as soon as look at you if I weren't here to protect you. Isn't that right, Ned?'

Wyatt grinned. 'Sooner.'

'Very brave, aren't you, Ned?' Price moved closer to him. 'Like to kill me too, wouldn't you? Go on – why don't you try to take one of the pistols from my belt?'

Wyatt looked tempted, but glanced at the soldier levelling his musket at him.

'I'll make it easy for you,' offered Price. 'Private Wilkins! Shoulder your musket. There now, Ned. Here – I'll clasp my hands on top of my head. Go on, Ned. It'd be worth it, wouldn't it? To be the man who cramped John Giles Price? You've often said you'll kill me if it's the last thing you do. Well, here's your chance.'

Wyatt's hand hovered inches from the grip of one of the pepper-boxes tucked in Price's belt. For a moment Killigrew thought the convict was actually going to go for it, even though he must have known that he himself would die seconds later, but then Wyatt lowered his hand to his side once more. 'Go to hell,' he muttered sullenly.

Price laughed. 'Haven't you worked it out yet, Ned? This *is* hell – and I'm the Devil, here to punish you for your sins! All right, my joker. Back to work.'

The convict sat down on the edge of the pier, lowered the round shot into the water until it was at the full extent of its chain and his ankle took the strain, and then eased himself off, landing in the water with a splash.

Price led his guests off the pier and they made their way along the sea wall. Price pointed out the different buildings as they passed: the new gaol, the convict barracks, the lumber-yard, the limekilns.

'What do you use the lime for?' asked Lord Hartcliffe. 'Cement?'

Price nodded, and gestured about them. 'All the buildings you see here were built by convicts using only the raw materials we find here on this island. We have our own quarry, and there are plenty of pine trees on the island for timber. It's sawn into planks at the lumber-yard. We're self-sufficient in food now too: sheep and cattle graze on the island, and we grow our own vegetables and corn at the agricultural station at Longridge, about a mile inland from here.'

70

'And the convicts do all this?' asked Fallon.

Price nodded. 'It keeps them out of trouble. You know what they say: the Devil makes work for idle hands! At present I've got them building a new gaol for my more recalcitrant guests. We're desperately short of cells for solitary confinement: a much less brutal method of punishing convicts than flogging, I'm sure you'll agree. But as things stand at present, when I sentence a man to solitary confinement, I have to put him in a cell with a dozen others.'

Government House stood apart from the rest of Kingston, a two-storey villa on a low knoll to the east of the settlement. Two eighteen-pounder brass cannon stood on the greensward in front of the house, glowering over the rest of the settlement. Price ordered his butler – a convict-trusty – to prepare rooms for his guests, where Fallon and Nairn might stay while they were on the island, and the officers of the *Tisiphone* could get dressed for dinner. Then he showed his guests into the parlour, and Mrs Price and her children were sent for.

'This lazar house of crime is no place for children to be raised,' said Price. 'Last year I even offered my resignation, so that Mary and I could return to VDL and raise the children in a more becoming environment. But Dr Hampton insists that no one can run Norfolk Island as well as I, and I have my public duty to think of.'

The children paraded into the room, three boys and two girls, their ages ranging from four to ten. They were followed by their mother, a handsome woman in her mid-thirties. Introductions were performed, but instead of dismissing the children back to the nursery immediately afterwards, they were suffered to remain. With a child's unerring sense for finding the one man in the room who could not abide infants, the youngest, Anna Clara, at once homed in on Strachan and started trying to crawl into his lap. The assistant surgeon squirmed in his chair until Price stood up and rescued him, lifting up the girl and returning to his seat to dandle her on his own knee.

'You're not one of those who thinks children should be seen and not heard, are you, Mr Strachan?' he asked jovially.

'Not at all,' said Strachan. 'I don't think they should be seen either.'

Mr and Mrs Price both laughed, thinking the assistant surgeon spoke in jest.

'You gentlemen must tell us all the latest intelligence,' said Mrs Price. 'Here on Norfolk Island, we hear so little of the outside world. Is there any news of my uncle?'

'Your uncle, ma'am?' asked Robertson.

'Sir John Franklin,' explained Price.

There was no need to explain further. Everyone knew of Captain Sir John Franklin, the renowned Arctic explorer who had sailed in search of the North-West Passage five years earlier, and had not been seen since.

'We've heard no news,' said Killigrew. 'But you mustn't abandon hope. It's not uncommon for the navy's exploring ships to over-winter in the Arctic; and if anyone could survive in those frozen waters for five years, it's Sir John.' On returning from a previous expedition in search of the elusive passage, Franklin had become famous as 'the man who ate his boots'.

They spent an hour making small talk about Arctic exploration over tea and cakes. None of the officers of the *Tisiphone* was part of the Royal Navy's circle of polar explorers.

At six o'clock they broke up and went to their rooms to get changed for dinner. Hartcliffe, Killigrew and Strachan were changing into the full-dress uniforms that had been laid out on their beds for them when Killigrew heard a carriage pull up outside, and crossed to the window. Looking out, he saw a man in convict-grey fatigues step down from a coach and four in the light from the front of the house. The carriage was Price's own: Killigrew recognised the Trengwainton coat of arms monogrammed on the door.

But for the fatigues, Killigrew would never had recognised the man as a convict: he carried himself with an air of arrogance, as if he disdained to be in a place like Norfolk Island. He was about to disappear out of sight beneath the verandah when something made him pause and look up.

He met Killigrew's eyes. The lieutenant recognised him at once from the caricatures in *Punch*: the broken nose, the broad shoulders, the narrow eyes and the low, sloping forehead. But there was something else about this man that the cartoons failed to capture – something in his eyes, a hint of a razor-sharp intellect that belied his rough-hewn appearance. Then his rugged face cracked into a grin, and he did not seem so ugly after all. He touched the brim of his convict cap mockingly to Killigrew, and stepped out of sight below.

'What is it?' asked Hartcliffe, lacing his half-boots.

'It seems we're to have a surprise guest to dinner tonight,' said Killigrew. 'Unless I'm very much mistaken, I just saw Devin Cusack arrive.'

They finished changing into their full-dress uniforms: navy-blue tailcoats, white pantaloons and kid gloves, and cocked hats tucked under their arms. They met Robertson and Westlake on the landing and the five of them made their way down to the drawing room. Cusack was studying a painting of winsome Nereides mourning over the body of Icarus, while Price sat in a chair reading a copy of

The Hobart Gazette that Nairn had brought from the *Tisiphone*. Cusack turned away from the painting and Price rose to his feet as the naval officers entered.

'Good evening, gentlemen,' said Price. 'May I present Mr Devin Cusack? Cusack, these gentlemen are Commander Robertson, Lieutenants Lord Hartcliffe and Mr Killigrew, and Mr Westlake and Mr Strachan, respectively the surgeon and assistant surgeon of HMS *Tisiphone*. I trust you gentlemen have no objections to dining with a rebel and a traitor? I thought that tonight's supper would be an ideal opportunity for Mr Fallon to meet Cusack.'

The five visitors shook hands with the infamous rebel; it seemed rude not to. Indeed, if there was any standoffishness, it came from Cusack, who looked down his nose at the naval officers, as if the Irishman were intently aware of his own aristocratic background. 'Killigrew, Killigrew . . .' he mused. 'I'm sure I've heard that name somewhere before.'

'You're probably thinking of my grandfather, Rear Admiral Killigrew.'

Cusack shook his head. 'No, that wasn't it. Wait a moment, now I remember. Last year. Hong Kong, wasn't it? I seem to recall something about a young lady being killed by Chinese pirates, thanks to your negligence.'

'There was no formal charge of negligence,' Robertson said sharply. 'Mr Killigrew did everything in his power to save that girl's life; and he'd be well justified in calling out any man who dared to suggest to the contrary.'

'Then please feel free to set me straight,' Cusack told Killigrew. 'I'd be fascinated to hear your side of the story; we Irish know what it's like to be slandered by not having our side of the story told.'

'It's something I prefer not to talk about.'

In the awkward silence that followed, Strachan nodded to the painting the Irishman had been studying. 'Looking for inspiration, Mr Cusack?'

Cusack smiled. 'Alas, I'm not the carpenter Dædalus was: I fear constructing a pair of wings to fly away from here would be quite beyond my powers. I was merely musing on the similarities between the Athens of King Minos and Mr Price's own kingdom here on Norfolk Island. Although whether Mr Price is a King Minos or a Minotaur I've not yet divined.'

Before Price could object to being compared to a monster which was half-man, half-bull, Nairn and Fallon appeared at the door.

'We haven't met,' Fallon told Cusack, pre-empting Price's introduction. 'I'm Malachi Fallon, a reporter for *The Irish-American*.'

'Mr Fallon is here to be reassured that you are being kept in a condition fitting for a political prisoner,' explained Nairn.

'Is that so?' asked Cusack, eyeing Fallon with amusement. 'If you're hoping for stories of dank, underground cells and thumb-screws, I'm afraid you're going to be disappointed. They keep me in a cottage by myself on the north side of the island. I have plenty to read and a certain amount of liberty, for what that's worth on a place the size of Norfolk Island. But I do miss my friends—'

Cusack broke off when he realised that everyone was staring at the doorway. He followed their gaze and his jaw dropped when he saw Mrs Cafferty standing there in a dark-blue evening dress of broché silk, the skirts domed by the mass of petticoats she wore underneath.

'Mrs Cafferty?' said Price. 'May I present Mr Devin Cusack? I believe you've already met everyone else present. Mr Cusack, this is Mrs Philippa Cafferty.'

Cusack bowed to kiss one of her kid-gloved hands. '*Enchanté, madame*. May I be permitted to ask what brings a young woman as lovely as yourself to a place like Norfolk Island?'

'Mrs Cafferty is to be governess to Mr Price's children,' said Fallon.

'Governess?' Cusack let go of her hand as if it burned him. He looked bewildered. 'Surely she . . . You're not suggesting that she join us for dinner, I trust?'

'Why not?' asked Price, evidently amused by Cusack's discomfort. 'Mrs Cafferty comes from an excellent family. Now that we've agreed to employ her – and she's agreed to accept our offer – we'll be considering her one of the family.'

Cusack looked as if he might have had further to say on the matter, but thought it best to keep his thoughts to himself. Mrs Price joined them presently – Killigrew gathered that the children had already been put to bed – and they went through into the dining room. Killigrew lingered to speak to Hartcliffe.

'Did you see the way Cusack reacted when Price told him Mrs Cafferty was a governess? The man's a damned snob!'

'Can you blame him? He comes from a proud family.'

'So do you. That doesn't stop you from treating people with respect, regardless of their rank.'

'Ah, yes. But then, you see, all my family think I'm a little peculiar. You're determined not to like this fellow Cusack, aren't you?'

'Can you blame me? He may have been let off lightly because his so-called revolution was such a débâcle, but it would have been a very different story if things had gone the other way that day at Ballingarry. The incident could have sparked off a rebellion the length and breadth of Ireland. There could have been a repeat of the events of the 'ninety-eight rebellion: brutal repression, sectarian

74

massacres, burnings, mass executions and other atrocities. Ireland's always been a powder keg of discontent, and Cusack and his friends were playing with fire – as well they knew. Using the threat of force of arms to put pressure on a democratically elected government . . . Oh, I'm not saying the men who want to see the Act of Union repealed don't have a valid point of view. If Ireland still had its own parliament, instead of a few token MPs in the House of Commons whose voices are drowned out by being a tiny minority, perhaps the effects of the potato blight might have been greatly reduced. But that doesn't excuse what the Young Irelanders did. Once you start giving in to the demands of a few people who chose to take up arms, where does it end? The next thing you know, you'll have the army dictating foreign policy to Whitehall!'

Hartcliffe held up an appeasing hand. 'God forbid! Not that the Foreign Office doesn't have me scratching my head in bewilderment from time to time, but I don't imagine those poltroons at Horse Guards could run things any better.'

They joined the others in the dining room, where half a dozen convict-trusties were assembled as servants to wait on them hand and foot as they sat down to eat at the large, linen-covered table.

'Does Mr Price often invite you to dine with him?' Fallon was asking Cusack.

'No.' Then, as if concerned not to appear rude, he added: 'Mr Price and I have a number of differences of opinion on political matters.'

'I can well imagine,' remarked Killigrew.

'How do you spend your time here?' asked Fallon.

'Reading and writing, mostly, or going for walks. The island itself is lovely: only the British could conceive of such a paradise as a penal colony.'

'So you wouldn't describe your incarceration here as a hardship?'

'It's certainly an imposition. But the greatest ordeal I've had to face in the six months I've been here is having to learn how to make my own bed and brew my own tea,' he added with a smile.

'If you returned to Van Diemen's Land, you could have a convict servant assigned to you,' said Nairn. 'All you have to do is give your parole.'

'Promise not to try to escape?' Cusack smiled. 'That I can never do, Mr Nairn.'

'You certainly won't escape from Norfolk Island,' Price promised him.

'Whereas if I were transferred to Van Diemen's Land, I might have a chance, you mean? Except that I'd have given my word not to; and I'm a man of honour.'

'A man of honour would never have taken up arms against his queen,' snorted Price.

'We've already had this discussion, Mr Price,' Cusack said boredly. 'And as for the rest of these gentlemen, well . . . I'm sure they don't care to hear what I have to say. In Mr Fallon's case, I should be preaching to the converted; as for the others, I should be preaching to the Pharisees rather than to the sick. If it's all the same with you, I'll be saving the rhetoric for men I might make an impression on.'

'And when rhetoric fails you, you resort to force of arms,' sneered Killigrew.

Cusack smiled. 'And you've never resorted to force of arms, Admiral?'

'He upset you, didn't he?'

Cusack had been taken back to his cottage on the north side of the island and nearly everyone else had gone to bed when Mrs Cafferty found Killigrew sitting on the verandah with his feet on the railing, a cheroot in one hand and Price's decanter of port close to hand.

Killigrew stood up. 'Who?'

She grimaced. 'You know very well who I mean. Devin Cusack.'

The lieutenant shook his head. 'I have to respect someone before I give a damn about what they think of me.'

'And you don't respect Cusack?'

'He's no better than the ruffians down there.' Killigrew gestured down to where the convict barracks loomed over the sea wall in the light of the full moon. 'But he gets treated with honour because his uncle is a lord and he dresses his villainy up in political ideals.'

'But you said yourself you're in favour of what he fought for: the repeal of the Act of Union.'

'It's his methods I object to, not his aims.'

'And are his methods so very different to the ones you use to keep the seas clean of slavers and pirates? I think you've got a lot more in common with him than you'd like to admit. I think you *do* admire him. I think there's a part of you that wishes you could risk everything to fight for a noble cause, as your father did in Greece.'

'My father was a dreamer. So's Cusack. Some of us have responsibilities, and have to live in the real world.'

'But your father's dream came true, didn't it? Greece got her independence from the Ottoman Empire. Who knows? Perhaps one day Ireland will also be independent of Britain. Would that be so terrible?'

'There are a good many Protestant Irishmen who would prefer to be ruled from Westminster by fellow Protestants than they would by

Roman Catholics in Dublin. You can't please everyone. What are you going to do? Draw a dotted line across the country and tell all the Protestants to live on one side of it, and all the Catholics to live on the other?'

She laughed. 'Now you're just being facetious.'

' "And if I laugh at any mortal thing,/'Tis that I may not weep." '

'Byron.'

'Another dreamer who died fighting for Greek independence.'

She moved closer to him. 'And what do you dream of, Kit Killigrew?'

'Oh, all the usual well-intentioned gammon. A world of peace, where men aren't driven by greed to rob, slaughter and enslave one another.'

'So that's what the "I" stands for: "Idealist"? And what place would there be for a man like you in a world like that?'

'None at all,' he admitted cheerfully. 'I could put my feet up. Fall in love, get married, raise a family. Do all the things that ordinary men take for granted.'

She looked up at him, her eyes shining in the gloom. 'But you're not an ordinary man.'

He wondered if she were paying him a compliment or if she were merely teasing him again, and wondered what she would do if he kissed her. He took her hand and gave it an experimental squeeze, and when she squeezed back he edged closer to her, moving slowly and deliberately so that she could not mistake his intentions and had all the time in the world to react one way or another. To his disappointment, she laid a hand on his breast and pushed him away.

'No . . . I'm sorry. I'm not some sixteen-year-old ninny fresh out of the nursery who's going to take one look at you and fall against your manly breast in a swoon.'

'It's just as well,' he said ruefully, trying to cover his embarrassment by resorting to light-hearted banter. 'My breast really isn't all that manly.'

'No? And what about those baubles you have hanging off it?'

He glanced down at his medals. 'These?' He pointed to them in turn. 'This one I got for being in the wrong place at the right time; and this one I got for being in the right place at the wrong time. I've also been mentioned in dispatches for being in the wrong place at the wrong time.'

'Have you ever been in the right place at the right time?'

'Well, I did remember to turn up to collect the medals . . . but it was a close-run thing on both occasions.'

She laughed. 'You know, I think I'll regret the fact you'll be sailing tomorrow. Against my better judgement, I'm actually starting to like you. As one grows fond of a mischievous kitten, you understand,' she added mockingly. Then she seemed to remember that she was not supposed to be happy. 'I'm sorry, Kit. It's not meant to be. Tomorrow you'll sail away from here and I . . . We'll never see one another again.'

'What's the matter? Surely you're not afraid you might fall in love with me? I'd credited you with better taste than that.'

'You have a very low opinion of yourself, don't you?'

'Don't be fooled,' he said with a self-deprecating grin. 'It's just false modesty.'

'You don't fool me, Kit Killigrew,' she said, and kissed him. It was a proper kiss, none of your pecks-on-the-cheek before fleeing, and he kissed her back enthusiastically. But he could not help feeling it was wrong. It was not a question of betraying the memory of the woman he had got killed in Hong Kong; he knew she would have wanted him to be happy. But after what happened in Hong Kong, he did not feel he had the right to be happy.

He was still debating with himself whether or not to break off the kiss when she resolved things for him by pushing him away. 'No. I can't do this to you. It's not fair.'

The rejection made his mind up: he wanted her. 'Oh, by all means be unfair to me!'

'You don't understand. It can't work out between us. Tomorrow you'll be sailing for the Fijis and you deserve better than to be my fi— my love of the hour. I'm sorry, Kit, I can't.'

She turned and ran back into the house.

Killigrew blinked and wondered what all that had been about. She did not strike him as the shy sort, but obviously something was upsetting her, something external to the two of them. He threw the stub of his cheroot away with a gesture of annoyance.

VI

Where Satan Never Sleeps

'Solomon Lissak! You're wanted!'

Lissak was already in his hammock when the call came from the far end of the ward in the prisoners' barracks. He had learned not to question orders: when you were called for, you went. He made his way between the rows of men lying in their hammocks to the door at the end of the ward.

The prisoners in general circulation – those not in the gaol-gang – were locked in the wards in the prisoners' barracks from six in the evening to sunrise without lights or any kind of supervision by the guards. When a new batch of convicts arrived, they were put in the wards with the hardened criminals, regardless of how petty their own crime might be. Lissak would lie awake at night and listen as the younger, prettier men were subjected to the inevitable initiation to the ways of Gomorrah Island. Not that he had ever undergone such an initiation: he had been well into his fifties by the time he had arrived on Norfolk Island, and even when he had been younger he had never been attractive, either to his own sex or the opposite.

The convicts in each ward selected a 'wardsman' from amongst themselves. The wardsman was supposed to be responsible to the commandant for anything that happened on the wards during the hours of darkness, but if he peached on any of his fellow lags he had to bear in mind that he still had to share the same ward with the men whose punishment he had helped bring about. If the infraction were severe enough to warrant the death penalty, then the executed man was sure to have plenty of friends to avenge him.

Lissak reported to the door at the end of the ward. The warder outside shone a light through the grille, dazzling him, and then the door was unlocked and opened. Lissak stepped through, and the door was closed and locked behind him.

'Price wants to see you.'

Lissak recognised Silas Jarrett's voice at once. 'Speeler' Jarrett had been a member of The Ring back in the days when Jacky-Jacky had been the ringleader, but Jarrett had only been small fry in those days and had slipped through the net when Price had punished the mutineers of 1846. Indeed, by secretly exposing several of his enemies as members of The Ring, Jarrett had both disposed of them and won Price's confidence; which made him a very useful person to Ned Wyatt. Even Lissak was not sure who Jarrett worked for, Wyatt or Price. It probably varied depending on the given circumstances.

'Price!' exclaimed Lissak. 'What does he want to see me for? And at this time of night?' Being dragged out of the ward to see Price would only convince everyone that he was one of Price's dogs, which boded no good for him when he got back; unless Jarrett could convince his fellow inmates he was innocent.

'Don't ask questions,' Jarrett told Lissak. 'Come with me.'

Lissak followed Jarrett past the guards and out of the prisoners' barracks. Outside the front gate, they turned left as if they were making for Government House.

'Got your betties?' Jarrett asked in a low voice.

'What betties?'

'Don't try to gammon me, Sol. I know you've been making a set of betties in the workshop. Doesn't it strike you as rum that you haven't been searched lately?'

'I figured the screws had a bellyful of cooling up my flanky every other day.'

'I told Price about the betties; that you were planning to escape with some of the others.'

'What? That's a bloody lie!' Lissak was planning to escape, true enough; but when he ran, he'd do it on his own. 'Who am I supposed to be making my lucky with, anyway?'

'Ah, that's the clever part. I said I didn't know; but if we waited for you to make your move, we'd find out soon enough. That was the only way I could stop you from being searched.'

They reached the corner of the wall surrounding the compound, but instead of continuing along the sea wall towards Government House, Jarrett suddenly grabbed Lissak and dragged him down the passage between the compound and the lumber-yard.

'You ain't taking me to see Pricey, are you?' Lissak guessed with trepidation. If Jarrett was not taking him to Price, then he had no authorisation to remove Lissak from his ward in the prisoners' barracks; and there was only one man on Norfolk Island for whom Jarrett would take a chance like that.

Jarrett led the way around the back of the prisoners' barracks. 'You saw that navy sloop arrive today?'

'Sure. I was working in the fields when it dropped anchor.'

'One of the men who arrived on it is an American reporter; except his real reason for being here is to rescue Devin Cusack.'

'That Irish rebel they got up at Cascades? He told you this himself, did he?' Lissak said sceptically. They were talking in whispers now, creeping through the shadows behind the three compounds that lined the sea wall.

'Someone in Hobart Town gave him my name as a man who could be trusted.'

Lissak gave a high-pitched, hooting chuckle. 'They got that wrong then, didn't they!'

'Keep quiet! Do you want to ruin everything? There's a whaling ship coming to Cascades Bay tonight to help Cusack and Fallon – that's the reporter – escape. Fallon told me if I had a couple of horses saddled to take us to Cascades, I could leave with them.'

'Plummy for you. What do you need me for?'

'You want to come, don't you?'

'You didn't answer my question.'

'Wyatt wants to go.'

'Wyatt is in the old gaol with the rest of the gaol-gang.'

'You're going to get him out.'

'I was afraid you were going to say something like that. And if you turn up at Cascades with Wyatt and me in tow, what do you think the arch-lagger of that whaler's going to have to say when he cools us? "Hop aboard, boys, the more the merrier"?'

'That's why you're going to fetch anyone else you find in Wyatt's cell in the old gaol.'

'There are ten men in that cell! If the arch-lagger balks at three extra passengers, what makes you think he's going to feel any happier about a whole crew of us?'

'He isn't. But if there's a dozen of us, he's not going to be in a position to argue, is he? Especially not when we've got Swaddy, Fingers, Bludger and Croaker with us.'

'Bludger Imrie and Croaker Norris? That does it! Take me back to my ward! I don't want any part of this.'

'You're not being given any choice, Sol. You can spend the rest of your days in this hellhole, but Wyatt and I are escaping, and we're doing it tonight. If you don't help us, I'll put it about that you're one of Price's dogs.'

'You bastard! You would, too!'

'Stop complaining, you old fool, and off you go.'

'What? Ain't you coming with me?'

Jarrett shook his head. 'I've got to go to Government House to fetch Fallon. I'll get the keys to the old gaol in case you have difficulty in picking the locks. We'll steal Price's carriage and meet you outside the old gaol in exactly one half-hour. Be waiting in the courtyard with Wyatt and the others.'

'How am I supposed to get past the screws? You know I ain't a croaksman.'

'Climb over the wall at the back. That shouldn't present any problems for the man who broke out of Port Arthur.'

'The man who broke out of Port Arthur was seven years younger than I am.'

'Then you'd better hope he hasn't forgotten any of his old skills in the intervening time. Because if you fail tonight, may God forgive you. Ned Wyatt won't.'

The grandfather clock in the hallway chimed midnight as Mrs Cafferty passed, startling her. She stopped abruptly, and realised that light was shining from under the door to Price's study. She listened, but heard no voices. Presumably he was working late, presenting her with an ideal opportunity. If she was going to act, she had to act now; the longer she left it, the harder it would become to do what she had to do.

She pushed all thoughts of Killigrew from her mind. It was not easy – yet she knew if she had succumbed to his advances, she would never have had the strength to carry out the plan which had brought her to Norfolk Island in the first place. The realisation that she had had the will-power to resist his charms somehow gave her the courage to push ahead with her plan.

She hurried upstairs and slipped into her room. There she lit an oil lamp and by its light she took her turnover pistol from her pocket, checked it was primed and loaded.

She opened the door a crack and peered out. The landing was dark and deserted. She slipped out of her room and eased the door shut behind her. The heavy tick-tock of the grandfather clock was the only sound in the house apart from the beating of her own heart and the snores emanating from the bedroom Robertson was sleeping in.

She descended the stairs, paused with one hand on the door to the library, took a deep breath, and entered.

Price was at the desk with his back to the door, so intent on his work he did not hear her come in. She closed the door quietly behind her and coughed to get his attention.

He turned sharply, and the monocle dropped from his eye when he saw the pistol in her hand. He stared at her in astonishment. 'What in Hades . . .?'

'Does the name Francis Holland mean anything to you, Mr Price?'

'Francis Holland? No. Why? Should it? What the devil is all this about?'

82

'I'm not surprised you don't remember; so many convicts must pass through your hands, it must be difficult to recall them all. But I had hoped you'd remember Francis. Perhaps if I tell you a little bit about him, it will jolt your memory.

'Francis Holland was an ensign in the Forty-Fourth Foot. Amongst his other duties he was given responsibility for the funds of the officers' mess: quite a responsibility for such a young man, but he bore it admirably, until, that is, fifty guineas were found to be missing. Francis denied all knowledge, of course, and when his brother officers gave him the chance to do the honourable thing, he refused, insisting on his innocence. So the colonel, in disgust at his cowardice, had him court-martialled, regardless of any scandal which might ensue.

'Francis was found guilty of embezzlement and sentenced to transportation to Van Diemen's Land for fourteen years. He served four at the penal settlement at Port Arthur, and because of his exemplary record while there, the commandant gave permission for him to serve as indentured labour at the farm of a local landowner. In the Huon River District. Your farm, Mr Price. Now do you recollect?'

'Oh, you mean *Frank* Holland? I knew he was an embezzler, of course, but not that he'd been an army officer. Still, I remember thinking there was something odd about him. He wasn't like most of the other convicts I employed at the time; or many that I've known since.'

'But you treated him the same as the others, didn't you? And one day, when he was too ill to work in the fields, you accused him of malingering and had him flogged. A sick man, and you gave him fifty lashes!'

'I made a mistake . . .'

'A mistake which cost an innocent young man his life!'

'So what? He was a criminal. A thief. The fact he was born a gentleman only makes his crime all the more disgraceful.'

'Shortly after news of Francis' death reached the officers of the Forty-Fourth, one of his fellow officers shot himself. He left a suicide note in which he admitted to stealing the fifty guineas to cover some gambling debts. Following a full inquiry, Ensign Francis Holland was exonerated of all blame and his name restored to the regimental roll of honour. But they couldn't bring him back to life. They couldn't bring him back to life because you, John Price, had taken it upon yourself to deprive him of his life. You set yourself up as judge and jury over him, and killed him as surely as I'm about to kill you.'

'For God's sake, I didn't know! Convicts malinger all the time, how was I supposed to know he was genuinely sick? They're all the same—'

'But that's just it, isn't it, Mr Price? They're *not* all the same.' She took a deep breath, the hand gripping her pistol steady although her heart was fluttering with fear.

'All right; what's this got to do with you?' Price refused to be cowed. 'Was he your lover? This was more than ten years ago – you must've been what, thirteen, fourteen?'

'I employed no deceit to obtain this position. There was no need to. You did not think to ask me what my maiden name was.'

The colour drained from Price's face. 'Holland?'

She nodded. 'He was my elder brother, Mr Price. The best friend I had in all the world. And you murdered him.'

Price swallowed. 'If you shoot me – even if you succeed in killing me – you'll never get away with it. The sound of the shot will bring the servants running. Do you think you can escape this island undetected?'

'I don't intend to. Two barrels, Mr Price: two bullets. One for you, and one for me. You see, I lost all interest in living seven years ago, after my husband died in my arms in the snows of the Khyber Pass. Since then, only one piece of unfinished business gave me a reason to go on living. When I saw your advertisement in the *Seneca Falls County Courier* it was like the answer to a prayer.'

'Then you'd better make certain of me with one bullet.'

'I intend to, Mr Price. One shot through the heart should do the trick. Don't worry, I'm an excellent markswoman—'

The door opened and little Emily Mary entered the room in her nightgown. Not understanding the significance of the pistol in Mrs Cafferty's hand, she regarded her father and the governess with saucer eyes. 'Mrs Cafferty? I'm thirsty!'

'Get out, Emily!' yelled her father. 'Get out now! Wake the servants!'

'Papa!' Unused to being shouted at, Emily started to cry.

'*Run!*'

Sobbing, the girl ran from the room.

'All right,' Price told Mrs Cafferty calmly. 'If you're going to shoot me, get it over with. Just don't do it in front of the children, that's all I ask.'

She drew a bead on his chest, and hesitated. She thought of Emily Mary, and the other children and their mother. Could she rob them of a father and a husband, the way she had been robbed of her own husband by a Ghilzai sniper, or of her brother by Price's brutality? Where did the cycle of violence end?

Right here, she told herself. *It ends when you rotate the lower barrel of the pistol into position and fire the second bullet into your own skull.*

But she could not do it. It was not a fear of death that stopped

84

her, but the realisation that if she killed Price she would be judging him. She would be no better than he was.

Tears welled in her eyes and she lowered the pistol.

Price stepped forward, forced her gun hand aside, and drove a fist into her stomach. She doubled up in agony, and he twisted her arm behind her back, clawing the pistol from her grip before he threw her to the ground.

'You murderous bitch! I ought to kill you right now . . .'

She rolled on her back to find him standing over her with the pistol levelled at her face. She saw murder in his eyes, and instinctively kicked up at his hand. The pistol was knocked from his grip and skittered across the floor to come to rest out of sight under the desk. She tried to crawl after it, but he caught her by the ankle and dragged her back. She rolled on her back to defend herself, and he sat down astride her waist, his hands reaching for her neck, when the door opened and Malachi Fallon entered with Price's convict-butler, Jarrett.

'Well!' Fallon remarked in amusement. 'Not quite the picture of wedded bliss we were led to expect, Mr Price!'

Price had frozen with his hands halfway to Mrs Cafferty's neck, so that they hovered over her breasts. He quickly folded his arms and leaped to his feet. 'This is not what it appears . . .'

'Don't worry, we don't mind if you want to roger your new governess,' said Fallon. 'Perhaps under different circumstances I'd have no objections to giving her a tumble myself. But at the moment I'm more interested in your keys.'

Price blinked. 'My keys?'

'The ones to the cottage where Cusack sleeps at night.'

'Cusack . . .? What in Hades do you want to see him for at this time of night?'

Fallon transferred his cane to his left hand. 'We're after rescuing him,' he explained airily.

'The devil you are!'

'If that's the way it has to be . . .' Fallon reached inside his coat and drew out a revolver. 'The keys, Mr Price. Don't be telling me you haven't got any. Jarrett here tells me you keep a spare set in the drawer of your desk there.'

Price looked genuinely bewildered. 'There aren't any keys to Cusack's cottage.'

'Don't lie to me! D'you take me for a fool?'

'It's true, I tell you! Why should we lock him in at night? We're on an island, damn your eyes! Where could he go?'

Jarrett coughed into his fist. He was a smooth-faced man somewhere in his forties, with his hair grown down to the collar of his blue 'trusty' jacket as if to compensate for the way it receded from his forehead. 'My apologies, gentlemen,' he said. Despite his convict status, his voice was urbane and plummy. 'I'm afraid I've been guilty of a small subterfuge. Mr Price is quite correct in stating that we don't need keys to get into Cusack's cottage. But we do need keys to get into the old gaol.'

'The old gaol?' said Fallon. 'Cusack's not in there.'

'No, sir,' said Jarrett. 'But Ned Wyatt and the others are.'

'You double-crossing son of a bitch!' Fallon turned the revolver on Jarrett. 'Freeing Wyatt and that scum was never part of our deal.'

Price lunged for Fallon's revolver. Without taking the gun off Jarrett, the Irishman swung the cane in his left hand at the side of Price's head. The commandant went down as if pole-axed.

Jarrett crouched over Price and felt for a pulse in his wrist. 'He'll live.'

'You sound disappointed,' Fallon said with amusement. 'Now tie the lass up and gag her, and let's be away. That ship won't wait for ever.'

Jarrett crossed to the window and took down one of the cords for tying back the curtains during the day. 'On your feet, ma'am,' he told Mrs Cafferty. She stood up and he tied her hands behind her back.

'Not like that,' said Fallon. 'Tie her to one of the chairs.'

Jarrett shook his head. 'She's coming with us as a hostage.'

'We don't need a hostage.'

'This ship . . . is it a steamer?'

'Of course not. What's that got to do with anything?'

'Well, that sloop you arrived on *is* a steamer.' Jarrett took two more cords from the windows and bound Price, gagging him with his own handkerchief so he could not raise the alarm when he came to. 'If we try to sail away from here without a hostage, what's to stop the *Tisiphone* from steaming after us and blowing us out of the water?'

'We've got plenty of time to get away from here before the sun rises, as long as we go now. Once we're below the horizon, they'll never find us. Besides, she can't ride with her hands tied behind her back.'

'We'll take Price's carriage. It's all ready. We'll drive down to the old gaol, as cool as you please, free Wyatt and the others, cross the island to Cascades Bay, get Cusack and signal the ship to send her boat in to pick us up.'

'You're crazy! We'll wake the whole garrison!'

'Wyatt's got it all worked out. If we do it properly, we'll be gone long before anyone realises anything's amiss.'

'You've spoken to Wyatt already?'

'Naturally. It was his idea. Who do you think runs this island? This sadist?' Jarrett kicked Price's recumbent body half-heartedly. 'It's not often we get a chance like this. Why waste a whole ship on one man? Look, Fallon, if you want to go without me, you can. Maybe you can find your way to Cascades Bay without my help, maybe you can't. But I'm not leaving Norfolk Island without Wyatt.'

'You owe him that much personal loyalty?'

Jarrett grinned. 'It's not a question of personal loyalty, Fallon. I know Wyatt. If I escape from this island and leave him behind, he might just find some other way to escape. And then he'll come and hunt me down. And when he's done for me, he'll be coming after you.'

'I'm not afraid of some petty coiner.'

'This isn't just any bit-faker we're talking about. This is Flummut Ned Wyatt. In London his name's uttered with the kind of hushed reverence most people reserve for the Devil. Except that the Devil doesn't exist, so no one is truly scared of him. But Ned Wyatt is very real . . .'

The door opened and Killigrew walked in. 'What's going on?' he asked. 'I heard voices and—' He broke off when he saw Price unconscious on the floor and Mrs Cafferty with her hands tied behind her back. 'Oh-ho!'

Fallon turned the gun on him. Killigrew kicked it from his hand and it flew across the room. Fallon swung his cane at Killigrew's head, but the lieutenant caught it in his right hand. He held it fast and tried to tug it from Fallon's grip, but the Irishman gave the silver head a twist and withdrew two and a half feet of razor-edged steel. Killigrew raised the empty ebony casing to defend himself. Fallon sliced it clean in two with a single blow of his sword, and held the point at Killigrew's throat.

Jarrett snatched up the fallen revolver and covered him also.

Killigrew dropped the remains of the ebony casing. 'Ah.'

'Ah indeed, Mr Killigrew,' said Fallon.

'Are you all right, Mrs Cafferty?' asked Killigrew.

'I'm fine,' she replied, astonished to find that she sounded a lot calmer than she felt. Everything seemed to have happened so quickly she was in a daze: one moment she had been planning to assassinate the commandant of the most notorious penal colony in the world, the next she was being held at gunpoint by a Young Irelander and an urbane convict.

'You're after Cusack?' Killigrew asked the two men.

'Amongst others,' said Jarrett, opening one of the drawers of the desk and taking out a large bunch of keys.

'Now hold hard!' protested Fallon.

Jarrett waggled the revolver at him. 'Time we renegotiated our contract, I think.'

While Jarrett and Fallon confronted one another, Mrs Cafferty tried to catch Killigrew's eye.

'Now I've got the revolver, perhaps I should leave both you and Cusack on this island,' said Jarrett.

At last Killigrew took his eyes off Jarrett and met her gaze. She flicked her eyes towards the double-barrelled pistol that lay beneath the desk. When she glanced back at him, he was still looking at her.

'You don't know the signal that will bring the boat in from the ship,' said Fallon.

Mrs Cafferty tried again. This time, when she flicked her eyes towards the desk, he followed her gaze, but his face remained impassive and he made no attempt to move. Fallon still had the point of his sword held unwaveringly at Killigrew's throat. Perhaps the lieutenant could not see the pistol from where he stood.

'And you don't know the way to Cascades,' Jarrett was saying. 'Let's face facts, Fallon: like it or not, we need one another. A fair deal: Cusack for Wyatt and the others. Either that, or we stand here arguing until the sun comes up and it's too late for anyone to escape.'

'All right,' acquiesced Fallon. Mrs Cafferty did not believe a word of it; but that would be Jarrett's problem, at a later date.

'Tie him up.' Jarrett indicated Killigrew. 'I'll keep him covered.'

'If you shoot me, the servants will come running,' warned Killigrew.

'True,' said Jarrett. 'But if you make a move and I *don't* shoot you, I think I'll be doomed anyway. I suggest that neither of us puts your theory to the test.'

'Get face-down on the floor,' ordered Fallon. Killigrew complied, and the Irishman tied his hands behind his back and his feet together at the ankles. He pulled out his own silk handkerchief to gag the lieutenant, but Jarrett stopped him.

'Leave it. We're running out of time. The horses are already hitched to the carriage. Put the girl in the back and bring it round to the front. I'll meet you there as soon as I've dealt with Ben Backstay here,' he added, gesturing at Killigrew with the revolver.

'You're not going to kill him, are you?' Fallon demanded suspiciously.

'Of course not,' Jarrett said impatiently. 'We need someone to tell Commander Robertson that we've got Mrs Cafferty, don't we? There's no point in having a hostage if no one knows we've got her.'

'All right.' Fallon took Mrs Cafferty by the arm and dragged her towards the door, holding the blade of his sword at her throat. 'Come on. We're going for a long ocean voyage. Act sensible and it may even be beneficial for your health.'

'Go on,' Jarrett sneered at Killigrew as soon as Fallon had closed the door behind him. 'Tell me what you'll do to us if we harm one hair on her head.'

'No matter where you go,' the lieutenant promised him, 'no matter how far you run, no matter where you hide, I'll hunt you down like dogs if it takes me the rest of my life.'

'Don't worry. The rest of your life won't be for much longer, I assure you.' Before Killigrew could protest, Jarrett gagged him with Fallon's handkerchief. He stood up and crossed to the desk. 'It's nothing personal, you understand. But I think we'll stand a better chance of making our escape if the garrison is occupied elsewhere while we're about it.'

He took the lamp off the desk, removed the stopper and started to splash oil across the bookshelves. Killigrew struggled against his bonds, but Fallon had done too good a job of trussing him up.

'It's true what they say about the Irish being trusting simpletons, isn't it? I've already double-crossed him once tonight, and yet he still believed me when I told him I had no intention of killing you.' Jarrett helped himself to a cigar from a silver box on Price's desk and snipped the end off it with a cigar cutter. 'But people have always trusted me. Even when I meant them nothing but harm. It's what comes from speaking like a gentleman, I suppose. Benefit of a good education, you see: the only thing my father bequeathed me,' he added bitterly, taking a match from a box. 'I could have been just like you, if I hadn't been born on the wrong side of the blanket. Just another case of the sins of the father visited on the son.'

Killigrew heard the sound of hoofs and the soft rattle of a carriage moving on to the track in front of the house. Jarrett heard it too, and looked up. 'Well, that's my ride.' He struck the match and applied it casually to the end of his cigar. After a few puffs, the end was glowing nicely. 'I'll be on my way now, but don't worry.' He tossed the still-burning match against the bookshelves, and the oil flared at once. 'I'll leave you a nice fire to keep you warm. You'd be amazed by how cold it gets here at night.' He stepped outside the door and pulled it to behind him. Killigrew heard him walk down the hallway and close the front door behind him.

VII

Breakout

From the corner of the wall surrounding the new gaol, Solomon Lissak peered across to the old gaol. He could not see the front of the gaol from where he crouched, but he knew there would be two privates from the garrison on sentry-go at the entrance to the courtyard.

He moved stealthily and silently through the shadows in front of the new gaol until he was directly behind the old. A seven-foot-high wall linked the buildings of the old gaol to form an enclosure no more than fifty feet square. He took a little run up to the wall, leaped, hooked his hands over the top of it, and hung there for a moment. He tried to pull himself up, but his ageing bones protested at the effort and he suppressed a gasp. *I'm getting too old for this gammon*, he told himself.

Bracing the toes of his boots against the stonework, he managed to boost himself up, and climbed on to the wall, peering through the stone framing over the courtyard below. After waiting to make sure the courtyard was deserted and that the men on guard outside the front gate opposite had not heard him climb the wall, he dropped down through a gap in the framing. He landed lightly on the flagstones below; his body might not be as strong and supple as it had been in his youth, but he had lost none of his stealth, and his bones made more noise creaking as he pushed himself to his feet once more than his boots had done hitting the flagstones.

He crept across to the outer door of one of the buildings, picked the lock – it was the work of about three minutes using the picks he had made – and let himself silently in. The corridor beyond was deserted. He tiptoed down to the second cell and peered through the grille in the heavy wooden door. 'Wyatt?' he whispered.

'Shh! The lock,' Wyatt hissed back.

Lissak picked the lock on the door – it took him even less time than the one on the outer door had – and let himself into a cell fifteen feet by five. There were ten convicts in there, lying on straw mats, all joined by their fetters to the same chain which was linked to ringbolts in the wall at either end of the long cell.

'Good work, Solly,' whispered Wyatt. 'Now get these clinkers off us.'

It took Lissak the best part of a minute to pick the locks on the fetters of the first man he came to, but all the locks were of the same pattern and as he went on he worked faster; in about seven minutes he had released all ten of them.

'Where's Speeler?' asked Wyatt.

'On his way.'

'Good!' Piggy, you come with me and Solly to help do for the guards; the rest of you wait here.'

None of them seemed inclined to argue: when Wyatt gave an order, it was invariably obeyed. Mangal 'Piggy' Griddha was an Indian, a tubby little fellow with a round, cherubic face. He did not look as though he would harm a fly, although Lissak knew that in Mangal's case appearances were deceptive. When Wyatt wanted someone killed and could not do it for himself – if he was in the water pit, for instance – then Mangal was his croaksman. A member of the *thuggee* cult, he could garrotte a man in seconds; he was the prime suspect for the murder of the warder who had earned Wyatt's wrath. In return, Wyatt used his influence to make sure Mangal got enough extra rations to maintain his rotund shape.

Lissak followed Wyatt and Mangal out of the cell block into the courtyard, where they crept across to the door set in the gateway.

Wyatt indicated the lock. Lissak nodded and went to work. While he was picking the lock, Wyatt produced a crude knife, fashioned from one of the tin plates the convicts were given to eat from; Mangal produced a strip of cloth torn from his fatigues and gripped it at both ends, wrapping it around his hands a couple of times.

The bolt on the lock snapped back with a sound like a musket shot in the silence of the night. The three convicts froze, waiting for a challenge from the two sentries on the other side of the door. But all they heard was the rattle of an approaching carriage: the soldiers had other things to occupy their attention. Wyatt eased the gate open a crack and outside Lissak could see one of the sentries, and beyond him Price's carriage approaching from the left. On the driving board of the carriage, Jarrett reined in the horses, and the sentry Lissak could see moved away from the gate to challenge him.

Wyatt tapped Mangal on the shoulder, and pointed to the sentry. Mangal nodded.

Go, mouthed Wyatt.

Mangal went out first, Wyatt immediately behind him. As the

second sentry stared at Mangal's back and started to unsling his musket, Wyatt caught him from behind, clapping one hand over his mouth to silence his warning shout. With his other hand, he buried the blade of his crude knife in the sentry's neck, slicing through his windpipe and silencing the man's cry of warning. Mangal brought down the other guard before he got halfway to where Jarrett had reined in the carriage. With one knee in the small of the soldier's back, the Indian looped his garrotte over his head and pulled it tight. The soldier struggled, and then the death rattle sounded in his throat and he lay still.

Wyatt wiped the blade of his knife on the dead sentry's tunic and then crossed to the waiting carriage. 'All set, Speeler?'

Jarrett nodded.

'Go and get the others, Sol.'

His hands and legs bound, Killigrew squirmed across to the library door and banged the soles of his feet against it repeatedly. The door was too solid to break, but the banging made an awful racket. He lay motionless and listened for any sounds of the household stirring, but all was still except for the flames that licked along the bookshelves. He tried yelling, but the silk handkerchief bound over his mouth muffled his cries. He glanced across to where Price lay: the commandant was still unconscious, and even if he did revive in the next few seconds, he too was bound and gagged. The bookshelves that lined the wall were fully ablaze now. The room was rapidly filling with acrid smoke that stung Killigrew's eyes.

Then he remembered the pistol beneath the desk that Mrs Cafferty had drawn his attention to. He squirmed across the floor to the desk and squeezed himself into the kneehole space, grasping for the pistol. His groping fingers touched the gun but only pushed it further out of reach. He wedged himself more tightly into the space and got a proper grip on it.

He fumbled with it. There did not seem to be any trigger he could find, until he pulled back the hammer and a small tang popped out under the breech. He pointed the gun into the wainscoting and squeezed the trigger, but it would not budge: it must have had some kind of safety catch. He explored it with his fingers, pushing and twisting at various parts of it and cursing through his gag.

A sliding catch moved back from the breech at the top of the butt. He pushed it back until it would go no further and pulled the trigger. This time the gun went off, but with little more than a disappointing pop. Wedged under the desk, his own body had muffled the sound. He squirmed out from under the desk, managed to rotate the two barrels, bringing the lower one into position. Then he lay on his side and rolled on to his front so he could aim the pistol at one of the windows. He fired again, through the curtains and shattered the window beyond. Someone *must* have heard that!

The flames were spreading towards the rug where Price lay. Killigrew squirmed across to him and put his shoulder to the commandant's body, laboriously pushing him away from the blaze. Even with the gag across his mouth, the smoke was starting to claw at his lungs and make him retch.

The door opened and Robertson stood there in a striped night-shirt and tasselled nightcap. 'What the blazes . . .?' He appraised the situation with a single glance, roared '*Fire!*' at the top of his lungs, and then entered the room to drag the unconscious Price out. He returned for Killigrew, dragging him into the hallway.

'Fire! Fire!' Robertson left Killigrew in the hallway and disappeared towards the back of the house.

Light spilled down the stairs as one of the bedroom doors opened, and Hartcliffe appeared on the landing above him. He glanced down and saw Killigrew and Price bound and gagged at the foot of the stairs. 'What in the world . . .?' The young aristocrat slid down the banisters in his nightshirt and vaulted over them at the bottom. He tore off Killigrew's gag. 'What's going on?'

'Fallon and Price's butler took Mrs Cafferty hostage and then set fire to the library to create a diversion while they rescue Cusack and Wyatt,' Killigrew explained, turning his back on Hartcliffe so that he could fumble with the bonds.

'Leave that,' commanded Robertson, returning from the kitchen with a carving knife. 'I'll untie these two. Get everyone out of the house. Start with the children.'

'Yes, sir!' Hartcliffe ran back up the stairs and started hammering on doors. 'Fire! Fire! Everyone out!'

'You say Fallon and the butler have gone for Cusack?' demanded Robertson, sawing through the cords on Killigrew's wrists.

'Yes, sir.' Killigrew rubbed his chafed wrists, and then took the knife from the commander to saw at the bonds on his ankles. 'I think they must have arranged for a ship to pick them up at Cascades, where Cusack's house is.'

'Right. I'll take care of everything here: as soon as we've got everyone safely out of the house, I'll go back aboard the *Tisiphone* with Hartcliffe and see if we can't head them off on the other side of the island. You grab a horse from the stables and alert the garrison. Tell the commanding officer to detail a platoon of men to come up here and help fight the fire; the rest can try to catch Fallon and the others at the old gaol.'

'Yes, sir.' Killigrew handed the knife back to Robertson so he could free Price, and sprinted to the back of the house. The kitchen door was not locked; he found a hurricane lantern hanging from a hook close to the door, lit it with a match, and went outside.

A full moon was shining, bathing the mews at the back of the house in its pale light, but he needed the lantern when he entered the stables. There were three horses left in there; he eliminated two of them at once: a skittish bay and a scrawny-looking nag. He quickly saddled the third horse, a likely looking grey, and led it out into the yard. He vaulted into the saddle and goaded it round the side of the house and down the path that led from the knoll to the buildings of the garrison which lined Quality Row, perhaps half a mile from the main settlement at Kingston. The horse broke effortlessly into a gallop and minutes later Killigrew was jumping down from the saddle to approach the two sentries on duty outside the gates to the barracks.

'Sound the tocsin!' he barked.

They gawped at him.

He pointed impatiently at the bell on the wall. 'You: sound the tocsin,' he said, pointing at one.

'Yes, sir!' The soldier nodded and sprinted to the bell.

Killigrew pointed to the other. 'You: find the duty officer and tell him there's a breakout in progress at the old gaol, and Government House has been set on fire.'

'Yes, sir!'

As the bell clanged loudly, Killigrew glanced down the road and saw a carriage moving towards the barracks from the direction of the old gaol. The only road that led out of Kingston passed right by the barracks, only a few yards from where he stood. There were about six men crouched on the roof of the carriage, and two more clung to each of the running boards on either side. Clearly Jarrett had not wasted any time in freeing Wyatt and the others from the old gaol. It looked as though he intended to escape with as many of his fellow convicts as possible.

Killigrew cursed himself for having left his pistols on board the *Tisiphone*. He ran back to the compound in front of the barracks and called across to the soldier frantically ringing the tocsin. 'Is your musket loaded?'

The soldier did not hear him above the clanging bell. Killigrew ran across to him and grabbed him by the shoulder. The soldier started and turned.

'Your musket! Is it loaded?'

'Yes, sir!'

'Give it here!' Killigrew snatched the musket and ran back out of the compound. The carriage was still a hundred yards away, moving slowly because it was so overloaded, but gathering speed nonetheless as the team of four horses drawing it got into their stride.

Killigrew stood in its path and waved his arms above his head, still holding the musket. The moonlight was so bright, it was impossible the driver of the coach could fail to see him.

He waited until the carriage was fifty yards away. 'Halt!' he roared. 'Or I'll fire!'

Perhaps the driver could not hear him above the rattle of harness and the thundering of the horses' hoofs; perhaps he could. Either way, he merely lashed the reins to urge the horses on even faster.

Killigrew raised the stock of the musket to his shoulder. It was tempting to shoot one of the horses, but if one went down the whole team would stumble and there was a good chance of a real smash if the carriage went over. He knew he could not risk that if Mrs Cafferty was a prisoner on board. He sighted down the barrel at the driver and waited until the carriage was less than ten yards away.

He fired. There was a bright flash and the stock slammed back against his shoulder. He leaped aside barely a second before one of the horses would have smashed into him, and reversed his grip on the musket to swing it like a club at the man clinging to the near side of the carriage. The musket whacked him in the side and he tumbled from the running board to land a few feet from where Killigrew stood. He tried to push himself to his feet, but before he could get up the lieutenant cracked him over the skull with the musket.

As the carriage continued down the road past the barracks, Killigrew saw a second figure lying in the road: his shot had found a mark. He crouched over the man: it was another convict in 'magpie' fatigues, a man he did not recognise. If this had been the man driving, then someone else on the roof had managed to grab the reins before they fell between the traces.

He looked back towards the barracks. Apart from the one dopey-looking private he had borrowed a musket from, there was still no sign of the garrison other than lights behind a couple of the windows. He cursed and, slinging the musket over one shoulder, ran back to where the horse stood, calmly cropping the grass at the roadside. Killigrew vaulted in the saddle, hauled on the reins to wheel his mount, and set off at a gallop after the carriage.

The horse was still fresh and the overloaded carriage moving so slowly that with within a quarter of a mile Killigrew was less than a furlong behind and gaining on it rapidly. There were still five convicts on the roof, including the driver, and another one clinging to the side of the carriage on the right-hand running board. Killigrew was close enough now to see that two of the convicts on the roof had muskets. And he himself was unarmed but for an empty musket.

He remembered what Robertson had told him back in Hobart

Town about taking unnecessary risks. Perhaps it was true: perhaps after Hong Kong he had grown weary of his own life. Then he remembered that Mrs Cafferty was almost certainly still a hostage in that carriage. It would take Robertson time to get back aboard the *Tisiphone*, and even if he sent Hartcliffe to signal the sloop from the signal station with instructions to get her engines started, it would still take the best part of two hours to get steam up from cold boilers; the *Tisiphone* would have to get to Cascades Bay under sail. If the convicts managed to get aboard whatever ship awaited them off the north coast, the chances were they could sail away into the darkness long before the navy sloop could head them off. The *Tisiphone*'s chances of finding the ship the next day without knowing which direction she had sailed in would be minimal. And who could say what kind of scum were amongst the convicts Mrs Cafferty would find herself with on that ship?

One of the convicts on the roof levelled his musket and there was a flash, a bang, and something soughed past Killigrew's head. Yes, he was taking a risk, but there was no doubt in his mind it was a necessary one. He goaded the horse on even faster. Another musket sparked, another bullet winged in his direction, but without hitting him, and now the convicts were as unarmed as he was.

Except there were six of them on the outside of the carriage – and almost certainly another five crammed inside with Mrs Cafferty – and he was alone. He had faced much worse odds, but usually in the knowledge that he had two dozen bluejackets and marines at his back. This time it was all up to him.

He had almost reached the back of the carriage. The road they were on forked, and the carriage took the right-hand branch, which angled up the side of one of the hills that surrounded Kingston. There was a rock-face to the right of the carriage and not enough room for Killigrew to pass on that side, so he passed on the other, on the narrow space between the carriage and the drop to his left, with the left-hand fork of the road below and getting further below with every passing moment.

The carriage had to slow on the gradient, so it was easy for Killigrew's horse to draw level and keep pace. He stood up, balancing himself in the stirrups. One of the convicts on the roof tried to slam the stock of a musket into his face. He ducked and the musket swept over his head, but almost lost his balance. He steadied himself with his left hand on the pommel of the saddle, and braced himself to jump.

It was then he saw a hand protruding from one of the carriage windows, pointing a revolver at him.

Before he could leap, one of the carriage's wheels hit a pothole. The hand holding the revolver was jolted, there was a flash and a bang, and Killigrew's horse stumbled. He felt himself flying through the air; a second later he crashed against the road, rolled over a few times and felt his legs sliding out into space. He clawed at the dusty track with his hands, caught hold of a spur of rock and found himself dangling over the left-hand fork of the road, about thirty feet below.

He scrabbled at the rock face below him with the toes of his half-boots, and managed to pull himself up to safety. The carriage was already a hundred yards up the track and getting further away with every passing second.

Killigrew crawled across to where his horse lay on its side. The beast was still alive, but it had been wounded in the shoulder and its breath issued raggedly from its nostrils. He swore, and glanced after the carriage again. The road turned to the right, heading up a steep slope to the crest of the hill above them, and the carriage followed it. And slowed, losing its momentum on the gradient.

Killigrew was back on his feet in the same instant he realised he was not yet out of the running. As his long legs powered him up the slope, a twinge in his ankle reminded him of his injury of three weeks ago, but he ignored it. He had to catch the carriage before it cleared the crest of the hill; nothing else mattered.

The road was steep and Killigrew was badly out of condition – too much alcohol and tobacco – and his ankle protested at the effort. Within seconds a stitch in his side pained him, and his lungs were on fire. He blocked out the pain, concentrating on that carriage, the convicts who had stolen it, thinking of what he was going to do to them when he caught up with it.

What *was* he going to do to them when he caught up with it? Alone, against eleven of them? He had no idea.

The pain was excruciating – his ankle, his thighs, his lungs – and the carriage was still fifty yards ahead of him, almost cresting the brow of the hill. Every nerve in his body seemed to be telling him to give up, he was wasting his time, he would never catch them. But Killigrew would rather have died than give up.

Then he saw that the carriage had come to a standstill just below the crest of the hill, the tired horses straining at the traces. The sight renewed his hope and he tapped hidden resources of strength to redouble his efforts. Four of the convicts jumped down from the roof and pushed at the back and sides of the carriage, while the man on the driving board urged the horses to pull them the last few feet to the level ground on the plateau beyond.

Forty yards ... thirty yards ... the convict who had been standing on the running board took something from someone inside the carriage and pointed it at Killigrew. There was a flash and a crack, but Killigrew did not even try to zigzag: at that range the man was wasting his time with a handgun.

Twenty yards . . . at last the carriage was starting to move again. It crested the brow of the hill, and the four convicts who had been pushing it scrambled back on to the roof. Killigrew was close enough to hear one of them shout 'Come on!' at the man with the revolver. The man squeezed off another shot at Killigrew. This time the bullet came close enough for the lieutenant to feel its wind. As the carriage moved off, the man tucked the revolver in the waistband of his trousers and stepped on to the running board.

Fifteen yards . . . ten yards . . . Killigrew was oblivious of the pain now, conscious only of the carriage and the men aboard it. It was gathering pace, but slowly, and he was still gaining on it.

Nine yards . . . six yards . . . four . . . three . . . the carriage gathered momentum; the gap was still closing, but more slowly.

Four yards . . . five yards . . . the gap was widening now. He had lost it. He had come so close, but a miss was as good as a mile. He cursed himself: if only he had put a little extra effort into it . . .

No, damn it! I'm not going to let these bastards get away now!

He remembered when he had been a midshipman aboard his first ship, the first time he had been ordered into the rigging. He had made it to the maintop, but then his fear of heights had overcome him and he had frozen, petrified. In the end, the topmen had been forced to tie a rope about him and lower him to the deck. For days afterwards he had been known as 'Quit Killigrew', until finally the taunting had forced him to overcome his fear. In the end he had proved himself more nimble at skylarking than any of his shipmates, including the topmen. And he had sworn then he would never give up again.

Four yards . . . three yards . . . two yards . . .

He leaped.

His hands touched the luggage netting at the back of the carriage and he twisted his fingers into claws, entwining them amongst the leather straps. He missed his footing on the ground and his legs were dragged through the dirt, but his grip on the netting was firm. He hauled himself up, lifting up his legs until he could brace them against the back of the carriage.

Made it! The thought filled him with strength and he forgot all about the pain in his legs. He started to climb up the netting to the roof of the carriage. Above him, one of the convicts tried to slam the stock of his musket into Killigrew's face.

The lieutenant let go of the netting with his right hand, rolling away and dangling from the other, while the musket missed his face by inches. He caught the musket by the stock and gave it a jerk. The convict lost his balance and fell from the roof, tearing the musket from Killigrew's grip and tumbling in the carriage's wake. Killigrew gripped the brass rail that ran around the roof, braced his feet against the back, and sprang up amongst the remaining three convicts crouched behind the driver.

All three of them were so astonished he had time to knock one off the roof of the carriage with a right cross before any of them had time to react. Another swung a musket at his head. Killigrew ducked, and the musket connected with the head of another man, and he too disappeared over the side. The convict with the musket was still staring in shock at what he had done when Killigrew caught him around the waist and pushed him down on to the roof of the bucketing carriage.

The convict was stronger, though, and filled with rage at his own carelessness in knocking one of his friends off the carriage. He pushed Killigrew away and rolled on top, pressing the barrel of the musket against the lieutenant's throat. As he felt himself choking, Killigrew could see another convict climbing up from the right-hand running board. Through the scarlet haze that threatened to swamp him, he recognised Ned Wyatt. With one hand on the brass rail, Wyatt stopped when his waist was level with the roof – he must have had his feet on the sill of one of the windows – and reached for the revolver tucked into the waistband of his trousers.

Killigrew gave up trying to push the musket away from his neck and landed blow after blow on the other convict's ribs, but the convict just kept on grinning savagely, forcing the barrel of the musket harder against the lieutenant's throat.

Wyatt levelled his revolver at Killigrew's chest.

Killigrew pinched the flesh on the underside of the other convict's upper arm through the fabric of his chequered jacket. The convict let go of one end of the musket with a yelp, enabling Killigrew to clip him on the jaw with a right hook. He pushed the convict off and to his left just as Wyatt fired. The convict shuddered, his face frozen in an expression of shock. He opened his mouth as if to protest, but only a thin trickle of blood came out.

Killigrew swivelled on his back and braced his shoulders against the rail on the left-hand side of the roof, using his feet to thrust the corpse at Wyatt. The coiner dropped out of sight and the corpse rolled over the low rail, but a moment later Wyatt was climbing up again. Killigrew kicked him in the jaw, snapping his head around, but the coiner kept on coming. He levelled the gun again. Killigrew kicked his wrist, sending the gun spinning into the night, and aimed another kick at his head, but this time Wyatt caught hold of his ankle and used it to pull himself up on to the roof. He punched Killigrew in the crotch, and fire exploded through the lieutenant's loins.

'Think you're tough, eh, pretty boy? I'll show you tough!' He kneeled over Killigrew with one knee on the lieutenant's groin, caught him by the collar with his left hand and drove a succession of blows into Killigrew's face with his right. Killigrew fought back, but his blows seemed to make no impression on the convict. A prison diet had left Wyatt emaciated, but he was tough and wiry for all that.

The convict seized Killigrew by the lapels and drew his head back to butt him on the bridge of the nose, but Killigrew butted him first. Wyatt lost his grip on his lapels and fell on his side. Killigrew pushed him on his back and tried to climb on top of him, but Wyatt braced the soles of his boots against his chest and pushed him off. Killigrew tripped over the rail and felt himself falling through space. He flailed wildly, managed to catch hold of the rail with one hand. The jerk almost pulled his arm out of its socket, but he clung on tightly, dangling from the side of the wildly swaying carriage. He got his feet on the running board and managed to grip the rail with his other hand. Through the open window in the carriage door, he could see Mrs Cafferty wedged between two convicts on the back seat. Fallon sat between Jarrett and another convict on the seat facing them.

'*Kit?*' she asked in astonishment.

'Hold on, ma'am. Have you out of there in a brace of shakes!'

Then one of the convicts interposed his snarling face between Killigrew and Mrs Cafferty, and drove a fist into Killigrew's jaw. Something smashed agonisingly into the lieutenant's fingers where they gripped the rail above. He glanced up and saw Wyatt standing over him, aiming a kick at the fingers of his other hand.

Killigrew pulled himself up with his arms and boosted himself back on to the roof of the carriage, butting Wyatt in the crotch as he did so. The two of them sprawled on the roof of the carriage, Killigrew on top of Wyatt. The convict seized the lieutenant by the neck with both hands and squeezed. Killigrew clawed at Wyatt's face, but the coiner pushed him off and punched him repeatedly in the face: a right jab, another right jab, and a left hook that came out of nowhere to send him slithering over the back of the roof. He managed to get hold of the luggage netting and was climbing up again, but Wyatt was waiting for him.

'You made a big mistake when you decided to take on Ned Wyatt, pretty boy!' The convict kicked Killigrew in the head. It was fortunate for the lieutenant that he was unconscious when he hit the ground.

VIII

Cliff-hanger

The carriage emerged from an avenue of trees and Lissak reined in and jumped down. He opened the door and thrust his grizzled face through. 'Cascades Bay!' he declared like a London omnibus driver. 'End of the line! Everyone out!'

Ned Wyatt jumped down from the roof. The lower half of his face was smeared with blood. 'What happened to you?' asked Jarrett

'What do you mean, what happened to me?' snarled Wyatt. 'I had a fight with that bastard navy officer, that's what happened to me! I didn't see you climbing up to help.'

'I had every confidence in your ability to deal with the situation,' Jarrett said smoothly.

Lissak looked Wyatt up and down. 'One man did that to you?' He gave a high-pitched, hooting chuckle. 'You're getting slow in your old age, Ned.'

'Cheese it, Sol. I got the better of him, didn't I? I don't think that bastard will be giving us any more trouble. Fingers, Swaddy: bring the girl.'

As the convicts exited the carriage, the two men who had sat on either side of Mrs Cafferty – one of them an ill-favoured man who had spent the entire carriage-ride sucking his fingers noisily – dragged her out after them. Along with Fallon, there were only six convicts now: Wyatt, Jarrett, Sol, Fingers, Swaddy, and a plump little Indian who looked as if he would not hurt a fly.

Fallon followed and nodded to a cottage that stood a short distance away. 'Is that where Cusack lives?' Jarrett nodded. 'I'll go and fetch him.' He set out for the cottage, but Wyatt caught him by the arm and dragged him back.

'Oh, no you don't. Sol can get your pal Cusack. You've got to signal the ship, remember? If it's still there.'

Fallon nodded and reached into the holdall he had been

103

clutching throughout the carriage ride. Jarrett caught him by the wrist and stopped him.

'I can't be signalling the ship without my bull's-eye now, can I?' said Fallon.

Jarrett tore the holdall from Fallon's grip and groped inside. He pulled out a second revolver. 'Are you quite certain this isn't what you were looking for?'

Fallon said nothing. Jarrett threw the revolver to Wyatt and pulled a bull's-eye lantern from the holdall, thrusting it into Fallon's hands. 'Go and signal that ship.' He pointed across a greensward to where a wooden derrick stood atop a precipice. Fallon walked across to the cliff top.

'I'll go and get Cusack,' said Lissak, and headed off to the cottage.

'Meet us by the derrick,' Wyatt called after him. Lissak nodded.

Wyatt, Jarrett and another convict followed Fallon towards the derrick, and Fingers and Swaddy started to drag Mrs Cafferty after them. She realised that once they got her on board the ship she was as good as dead; now was her last chance to escape. It was in a spirit of desperation rather than in any hope of success that she suddenly pulled her arm free of Swaddy's grip, balled her hand into a fist and drove it with all her might into the convict's jaw. She had had cause to slap a few men in her time, but this was the first occasion she had ever punched anyone and she was surprised by how much it hurt. Nevertheless, Swaddy stumbled and fell, dazed.

Fingers pulled her towards him and grabbed her right wrist. She lifted her knee into his crotch, the way she had once seen Lady Florentia Sale deal with an excessively brutal guard during their captivity at Budeeabad. The trick worked equally well on Fingers and he let go of her, clutching at his loins as he sank to the grass with a high-pitched scream.

She turned and ran. She could drive a carriage, but she knew the other convicts would catch her before she could climb on to the driving board and turn the carriage round. She headed for the trees instead. She knew that if she hid amongst the bushes in the darkness beneath the boughs, the convicts would have difficulty finding her before sun up; and they would not want to wait around until then.

She had almost made it when something slammed into her from behind and she pitched forwards on her face with a cry. Someone climbed on top of her and pinioned her to the ground. He rammed something hard into the small of her back. 'You know what this is?' Wyatt snarled into her ear.

'I very much hope it's the muzzle of your pistol.'

'Very funny!' He climbed off her and dragged her to her feet. 'Try that again and I'll croak you. After I've let Fingers and the others have their fun with you, of course. You know what Fingers was lagged for, don't you? Raping little bitches like you. He likes to hurt 'em. He's been five years on this bloody island, and that's a long time to go without a woman.' He stroked her cheek with the back of one hand, and leered. 'Come to think of it, I might have a go myself.'

She sank her teeth into his fingers, biting down until she tasted blood in her mouth. He just grinned. 'You think that hurts?'

She could only abide having his vile fingers in her mouth for so long, and at last gave it up and spat them out. He tucked the revolver in the waistband of his trousers and shrugged off his jacket, turning his back to her so she could see that it was nothing but one mass of crisscrossed scars.

'Eight hundred and thirty-six lashes of the cat,' he said proudly. 'Thirty-six the first time, a hundred the second, two hundred the third, and another five hundred three weeks ago. And I never once peeped.' He shrugged his jacket back on and jerked his head to where the other convicts stood. 'You ask any of the lads. So if you think you can hurt me, think again.' He pushed her after the others.

They reached the wooden derrick on the cliff top. In the moonlight, Mrs Cafferty could not fail to see the three-masted ship hove to about half a mile out to sea.

'You've signalled her?' demanded Wyatt.

Fallon nodded. 'They're sending a boat ashore.'

'Winch the cradle down to them, Swaddy.'

Swaddy nodded and swung the arm of the derrick out, so that it reached beyond the rocks a hundred feet below, where breakers foamed whitely in the darkness. He started to turn the winch that lowered the cat's cradle from the derrick.

'Mal?' a voice called behind them, and they turned to see Sol returning with Devin Cusack in tow.

The two Young Irelanders embraced like old friends. 'It's good to see you again, Dev,' said Fallon. Tears shone on his cheeks in the moonlight.

'How touching,' sneered Jarrett.

Cusack jerked his head at the convicts. 'What are they doing here?'

Fallon grimaced. 'I needed Jarrett to show me the way here. He insisted that we bring some of his friends. Although what Captain Quested will say when he finds out we've got six more passengers than he's expecting remains to be seen.'

'You let me worry about that,' said Wyatt, waggling his revolver. 'You'll be Devin Cusack, then?'

'And you are?'

105

'Ned Wyatt.' He gestured at the other convicts. 'Speeler Jarrett you probably know already. These others are Solly Lissak, Swaddy Blake, Piggy Griddha and Jemmy Fingers.'

'What are you all in for?'

'Where I come from, that's not a polite question.'

'I can't help being curious about what kind of scum I'll be unleashing on the rest of the world if I let you come with us.'

'Hear that, lads?' asked Wyatt. '*He*'s letting *us* go with *him*.' The other convicts laughed at the suggestion. Wyatt pulled back the hammer of the revolver. 'Maybe I should just kill the pair of you here and now.'

'There are more than two dozen men on that ship out there,' warned Fallon. 'D'you think the skipper's going to be happy to take you wherever you are wanting to go, if there's nothing in it for him?'

'He's taking you, isn't he?'

'Only because he's getting paid five thousand dollars when we get to San Francisco. I'd like to see you match that.'

Wyatt eased off the hammer of the revolver. 'All right. You talk the skipper of that ship into taking us with you, and no one gets hurt. Deal?'

'I can't make any promises. Captain Quested is a hard man.'

Wyatt grinned. 'Not as hard as I am, I'll bet.'

Fallon smiled. 'Let's just say that if the two of you were in the ring together, I wouldn't like to have to wager money on either one of you.'

Cusack noticed Mrs Cafferty. 'What's she doing here? Don't tell me she's in on it?'

'She's our hostage,' said Wyatt.

'We're not needing a hostage.'

'Oh, yes we do.' Wyatt indicated Fallon. 'Or did your pal here forget to mention the Royal Navy paddle-sloop that's anchored in Sydney Bay on the other side of the island? They'll be coming after us, and when they do she could be the only thing that stops them from blowing us out of the water.'

Cusack stopped abruptly and turned back to stare at Fallon. 'The *Tisiphone*'s still here?'

'I'm afraid so.'

'Then the escape's off. At least until tomorrow evening. Can you sneak back to Kingston without anyone knowing you left?'

'Certainly. But that's the least of our worries. It took the *Tisiphone* longer to get here than I anticipated. Tonight's the last night our ship sails in under cover of darkness. It's now or never, Dev.'

' "The best laid schemes o' mice an' men gang aft a-gley", Mal. We'll just have to hope we can get far enough away before they realise we're gone.'

106

'I doubt that,' said Wyatt. 'The tocsin was ringing in the barracks when we passed.' He turned to the Indian. 'The garrison could come by at any moment, Piggy. Keep an eye on the road. You see anyone coming, I want to know about it, understand?'

Mangal nodded and made his way back to the carriage, peering around the back of it down the tunnel of trees.

'It will take them a while to get organised,' said Jarrett. 'And I left them something to distract their attention: a little fire at Government House.'

Fallon stared at him in horror. 'You mean, after we left Price and Killigrew tied up in the library, you set the place on fire? You murderous devil!'

'Don't worry,' said Jarrett. 'Killigrew got free somehow. I don't imagine he left Price and the others to their fate.'

'I don't think we need to worry about Killigrew,' said Cusack. 'I met him at dinner tonight. I know his sort. A gutless fop, all mouth and no pantaloons. He probably only joined the navy because he thought the uniform would make him popular with the ladies.' The Irishman grinned. 'Or with the boys.'

'You think so?' demanded Wyatt. 'It so happens that your gutless fop just chased us halfway out of Kingston, single-handedly killing two of our mates and throwing another four off the roof of the carriage.'

Cusack blinked. 'Killigrew? Are you sure it's the same man we're talking about?'

'That was Killigrew all right,' said Jarrett.

'Well, we needn't worry about him any longer,' asserted Wyatt. 'I did for him. We were going at a hell of a lick when I kicked him off.' He smiled at the recollection. 'I'll bet he broke every bone in his body.'

The winch was all played out now, and the rope hanging from the derrick arm swayed as someone below caught it with the aid of a boat hook. Wyatt crossed to the precipice and looked down. 'All right, they've secured the boat to the cradle. Winch them up, Swaddy.'

Blake reversed the winch. The gear mechanism was designed so that one man could lift several hundred pounds effortlessly, and he had no problem lifting the boat with five men in it, but it rose slowly: one turn of the handle raised it about one inch. It would take twelve hundred turns to raise the boat to the top of the cliff.

'Five thousand dollars,' mused Cusack. 'That's a divil of a lot of money, Mal.'

'Ten thousand in total,' Fallon told him. 'He's already had half in advance.'

'Ten thousand dollars! Holy flip me pink! Where's it coming from?'

'Don't worry about it. When I approached the Irish Directory with my plan, they were falling over themselves to put up the money. This is just the beginning, Dev. If we can get you out, why not the others? There are already plans afoot to rescue Smith O'Brien from Maria Island.'

'The authorities in Hobart Town might respond by revoking the paroles of the other prisoners. They'll be waiting for us next time.'

'You know the British – they'll be so mulvathered that we were able to do it once, they won't expect us to try the same thing again – and again, and again. And even if they are, we can outfox 'em every time. God knows, it's not difficult. We'll make 'em the laughing stock of the whole world! Holy Mary, what wouldn't I give to be here to see Price's face when he finds out I've spirited you away!'

Cusack shook his head grimly. 'You don't want to be here when that happens. The man's astray in the head. The things he does to the other convicts . . . not that he ever dared to lay a finger on me, no matter how much I provoked him, although I got the feeling he'd've liked to.'

'You can tell me all about it on the way to San Francisco.'

'San Francisco,' mused Cusack. 'And where the divil might that be? Mexico?'

'Jesus, Dev!' exclaimed Fallon. 'You *have* been out of circulation for a long time, haven't you? California? The Gold Rush?'

'I heard something about that,' admitted Cusack. 'It's true, then? More gold than Tom Tiddler's ground?'

Fallon grimaced. 'Not exactly. But there's plenty have already made their fortunes several times over, and more on their way. San Francisco's crowded with prospectors right now: Yankees, negroes, Chinese . . . and lots of Irish. Just about everyone who emigrated to America during the Hunger is now heading west to California.'

'What ship is it?'

'The *Lucy Ann* – a Yankee whaler. I got the impression this isn't the first time her skipper's turned his hands to a bit of dirty work.'

'Is he trustworthy?'

Fallon grinned. 'I'd be suspicious of the morals of any man who agreed to break a convicted traitor out of a penal colony. He's got no great love for the British, that much I do know.'

Cusack glanced at Wyatt and the other convicts. 'One thing I've learned, my enemy's enemy isn't always my friend.'

'True enough. He's a mercenary divil, to be sure.'

It did not take Swaddy long to winch the boat up to the level of the cliff edge. The whaleboat was nearly thirty feet long, tapered at both ends, with four oarsmen – three white men, and a Polynesian – sitting on the thwarts, and a fifth man at the tiller. Except for the steel hook where his left hand should have been, the man at the tiller did not look prepossessing; but then neither (in Cusack's opinion, at any rate) had Killigrew.

'Well, Mr Fallon!' the man at the tiller declared in an American accent. 'This is quite a reception committee you've arranged for us. Who are the lucky two who get to come to California with us?'

'We're all coming,' said Wyatt.

'Are you now?' The man smiled. 'I think my boys might have something to say about that. Explain it to him, boys.'

The four oarsmen abruptly snatched muskets from the bottom boards and presented them at the convicts.

'I don't like to be double-crossed, Mr Fallon,' explained the man at the tiller.

'It wasn't his doing,' said Wyatt. 'We insisted he take us. You're Captain Quested?'

The man at the tiller glanced at Fallon. 'You told him my name?'

'I didn't think—'

'You're right,' agreed Quested. 'You didn't think. You're a half-wit, Fallon. Now he can identify me, if we leave him behind . . . alive.'

Wyatt pulled back the hammer of his revolver and levelled it at Quested's head. All four oarsmen pointed their muskets at the convict.

'For God's sake!' pleaded Cusack. 'Killing each other isn't going to resolve anything. Could we at least settle our differences until we get on board your ship? The garrison's on its way here even as we speak, not to mention the *Tisiphone*.'

Quested glanced back at Fallon. 'The *Tisiphone*'s still here?'

Fallon shrugged awkwardly. 'They came here under sail power alone. It took longer than I expected . . .'

'Spare me your pathetic excuses,' sneered Quested. 'You're worse than a half-wit, Fallon. You're a quarter-wit! Maybe I should cut my losses and leave all nine of you here on this island.'

Wyatt grinned. 'And how are you going to winch the boat back down to the sea?'

'You're right,' allowed Quested. 'We do seem to be in something of a predicament, don't we? What's your name?'

'Ned Wyatt.'

'Are you the leader of these men?'

Wyatt nodded.

'Oh-kay, Mr Wyatt. You seem like an honest guy, to judge from the way you owned up to forcing Fallon to bring you. Although I don't doubt that's what you wanted me to think when you did it. But I'm willing to cut you a deal. It so happens I'm four hands short at the moment—'

109

Fallon opened his mouth to protest, but Quested waved him to silence. 'Oh, I've got more than enough men to work my ship to California; but I was kind of hoping to do some whaling on the way, cut my losses on this voyage. For that I need a full complement. Maybe the six of you can take the places of the four men I lost in Hobart Town. So here's the deal: I'll take you all to 'Frisco with Mr Cusack and Mr Fallon, but it will be a working passage. You'll take your orders from me. If any one of you or your friends gives me any trouble, he goes over the side. There is but one God in Heaven and one master on board the *Lucy Ann*, follow me?'

Wyatt nodded. 'Mister, you got yourself a deal.'

'Don't get too enthusiastic, Mr Wyatt. I have two more conditions that require your agreement yet. First, your gun. Now.'

Wyatt laughed hollowly. 'You must be joking!'

'Only my men carry guns on my ship.'

The convict hesitated. 'What's the second condition?'

Quested held out his hand. 'The gun first. Believe me, the second condition is not negotiable.'

'Don't give it to him, Ned!' protested Jarrett. 'You don't think we can trust this fellow, do you?'

'We don't have any choice, Speeler.' Wyatt handed the revolver to Quested and stepped back from the brink, spreading his arms wide. 'Now you've got all the guns, Captain. What are you going to do? Shoot me?'

'You've got sand, Mr Wyatt, I'll say that for you. Sand . . . and brains.' Quested tucked the revolver inside his coat. 'The second condition is that there isn't room for all nine of you in this boat. Two of you will have to stay behind – and even then we're going to be dangerously overloaded on our way out to the *Lucy Ann*.'

'We can make two trips, can't we?' asked Wyatt.

'If I might remind you gentlemen, time is of the essence,' ventured Fallon.

'So let's stop arguing about it and get on with it,' said Quested. 'Which two are staying behind?'

'Oh, no you don't,' said Wyatt. 'We'll leave one of your men ashore, in case you have second thoughts about sending the boat back once we're on board your ship.'

'Oh-kay, but one of you will have to take his place at an oar.'

'I'll do it,' said Vickers. 'I can row.'

'Give your oar to the gentleman and climb out of the boat, Jeffries,' Quested told one of his oarsmen.

'Why me?'

'Because you ask too many stupid questions, that's why. Now do as I say.' Jeffries climbed out of the boat and Vickers took his place.

110

'We still need one more man to stay behind,' said Cusack.

'I'll stay,' said Fallon.

Cusack shook his head. 'No, Mal. Not you. One of these gatecrashers can do it.'

Fallon smiled. 'You want to try persuading them? Better I stay – all they'll have on me is aiding and abetting a prison breakout. Besides, I told you I wanted to see Price's face, did I not?'

Cusack shook his head. 'No, Mal! You don't know what you're saying!'

'He stays,' Quested snapped impatiently. 'I don't see anyone else volunteering.'

'You'll send the boat back for him?' Cusack asked as he climbed into it.

'Certainly. I might even send a couple of men with it. Jeffries and he can winch it to the top so they can get in, then my men will winch it down and climb down the cable. Oh-kay?'

Cusack still did not seem convinced. 'If anything goes wrong,' Fallon told him, 'if that navy sloop shows up on this side of the island, you tell Captain Quested here to set sail and go without me, d'you hear?'

'If a navy sloop shows up, I shan't ask Mr Cusack his opinion before I set sail,' Quested assured him. 'What's the heifer for?' he asked as Mangal handed Mrs Cafferty into the boat.

'Hostage,' grunted Wyatt.

'I don't want a heifer on board my ship,' said Quested. 'Don't you know it's bad luck?'

'It'll be worse luck if that sloop turns up and we don't have a hostage to protect us.'

Quested looked inclined to argue, but he just scowled and banged the palm of his hand against the boat's side. 'We're wasting time – lower away, Jeffries!'

The sailor swung the derrick arm out beyond the rocks below, and started to turn the winch. The boat began its long, slow descent into the darkness. When they finally reached the water, they released the boat from the cat's cradle and Vickers and the three oarsmen started to pull for the *Lucy Ann*. Mrs Cafferty sat wedged uncomfortably between Blake and Mangal in the stern sheets as the boat pitched over the white-capped waves in the darkness. The boat skimmed across the waves at an impressive rate, but they were severely overloaded and water splashed over the gunwales to gather around their feet.

Quested picked up a bailing scoop and handed it to Blake. 'Put that to some good use.'

'What is it?'

'What is it?' echoed Quested. 'It's a bailing scoop, you half-wit.'

111

'Why me?'

'Stop arguing, Swaddy, you idle bastard, and do as he says,' snapped Wyatt. 'You heard what he said. While we're on his ship, we do what he tells us. I'd say now would be as good a time to start as any.'

As Blake began to bail, Quested nodded thoughtfully. 'I like your attitude, Mr Wyatt. Keep it up and I think you and I are going to get along just fine.'

It was not long before the *Lucy Ann* loomed over them out of the darkness, a three-masted barque a little over a hundred feet in length, with three more whaleboats hanging from the davits on her port side. Quested steered the boat around the whaler's stern, and Mrs Cafferty expected to see two more boats on that side, but there were none, just an empty pair of davits for the boat they were currently in. Vickers and the other oarsmen manoeuvred the boat until she was immediately below the starboard gangway, where a long section of the bulwark seemed to be missing beneath a kind of scaffolding that hung out over the water.

A rope ladder had already been lowered from the gangway. A man appeared above them. 'Everything oh-kay, Cap'n?'

'Everything's fine, Mr Macy. We seem to have picked up a few more passengers than we'd originally anticipated, but no problems other than that.' He indicated Mrs Cafferty. 'We'll need a bosun's chair here.' He turned to the three oarsmen in the boat. 'Soames, Rodman: you two stay in the boat. There's no sign of the *Tisiphone* yet. As soon as the rest of us are on board the *Lucy Ann*, you two row back to the shore and pick up Jeffries and Mr Fallon. We'll keep an eye out for the *Tisiphone* or the garrison. If either shows up, we'll signal you – you forget about those two men and come straight back here, follow me?'

'Aye, aye, sir.'

While the sailors on deck rigged a chair and hoist to lift Mrs Cafferty into the ship, Quested and the Polynesian sailor climbed the ladder to the gangway and were followed by Cusack and the six convicts. The boatswain's chair was lowered from a yard, and Soames and Rodman helped Mrs Cafferty into it. Once she was safely over the deck of the *Lucy Ann*, the two oarsmen started to row back.

Two sailors came forward to help Mrs Cafferty down from the boatswain's chair, both swarthy-looking Latin types, but a glance around the deck revealed that, in addition to Quested and one of his officers, six of the other seven men she could see were Anglo-Saxon. The seventh was a Polynesian, a muscular man whose savage, tattooed face was at odds with his Western-style, almost dandified clothing.

Quested turned to a subordinate officer. 'Get the telescope from the binnacle and keep a sharp lookout, Mr Forgan.' He pointed off the port quarter. 'When the *Tisiphone* comes, she'll heave into view round that headland. If she gets here before Rodman and Soames get back with Jeffries and Fallon, sing out.'

'Aye, aye, sir. Want me to send up a rocket, or just signal them with a lantern?'

'Neither. If the *Tisiphone* puts in an appearance, we'll have a hard enough time giving her the slip as it is, without waiting for those lubbers to reach us.'

Killigrew saw stars. After a while, they stopped dancing and assumed their fixed places in the heavens. He recognised the constellations well enough – Aquila, Serpens, Ophiuchus.

He searched himself all over for broken bones. A large bump had risen on his temple where Wyatt had kicked him, and he had put his knee through his pantaloons in the fall from the speeding carriage. The skin beneath was badly grazed, but the injury was hardly life-threatening.

He tried to get up, and at once pain lanced up through his neck to explode in his skull like a *feu de joie*. He settled back down with a groan. He had thrown at least three of the convicts from the roof of the carriage; that was more than his fair share. Someone else could . . .

Mrs Cafferty.

'Christ!' Ignoring the pain, he leaped to his feet and broke into a hobbling run. It was bad enough to have the death of one young woman he had failed to protect on his conscience: he certainly did not want to add another.

A hundred yards further on he came to a crossroads, but it was easy to see which way the carriage had gone: even in the moonlight he could see the tracks it had left in the dusty road. He turned left and followed it.

He jogged when he had the energy and walked when he had not. He was still winded from the dash up the hill after the carriage and the fall had left his knee stiff and aching. Under any other circumstances he would have given up and turned back to Kingston for a hot bath and a glass of whiskey. A very large glass. But a woman's life was at stake.

He had not gone far, however, when he heard hoof beats behind him and turned in time to see a horseman galloping up. Killigrew flagged down the rider, a young ensign from the garrison, who fumbled clumsily for a pistol which he dropped to the ground in his panic. 'Who goes there?' he squeaked, struggling to draw his sword.

Killigrew stooped to gather up the fallen pistol and proffered it to

113

the ensign. 'Lieutenant Killigrew, HMS *Tisiphone*.'

The ensign relaxed and bent down to take his pistol. Killigrew seized him by the wrist and pulled him from the horse before swinging himself up into the saddle in his stead.

The ensign picked himself up and tried to straighten his shako, which had fallen over his eyes. 'I say! What the deuce do you think you're doing with my prad?'

'Just borrowing it.' Killigrew dug his heels in the horse's flanks and galloped away.

It only took a couple of minutes to cover the remaining distance to Cascades Bay, but even as the houses came into view he knew he was wasting his time: the convicts would be long gone. The chances were he would find Mrs Cafferty's body with its throat slit; either that, or they would have taken her on board for their vicious amusement.

He goaded the horse on.

He entered a tunnel of trees and saw the gleam of the deep purple night sky, only light by comparison with the starkly silhouetted trees up ahead. The whitewashed cottages of the settlement at Cascades loomed in the moonlight beyond, and he reined in and dismounted at once. If the convicts were still there, he did not want the clop of his horse's hoofs to alert them to his approach. He tied the horse's halter to a tree and continued hurriedly on foot.

There was no sign of anyone in the settlement. Breakers boomed over rocks somewhere in the distance, but otherwise the night was silent. He looked around, at a loss, and then heard a horse whinny softly in the night somewhere ahead of him. He followed the sound to the far side of the settlement and, seeing the carriage abandoned in the starlight, walked across to it. He did not expect to find any of the convicts still inside, but braced himself before looking through the windows, dreading to find Mrs Cafferty's mortal remains in there.

It was empty.

'I don't get it,' a voice with a Yankee accent said close by; close enough to startle him. 'If we winch the boat up here, and they get out and winch us down – who's going to winch them down?'

'They're sailors, aren't they?' Killigrew recognised Fallon's brogue at once. 'They can shin down the cable.'

The voices came from beyond the carriage. Killigrew peered around it to see Fallon standing by the derrick, switching the sword from his cane at the grass as he watched a second man, wearing a striped jersey and an oilskin hat, turning the winch. Out at sea, Killigrew could just make out a three-masted ship hove to in the moonlight.

'Why didn't your lot just shin down the cable as soon as the boat

114

landed?' grumbled the American at the winch. 'That would've saved the trouble of winching the boat all the way up and down.'

'And ruin my perfectly good suit?' Fallon brushed fastidiously at his lapels. 'Heaven forbid, me old son!'

'Suit my eye!' grumbled the American. 'You're scared of heights!'

'It's not the height that bothers me, Mr Jeffries. It's all those nasty, jagged rocks waiting at the bottom.'

Jeffries had his back to Killigrew and was so engrossed in his work he did not hear him approach, but Fallon whirled abruptly, bringing up his sword. Killigrew raised his hands. 'You wouldn't kill an unarmed man, would you?'

The American turned at the sound of his voice, but Fallon motioned him away. 'You just keep turning that winch, me old son. I'll be dealing with this feller here.' Smiling, he threw his sword to one side, and raised his fists in the traditional boxing stance. 'I should warn you, I used to box for Stonyhurst.'

Killigrew raised his own fists, and the two of them circled on the cliff top. 'Lower deck rules?' asked the lieutenant.

'Lower deck . . .?'

Killigrew kicked Fallon in the crotch and punched the Irishman in the side of the head as he went down. 'Not very sporting,' groaned Fallon.

'There's a time and a place for being sporting,' said Killigrew. He kicked Fallon in the head, knocking him out. 'And this isn't it.'

Killigrew realised the ratchet had stopped clicking, and glanced up to see that Jeffries had left off turning the winch to run for Fallon's sword. Killigrew ran after him, but the American got there first and turned to face Killigrew, slashing at him with the blade. Killigrew jumped back beyond the reach of the arcing tip. Jeffries slashed again, but again the lieutenant dodged the blow easily.

Killigrew was grinning. 'Come on, man! Let me have it! Surely it can't be that difficult to kill an unarmed man? Don't slash, thrust! Have you never heard the saying: "The point always beats the edge"? Run me through, damn your eyes!'

Jeffries lunged. Killigrew side-stepped and caught him by the wrist. The two of them grappled chest to chest on the cliff-edge, but the American was stronger. He grinned as he gradually forced Killigrew around so that his back was to the precipice. The lieutenant's feet slipped on the loose turf, and Jeffries gave him a push. Killigrew teetered, his arms flailing wildly, and he caught hold of the only thing within reach: Jeffries' neckerchief.

The American was caught off balance. He staggered forwards, crashed into Killigrew, and the two of them went over the cliff together.

IX

The *Lucy Ann*

Killigrew and Jeffries fell about ten feet from the top of the cliff and then a hard edge smashed against the lieutenant's side. He hooked his arms over it in desperation – agony shot through his shoulder, a painful reminder of an old injury – and was aware of Jeffries spinning over and over to where the breakers crashed against the rocks ninety feet below.

He clung to the gunwale of the whaleboat suspended from the derrick, where the two sailors sat, dazed. Impelled by his impact, the boat swung outwards, and then swung back like a pendulum. It crashed against the cliff face – or rather, would have done, if Killigrew had not acted as a human fender. Pain exploded in his chest and he slipped, catching hold of the gunwale with his hands barely in time to stop himself from plunging to his death.

The sailors recovered from their shock. 'It's a goddamn navy officer!' said one.

An oar was smashed against one of Killigrew's hands where they gripped the gunwale. He tried to haul himself up, got one arm over the gunwale and jerked his head aside before a second blow from the oar landed. He grabbed the oar and tried to haul himself up, but the sailor quickly released it. Killigrew dropped back down, dangling from the fingers of his left hand. He let go of the oar and it fell towards the rocks below.

A head appeared above him. He reached up behind it and pulled it down with his right hand, forcing the sailor's throat against the gunwale. The sailor gurgled horribly as Killigrew used his head for purchase to pull himself up into the safety of the boat. The other sailor tried to pull his friend up; Killigrew butted him in the chest with his head and fell on to the bottom boards.

The three of them sat facing one another in the wildly swaying boat: Killigrew in the bows, the two sailors in the stern, one of them rubbing his Adam's apple gingerly. Killigrew noticed that Fallon's sword had fallen into the boat, and he snatched it up, panting hard. 'You're both under arrest.'

Then he noticed a musket lying under the thwarts between them. He made to grab for it, but one of the sailors got there first and raised the stock to his shoulder, levelling the barrel at him. The sailor pulled the trigger, and grimaced when nothing happened: the hammer had not been cocked. He wasted precious seconds drawing it back, while Killigrew shrank into the prow and carefully hooked his feet under one of the thwarts.

His musket cocked, the sailor took careful aim once more.

Killigrew slashed at the ropes on either side of him with the sword. They parted and the boat swung down, suspended vertically by the stern. The two sailors fell headlong past the lieutenant, screaming.

Hanging upside down by the toecaps of his half-boots, Killigrew let go of the sword and caught hold of another thwart with his hands. He unhooked his toes from under the first thwart and dropped his legs until he hung the right way up. He dangled there, his heart pounding in his chest as the boat swung sickeningly. Then, when he had caught his breath, he started to climb up the thwarts as if they were the rungs of a ladder. When he reached the stern he managed to grasp one of the ropes supporting the boat and hauled himself up agonisingly.

Then he saw Fallon standing on the cliff-edge, peering down at him.

The Irishman took a clasp knife from a pocket and started to saw at the cable that ran from the winch to the derrick. Seeing his peril, Killigrew started to shin up the cable to the peak of the derrick arm, but it was at least fifteen feet above him and he knew the cable would part long before he got there, hurling him to his death on the rocks below.

Hoof beats sounded, and a lone horseman came galloping out of the trees. It was another officer from the garrison. He quickly took in the situation, drew a single-shot percussion pistol from a holster, and thumbed back the hammer.

Fallon had stopped sawing at the cable and whirled to face him. Seeing the gun in the officer's hand, he threw down the knife and spread his arms.

The officer took careful aim, his tongue protruding between his lips as he concentrated.

'No, you fool!' Killigrew roared in horror.

The officer fired. Fallon's head was jerked back and he stumbled to slump across the drum of the winch with blood dripping from his head.

Killigrew shinned the last few feet to the peak of the derrick arm.

When he had reached it he sat astride it and edged down it as cautiously as an old maid. He had taken enough chances for one night; enough for a lifetime. Once he was well clear of the precipice, he dropped to the ground and lay there, sobbing for breath, until he was aware of the officer standing over him. The officer blew across the muzzle of his pistol as if to clear away the smoke, which the sea breeze had long since dispersed.

'Not a bad shot, what? Even though I do say so meself.'

'Were you aiming for his head?' asked Killigrew.

'Of course!' The officer smirked. 'I always aim to kill!'

'We needed him alive.' Killigrew gestured wearily to where the ship out at sea braced her sails to the wind, moving away from the island. 'He was the only one who could have told us where they're sailing with Mrs Cafferty.'

Quested snapped the telescope shut by pressing it against his chest with his right hand, and passed it back to Forgan. 'Set royals and t'gallants and spread stuns'ls,' he ordered crisply.

'Hold hard!' Cusack protested as the nine sailors on deck hurried to obey Quested's orders. 'What about Fallon? And your three men?'

'They won't be joining us, Mr Cusack. Not ever.'

'So say you! I want to see for myself.'

Quested looked inclined to refuse him at first, but then shrugged as if he could see no harm in it. 'Let him have the telescope, Mr Forgan.'

'What course, Cap'n?' Forgan asked Quested, as Cusack levelled the telescope over the taffrail.

'North-west. We'll run before the wind, get as far away as possible before the *Tisiphone* gets here.' He glanced up towards the night sky, and pointed to where a dark band of clouds rolled towards the full moon. 'Be sure there are no lights showing. With any luck we'll lose any pursuers in the darkness.'

Standing with the other six convicts, Solomon Lissak watched as Cusack lowered the telescope. The Young Irelander looked sick at heart and Forgan had to relieve him of the telescope before he dropped it.

'Satisfied now, Mr Cusack?' asked Quested. The Irishman nodded. 'Good. Now perhaps you'd like me to show you to your cabin?'

'What about Mrs Cafferty?' asked Cusack.

'We'd best put her in my stateroom,' said Quested. Seeing that Cusack looked inclined to protest, he added: 'I'll have to move into the berth in your cabin set aside for Mr Fallon.'

'What about them, Cap'n?' Forgan indicated the convicts.

Quested glanced at them over his shoulder, as if he had forgotten all about them, and called across to the Polynesian with Western clothing and a tattooed face. 'Utumate! Show the rest of our guests to the fo'c'sle. Tell Doc to give them something hot to eat, and dig a change of clothes for them out of the slops chest. They look like a bunch of half-starved scarecrows. Then sling some hammocks for them and let them sleep until the forenoon watch. Tomorrow they go to work: three in one watch, three in the other.'

'Keeping us separated, Captain?'

Quested grinned. 'Spreading your inexperience, Mr Wyatt. You're in my world now – the world of the whale road. I'd advise you not to forget that, if you want to live to see California.'

Killigrew sat on the greensward atop the cliffs and watched helplessly as the barque hoisted her sails and moved off into the darkness. He heard hoof beats behind him and a moment later Price arrived on horseback with some more officers from the garrison.

'What happened?' the commandant demanded crisply.

'They got away.' Killigrew gestured to the barque.

'How many?'

'I don't know. Maybe half a dozen of them.'

Price turned to one of the officers. 'Check Cusack's cottage.' The officer nodded and hurried off.

'This man's still alive!' called one of the officers, crouching over Fallon's body.

Killigrew was on his feet in an instant. The light of a bull's-eye revealed that the bullet had merely creased his skull, and while the blood that covered one side of his head made him look ghastly, he was still breathing weakly.

'Take him to the cellar beneath the old gaol,' ordered Price. 'Put him on the frame with a tube-gag. Maybe he can tell us where that ship is headed.'

Killigrew had no idea what the frame or the tube-gag were, but he did not like the sound of either. 'He needs medical attention. Shouldn't you take him to the infirmary?'

'I've spent half my life dealing with criminals, Mr Killigrew. Before I was appointed commandant of this establishment, I was muster master in the Convict Department and, *de officio*, an assistant police magistrate. I know how to get information out of men reluctant to surrender it.'

Fallon was slung across the saddle of a horse while two officers took him back to Kingston. Shortly afterwards the officer returned from the cottage. 'Cusack's gone, sir.'

'But of course!' said Price. 'He was the one they came for.'

A bank of cloud rolled in front of the moon, hiding the barque from sight.

'Where in Hades is the *Tisiphone*?' demanded Price.

'She'll be here,' said Killigrew. 'When she gets here, we'll have to let Robertson know which direction the barque sailed in.'

'And how do you intend to do that? You're going to signal her?'

'Unfortunately there are only about a dozen naval night signals which are generally recognised, and you need four lights for each of them,' Killigrew said tightly. It had never occurred to him until that moment what a parlous state naval night signalling was in. 'I'll have to go out to the *Tisiphone* by boat.'

He pushed himself to his feet and crossed to the derrick. The rope running from the winch to the derrick arm was sawn halfway through and was in danger of snapping.

'I need a dozen men, Major!' he called to the commanding officer of the garrison.

'Right!' The major turned to one of his sergeants, who had now arrived with a platoon of breathless soldiers. 'Pick twelve men and assist Mr Killigrew.'

'Yes, sir.' The sergeant selected a dozen privates and led them over to the derrick. 'What do you want us to do?'

Killigrew indicated the rope running to the derrick arm. 'This rope isn't going to hold unless I knot it. I need you to hold it while I cut it through and tie it off again.'

The soldiers complied, and Killigrew cut through the rest of the rope, allowing the soldiers to take the strain while he ran enough slack off the winch to tie the line in a secure knot.

'Here comes the *Tisiphone*!' The major pointed to where the sloop's lights showed in the night, off to their right.

One of the privates winched the boat up as far as it would go, and then he and the other soldiers swung it back over the land, the dangling prow scraping across the ground. Then they lowered it again, and Killigrew saw that the name of the ship had once been painted on the boat's stern, but it had been sanded off to prevent identification. Whoever the master of the barque was, he did not miss a trick.

Killigrew quickly effected repairs to the cat's cradle. Most of the boat's tackle had fallen out when he had cut through the cradle earlier, but there were still two oars and a couple of whaling irons wedged under the thwarts. 'I don't suppose any of you can row?' he asked.

'I can row,' said Price, climbing into the boat. 'Have your men swing us back out over the cliff and lower us to the sea below, de Winton.' He ordered the major and turned to Killigrew. 'Hope you know how to tie a good knot, Mr Killigrew!'

'They'll hold,' the lieutenant assured him, joining him in the boat.

The soldiers started to winch them down. 'You're in charge until I

121

get back, de Winton!' Price called up. 'As civilian commandant I'm exercising my authority to declare a state of martial law on the island. There'll be no work details tomorrow morning: I want all the convicts locked up until we've taken a roll call, established the full extent of the breakout. There may be other men loose on the island who didn't get on the boat. Find them, before they let some of their fellow lags out of the prisoner barracks and spark off another mutiny!'

As they were winched down to the sea below, the *Tisiphone* drew ever nearer, until she hove to only a few hundred yards off. Killigrew could see sparks flying from the sloop's funnel. When the boat reached the waves, he cast off the cat's cradle. At least Price had not been lying when he claimed to be able to row: he was a skilled oarsman, and stronger – and less exhausted – than the lieutenant. It took them a couple of minutes to reach the *Tisiphone*, and they both climbed up the side ladder while Petty Officer Olaf Ågård – a tall, blond Swede whose eyes were narrowed from years of squinting across the seas – climbed down to the boat to secure it. The men on deck were all at their quarters, ready for action, and Robertson awaited Killigrew and Price on deck. 'Well?'

'There was a ship all right, sir,' Killigrew told him. 'A barque. She sailed from here not twenty minutes ago, heading north-west.'

'Mr Cavan, go below and ask Mr Muir to set on, full speed ahead,' ordered Robertson.

'Aye, aye, sir.'

As the midshipman descended the after hatch, Robertson turned to the quartermaster. 'You have your heading, Holcombe. North-west.'

A few seconds later the *Tisiphone*'s paddle-wheels splashed into life, and the quartermaster ordered the helmsman to steer two points to port.

'You really think you can catch her?' asked Price.

'It's not a question of catching her,' Killigrew told him. 'The *Tisiphone* can make eight and a half knots under steam. Even running before the wind, a barque could make no more than four, maybe five knots in these winds. No, Mr Price. The difficulty will be finding her in this darkness. She's sailing without lights.'

'I think you'd better see this, sir,' said Ågård; there was no trace of his native Sweden in his accent; if anything, he spoke with a Yorkshire accent picked up from the Hull whaler-men from whom he had first learned English. He had taken a whaling iron from the boat, and he held it out to Killigrew.

'A harpoon, Ågård. So we know the ship we're after is a whaler. That hardly helps us: whalers must be ten a penny in these waters.'

'Look again, sir. It's common practice for whalers to stamp the

122

names of their vessels on their craft.' He ran his finger along the haft of the harpoon until he found the imprint. 'Here we are: the *Lucy Ann.*'

'Christ!' exclaimed Killigrew.

Price glanced up at him in surprise. 'Mean something to you?'

'Killigrew, wasn't that fellow you killed in Hobart Town from a whaler named the *Lucy Ann*?' asked Robertson.

The lieutenant nodded. 'Peleg Starbuck – Captain Quested's nephew.'

'Is Mrs Cafferty on that ship?' asked Robertson.

'No sign of her ashore, sir,' Killigrew said grimly. It was bad enough that she was in the hands of escaping convicts, but if they were escaping on board Quested's ship . . .

'So if we do catch this ship, we can't simply blow them out of the water,' Robertson said with evident regret.

'You needn't shed any tears for her,' snapped Price. 'She tried to murder me earlier!'

'What?' spluttered Robertson.

'You mean, she was in on it?' asked Strachan.

Price shook his head. 'No, I don't think she knew anything about it. The bitch came here solely with the express intention of assassinating me!'

Killigrew could not believe it. 'Why?'

Price shrugged. 'I used to employ convicts as labourers on my farm on the Huon River before I was appointed commandant here,' he explained. 'Seems her brother was once one of the men assigned to me, a young army subaltern who embezzled the mess funds and didn't have the sand to take the honourable way out. He died – he was a sickly sort of fellow – and she holds me responsible.'

'And you say she tried to kill you for it?'

'That pistol you found under my desk? The one you used to raise the alarm? Hers. I was just disarming her when Fallon and Jarrett burst into the library. So you can blow that barque to kingdom come for all I care.'

'I'm sure that won't be necessary,' said Robertson. 'We'll just have to board her, that's all. It will be tricky, but I think my men can handle themselves against a crew of whalers and . . . how many convicts got away?'

'Seven,' said Killigrew. 'Cusack, Wyatt, Jarrett, and four others.'

Robertson turned to Ågård. 'You've served on whalers, haven't you, Ågård? How large a crew do they usually carry?'

'Yankee whalers usually carry six men to a boat, and three ship-keepers or thereabouts, sir. That's twenty-seven.'

'If it is Quested's *Lucy Ann*, then he lost four men in Hobart Town, don't forget, sir,' put in Killigrew. 'With sailors in such short supply these days, I don't imagine he had time to find replacements for Wadrokal, Starbuck and the other two. And I managed to take care of another three up on the cliffs just now. So he's short-handed by seven.'

'Except he's just added seven convicts to his crew. I don't imagine they'll be much use as sailors, but I'll wager they know how to fight. Will they carry much in the way of arms, Ågård?'

'Most whalers carry a few muskets and pistols in the great cabin, sir, in case of mutiny. And they'll have plenty of whaling craft: irons, flensing knives, cutting-in spades, that sort of thing.'

'Permission to lead the boarding party, sir,' said Killigrew.

'Not granted, Second. Lord Hartcliffe can lead the boarding party: you look like you're all in. Besides, first we've got to find them. You'd better get down to the sick-berth and let Mr Strachan take a look at that.' He indicated the cut on Killigrew's temple where Wyatt had kicked him.

'Aye, aye, sir.' Taking into account the relative speeds of the two ships, and the fact the *Lucy Ann* had a half-hour start on the *Tisiphone*, Killigrew reckoned it would be at least another thirty minutes before they caught the barque; assuming they were even sailing in the right direction. Without lights, all the *Lucy Ann* had to do was change her heading, and the first the crew of the *Tisiphone* would know of it was when dawn came to reveal no sign of the barque in any direction.

Killigrew made his way down to the sick-berth, where Strachan was poring over a book. 'What happened to you?' he asked when he saw the lieutenant.

'I was kicked in the head.'

Strachan sighed and cleaned up the wound with iodine, making Killigrew wince. 'Och, stop being such a baby! You know, I seem to spend more time patching you up than the rest of the crew put together.' He put a sticking plaster over the cut. 'How is it you can't go for a fortnight without getting in a scrap?'

'I don't know,' Killigrew said wearily. His whole body was a mass of cuts and bruises, and his thighs ached from all the running he had done. 'Just lucky, I suppose.'

'There, all done. Please try to avoid getting into any more fights, for the next few days at least.'

Killigrew smiled wanly. 'I don't think that's a promise I can keep.'

Killigrew's worst fears came to pass when dawn rose a few hours later: the *Lucy Ann* had changed direction in the night, giving them the slip. The sea was empty in every direction except where the peak of Mount Pitt – the highest point on Norfolk Island – was visible over the horizon astern.

'I've decided we're going back to Kingston,' Robertson announced to his officers and Price in the day-room. 'We're wasting our time searching for the *Lucy Ann*.'

'You're just going to give up?' Price asked in disgust. 'Just like that?'

'What else would you have me do?' Robertson replied quietly.

'Quarter the seas for them! Last night, you yourself said the *Lucy Ann* couldn't manage more than five knots running before the wind. It's only four hours or so since she sailed. She can't be more than twenty miles away.'

'But in which direction, Mr Price?' asked Robertson.

The master, Mr Yelverton, took a scrap of paper and a pencil and drew a small circle on it. 'That's Norfolk Island, see? And here's Cascades Bay. There's been a strong breeze blowing fairly steadily from the south-east all night. Now, if the *Lucy Ann* sailed south-east, to windward, she'd have to tack.' He drew a diagonal line down and to the right of Norfolk Island, and then scribbled three hard lines across it less than an inch from the island, as if by doing so he could bar the passage of the ship.

'She couldn't manage much more than one knot as the gull flies. Even after four hours, we'd still be able to see her from the cliffs. So it's fairly safe to assume she's running before the wind. That still gives us sixteen points of the compass to search in.'

He drew a large circle around Norfolk Island, and then a line bisecting the circle, from south-west to north-east; the north-western half of the circle he hastily shaded with hatching. 'What's left is our search area. Let's say the *Lucy Ann* can manage five knots running before the wind. That's damned generous, but we have to assume the worst. If they sailed north-west, they could be twenty miles away by now. That gives the *Tisiphone* about six hundred and thirty square nautical miles of ocean to search. In another four hours, it will be more than two and a half thousand square miles. After twenty-four hours, more than twenty-two thousand square miles. And so on and so forth, increasing geometrically with every passing hour.' He stabbed at his diagram with the pencil, snapping off the point.

'It's a big ocean, Mr Price,' said Robertson. 'Finding a needle in a haystack would be easy by comparison.'

'So you're just going to let them escape?'

'I didn't say that. We'll head back to Norfolk Island. Perhaps Mr Fallon can give us some clue as to where they've gone. Return on deck and have us put about, First. Have the men stand down – they've been at their stations for over four hours now. The rest of you are dismissed.'

Killigrew made his way to the wardroom and poured himself a

large whiskey from one of the decanters. A moment later there was a knock at the door. Killigrew quickly put his glass down behind him. 'Who is it?'

'Me,' said Strachan. As assistant surgeon, he belonged to the gunroom mess and could not enter the wardroom without being invited to.

'Come in, Strachan.' Killigrew picked up his glass again and took a swig as the assistant surgeon entered. When Strachan looked at him disapprovingly, Killigrew held up the decanter. 'Can I offer you a glass?'

Strachan shook his head. 'It's a little early in the day for me. What is it you sailors say? Sun not over the forearm?'

'Foreyard,' Killigrew corrected him.

'You know, I've been meaning to have a word with you about your drinking.'

'Don't you start. I've already had the Old Man weighing me off . . .'

'If you won't listen to your commanding officer, will you at least listen to a friend? You won't find the answers you're looking for in the bottom of a glass, Killigrew.'

'I don't drink to find the answers. I drink to forget the questions.'

'Very glib! You want to get kicked out of the service?'

'I was ready to give it up for her . . .' Killigrew said morosely. He did not have to explain to Strachan that he was thinking of the girl in Hong Kong. 'Every night I dream about her. Every night we're back there on that clipper, and she's got that gun to her head. And I try to save her. And do you know what?'

'You fail?'

Killigrew shook his head. 'No. That's just it. I could live with nightmares like that. But in my dream I save her, and for a few moments I'm happy because I think that losing her was just a nightmare, and we're going to be together. And then I wake up, and I'm alone in my bunk, and that's when I realise she's dead and she's never coming back. Every morning I wake up, it's as though I've lost her again. Every day I have to face another day without her, I have to face knowing that if I'd been faster, if I hadn't hesitated for a fraction of a second, she might still be alive today. Instead I have to face another day without her. And another, and another. For the rest of my life. I can't live with that pain any longer.'

'She's *dead*, Killigrew. I'm sorry for it, but life goes on. Drinking won't bring her back. And if she were here, what do you think she would say if she saw the state of you now?'

'She'd probably say it served me right.'

'She'd want you to get on with your life. Damn it, Killigrew, act like a man!'

'You weren't the one who got her killed.'

'Neither were you. Pull yourself together.'

'She'd never have died that day if it hadn't been for me.'

'No; she'd have been killed two months earlier. Instead you had two months together; there must be some precious memories which count for something.'

'Precious memories! Fourteen years at sea, and that's all I've got to show for it! Precious memories indeed!'

'And how many lives did you save during the *tai-pan* affair, or in your work on the Guinea Coast? Don't they count for something?'

Killigrew put a hand on his friend's shoulder. 'I'll tell you something, Strachan: I'd trade them all in – yes, and my own worthless life – to have her still alive today.'

'No you wouldn't. "The greatest happiness of the greatest number", remember?'

'Bentham! That old cynic! What did he know? What about *my* happiness, Strachan? Aren't I entitled to a little happiness?'

'If you want to be happy then *be* happy, instead of feeling sorry for yourself. Yes, for *yourself*! If it was her you were feeling sorry for, I could understand; but it isn't. It's yourself, and there's nothing more disgusting than the sight of a self-pitying drunkard. I've been reading *Dombey and Son*, and there's a phrase in there that made me think of you. What was it? Ah, yes, now I remember: "Melancholy – the cheapest and most accessible of luxuries." We all have fits of the mollygrumps from time to time, but you're trying to make a career out of them.'

'A pretty speech,' sneered Killigrew. 'Go tell it to Exeter Hall . . .'

'You're taking this worse than Mr Price.'

'He wasn't the one responsible for Mrs Cafferty being taken hostage.'

'Oh? And what did you do? Say to those convicts: "Oh, whatever you do, please don't take Mrs Cafferty hostage"?'

Killigrew grimaced. 'I might as well have done. It's just like Hong Kong all over again.'

'Do you want me to fetch you an opium pipe?'

White-faced with sudden rage, Killigrew glared at him.

'Well, that's what it's all about, isn't it? It's not Mrs Cafferty you're worried about, it's yourself. When those convicts seized her last night, you saw a way to redeem yourself for what happened in Hong Kong. Only it didn't quite work out like that, did it? So you're starting to wonder if there's something wrong with you; you wonder if you failed both that lassie in Hong Kong and Mrs Cafferty in some way. You want my opinion? You did.'

The lieutenant looked at him sharply, now too bewildered to be angry.

'Failure's a part of life, Killigrew, just as much as success is.'

'I don't like to fail.'

'No one does. But it's something we all have to face from time to time. The real test of character comes in how we cope with that failure: the realisation that even the best of us is only human.'

'And I've failed that test too, you mean?'

'No one faults you for being upset. All I'm saying is that sometimes you have to disremember the past, and learn to live for the future.'

X

A Means to an End

It was nearly ten in the morning by the time the *Tisiphone* dropped anchor in Sydney Bay once more. Killigrew went ashore in the gig with Price, Robertson, Strachan and the marines appointed to act as the officers' servants, who were detailed to collect the personal belongings that had been left behind at Government House the previous night. The house itself was more or less intact, but there was smoke-blackening around one of the windows, which Killigrew guessed looked out from the library. There were no convicts in sight anywhere, not even blue-jacketed overseers, but the soldiers of the garrison were much in evidence. The sound of roll call being taken drifted across from the direction of the compound surrounding the convict barracks.

The naval party met the garrison's commanding officer coming from the direction of Quality Row with his adjutant. 'Ah, Commander Robertson! I wondered if I might have a word?'

'Certainly, Major,' returned the commander. 'May I ask what it's in connection with?'

'I'm going to have to submit a report to my colonel about last night's events. Since both my report and yours is likely to end up before the lieutenant-governor – and quite possibly even the colonial secretary – I thought it might be sensible if we were to compare notes.'

Robertson frowned. 'Are you sure that's necessary? If we both stick to the truth, there's no reason why our reports should contradict one another.'

'Well, you know how these things can look different depending upon your perspective. Perhaps we could retire to my house to discuss it over a pot of tea?'

Price smiled. 'I'll leave you gentlemen to it, shall I? I've got a report of my own to prepare, and I need to speak to Mr Nairn. I don't suppose you know where I can find him, Major?'

129

'In the superintendent's house, the last I heard.'

'What about Fallon, sir?' Killigrew asked impatiently.

'Fallon can wait,' Price assured him. 'The longer he's had to mull over the situation he's put himself in, the more willing he'll be to talk.'

'And the further away the *Lucy Ann* will be!' protested Strachan.

Price smiled. 'Given that the *Tisiphone* is twice as fast as the *Lucy Ann*, and there's no land within four hundred miles of here, wherever the *Lucy Ann*'s bound, I think you can be sure of getting there ahead of her even if you don't leave until tomorrow morning.' He touched the brim of his straw hat and struck out across the greensward towards the old gaol.

'Wait a minute, Mr Price!' Robertson called after him. 'You said you'd let me have copies of the files on Cusack and the other six men who escaped.'

Price turned back. 'I'll bring them to you.'

'No need. Killigrew will come with you and you can give them to him.'

The commandant hesitated before replying. 'Very well,' he said at last.

Robertson followed the major and his adjutant back in the direction of Quality Row, arguing about what they should say in their reports, while Killigrew and Strachan went after Price as the commandant headed to the superintendent of convicts' house.

'I thought you were going to the old gaol, sir?' Killigrew asked Price.

'You want those files, don't you?'

The three of them found Nairn in one of the offices in the house, restoring his shattered nerves with a snifter of brandy. 'A pretty to-do, eh, gentlemen?' he declared heavily. 'A pretty to-do! The comptroller-general will certainly have something to say about this! Devin Cusack snatched right from under our noses, and six of our most vicious incorrigibles to boot! A pretty to-do!'

'The comptroller-general?' said Killigrew. 'After last night's débâcle, I would have expected to be weighed off by the lieutenant-governor himself at the very least!'

'If you're going to blame anyone for what happened last night, Mr Nairn, let it be me,' said Price, digging some manila folders out of a wooden cabinet. 'Mr Killigrew did everything in his power to prevent those desperadoes from absconding.'

Nairn nodded. 'I'm aware of Mr Killigrew's efforts. Major de Winton tells me that if it hadn't been for the lieutenant, we'd've had twelve convicts escape last night, instead of just six.'

'You managed to round up the other six?' asked Killigrew.

'What was left of them,' said Nairn. 'You killed three of them;

not to mention those three sailors from the ship that rescued them.'

Killigrew shook his head. 'Wyatt shot one of them, though that was partly my doing, I suppose . . .'

'You needn't shed any tears on their account, Mr Killigrew,' said Price, putting a couple of folders on the desk. 'They murdered two soldiers from the garrison breaking the others out of the old gaol. Are the results of the roll call in yet, Mr Nairn? We know Cusack, Wyatt and Jarrett were amongst the escapees. What about the others?'

'Wait a moment, I've got a list here somewhere.' He shuffled through some papers on the desk. 'Ah, yes, here we are. Blake, Harold; Vickers, James; Jarrett, Silas; Lissak, Solomon; Griddha, Mangal; and last but by no means least, Wyatt, Edmund. Oh, and Cusack, of course.'

'Is it bad?' asked Strachan.

'About as bad as bad can be,' Price told him, digging out another four files.

'Let's go and speak to Fallon,' suggested Killigrew.

'I'll deal with Fallon,' said Price. 'You gentlemen had better go back on board the *Tisiphone* and get ready to sail. I'll have a destination for you within the hour.'

'We're ready to sail now,' said Killigrew. 'Is there something you'd prefer us not to see in the cellar beneath the old gaol?'

Price looked awkward and glanced across to Nairn. 'Under the circumstances, I think you'd better let them see,' said the assistant comptroller-general.

Price shrugged and picked up the files he had gathered, slipping them under one arm. 'All right, gentlemen.' He headed for the door.

Killigrew and Strachan followed Price to the old gaol next door. 'I hope you gentlemen aren't squeamish,' said the commandant, opening a door to one of the two buildings that flanked the courtyard.

'We've both seen plenty of blood in the course of our careers,' Killigrew assured him.

'Heaven forbid it should come to that,' said Price. 'I have little relish for brutality, whatever my critics in Hobart Town may say to the contrary.'

They followed him down a narrow stone stairway into a cellar with freshly whitewashed brick walls, illuminated by a couple of oil lamps hanging from the ceiling. Two civilian overseers were standing guard over Fallon, who had been strapped to a horizontal iron frame six feet by two, with his head projecting over one end of it. He had been stripped naked but for a grimy, bloodstained bandage around his head, and a kind of gag in his mouth which consisted of a hardwood cylinder four and a half inches long and an inch and a half in diameter. The tube had been forced into his mouth like a horse's bit, with only a hole drilled through it to allow him to breathe.

His face was beaded with sweat and the tendons stood out in his neck from the effort of keeping his head up. The tube-gag had been forced roughly into his mouth, so that his lips were bloody and flecks of blood bubbled through the hole in the tube with each whistling, ragged breath.

Strachan blanched. 'Jings!'

'We call this "the frame",' explained Price. 'If he relaxes and allows his head to fall back, it cuts off his breathing. It may not look much, but you try it at home some time, with your head sticking off the end of the bed. The first few minutes are easy enough; but if you can keep it up for more than half an hour, I'll be impressed.'

'How long's he been like this?' asked Killigrew.

'Since he was brought here last night.'

'But this is monstrous!' protested Strachan. 'It's torture, sir! Nothing less! Damned, barbaric, inhuman torture!'

'If you know of any better way to find out where Cusack and the other convicts have gone, I should be more than happy to try it,' Price assured him.

'Tell him, Killigrew,' pleaded Strachan, his native Perthshire accent creeping through his anguish. 'By the hookie! Tell him tae let the puir de'il up! It's inhuman, I tell ye!'

'He's right, Strachan,' said Killigrew. 'It's the only way to find the *Lucy Ann*.'

The assistant surgeon stared at his friend in horror. 'No' you too! I'd've expected nothing less from this fiend in human form, but you . . .!' He shook his head. 'I want nae part of this. Better that Cusack and the others should escape than we become even worse monsters than the worst of them!'

'You have no concept of what kind of men we're dealing with here, Mr Strachan,' said Price. 'They're not called "incorrigibles" for nothing. I'd sooner die than have their being let loose on the world at large on my conscience.'

'How bad can they be?' demanded Strachan. 'Surely if they were truly vicious, they'd've been hanged for their crimes rather than transported?'

'Oh, there's not one of them who wasn't condemned to be executed to begin with. But there's a spirit of liberalism running through the British legal system these days, and they all had their sentences commuted to transportation for life. A mistake: out here in the colonies, they've confirmed their viciousness and become steeped in evil.' Price took the folders from under his arm. 'Wyatt

I've already told you about. Let's see, who else is there? Silas Jarrett, also known as Speeler: a swindler specialising in using his well-spoken manner to rob ladies of a certain age of their savings; he's the one who left us to be burned alive last night, Mr Killigrew. Then there's James Vickers. Fond of the ladies, is our Jemmy Fingers. They're not so fond of him, but that never troubled him. He likes to hurt women. Eventually he was arrested as the perpetrator of a series of particularly vicious rapes.'

'Vicious rapes,' echoed Killigrew. 'Isn't that tautological?'

Price smiled grimly. 'Not in Vickers' case. If it were any woman other than Mrs Cafferty on that ship with him, I might feel sorry for her.'

'No woman deserves to be raped, whatever sins may be on her conscience,' snorted Strachan.

Price shrugged. 'Next we have Solomon Lissak, the most notorious cracksman in living memory. The police had been after him for years. He was arrested for stealing goods to the value of five hundred guineas; even after he was arrested, he refused to name his accomplice or to surrender the booty. This isn't the first time he's made an escape attempt, gentlemen. When he was first arrested, he escaped from the police office where they were holding him and almost got away. Again, he escaped from the prison hulk he was held on in Gallion's Reach and got halfway across the Kent marshes before the local yeomanry ran him to earth. He escaped twice more from the prison at Port Arthur; the second time he got as far as Sydney before the police picked him up following a bar-room brawl. After that they sent him here to Norfolk Island, thinking it was the one prison he couldn't escape from. Three years ago he knocked out a civilian overseer and stole his uniform; the brig he stowed away on was only two days out of Hobart Town when he was caught.

'Harold Blake, also known as Swaddy Blake. An old soldier – not that he ever served in any regiment longer than was necessary to collect his first pay and steal whatever arms and equipment he could lay his hands on. Between his brief stints of military service he used to beg in the streets of London by claiming to be a veteran of the Afghan War with a debilitating wound and a wife and four children to support; a fine dodge until one day he had been recognised as a thief and deserter by a sergeant of the Seventy-Seventh Foot. The sergeant, being a real veteran of that war, and having a real wife and four real children, took exception to Blake's dodge. There was a fight; Blake hit the sergeant with a cosh. He pleaded self-defence to manslaughter, was found guilty and sentenced to death regardless, but then his sentence was commuted to transportation for life.

'And finally, Mangal Griddha, also known as Piggy. He was arrested as a *thug* in India by Sir William Dampier; he turned approver. For betraying his fellow *thugs*, he was pardoned, despite having confessed to over a hundred garrottings; but he soon went back to his old ways. The next time he was arrested it was for being in possession of stolen goods. No one could prove he had strangled the merchants he had taken the goods from, so he was transported for receiving.

'So if I have to torture Mr Fallon here, who played such a large part in helping them to escape last night, in order to stop them from being unleashed upon society once more, then I shan't lose any sleep over it.'

'That's as may be,' allowed Strachan. 'But there are laws. Fallon hasn't even been tried yet . . .'

'I'm sure you'll agree there's no question over his guilt. And time is of the essence. You ask Killigrew here: the further the *Lucy Ann* gets away from this island, the less chance there is of us ever catching them.'

Strachan shook his head in disgust and made to leave. Noticing an iron frame with two small iron hoops at each end of it, and one larger iron hoop, he stared at it. Then he turned back to Price. 'I've seen one of those before. In the Tower of London. It's a scavenger's daughter, isn't it?'

Price nodded. 'Extremely effective for extracting confessions from conspirators. Why do you think there have been no mutinies on this island since I took over as commandant? If the frame doesn't get the truth out of Fallon here, I'll try him in the scavenger's daughter for a few hours.'

'You know what that will do to him? He'll be crippled for life!'

Price shrugged. 'Not if he tells us where the *Lucy Ann*'s bound.'

Strachan stared at him. 'I was warned I'd find the worst scum of the Empire on this island; but I never imagined that the vilest fiend of all would turn out to be the commandant!'

Price took two steps towards Strachan and raised a fist to strike him. The assistant surgeon flinched, but Killigrew caught Price by the wrist and stayed the blow. 'Let him go,' he told Price softly.

Strachan paused on the stairs and turned back. 'And you're no better than he is, if you stand by and allow him to commit atrocities like this!' he snarled at Killigrew, before turning and hurrying up out of the cellar.

Killigrew released Price's wrist, and the commandant chuckled. 'Seems your friend has no stomach for this kind of work.'

'Let's just get it over with,' said Killigrew, feeling sick.

Price nodded. 'Take his gag off,' he told one of the overseers. 'Let's see what he's got to say for himself.'

The tube-gag was taken from Fallon's mouth, and the Irishman at once spat a mouthful of blood and saliva at the commandant's face. Immediately one of the overseers smashed a wooden truncheon down on Fallon's stomach. The Irishman bucked in his straps in agony and let out a sob.

'Do that again, and next time I'll aim for your knackers,' snarled the overseer.

Price wiped his face with his handkerchief. 'Now then, Mr Fallon – if that is your real name – perhaps you'd like to tell us where Captain Quested is taking Cusack on the *Lucy Ann*?'

'Somewhere where you won't be able to reach him!' Even after several hours on the frame, there was still plenty of fight left in the Irishman.

Price smiled. 'You don't seem to grasp the seriousness of your situation. You're on Norfolk Island now. There's no God here: just John Giles Price. I could kill you – tell the authorities in Hobart Town that you died as a result of an accident – and no one would question it. But it's not part of my plans that you should die. That would be too quick. But I will make you suffer, and the suffering's going to last a long, long time. Unless, that is, you'd like to tell us where the *Lucy Ann* is bound.'

'Go to the divil!'

Killigrew decided to try to reason with him. 'Those six convicts who escaped with Cusack – you heard Price talking about them just now: a vicious coiner, a rapist, a cracksman, an army deserter, a swindler and a *thug* strangler. How long do you think Mrs Cafferty is going to last on a ship with men like that? How long do you think Cusack is, for that matter?'

'You'd say anything to convince me to betray Cusack. That whole scene you just played out with Mr Strachan: an act for my benefit, I've no doubt.'

'I'm going to get the truth out of you sooner or later, Fallon, so you might as well talk now,' said Price. 'Do you know what happens when a man is crushed into the scavenger's daughter? Your internal organs will be massively damaged from having your knees jammed against your chest. Cramps will seize your limbs, and you'll bleed from your mouth and your anus. Sooner or later you'll forget your misplaced loyalty to Cusack.'

Fallon grinned. 'But as you said yourself, the further away he gets the less chance you have of catching him. So I guess it'll have to be later rather than sooner.'

Price sighed. 'This is going to take longer than I thought,' he told Killigrew, handing him the folders. 'Two, maybe three hours.' He checked his watch. 'But I'll wager you ten guineas he talks before noon.'

135

Killigrew had seen more than enough. 'I'll leave you to it.'

Price nodded and turned to the overseers. 'All right. Let's have him up and put him in the scavenger's daughter.'

In the courtyard upstairs, Killigrew gratefully pushed the door to behind him and sucked the fresh air into his lungs, biting back the bile that had risen to his gorge. He was no stranger to bloodshed, but there was something about the very thought of one man deliberately and cold-bloodedly inflicting pain on another that always made him sick and angry.

He left the old gaol and found Strachan on the sea wall, gazing out across the lagoon. 'Don't talk to me!' the young Scotsman snarled when Killigrew joined him. 'Torture! In this day and age! It's barbaric, I tell you!'

'What's barbaric, Mr Strachan?' asked Killigrew. 'Interrogating a prisoner to find out where Mrs Cafferty's being taken? Or leaving that poor woman in the hands of scum like Ned Wyatt and Jemmy Fingers? Don't talk to me about Fallon's rights. It's thanks to Fallon that Mrs Cafferty is a helpless captive in the hands of that scum – assuming they haven't already raped her, slit her throat and thrown her into the sea. What about *her* rights? It's easy for us to condemn a man like John Price—'

' "Easy" is too mild a word for it. It's our duty, damn it. If the people back in the comfort of their homes in Britain knew what was going on out here . . .'

'Did it ever occur to you that the reason the people back home in Britain are able to live in such comfort and security is because of men like John Price who do Society's dirty work?' Killigrew asked his friend. 'Nearly everyone we met in Hobart Town spoke highly of Price's ability as a penal administrator. You know, just maybe he knows what he's doing. It can't be easy keeping control of an island full of men like Ned Wyatt. You don't get the better of men like that by playing the game by the rules, Strachan. The villains of this world win every time, because they're not hidebound by the same rules of decency as the rest of us, whatever Dr Arnold might say. So the only way to beat them is to be even more ruthless than they are.'

'And become as bad as they are? So what happens? You rid the world of evil men, and find you've replaced them with men even more evil than the ones you set out to replace.'

'Evil's rather a subjective word for a scientific man like yourself, Strachan. Where does it fit into your atheistic philosophy, exactly?'

'I don't have to be a God-fearing Christian to know that there are certain rules Society must impose on its members if we're to maintain any semblance of civilisation. That's what sets men apart from animals; most men, at any rate.'

'Exactly my point. Not all men are so very different from animals. The only way to protect your society against them is to employ men with a little bit of the animal in them.'

'Men like John Price, you mean?'

'What would you prefer? John Price torturing criminals here on Norfolk Island? Or men like Jemmy Fingers raping innocent young women back in Britain?'

'I'd rather do without both, if it's all the same with you.'

'But if you had to choose?'

'Price, of course.' Strachan was nothing if not a pragmatist. 'But what if the Law makes a mistake? Suppose an innocent man gets wrongfully convicted, and ends up in a place like this through no fault of his own? That's why even criminals must have certain rights.'

Killigrew thought of the man who had killed the woman he had loved in Hong Kong; the one who had put a bullet in her skull, at any rate. 'I don't see the necessity.'

'Jings, Killigrew! You're a cold-blooded bastard. I'm starting to wonder: is it Price we're talking about, or you?'

Killigrew had no reply to that. Strachan turned his back on him and walked away, stopping occasionally to pick up a stone and skim it across the lagoon. Killigrew took a pull from his hip flask and lit a cheroot.

Robertson returned after half an hour. 'Everything sorted out, sir?' Killigrew asked him.

'As far as I'm concerned, yes. That damned scoundrel de Winton wanted me to falsify my report to protect himself and Price!'

'It might not be a bad idea to go along with them, sir,' Killigrew said quietly.

'You're joking, I take it?'

'Not at all, sir. Otherwise as soon as we've gone they might just agree to make sure their reports both put the blame on you.'

'Well, perhaps I am partly to blame – not that it's my responsibility to help Price keep his convicts locked up.'

'We were the ones who brought Fallon here.'

'Acting under the lieutenant-governor's orders. Anyhow, I'm damned if I'll falsify an official report.'

It suddenly occurred to Killigrew that perhaps one of the reasons Robertson was still only a commander in his mid-forties was his total incorruptibility. He wondered what he would do if he ever found himself in a similar situation: would he sacrifice his whole career to maintain a truth which no one back in England wanted to know about?

Robertson noticed the folders under Killigrew's arm. 'Are those the files on the convicts who escaped with Cusack?'

'Yes, sir.' Killigrew held them out to Robertson, who shook his head.

'You hold on to them for now, Second. What about Fallon? Did Price interview him yet?'

'Interview him!' snorted Strachan, who had hurried across the moment he had seen Robertson talking to Killigrew. 'Torturing him, more like. They've got a scavenger's daughter in the cellar there!'

'Don't be ridiculous, Mr Strachan,' said Robertson. 'This is eighteen fifty, not fifteen eighty. The Spanish Inquisition ended a long time ago.'

'But it's the truth, sir! If ye dinna believe me, go see for yourself!'

Astonished by Strachan's vehemence, Robertson glanced at Killigrew. The lieutenant knew that if Robertson found out what Price was doing, he would try to stop it – he might even succeed. In a battle of wills, it would be hard to judge which of the two would win – and then they would have no chance of catching the *Lucy Ann*. But he could not deny it, either. Part of him wanted the torture to stop, to find a more humane way to learn which way the *Lucy Ann* had gone. 'It's true, sir,' he admitted.

Robertson set his jaw. 'Right. We'll see about that.' He began to stride across to the old gaol. Strachan followed, but Robertson rounded on him. 'Not you, Strachan. I want to speak to Price alone. You go back aboard the *Tisiphone*; I'm sure you have duties to attend to. You too, Second. I want a full report of what happened last night waiting for me on my desk by the time I come back on board.'

Killigrew and Strachan climbed into the gig and sat in silence as they were rowed back to the ship. Neither of them felt much like talking to the other. Killigrew preceded Strachan up the side-ladder to the entry port and ordered the coxswain of the gig to go back to wait for Robertson.

Hartcliffe and Ågård were talking to Able Seaman Molineaux until Killigrew stepped on to the quarterdeck. Killigrew exchanged 'good mornings' with Hartcliffe, and turned to the quartermaster. 'You used to be a spouter, didn't you, Ågård?'

'Aye, sir.'

'The ship we're after is a whaler. Any notion of where it might be headed?' Killigrew was thinking that the best place to hide a whaler was in a fleet of whalers.

'I was on the Greenland fishery, sir, hunting right whales. Here in the Pacific, chances are the ship we're after is a Yankee, a sperm whaler. Not that it makes any odds: whalers don't usually hunt in packs.'

'But what waters would we find them in? Don't whales have

138

seasonal patterns of migration or something like that?'

Ågård grinned ruefully. 'Maybe they do, sir, and maybe they don't. No one knows it for sure, though I heard tell that some Yankee is making some kind of study into the subject. If he can tell whalers the best place to find whales at any given time of year, he'll be a rich man.'

Killigrew smiled sadly. 'That's not much help to us, Ågård; but thank you anyhow.' He turned towards the after hatch when Molineaux called after him.

'Sir?'

'Yes, Molineaux?'

'Reckon I could hazard a guess at where they're headed, sir.'

Killigrew smiled with amusement. That was Molineaux all over: always trying his best, even when it was hopeless. 'Go on, Molineaux.'

The seaman spoke at length, and with all of Killigrew's interjections it took him nearly ten minutes to finish. When he had done so, Killigrew stood in thought for a few moments.

'What do you think, sir?'

Killigrew turned to the yeoman of the signals. 'Signal the shore, Flags. Tell Commander Robertson that we might just know where the *Lucy Ann*'s headed.'

When Mrs Cafferty woke up it took her a moment to realise where she was. The sun shone behind the small curtain drawn over the porthole, and there was enough light for her to take in her surroundings. She lay on a bunk in a cabin about eight foot by six, with a wardrobe, desk, and a shelf with some books on. At first she thought she was back on board the *Tisiphone*, and that the events of the previous night had all been part of a bad dream. Then she realised that this stateroom was different from Killigrew's cabin, and that she was a prisoner on board the *Lucy Ann*.

She glanced down at herself: she lay on top of the covers, still fully dressed in the evening gown she had been wearing to the dinner party at Government House on Norfolk Island. It seemed more like days than hours ago. She kneeled on the bunk to draw the curtain and peer out of the porthole: the sun dazzled her. If it were morning – and she did not think she had been asleep more than a few hours – then the *Lucy Ann* was heading north. No matter which way she craned her head, she could see neither land nor any other ships, only mile after mile of rolling blue ocean.

She was amazed that she had been able to sleep at all, given her situation; but exhaustion had overcome her. The nights on board the *Tisiphone* had been long, as each day took her nearer to her long-awaited confrontation with John Price. Now that the ordeal was over and done with – and somehow she did not feel disappointed that she had been unable to kill him – the tension had oozed out of her.

Now all you've got to do is escape from a whaler crewed by a gang of savages, cut-throats and convicted criminals in the middle of the Pacific Ocean and make your way back to civilisation, she thought ruefully to herself.

At least it was obvious they meant her no immediate harm. If Cusack and Quested had any intention of allowing Wyatt and his cronies to rape her, then it would have happened last night. The fact that they had not already slit her throat and dumped her body over the side gave her some reassurance; perhaps they intended to let her go when they no longer needed her as a hostage. But now she could identify Quested and his ship, she wondered if he *would* let her go. As an American citizen, he might consider himself beyond the reach of British law, and once Cusack had been safely delivered to San Francisco it was unlikely that the Royal Navy would put much effort into hunting down the men who had helped him escape. That would be closing the stable door after the horse had bolted, and the ructions with the US State Department likely to arise from such an act would outweigh the benefits of seeing justice done.

On the other hand, perhaps Quested and his crew were simply squeamish about killing a woman, and were putting the deed off for as long as possible.

But if they thought she would let them kill her without putting up a fight, they had another think coming. She knew it was unrealistic to expect the *Tisiphone* and her crew to come to her rescue, the way Sir Richmond Shakespeare and his Kuzzilbash cavalry had rescued her and the other captives at Bameean seven and a half years ago. If the *Tisiphone* were going to catch the *Lucy Ann*, it would have done so by now. If anyone were going to get her out of this predicament, it would have to be herself. She knew there was no one on board the whaler she could trust, but she might be able to play them against one another. She would have to use her wits if she was going to stay alive for the next few weeks.

She studied the room she was in, hoping it would give her some insight into the kind of man she had to deal with in Captain Quested. His personality seemed to leave little stamp on the stateroom. There was no smell of tobacco, so he did not smoke, and there was no evidence that he was a drinker. No framed calotypes or daguerreotypes of loved ones, no personal letters in the drawers of the desk. The clothes in the wardrobe were sober and unostentatious, but of good quality. He was a man who liked neither to stand out in the crowd nor to spend money on luxuries, but clearly he preferred to spend good money on something which would last

140

him. There were no novels amongst the books on the shelf – a disappointment, as she knew this might prove to be a long voyage and would have liked something to take her mind off her woes – just tomes of maritime law, and a few books of political philosophy including (rather worryingly) Machiavelli's *The Prince*.

There were two doors leading out of the stateroom. The first led only into a privy. She tried the second door, and was surprised to find it unlocked. She opened it, cautiously at first, to reveal the great cabin beyond. It seemed rather larger than she had remembered it to have been the night before, until she realised that the bulkhead between it and the compartment forward of it was nothing more than a partition which folded up against the deck head. A large window looked out astern with a window seat below. There was a large table in the centre of the compartment, and the fact that two of the chairs surrounding it did not match the other four suggested that the table was not used to seating more than four at a time.

The door out of Quested's quarters was on the other side of the great cabin. She tried the doorknob, but it was locked. She crossed back to the window and tried to open it. It would not open, although there was no lock: it seemed to be jammed, with oakum wedged round the frame.

She looked around the cabin, searching for something she could use as a crowbar to pry the window open. There was a rack of muskets in one corner, but they were securely held in place with a padlocked chain that ran through the trigger guards.

Mrs Cafferty returned to the cabin. A board ran down the side of the bunk, to stop the occupant from being tossed out of bed at night, but the board lifted out of its slots. She took it into the great cabin, braced one end of the plank against the backrest of the seat below the window, and hooked it behind the handle. She pulled on the top end of the plank, but the window would not budge, even with her full weight on it. She braced a foot against the window frame, exerting all her strength, and the board creaked and suddenly there was a loud snap. She fell back, cracking the back of her head against the table, and sprawled on the deck.

She lay there for a moment, thinking that she had broken the plank and that all she had achieved was the lump she could feel rising on the back of her head, and a splitting headache. Then she felt a fresh draught of air, and when she looked up and saw the window swinging open she forgot all about the headache.

She scrambled back on to the seat and thrust her head out of the window. Still she could see nothing but sea in all directions. Then she heard a key turning in the lock behind her, and withdrew her

141

head from the window in time to see Quested enter.

He glanced at the open window with a faint smile. 'If you're going to jump out and swim for Norfolk Island, I suggest you do so now,' he told her. 'It's twenty-five miles astern, and falling further behind with very passing minute. And you won't find any other land within five hundred miles of here.'

There was something about the whaling skipper that made her feel uneasy – a sense that he for one would not be squeamish about murdering a woman, should he consider it necessary – but she was determined not to let him see how frightened she was.

Quested was followed into the great cabin by a chunky negro who approached the seat where Mrs Cafferty kneeled. 'Uh . . . excuse me, ma'am?'

She thought he wanted to close the window, but when she climbed off the seat to get out of the way, he lifted up the seat itself to reveal a capacious locker below. He lifted out two hampers – one containing a tablecloth and napkins, the other glassware and crockery – and a case of cutlery. As he started to set six places at the table, a man Mrs Cafferty did not recognise at first entered. Tall and well built, his hair neatly brushed in waves and lightly pomaded, his whiskers trimmed, he was dressed in a bottle-green frock coat, marbled pale grey trousers, a white muslin cravat and kid gloves. He grinned at her.

'Good morning, Mrs Cafferty. I trust you slept well?'

Only when he spoke did she recognise him from his Irish accent, and even then it was difficult to marry the handsome gentlemen before her with the rough-looking individual in grey convict fatigues she had met the evening before. 'Mr Cusack?' she stammered in astonishment.

'What do you think?' He turned this way and that, preening himself like a peacock, so she could admire the cut of his clothes. 'I've lost a little weight since I was arrested, but not a bad fit for all that.'

'You look . . . very handsome,' she said weakly.

He beamed proudly. 'Thank you. You look very well yourself this morning, under the circumstances.'

She realised he was just being polite. 'I must look a fright.'

'You, ma'am?' Cusack pulled out a chair for her, and she sat down. 'Inconceivable. Although, if there is anything you require while you're on board this ship, I'm sure Captain Quested will have no objections to your imposing on him.'

'This is a whaling ship, not a 'tarnal enamelling studio,' growled Quested. 'She's already got my stateroom so she can use the cuzjohn in privacy. What more can she ask for?'

Cusack coughed awkwardly, and whispered something in

142

Quested's ears. The captain sighed, and nodded. 'I'll see what I can do.'

The door opened, and three men entered: Mrs Cafferty recognised one of them as Mr Forgan from when she had come on board.

'Well, come on in, gentlemen,' said Quested. 'We haven't got all day. Sit down, sit down. You've all dined with a woman before now, I hope.'

'Aren't introductions in order?' suggested Mrs Cafferty.

Quested sighed again. 'Mr Macy, Mr Forgan and Mr Gardner: my chief, second and third mates respectively. Gentlemen, this is Mrs Cafferty and Mr Cusack.'

The three mates sat down at the table while the negro served breakfast: flapjacks and coffee. Quested took a mahogany box from the seat-locker and opened it. Mrs Cafferty gasped when she saw what lay on the green-baize lining within.

Hands.

There were eight of them, all in black leather gloves, all in different attitudes: one flat, one relaxed, one clenched in a fist, one holding a dagger. Quested unscrewed the hook from the stump of his left arm and selected another hand from the box – one holding a fork – to replace it.

Mrs Cafferty cleared her throat. 'If it's not a rude question, Captain Quested, might I enquire as to how you came to . . . ah . . .?' She was not sure how to finish the sentence without risking giving offence to the volatile captain.

Mr Forgan came to her rescue. 'A shark took it off, ma'am. A great white, off the coast of Tanna in the New Hebrides.'

'That was no shark, Mr Forgan,' growled Quested.

Forgan flushed. 'Whatever you say, Cap'n.'

Cusack was intrigued. 'If not a shark, then what?'

'Shall we start?' suggested Mr Macy, indicating that it was a subject best steered clear of, at least in the captain's presence.

All four of the ship's officers were about to tuck in when they noticed that Cusack and Mrs Cafferty had clasped their hands to say grace. Cusack had done so first, but Mrs Cafferty had quickly picked up on his lead. She was not a very religious woman – all the things St Paul had to say about women put her off taking Christianity too seriously – but she was already starting to look at Cusack as a possible ally against the convicts and the whaler-men, and it would do no harm if he thought she were every bit as pious as he. And just in case there was a God and he was listening, it would not do her any harm to have Him as an ally too.

'Keep me, Lord, attentive at prayer, temperate in food and drink, diligent in my work, firm in my good intentions.'

'Amen,' said Mrs Cafferty, and there was a muttering of 'amens' around the table; only Quested himself did not join in the prayer, watching the rest of them with a sneer of contempt.

'It's not often we have the pleasure of a *señora* on board,' Mr Forgan hazarded in the awkward silence that followed.

'I wish I could say the pleasure was mutual, Mr Forgan,' she returned with a smile. 'However, I find it hard to consider myself a guest when I am being held against my will. I would have thought "prisoner" would be a more apt description of my current circumstances.'

Quested leaned back in his chair. 'Well, now . . . you're no less free to come and go than any passenger on board a transatlantic steamer.'

'Except that most passengers on board transatlantic steamers had the choice of undertaking the voyage in the first place,' said Mrs Cafferty. 'Might I enquire as to what fate you intend for me? Not that I expect you to admit to it if you plan to murder me and throw my body overboard – suitably weighted down, naturally – but it might help me prepare myself mentally for such a fate if you were to give me a hint now.'

'No one's going to be throwing you overboard, ma'am,' Cusack said firmly. 'You have my word on that.' He glared at Quested as if daring him to contradict; Mrs Cafferty wondered if they had already debated the matter.

'And do you intend to keep me locked up in your stateroom twenty-four hours a day all the way to California?'

'The boatsteerers take their meals in here after we do,' said Quested. 'While they do so, you'll be allowed to walk the quarter-deck to get some fresh air, weather permitting. Under close supervision, of course.'

'Of course,' she agreed mockingly. 'Who knows? I might jump overboard, and swim all the way back to Norfolk Island.'

'I propose a toast,' Cusack said suddenly, tapping his wineglass with his knife to make the crystal ring. 'Here's to freedom—'

Quested lunged across the table and brought his left hand down sharply over the ringing wineglass. It shattered under the blow. 'What in hell do you think you're playing at?' he snarled.

Cusack looked bewildered. 'I merely wanted to thank you for my deliverance . . .'

'Don't you know it's bad luck to let a glass ring on board ship? It sounds the death knell for a sailor who'll drown, and I've lost enough men on this voyage as it is.'

'Lucky the cap'n stopped it from ringing,' Macy said with a weak grin, as if apologising for Quested's superstitious nature. 'That means the devil will take two soldiers instead.'

The attempt at humour fell flat. In the awkward silence that ensued, Mrs Cafferty noticed that Quested had cut his palm. She picked up a napkin and tried to take his hand to bind the wound, but he snatched it away from her. 'Leave it!'

'But you're bleeding!'

'Leave it, I say! I'll get the cook to look at it.' He pushed back his chair and stormed from the cabin.

'You'll have to forgive the cap'n,' said Macy. 'He can be a little . . . superstitious.'

'So I'd noticed,' Mrs Cafferty said drily. 'You were going to tell me how he came to lose his hand?'

'It was a shark,' said Macy. 'And don't let anyone tell you otherwise.'

XI

Pursuit

'Tell the captain what you just told me,' Killigrew ordered Molineaux.

In Robertson's day-room on board the *Tisiphone*, the seaman eyed the expectant faces of the officers nervously. It was not that he was afraid of gold braid. Robertson could be intimidating, but after serving on the *Tisiphone* for twenty months the seaman had learned that the commander's bark was worse than his bite; and the rest of the executive officers – Hartcliffe, Killigrew and Yelverton – were oh-kay. But what had seemed like a brilliant piece of deduction on the deck earlier was now starting to look riddled with holes.

Robertson's scepticism was hardly encouraging. 'Go on, Molineaux,' he ordered, throwing the manila folders Killigrew had given him on to the table. 'I'm intrigued to know what piece of information that escaped myself and my officers was so easily picked up by an able seaman. Besides, since we're not going to get anything out of Mr Fallon, it seems you are now our only hope, God help us.'

'Is Fallon still not talking, sir?' asked Killigrew.

'Fallon's done all the talking he'll ever do, Mr Killigrew. He's dead. It seems he put up a struggle when Price and his two guards tried to transfer him from one instrument of torture to another, and the guards were a little overenthusiastic in subduing him.'

Killigrew looked as if he had been gut-punched. Molineaux had seen that look on the young officer's face before, and knew that in some way he was blaming himself for what had happened. But then Killigrew could feel guilty if a child starved on the streets of Peking while he himself was dining in comfort in a restaurant in London.

'Needless to say, I shall be lodging a strongly worded protest about Mr Price's methods with the comptroller-general of convicts when we get back to Hobart Town,' added Robertson.

'I shouldn't bother if I were you, sir,' drawled Hartcliffe. 'From what I hear, Dr Hampton knows damn' well about the brutality here on Norfolk Island, and turns a blind eye. He gave Price his full backing during that row when the Reverend Mr Rogers published that book condemning the brutality on the island last year.'

'Considering that the reverend had been dismissed as the Anglican chaplain on the island only a few months earlier, it's hardly surprising that Hampton disregarded the book as sour grapes on the reverend's part; perhaps a complaint from me will bear out Roger's accusations as being not entirely without foundation. Nevertheless, point taken, First. I shall address my letter to Sir William Denison. Damn it, I'll even send a copy to Lord Palmerston if needs be. However, we're getting off the point. Molineaux, perhaps you'd care to proceed?'

The seaman gestured to the charts on the table. 'May I, sir?'

'By all means.'

Molineaux picked up the folders Robertson had put on the table and was about to transfer them to the bureau in one corner when something caught his eye.

'I'll take those,' said Robertson.

The seaman did not hear him. He felt as though he had just been struck by lightning.

'I said, I'll take those,' repeated Robertson, holding out one hand.

Molineaux stood as if rooted to the spot, staring at one of the files he held. Robertson had to drag the manila folders from him by force, and did not look pleased about it.

'Are you all right, Molineaux?' asked Killigrew.

'Huh?'

'I said, are you all right?'

Molineaux finally remembered where he was. 'Me, sir? Right as rain.'

'Then stop mooning about like a lovelorn footman and get on with it, damn your impudence!' snapped Robertson, hammering a fingertip against the charts on the table. 'And when I speak to you in future, I expect you to respond promptly and attentively, hoist in?'

'Aye, aye, sir.' Molineaux hid his awkwardness behind the charts, shuffling through them until he found one that covered the whole of the Pacific. 'It's all a question of where the convicts *aren't* going, sir. The way I see it, if we take away the places we know they're *not* headed, we'll find there aren't that many places they *can* go. For one thing, we know they're going to avoid any British territory like the plague: so they won't head west to the Australias, or south to New Zealand. They could try heading around the south of Van Diemen's Land and western Australia to get into the Indian Ocean, but they'd be battling against the Westerlies all the way. I can't see them heading north-west past New Guinea and through the East Indies either: any shipping they're likely to run into is going to be British

148

ships or pirates, and I can't see them wanting to fall in with either of those. So now we've got to ask ourselves just where they *are* bound. You're an Irish rebel looking for a safe place to live, beyond the reach of British justice, somewhere where you'll get a warm welcome. Where would you go?'

'The United States,' Hartcliffe said firmly. 'America's full of Irish emigrants, not all of them poor peasants who left Ireland during the famine. Some of them are quite wealthy, in fact; and someone must've put up the money for this rescue attempt. It can't be cheap to charter a whaling ship and her crew for the best part of a year.'

Molineaux nodded. 'That's the way I see it, sir. But east coast or west? I'm putting my money on the west.'

'Based on what reasoning?' demanded Robertson.

'Two things, sir. Firstly, to reach the east coast, they'd have to sail south-east. Fine once they get into the Roaring Forties: they'll have the Westerlies behind them all the way to Cape Stiff. But first they've—'

'Do you think you could spare us your seaman's slang and give Cape Horn the decency of its proper name?' growled Robertson.

'Sorry, sir, Cape Horn I mean. But first they've got to get there, and at this time of year they'll be battling against the trade winds every step of the way. Then, once they reach Cape Sti— Cape Horn, they've reached a bottleneck between the cape and the northern limit of the pack ice. It'll be winter here in the southern hemisphere at this time of year, with only a few miles between the two. They can't risk the possibility we'll guess that's where they're going, and wait for them there. I'll admit neither reason's convincing on its own, but put 'em together . . .'

'All right, Molineaux, I'm with you so far,' allowed Robertson. 'The west coast of America it is. But how does that help us? We can hardly blockade all the ports of California: once they reach Yankee territorial waters, they're out of our jurisdiction.'

'Bear with me, sir. Now, what's the quickest way to Californy from here? They could sail direct; but as soon as they cross the line they'll come up against the north-east trade winds. If this cove Quested is a whaler then he knows the winds in this ocean, and he'll go for the great circle route: run before the south-east trades as far as the Marshall Islands, and once he's got the northern Westerlies behind him he'll have an easy run all the way to Californy.'

'That still gives us a lot of water to cover, Molineaux.'

'I'm not done yet, sir. He's not going to sail all the way to Californy without touching at land somewhere, is he? He's going to want to pick up fresh water and fruit. Also, he's just swapped three experienced hands for six convicts and an Irish rebel. Whalers usually carry a lot of greenhorns anyway; having some extra ones

149

isn't going to help him. He's got to stop somewhere where he's got a chance of taking on some experienced spouters.'

'We're looking at Pacific islands, Molineaux, not Massachusetts. Spouters looking for work are hardly going to be ten a penny in the South Seas.'

'Actually, sir, he's on to something,' said Killigrew. 'I've read a couple of books by an American chap who's served on whalers. Melville, I think his name was. Anyhow, to hear him tell it, spouters are constantly deserting their ships on Pacific islands and waiting for the next whaler to come along. Discipline's harsh on whalers, and the temptation to think the grass will be greener on another vessel must be strong. There are plenty of likely places in the South Seas where a spouter can wait for a whaler to come by: all these islands are riddled with trading stations which have try-works.'

'I thought whalers carried their try-works on deck?'

'They do, sir,' said Molineaux. 'But trying out blubber on the deck of a ship at sea is a chancy business. A lot of these traders have try-works at their stations which they let whalers use for free. That encourages the whalers to stop at their trading stations to pick up provisions while they're about it.'

'All right.' Robertson stood up and started shuffling through the charts himself. 'Let's see, what are the first islands they'll come to if they run before the trade winds?'

'New Caledonia, sir,' said Yelverton. 'There are a couple of trading stations on the Isle of Pines.'

'*Two* trading stations?' queried Robertson. 'How big an island is it?'

Yelverton grinned. 'Not big enough for two trading stations. The master of a sandalwood trader I spoke to when we were in Sydney told me all about it. There's been real competition for sandalwood in New Caledonia and the New Hebrides over the past few years. The two main competitors are Captain Paddon and Robert Towns, although there are one or two others trying to pick up scraps of the trade, like hyenas hovering by during a fight between two lions: hyenas like John Kettle and Thaddeus Thorpe.'

Robertson glanced at Killigrew. 'Your friend,' he said drily. The lieutenant shrugged.

'Is there enough demand for sandalwood to justify all this competition?' the commander asked Yelverton.

'It fetches a high price in Shanghai, sir.'

Killigrew nodded. 'The Chinese burn it as incense in their joss-houses. I understand these islands are also a source of *bêche-de-mer*, which is considered a great delicacy in China.'

Robertson knitted his brows. '*Bêche-de-mer*?'

'Sea slug, sir.'

'I'm sorry I asked.'

'Actually, it's not bad. A little salty, though.'

'Thank you, Killigrew, we all know what an expert you are on Chinese culture. Returning to the issue in hand: what are you saying, Molineaux? You think the *Lucy Ann* is headed for the Isle of Pines?'

'Either there, or one of the trading stations in the New Hebrides.'

'Plenty of trading stations there,' said Yelverton. 'Paddon's got his main base at Aneiteium; there's one on Tanna at Port Resolution – I think that's owned by Kettle – and of course there's Thorpetown on Éfaté.'

'That gives us four places to look, Molineaux. Unless you can narrow it down further?'

The seaman shook his head.

'Give Molineaux his due, sir,' said Killigrew. 'He's narrowed it down from the whole of the Pacific to four locations. That's better than any of us could do.'

Robertson sat down once more and steepled his fingers. 'I don't know, gentlemen. It's flimsy – damn' flimsy.'

'There's no harm in trying, sir,' said Killigrew. He spoke with an enthusiasm Molineaux had not seen in the young officer for many months. 'I don't think that any of us would argue that the *Lucy Ann*'s headed north. And another thing, sir. Wadrokal – the Polynesian negro I tried to help in Hobart Town – he was from the New Hebrides. Aneiteium, I think he said. Chances are that's where Quested took him on. If Quested's on the run, don't you think he's going to want to head for familiar territory? Even if he doesn't stop at any of those islands, if they're as busy as Yelverton seems to suggest then someone at one of those trading stations is bound to have seen something or heard word of the *Lucy Ann*. And we were going to visit the New Hebrides on our way back from the Fijis. All we have to do is visit the New Hebrides first, and then go on to the Fijis.'

'It's not much of a plan,' said Robertson. 'However, in the absence of a better one . . . the New Hebrides it is.'

'If I wanted to work for a living, I would have turned honest years ago,' grumbled Swaddy Blake. He stood next to Lissak, part of a human chain that stretched from the fresh-water butts in the waist to the scuttlebutt at the taffrail, passing buckets down the line to replenish the latter from the former.

It was just after eight in the evening, more than eighteen hours since the *Lucy Ann* had sailed from Norfolk Island. Wyatt, Jarrett and Mangal had retired to the forecastle with the rest of the starboard watch. Lissak, Blake and Vickers had been appointed to the larboard watch.

'You're not working for a living,' Lissak told Blake. 'You're working for your life. Lucky for us half the crew are ticket-of-leave men and don't seem to mind having half a dozen lags on board. But their feelings towards us might change if we ain't seen to be pulling our weight.'

'What will you do when we get to Californy?'

'Ain't you heard? There's gold there.'

'Go gold-mining?' Blake grimaced. 'Sounds too much like hard work to me. Easier to take gold after others dig it from the ground.'

'Go back to prigging? After fourteen years in the colonies?'

'You are not thinking of going straight?'

'I've lived by lying and thieving all my life,' said Lissak. 'But when a cove gets to my age, he gets to thinking about death. Thinking about what comes after. I don't know; maybe we should give some thought to trying to redeem ourselves . . .'

Blake stared at him, aghast.

Lissak cracked his face into a grin. 'Only kidding. I'll bet the Yankees' peters aren't nearly as difficult to crack as the ones they have in England.'

'If it's work th'art looking for, thee couldst do worse than sign on wi' Cap'n Quested for his next voyage,' said Noah Pilcher. An ancient Nantucketer of Quaker stock, as one of the *Lucy Ann*'s harpooners Pilcher acted as a petty officer on board, and he was supervising the men as they worked. 'There's good money to be made in whaling, if thee ships wi' the right captain.'

'And Captain Quested is the right captain, is he?'

'He's the best,' Pilcher asserted proudly. 'I've been on whaling voyages where we cruised for four years without spying a fall, and crawled back to Nantucket without enough oil in the hold to keep a lantern going for half an hour. But not with Quested. It's as though he's got the second sight – always seems to know where the whales are. And he can catch them too. Didst ever hear tell of Mocha Dick?'

'No,' said Lissak. 'Who is he? A prizefighter?'

Pilcher chuckled wheezily. 'Aye, that he was. The biggest prize-fighter there ever was, for he measured twelve fathoms from his head to his flukes. Aye, a whale he was, the biggest parmacetty I ever clapped eyes on. And the meanest: for he developed a taste for whaling boats, and the men that rode them. More than a hundred men he's said to have dragged to a watery death. Oh, thee may look at me with disbelief in thy eyes, for I've heard the yarn spun in a thousand taverns and each time it became more and more far-fetched. But take it from one who knows, for I was there the day Mocha Dick was slain.

'For twenty years he'd been the terror of the cruising grounds off the coast of Chile; 'tis even said it was Mocha Dick that sank the *Essex*. The day we sighted his spout three days out of Valparaiso, we didst not know it was Mocha Dick, otherwise no doubt we wouldst have sailed on without lowering. But as soon as we drew near, when we saw the whiteness of his hump – for he was white as the surf, was Mocha Dick – we knew what we were up against. There were those of us who were for turning back to the ship and letting well alone; but the first mate ordered us on, saying that the oil from such a whale would pay for the whole cruise.

'Well, the second boat caught him first and the boatsteerer threw his iron straight and true. But that only enraged Mocha Dick, for instead of being gallied like any normal whale, he turned on us at once. The first mate's boat he crushed in his jaws – aye, and the first mate along with it – and the second mate's boat – the one I was in – he smashed with a flick of his flukes. But Mocha Dick was not the only one with a temper on the sea that day, for when Quested – who was third mate – saw what the whale hadst done, he only ordered his boat to press on. The boatsteerer got his iron in the whale's back, and this time he ran. Quested's boat was off on a Nantucket sleigh ride, and we thought that was the last we'd see of any of them; but then the loggerhead broke, and Quested got caught in the line and was dragged overboard. Mocha Dick sounded, diving deep down to the bottom of the ocean, and Quested was dragged after him. For two hours the whale stayed under – for that was another thing about him: he could stay under longer than any other whale I heard tell of – and we were sure Quested was drowned. But when the whale breeched, there he was: no longer caught in the line, but pulling himself along it, hand over hand. Right on Mocha Dick's back he climbed and when he was astride the whale's hump, he tore out one of the score of irons embedded there from an earlier fight, and plunged it down again, seeking the whale's heart. For three hours the battle raged, man versus leviathan, but at last we saw fire in the chimney – that's what we say, when the whale's spout turns crimson wi' blood: "Fire in the chimney!" – and as Mocha Dick thrashed about in his flurry, Quested was thrown from his back. But he lived to tell the tale. Two hundred barrels of oil we got from that whale, and from that day on Mr Quested was known as the man who slew Mocha Dick.'

'Gammon!' snorted Lissak.

Pilcher grinned. 'Aye, perhaps I exaggerate a mite; but the yarn's true enough in its essence. Cap'n Quested slew Mocha Dick, bullies, and that's nothing to be sneezed at.'

Lissak glanced across to where Quested's slight figure paced the quarterdeck. It was almost impossible to believe he could have killed such a ferocious whale; but whaling was his craft, after all, and he must have been good at it to have risen to the rank of captain. But perhaps what was most significant of all was that an old salt like Pilcher, who had plenty of whale-kills to his own credit to hear his shipmates tell it, was prepared to believe it. Lissak had never regarded Quested dismissively – he had known enough dangerous men in his time to know another when he saw one – but now he regarded the captain in a new light.

'Is that how he lost he left fam?' Lissak asked Pilcher. 'Fighting Mocha Dick?'

Pilcher grinned. 'No, that was a couple of years ago, off Tanna. We were trading with the natives for sandalwood in those days, when some of them turned nasty on us and we had to swim for the ship. While we were in the water, a shark swam right up to him and bit that hand clean off. Cap'n's been a little bit crazy ever since that happened – though some would tell you he never was quite right in the head. But that don't stop him from being a good cap'n. Fact is, I reckon in our trade you have to be a little bit nuts to succeed.'

'What do you mean, nuts?'

'Why, *non compos mentis* – mad as a March hare. Y'see, Cap'n Quested, he don't reckon it was a shark that took his hand at all.' Pilcher chuckled. 'Fact of the matter is, he's got this crazy notion it was a—'

'On deck there!' cried the lookout at the main-top. 'Sail ho!'

'Where away?' demanded Mr Macy, the chief mate.

'Fine off the starboard quarter!'

'How far off?'

'About twelve miles, sir; sailing north-west by north.'

'Mr Pilcher! Tavu! Douse all lights, there!' Quested bellowed as Macy took the telescope from the binnacle to level it over the taffrail.

Pilcher and Tavu – another harpooner, a muscular young South Sea Islander – ordered the hands on deck to extinguish all deck lights, and then went below to see to it that no lights were left burning in the 'tween decks.

With the deck lights extinguished, the only illumination came from the gibbous moon in the cloud-racked night sky. 'Wonderful!' said Cusack, emerging from the after hatch. 'What's to stop us from running aground in the dark?'

'Deck lights are no protection against running into a reef, Mr Cusack,' said Quested. 'But fear ye not, there's neither reef nor rocks within seventy miles of here, and those are on Norfolk Island; before us, nothing but clear blue water all the way from here to New Caledonia. There's more danger of running into another vessel, and that's unlikely enough in these waters. What do you see, Mr Macy?'

'Nothing, cap'n,' admitted the chief mate, handing the telescope to Quested so he could see for himself. 'She must be half tops'ls under.'

As Quested stared through the telescope, Wyatt came up from the forecastle and joined them on the quarterdeck. 'What's going on?' he demanded.

'The lookout thinks he's seen another ship,' whispered Cusack.

Quested looked for himself, and then addressed the lookout at the maintop. 'What do you make of her, Inácio?'

'She's a steamer, *senhor*. I can see her lights and sparks flying from her funnel'.

'The only steamers in these waters are navy vessels,' said Macy. 'Ten gets you one she's that Limey navy sloop that was anchored in Sydney Bay, out quartering the seas for us.'

'*Un momento*,' called Inácio, still staring through the telescope. 'She change course, *senhors* – now she head north-east by east.'

'Must be tacking.'

'Steam vessels don't tack, Mr Wyatt,' said Cusack. 'Least of all when they're running before the wind as we are. They're quartering the seas for us. They must have worked out which way we'd head.'

'It didn't take a genius to guess that we'd run before the wind,' snorted Quested. 'Don't worry: we'll soon lose them amongst the islands; and I have friends there who may be able to help us.' He turned to where the steersman stood at the helm. 'Steer six points to port, Addams. We'll run west-nor'-west until morning, then turn north by east; we should be far to the west of where the *Tisiphone* is looking for us.'

Killigrew was back on board the ship in the Cap-sing-mun Anchorage, but this time it was Mrs Cafferty who had a gun to her head, and Ned Wyatt who held it. The convict smirked at Killigrew over her shoulder. 'Last chance, Lieutenant. I mean what I say.'

'Go ahead,' Killigrew replied, off-hand. Wyatt had only one bullet in his gun, and the lieutenant was confident that he would not waste it on his hostage.

Except this time he knew better. He knew there was a second man creeping up behind him with a shotgun, and his words would only provoke Wyatt into pulling the trigger and killing her. Yet still he spoke the words, as if he could no longer control his own lips.

'Shoot her. She means nothing to me.'

'As you will . . .'

The sound of the pistol shot was deafening in the confined space. The bullet smashed through Mrs Cafferty's skull, splattering her brains all over the bulkhead, all over Killigrew.

And he knew he had killed her.

Wyatt fired again, and again, and again, and then the series of shots had become a banging sound: someone rapping on a door. Killigrew lay on the bunk in his cabin, fully dressed but for his pea-jacket and half-boots. His shirt was drenched with his sweat and he was shaking all over. He felt vaguely sick.

'Sir?' Private Hawthorne's voice. 'You asked me to wake you just before dawn.'

'Thank you, Hawthorne. I'll be on deck directly.'

He heard the private's footsteps crossing the wardroom back to the far door, and Killigrew reached across to the fold-down desk where he had left his fob watch. It was just coming up to half-past five.

It was three days since the *Tisiphone* had sailed from Norfolk Island and they had made good time under steam, despite following a zigzag course in search of the *Lucy Ann*. They spotted two other vessels: both whalers, but neither was the *Lucy Ann*, so Robertson had contented himself with overhauling them and enquiring with his speaking trumpet if either of the masters had seen the ship they were looking for. Both men had seen three-masted whalers, but that had been off the coast of New Zealand a couple of weeks earlier, and the masters had recognised the ships in question and known none of them was the *Lucy Ann*.

Killigrew stripped down to his waist, washed the sweat from his body with a face cloth and cold water, towelled himself dry and dressed before going up on deck. It was still dark, the first traces of the coming dawn little more than a hint in the eastern sky, but morning came swiftly in the tropics and Killigrew knew it would be broad daylight within an hour. The *Tisiphone* had reached the island three hours ago, but according to the chart the only way into the anchorage on the south side of the island was via a narrow channel through the reef, and neither Robertson nor Yelverton had any intention of attempting to navigate it before sun-up. They were not in any hurry: for the *Lucy Ann* to have reached New Caledonia so soon, she would have had to have averaged an unlikely five and three-quarter knots.

The sun rose and revealed the Isle of Pines in all its glory: a plateau rising up to about eight hundred and fifty feet, surrounded by a lowland belt of lush vegetation. White, sandy beaches alternated with jagged rocks, and the araucaria trees that gave the island its name rose to over two hundred feet in places.

Studying the shore with the telescope, Killigrew saw a small village of circular huts with conical, palm-leaf thatched roofs. Even as he watched, the men of the village – Polynesian negroes, naked but for the penis-wrappers girdled at their waists – pushed outrigger canoes into the sea and paddled out into the reef, where they at once began to fish with nets. Seeing the *Tisiphone*, they waved, but did not get overexcited at the sight of a ship: evidently whalers and sandalwood traders called here often enough for the arrival of the white man to have ceased to be the great event it must have been when Cook had been one of the first white men ever to visit the New Hebrides.

'At last the natives seem friendly, sir.' Killigrew handed the telescope to Robertson so he could see for himself.

'Aren't there cannibals in these islands?' asked Robertson.

'I understand the natives on this island still practise cannibalism from time to time,' said Yelverton. 'But the missionaries have been here unmolested for two years now, and Paddon's trading station was set up a year before that. I think we'll be safe.'

'That's easy for you to say,' grunted Robertson. 'You're not the one going ashore!'

'Erromanga's the place we've got to steer clear of, sir. The Martyrs' Isle, they call it, ever since a couple of missionaries were killed and eaten there about ten years ago. They say the savages on that island are the most aggressive and warlike in the world.'

'Any missions or trading stations on Erromanga these days?'

Yelverton chuckled. 'You must be joking, sir. I understand some of the more adventurous traders touch there for sandalwood, but they deal with those natives at their peril.'

'So it's unlikely that the *Lucy Ann* will touch there?'

'From what I've heard, sir, we can be sure it's the one island in these waters they *won't* touch.'

'If they're going to give it a wide berth, then so can we.' Robertson snapped the telescope shut and handed it to Midshipman Cavan to replace it in the binnacle. 'Instruct Mr Muir to start the engines, Mr Cavan. Ahead slow.'

'Aye, aye, sir.' Cavan descended the after hatch to the engine room.

'Take her in, First.'

Standing at the helm with the quartermaster of the port watch, Lord Hartcliffe acknowledged the order and conned the sloop towards the reef. As soon as smoke issued from the funnel and the paddle wheels began to churn the water at her sides, the native fisherman stopped what they were doing, staring and pointing in amazement and alarm.

'Haven't they seen a steamer before?' Robertson demanded irritably.

'Probably not, sir,' said Yelverton.

The channel through the reef was a narrow one, but the combined efforts of Hartcliffe, the quartermaster and the helmsman were enough to see them through. By the time the sun was fully over the horizon the *Tisiphone* had dropped anchor in the lagoon behind the reef. Ashore, there was a large village of more circular huts, and a few buildings which were clearly European in design, even if the materials were native: a small church for the mission, a house for the missionaries, and the trade house, a tumbledown shack.

'Prepare my gig, Mr Darrow,' Robertson told the boatswain. 'Perhaps you'd care to accompany me ashore, First?' he asked Hartcliffe, before turning to Killigrew. 'You have the anchor watch, Second. Better load the port-side thirty-two-pounder and have her run out. If the natives turn nasty, it might be as well to remind them of the power of European ships.'

'Aye, aye, sir.'

Robertson and Hartcliffe descended the side ladder to the gig and were rowed across the aquamarine waters of the lagoon to a white sand beach, where the men of the village already converged on the newcomers from all parts of the village. Killigrew ordered the port-side thirty-six-pounder's crew to load it as per Robertson's instructions, but in the event the precaution proved unnecessary: even from the *Tisiphone*'s bulwarks, it was clear the natives were friendly. Even as they crowded round Robertson and Hartcliffe, a man in a long, black cassock emerged from the church and strode across the sand to greet them.

While Robertson spoke to the French Roman Catholic missionary – with Hartcliffe acting as interpreter – Killigrew allowed his attention to wander to the wide expanse of sea on the opposite side of the reef. The *Lucy Ann* was out there somewhere, with Cusack and the six escaped convicts on board. And perhaps – just perhaps – Mrs Cafferty was still alive and on board. Whether or not the *Tisiphone* caught them depended on Molineaux's educated guess that the whaler was bound for these islands. If Quested was familiar with these waters, then there was every chance that they might run into someone at one of the other trading ports who knew the *Lucy Ann*, and who might be able to give them some clue as to where the whaler was likely to land: a favourite place for replenishing the casks with fresh water, or for trying-out blubber.

Cavan's voice broke Killigrew from his reverie. 'Looks like they're coming back already, sir,' he said in some surprise.

Killigrew looked for himself. Robertson and Hartcliffe were indeed being rowed back out to the *Tisiphone*. They had not even had time to talk to the man who ran Paddon's trade house – not that there was any sign of him – which could only mean that the priest had been able to provide them with some news of interest.

'Have they seen a ship which might be the *Lucy Ann*, sir?' Killigrew asked eagerly as the gig bumped against the *Tisiphone*'s side.

'We're the first ship to touch here in over a month,' replied Robertson, heaving his bulk up through the entry port. 'But some of the natives say that according to the bush telegraph, a ship dropped anchor in the Bay of Crabs, on the north side of the island.'

'Bush telegraph, sir?' asked Midshipman Cavan.

'Tam-tams, Mr Cavan.'

'Is it the *Lucy Ann*, sir?' asked Killigrew.

'The natives couldn't even tell me if she was a whaler. All ships look the same to them. Unlikely that the *Lucy Ann* could have got here so swiftly, of course, but we need to be certain. Weigh anchor, Mr Darrow!'

XII

The Bay of Crabs

Able Seaman Wes Molineaux was off duty in the forecastle, idly strumming his guitar while watching his messmates playing cards, when the *Tisiphone*'s engine started up again. Private Hawthorne emerged from the galley carrying a steaming mug of tea, and in that instant Molineaux was struck by a moment of inspiration.

He put his guitar to one side. 'Hawthorne? Corporal Summerbee wants to see you topsides.'

Endicott looked up in surprise. 'What are you talking about, Wes? You know Summerbee doesn't—'

Molineaux surreptitiously dug an elbow into his friend's ribs. '. . . Like to be kept waiting,' he finished Endicott's sentence for him.

Hawthorne was a well-intentioned young man, a country lad born and bred, but hardly the sharpest tool in the box. 'I've got to take Tommy Pipes his char . . .' he stammered, plainly panic-stricken at the thought of having to decide his own priorities.

'I'll take the Old Man his char,' Molineaux assured him. 'You'd better look lively and see what Summerbee wants.'

Hawthorne looked relieved. 'Thanks, Molineaux. You're a pal.'

The seaman clapped him on the shoulder as he relieved him of the mug of tea. 'Hey, what are friends for?'

As Hawthorne ascended the companion ladder to the forward hatch, Molineaux headed aft with the mug. He knew he was taking a big risk, but something had been preying on his mind ever since the *Tisiphone* had steamed from Norfolk Island, and he could see only one way to set his mind at rest.

Private Barnes was on duty outside the door to the captain's day room. 'Mug of split pea for the Old Man,' Molineaux told him.

The marine opened the door for him. 'Where's Hawthorne?'

'Had to go topsides,' explained Molineaux, deliberately implying that the marine had been caught short and was paying a visit to the head.

He stepped into the day-room. The door to Robertson's cabin was open, and he could hear the captain moving about in there. 'Mug of char, sir?'

'Put it on the desk,' Robertson's gruff voice called back from the cabin.

Molineaux crossed to the desk in the far corner, put down the mug, and after a quick glance to the cabin door to make sure Robertson had still not emerged, he moved some papers aside to look at the files beneath.

If there was one thing Molineaux was suspicious of, it was coincidence. It had been no coincidence that the peelers had knocked on the door of the stable where he and Foxy had been lying low the morning after the theft from Her Majesty's Theatre: someone had tipped them off. Yet at the same time, he could not help thinking of an Irish priest he had once met in Kilburn named Father Shepherd-Henderson; and of another Irish priest he had met in Cork two years later, also named Shepherd-Henderson, and completely unaware that he had a namesake in London. The double-barrelled name was unusual enough in itself; the fact that both men had gone into the clergy was a remarkable coincidence.

Molineaux was hoping he had stumbled across another remarkable coincidence, but he was disappointed. That was to say, it was a coincidence, true enough – a remarkable coincidence – but not the coincidence he had been hoping for. He swore under his breath.

'Molineaux!'

Robertson had emerged from his cabin – for a big man he could move like a cat when he wanted to – and now stood staring at the seaman. 'What the blazes do you think you're doing?'

Molineaux was so startled that he almost dropped the folder he was holding, but he quickly recovered himself and squared off the papers within by knocking it against the surface of the desk. 'Clearing a space, sir,' he said innocently, putting the file to one side with exaggerated care.

'The devil you are! I saw you going through my papers! What's the meaning of it, hey?'

'I wasn't reading it, sir. I just dropped the folder as I was clearing a space, and the papers fell out. I was trying to put them back in the right order, sir.'

'You're a very bright young man, Molineaux. I was very impressed with your reasoning the other day, but don't let it go to your head. You leave the thinking to us officers and attend to your duties. And if I catch you nosing through my papers ever again . . . so help me God, I'll have you keelhauled and strung up from the yard-arm! Hoist in?'

'Aye, aye, sir.'

'Now get out of my sight.'

Molineaux withdrew.

Back in the forecastle, he met Hawthorne coming down the companion ladder. 'Corporal Summerbee didn't want to see me, Wes,' the marine protested plaintively. Knowing Summerbee, he had probably given Hawthorne a flea in his ear for wasting his time.

'Didn't he?' Molineaux asked innocently. 'Sorry. I must've got confused.' With a shrug, he rejoined Endicott and the others at the mess table, and Hawthorne went on his way.

'You never got confused in your life, Wes,' snorted Endicott. 'What the bloody hell are you up to?'

'None of your business, Seth.'

'You're going to get yourself in trouble one of these days.'

Molineaux shrugged indifferently. 'I've been there before.'

Mrs Cafferty listened to the sailors singing a shanty as they worked while she enjoyed one of her rare breaks on deck. The song was unfamiliar: something about a man who shipped on a whaler and, after various trials and tribulations, ended up marrying the captain's daughter and became first mate. The tune was jaunty enough, and she found herself whistling along to it in an effort to keep her spirits up.

She heard footsteps on the companion ladder and turned in time to see Quested emerge from the after hatch. His face white with rage, he stormed across to where she stood and grabbed her by the shoulder with his right hand. 'What in tarnation do you think you're doing?' he screamed.

'N . . . nothing!' she stammered, stunned and bewildered by his anger. 'I was just standing here—'

'Nothing? Nothing! You were *whistling*, damn you!'

'What of it?'

'Don't you know it's bad luck to whistle on board ship? And worse luck when it's a woman whistling! Death and devils! Do you want us all to be drowned?'

'Well, how was I to know?' she demanded. 'If you wish me to respect your ridiculous superstitions, Captain Quested, I suggest you give me a complete list so that I know what not to do in future.'

'The black vomit wrench ye! I ought to throw you overboard right now!'

'Keep your shirt on, Quested!' snapped Wyatt. 'She wasn't to know. Hell, even I didn't know that one—' He broke off and stared past her shoulder. '*And what the hell's that?*'

Mrs Cafferty and Quested both turned and saw a sail in the distance.

'Goddamn it!' snarled Quested. 'Who's supposed to be on

lookout?' He craned his head to where Blake sat at the maintop, fast asleep. 'One of yours, Mr Wyatt!'

'Swaddy! Get your idle backside down here now!' roared Wyatt.

'Go up and take his place, Osório,' Quested told one of his own men, striding across to the binnacle. He took out the telescope and wedged it under one arm to extend it. He raised it to one eye, and looked relieved.

'It's only a brig. Probably another whaler, bound for the Japans. Still, we'd best give her a wide berth. Four points to larboard, Palmer!'

'Aye, aye, Cap'n.'

Blake swung himself under the ratlines and dropped down to the deck, walking across to where Wyatt stood. 'You wanted to see me, Ned?'

'Not as much as I—' Quested began angrily, but Wyatt motioned for him to stand back.

'I'll deal with this, Cap'n. Did you have a plummy doss, Swaddy?'

Blake grinned sheepishly. 'Sorry about that, Ned. I must've dozed off for a few seconds there.'

'You realise, of course, that if that'd been the *Tisiphone* instead of another whaler, we'd all be as good as scragged by now?'

'What can I say?' Blake shrugged. 'Lucky for us it wasn't, eh?'

Wyatt rubbed the powder burn on his cheek with the heel of his palm. 'You know the *Tisiphone* will be out there looking for us, don't you? What if she runs into that whaler, and the cap'n tells the crew of the *Tisiphone* he saw a ship answering our description hereabouts?' He caught a fistful of Blake's hair, pulled his head down and caught him in a headlock. 'Cap'n Quested gave you a perfectly simple job to do, Swaddy. He knew you weren't a lagger, so he asked you to climb up to the maintop and keep a look-out for other ships. That wasn't so very difficult, was it? *But you still managed to muck it up, didn't you? You idle bastard!*' he raged. '*You want to sleep? I'll let you sleep? You can sleep for ever!*'

Wyatt gave Blake's head a wrench. There was a peculiar snapping sound, and Blake seemed to go limp. Wyatt loosened his grip, and Blake slumped to the ground, his head twisted at an impossible angle. It took Mrs Cafferty several seconds to realise his neck was broken. She fought back the bile that rose to her gorge and reached out to hold on to a pin-rail for support.

'You know, I'd've settled for a whipping myself,' Quested remarked mildly.

Wyatt grinned, his fury abated as swiftly as it had blown up. 'You can whip my pals till your arm drops off, Cap'n. Won't do you no good; some of 'em have been flogged so much they've gotten to like it! But none of the others will fall asleep on watch now, I promise you.' He turned and stalked back to where the other incorrigibles were gathered on the forecastle, their faces white with fear.

Quested turned to Mrs Cafferty. 'Another ridiculous superstition to add to your list, missy. Don't make Mr Wyatt angry: it's bad luck.'

It took the *Tisiphone* the best part of two hours to extract herself from the lagoon and circumnavigate the reefs surrounding the island to reach the Bay of Crabs, where the island's second trading station was located, every bit as ramshackle as the one on the south side of the island. There was not one but two ships anchored in the bay: a small brig, and a familiar-looking topsail schooner flying the white ensign.

'Isn't that the *Wanderer*, sir?' asked Killigrew, his disappointment at not finding the *Lucy Ann* forgotten in his surprise at finding Thorpe's yacht there.

Robertson studied the schooner through the telescope, and nodded. 'And it looks as though we're being invited on board,' he added, as the *Wanderer* hoisted signal flags. 'Your turn to accompany me, Second.'

The gig was lowered once again, and as Killigrew and Robertson were rowed across to where the schooner was moored, the lieutenant had his first chance to admire the *Wanderer*'s fine lines properly; he was willing to bet she was a fast sailer. A figure in white – which, from its bulk, could only be Thaddeus Thorpe – stood on the forecastle with one foot on the rail of the head and a gleaming brass telescope raised to his eye, gazing across to an islet off the coast of the main island.

The gig reached the yacht's side ladder, and a man in an immaculate white uniform, with brass buttons on the double-breasted jacket and a white pilot cap, appeared at the entry port above them.

'Permission to come aboard?' asked Robertson. The *Wanderer*'s signal flags might have invited them aboard already, but even a gruff old salt like Robertson knew that courtesy demanded he ask again.

'Permission granted,' replied the uniformed man. 'You are most welcome, gentlemen.'

Robertson and Killigrew ascended the side ladder, ordering the gig's coxswain to wait for them. 'You're the master of this fine vessel?' Robertson asked the uniformed man.

'The first mate, Commander. Captain Thorpe is the master.' The first mate spoke with the respectful but unobsequious tones of the better sort of butler. 'Mr Irwin, sir, at your service. Captain Thorpe has asked me to conduct you to the fo'c'sle.'

As they followed Irwin forward, Killigrew took in the upper deck at a glance. Like any naval captain, Robertson liked to keep his

165

decks gleaming, with all rope ends neatly squared away and all metal brightly polished, but so spotless was the upper deck of the *Wanderer* it put the *Tisiphone* to shame. It was so spick and span, Thorpe might have been expecting the Queen and Prince Albert on board. Like Irwin, the rest of the crew were immaculately uniformed, but no less competent-looking for all that.

But the thing that really caught Killigrew's eye was the impressive display of ordnance on deck. There were four brass deck guns – two six-pounders and two four-pounders – on carriages carved in the shape of dolphins; two two-pounder rail guns on each side, and a brass twelve-pounder traversing gun on the forecastle.

They found Thorpe in exactly the same attitude in which they had seen him from the gig, but the reason was clear: a fair-haired, pink-faced young man sat at an easel, painting the entrepreneur's portrait in oils.

Thorpe lowered the telescope long enough to glance at Robertson and Killigrew. 'Welcome aboard the *Wanderer*, gentlemen!' he effused. 'You'll forgive me if I don't shake hands; as you can see, Mr Greeley is engaged in painting my portrait – and a deuced long time he's taking over it too. Blast it, Osgood! At least finish painting my head, so I can put my hat on before I get sunburned.'

'Osgood Greeley?' stammered Killigrew. '*The* Osgood Greeley?'

The artist smiled, without pausing in his work. 'Well, *an* Osgood Greeley, at any rate,' he admitted.

'But I've seen your work exhibited in London,' said Killigrew. 'Seascapes and suchlike. Magnificent use of colour to depict the play of light on clouds and on water.'

The young artist flushed. 'You're too kind, Mr . . .?'

'Oh, good heavens, do forgive me!' exclaimed Thorpe. 'I'm being dreadfully remiss. I think we had better call it a day; or a morning, at least. We'll resume after dinner, eh, Osgood?' Thorpe dropped his pose, snapping the telescope shut. 'You will stay for dinner, won't you, gentlemen?' he asked Robertson and Killigrew.

'I'm afraid we're in too much haste, Mr Thorpe,' said Robertson.

'Then at least stay for tea. Have a pot of tea for four sent to the great cabin, Irwin.'

'Aye, aye, sir.' The first mate rolled his eyes as he passed Killigrew, as if to say: *Forty years a seaman, and he uses me like a steward.*

'Let us adjourn to the cabin, eh, gentlemen? By the way, Osgood, this is Commander Robertson of the *Tisiphone* and his second lieutenant, Mr Killigrew, both of whose acquaintance I had the pleasure of in Hobart Town. As you've gathered, gentlemen, this is Mr Osgood Greeley, the artist.'

On the way down to the great cabin, Robertson and Killigrew exchanged handshakes with Greeley.

The great cabin would not have looked out of place on board the royal yacht *Victoria and Albert*, with oak panelling on the bulkheads and plush velvet furnishings. An off-key note was sounded by the native clubs that decorated the bulkheads, however: ornately carved, the fantastic designs on them could not disguise their deadly purpose.

'I see you're admiring my collection of native artefacts, Mr Killigrew,' beamed Thorpe.

'I've studied a little ethnology, although I'm unfamiliar with the cultures of the Pacific,' admitted Killigrew. At an age when most of his peers had thrilled to read of Nelson's exploits, Killigrew had always preferred Captain Cook's voyages of discovery. He had always been fascinated by tales of far-off, exotic places, spending hours poring over the globe in his grandfather's library at Killigrew House in Falmouth, looking up the place names in the *Encyclopaedia Britannica*, and dreaming that one day he would have a chance to visit them.

He indicated the clubs on the bulkheads. 'War clubs?'

'Pig-killing clubs,' Thorpe corrected him. 'The New Hebrides are a positive treasure trove for the budding ethnologist. A pity you did not come to these islands in the autumn; our autumn, that is – spring to the people of the New Hebrides. The Nekiowar Festival of Tanna is well worth viewing.'

Thorpe motioned for his guests to be seated at the mahogany table, and joined them. 'But by far the queerest thing I've ever heard of is the Naghol Ceremony of Pentecost Island. It all harks back to a legend of theirs concerning a man named Tamalié who lived in a village called Bunlap in the south of the island. His wife found him intolerable to live with, the legend neglects to say why . . .'

'Perhaps he snored,' suggested Killigrew.

Robertson scowled at his second lieutenant's flippancy, but Thorpe only chuckled. 'Perhaps, Mr Killigrew. Tamalié's wife tried to abscond on numerous occasions, but each time he pursued her and caught her. On one occasion he chased her up an enormous banyan tree. At the very top, she threatened to jump off. She dared him to follow, saying if they both survived then it would be a sign from the gods that they were meant to be together, and that being so she would never run away again. He accepted the challenge. They both jumped. But the woman had taken the precaution of tying a length of yam vine to her ankle. She survived; Tamalié fell to his death.'

'That's what comes from trusting a woman,' grunted Robertson.

'For many years after Tamalié's death, the women of the village commemorated the jump each year by imitating it,' continued Thorpe. 'But whenever they did so, the wind would whistle eerily through the trees. The village elders took it as a sign that Tamalié's spirit was made unquiet by the ritual, and ruled that henceforth only men would be permitted to perform the land dive. They still do it to this day, towards the end of the rainy season. It is a sort of coming-of-age ritual combined with a fertility rite, to guarantee a fruitful yam harvest. The vines have to be just the right length: too long, and the land-divers crack their skulls on the ground; too short, and their hair won't touch the ground to fertilise it.'

'Do they dive from very high?' asked Killigrew.

'I'm informed they dive from over eighty feet, if they're experienced; although I've never seen it for myself.'

'Eighty feet! It's a wonder they don't break their legs when the vine snaps taut.'

'It does happen from time to time, I'm told,' said Thorpe. 'But I'm given to understand that yam vines are springy, so that instead of snapping tight, they stretch. The land diver must be careful, nonetheless. If the vine is *too* springy, it can snap him back against the tree and break every bone in his body.'

'Sounds like a capital lark,' said Killigrew. 'I wouldn't mind trying it myself some time . . .'

'You would too, you Bedlamite,' Robertson muttered, as a white-coated steward entered with a pot of tea and four bone-china cups on a tray.

'So, gentlemen, what brings you to the Isle of Pines?' Thorpe asked when the steward had poured out the tea and retreated. 'I had thought the *Tisiphone* was bound for the Fijis. Or is it a military secret?' he added, with a humorous twinkle in his eyes.

'No secret, sir,' said Robertson. 'We were ordered to touch at Norfolk Island on our way to the Fijis. While we were there, there was a breakout. A whaler picked up Devin Cusack and six dangerous convicts.'

'Devin Cusack? The Young Ireland chap? Good gracious! Well, I never!'

'We tried to give chase, but lost the whaler in the dark. We're searching for her now.'

'You think she may have come here, to New Caledonia?' asked Thorpe.

'It's one possibility,' admitted Robertson. 'Although I think it more likely they'll try to get at least as far as the New Hebrides before they touch land.'

'Saints preserve us! You don't suppose they could be headed for Thorpetown, do you? I'm on my way there now; I'd hate to think that I might arrive and find such a band of cut-throats and desperadoes awaiting me there!'

'It's a possibility I haven't ruled out. But they won't be there yet.

It's less than three and a half days since the ship we're after sailed from Norfolk Island. We were hoping to catch them before they got this far, but we must have passed them in the night. Assuming they *are* headed for the New Hebrides.'

'What will you do now? Turn back?'

Robertson shook his head. 'I don't want to risk passing them again. Our best chance of catching them lies in waiting for them in the New Hebrides.'

'There is no scarcity of islands in the New Hebrides, Commander. How will you know which one to wait at?'

'I think we can narrow it down to one of three islands: Aneiteium, Tanna or Éfaté. I'm taking the *Tisiphone* to Thorpetown and leaving my first lieutenant at Aneiteium with a couple of dozen men, and Mr Killigrew here at Tanna with another couple of dozen.'

'If you're stopping at Aneiteium, I should advise you to be wary of Captain Paddon,' said Thorpe. 'The man's an unscrupulous rogue. He dreams of establishing a monopoly in the sandalwood trade in these islands, and resents any kind of competition. As a merchant, I'm used to dealing with sharp practices on the part of my rivals, but Paddon will stop at nothing to get what he wants. The man is entirely without morals or standards. You may have heard that a couple of years ago I was accused of kidnapping natives from the island of Tanna to use as slave labour?'

'I'm also aware that an investigation was carried out into your exportation of island labour by Captain Maxwell of HMS *Dido*, and that you were completely exonerated as a result,' said Robertson.

Thorpe beamed. 'Kind of you to remember, sir. Well, in no way did I deny that *someone* was kidnapping islanders from Tanna; what I find most irksome is the fact that, after I established my own innocence in the raids, no one seems to have been concerned with finding the true culprit.'

'And you think this fellow Paddon might have been behind it?' asked Robertson.

Thorpe spread his hands. 'Of course I can prove nothing, but . . . it is difficult to see who else is trading in these islands who has the resources to carry out such a despicable trade on such a scale; or who else is ruthless enough. Indeed, gentlemen, I should not be surprised to learn that the reason the finger of guilt was pointed at me in the first place was because Paddon deliberately planted evidence incriminating me. There's nothing that would please him more than to see my being ousted from the island trade; then he'd have a free hand to continue to ravage these islands.'

'What sort of a man is this Paddon?'

'A man of mystery, Mr Killigrew. He claims he was born in Portsmouth and that he once served in the Royal Navy – although if it is true, I very much doubt he served on the quarterdeck. The man is no gentleman; his trading station on Aneiteium is nothing but a den of vice and iniquity. Speak to the Reverend Mr Geddie at Anelghowhat; he'll confirm everything I've told you. The only thing I do know about his past is that he used to run opium into China, before he realised there were greater profits to be made in the sandalwood trade. His trading station at Aneiteium is situated on a sandy islet off the south coast of the main island, a place called Inyeug – it means "Mystery Island" in the tongue of the natives. They believe it's haunted; he bought it from them for an axe, a rug and a few beads.'

'If he is slaving, then it's our duty to put a stop to it,' said Robertson. 'You say these raids took place on Tanna?'

Thorpe nodded.

'I'm planning to leave Mr Killigrew here at the trading station at Port Resolution,' mused Robertson. 'He has considerable experience of dealing with slavers on the Guinea Coast; I'm sure he'll be happy to look into the matter while he's waiting for the *Lucy Ann* to show up at Port Resolution.'

'The *Lucy Ann*!' exclaimed Thorpe. 'That's the name of the ship that rescued these convicts from Norfolk Island?'

'You've heard of her?' asked Killigrew.

'But of course! Wasn't *Lucy Ann* the name of the ship captained by the uncle of that youth who assaulted you in Hobart Town when last we met? I wish you joy of your hunt, gentlemen. If Captain Quested is the man who spirited Devin Cusack and these six other convicts away from Norfolk Island, it sounds to me as if you've got your work cut out for you.'

Mrs Cafferty was sitting on the bunk in Quested's stateroom with her knees drawn up to her chest when she heard the door to the great cabin open and saw a light beneath the stateroom door. It was three o'clock in the morning – she had just heard the ship's bell clang six times – and all was dark outside the porthole in the bulkhead above her, but she was wide awake.

She heard footsteps crossing the deck of the great cabin and a jingle of keys turning in the lock. It was not Quested, she knew: he never disturbed her except to let her out for meals during the day – and besides, by now she had learned to recognise his footsteps, a sound that never failed to send a shudder down her spine. Part of her hoped it was Cusack, but when the door opened she was disappointed to recognise Vickers. He stood in the doorway, looking at her, the little finger of his right hand thrust deep into one cheek.

170

'What do you want?' she asked.

'Came to see if you were all right, didn't I?'

'It's three o'clock in the morning,' she protested.

'You weren't sleeping.' She was fully dressed, albeit in a change of clothes from the evening gown she had been wearing when she had first been kidnapped five nights ago. Instead she wore a pair of trousers from the pusser's slops with the hems rolled up, and a striped woollen guernsey that was three sizes too large for her. She had not forgotten what crime Vickers had been transported for, and hoped that the baggy, masculine clothes would deprive her of any feminine allure she might possess.

'That's beside the point,' she told him.

'I brought you a drink,' he told her. 'You look like you could do with one.' He stepped aside and gestured to where he had set a bottle of wine and two mugs on the cabin table. Looking through the stateroom door, she saw the curtains over the stern window were open, and through them she could see a distant light in the darkness outside. She wondered if it was another ship. If there was some way she could signal to it, perhaps . . .

Vickers followed her glance, and seemed to read her mind, or at least come close. 'That's the Isle of Pines,' he explained to her. 'Four miles off the larboard beam, so if you were thinking of jumping overboard and swimming ashore, I'd think again if I were you.'

Four miles, she thought to herself. She knew she was a strong swimmer, but she did not know if she was capable of swimming four miles. She climbed off the bunk and walked into the great cabin.

Vickers uncorked the wine and poured them each a mug. He raised his own to his lips. 'Mmm! Not bad. Not bad at all. What's the matter, ma'am? Not drinking?'

'I'm not thirsty, Mr Fingers.'

'You don't know what you're missing.' He sat down on the edge of the table, facing her as she sat on the window seat. 'Please, call me Jemmy. You got a Christian name, ma'am? Seems kind of foolish, us being alone together and me having to call you "ma'am" or "Mrs Cafferty" all the time.'

'I don't think we are sufficiently well acquainted for you to address me by my Christian name, Mr Fingers.'

'Yur, well, I were thinking we could get better acquainted.'

'Does Captain Quested know you're in here?'

'He's tucked up in his cabin, sleeping.' He leered. 'So you don't have to worry about anyone disturbing us.' He locked the door behind him, and then sat down beside her. 'I've seen the way you've been looking at me . . .'

She stood up and moved away. 'With revulsion?'

He leaped angrily to his feet. 'What's the matter with you? Think you're too good for me, is that it?'

'Well, since you mention it . . .'

'Don't act all virtuous on me! You think I don't know what you and Cusack get up to when you're alone together in here?'

'Apparently you don't, since all we do is play draughts.' She moved so that the table was between her and Vickers. He started to dodge one way round the table; she dodged the other way, but his move was a feint and he doubled back like lightning, catching her by the wrist. 'Let go of me!'

He forced her back against the bulkhead. 'All right, drop the act. You know you want it really.'

'Wanting "it" is one thing, Mr Fingers. Wanting "it" from *you* is another matter entirely. If you don't let me go this instant, I shall be forced to summon assistance.'

He brought up his right hand: he was holding a clasp knife, and he laid the flat of the blade against her throat. 'You scream, missy, and it'll be the last sound you ever make.' He pushed her towards the table and made her bend over it. 'Come on, stop making such a fuss,' he said, reaching down to the waistband of her borrowed trousers. 'Who knows? You might even enjoy it.'

She snatched the bottle off the table and spun around, swinging it against the side of his head. The bottle remained intact; Vickers staggered under the blow, momentarily dazed, but quickly recovered himself.

'You little bitch! I only wanted to have a little fun, but you had to play all hoity-toity. Well, for that I'm going to have to hurt you . . .'

Solomon Lissak was being pursued. He had no idea what chased him, only that he had to get away from it. He tried to run, but his limbs were like lead, glued to the ground, and it took all his strength just to put one leg in front of the other.

He felt a hand grip him by the shoulder from behind, and his stomach lurched when he realised it was all over. He turned to look into his assailant's eyes, and looked into the eyes of a younger version of himself.

He heard a woman scream. The scream had no place in his nightmare and, with the realisation that a nightmare was all it was, he woke up. He lay in a hammock in the forecastle of the *Lucy Ann*.

'What the bloody hell was that?' Wyatt's voice demanded in the darkness.

Another sound came from aft, a muffled splash. Footsteps thundered on the deck above.

'That was a woman's scream,' said Wyatt. He struck a match and applied the flaring flame to a spermaceti candle. The flickering light from beneath his chin gave his features a demonic look. 'And the only woman on board is Mrs Cafferty,' he added.

'We'd better go and take a look,' said Jarrett.

Grumbling, Lissak climbed out of his hammock and pulled on his trousers. 'You coves go first.' Wyatt and Jarrett glared at him deprecatingly. 'I'm an old man!' he protested.

Jarrett noticed that the hammock next to his own was empty. 'Where's Fingers?'

'I think I can guess,' Wyatt said grimly.

The three of them made their way aft in time to meet Quested and Cusack emerging from their cabin. Utumate descended the companion ladder from the deck, with two more spouters crowding behind him.

'What's going on, Utumate?' demanded Quested. 'I thought I heard a scream, then a splash.'

The Polynesian specksnyder nodded. 'It come from your cabin, Cap'n. Sound like someone fall overboard.'

Quested and Cusack exchanged glances, and then they all hurried down the corridor to the door at the far end. Cusack grabbed the handle, but the door was locked. He threw his shoulder against it ineffectually.

'Out of the way.' Wyatt motioned the Irishman aside, and then slammed the sole of his foot against the door, just below the handle. It sprang open, but only a couple of inches. 'There's something blocking it,' said Wyatt, and thrust his head through the gap. 'Looks like Fingers.'

'Is he dead?' asked Cusack.

'Can't tell.' Wyatt snapped his fingers at Utumate, and the two of them put their shoulders to the door.

'Hold on, Mrs Cafferty!' called Cusack. 'We'll be there in a moment!'

There was no reply. That did not surprise Lissak: if Vickers was dead or unconscious, then only one other person could have made the splash.

Wyatt and Utumate managed to force the door open. They all stumbled inside. Vickers lay behind the door, a bruise weeping blood on his temple, his head surrounded by the shards of what might once had been a chamber pot. Wyatt crouched over him, feeling for a pulse in his wrist. 'He'll live,' muttered Wyatt.

'Mrs Cafferty?' called Cusack. 'It's all right, it's safe now. You can come out . . . ma'am?' He crossed to the open door of the state-room and peered inside. 'She's not in here.'

'Mr Cusack?' said Lissak.

The Irishman turned back to face him. Lissak nodded to the open window.

'Jesus Christ!' hissed Wyatt. 'The crazy bitch is trying to swim for it!'

Quested crossed to the window and peered out before turning back to Utumate. 'Where are we? Off the Isle of Pines?'

The specksnyder nodded. 'She never make it, Cap'n. It be four mile off. Even if shark not get she – even if she make it past reef – savage be waiting when she get ashore.'

'Put the ship about,' ordered Cusack. 'We have to pull her out of the water before she drowns!'

The harpooners called all hands on deck. They tacked the ship to windward, coming about and sailing back to the point where Utumate had heard the splash, as best he could remember. Whatever light Mrs Cafferty had seen on the Isle of Pines was no longer visible, and while they could just make out the mass of land to starboard, there were no landmarks visible by which they could orientate themselves. The *Lucy Ann*'s three remaining boats were lowered from the davits and their crews started to quarter the dark waters between ship and land, using bull's-eyes and flambeaux to illuminate the scene.

'There's no sign of her!' Macy called across impatiently to where Cusack, Lissak and Utumate stood at the bulwark of the *Lucy Ann*.

'She drown, Mr Cusack,' said Utumate. 'That, or shark get her.'

The Irishman ignored the specksnyder. 'Widen your search pattern! Go further in towards the island!'

'We're almost on the reef as it is,' Quested said mildly. 'No one can swim four miles, least of all some chit of a girl.'

'Byron swam the Hellespont,' replied Cusack. 'That's about four miles. And he had a gammy leg.'

'Who the hell's Byron?' asked Lissak.

'We're wasting time,' Quested said dismissively. 'Search for the bitch, by all means. I'm going back to my bunk.' He turned away from the bulwark. Lissak saw Forgan follow the captain below, and turned to Cusack.

The Irishman had other things on his mind. 'I got her into this mess,' he muttered. 'I can't leave her to die.'

In the past Lissak had often been accused of talking too much, but this time he knew there was nothing he could say which would help, so he clapped Cusack sympathetically on the shoulder and then followed Quested and Forgan to the after hatch.

The old lag stole down the companion ladder on the same catlike feet which had served him so well as a thief. He could hear muffled voices coming from one of the cabins: Quested and Forgan. He could not make out what they were saying, so he crept closer.

'. . . shouldn't underestimate her, Cap'n. She's ain't *loco*. No matter how desperate she was, she wouldn't have jumped overboard

174

unless she judged she had a good chance of reaching the island.'

'Landlubbers often misjudge the perils of swimming in the sea. The chances of her swimming four miles, getting past the sharks and making it across the reef—'

'Are tiny, yes. But there *is* a chance. And if she makes it to the mission, or to Paddon's trade house . . . she can identify the *Lucy Ann*, Cap'n. She can identify *us*. Is that a chance you want to take?'

There was silence for a moment, and then Lissak heard someone in the cabin take a step towards the door. He quickly started to walk boldly down the corridor to the great cabin at the far end, and bumped into Quested as he emerged from the door.

The captain looked at the old lag suspiciously. 'And what do you think you're doing, creeping around down here? Why aren't you up on deck with the others?'

'I thought someone had better check on Fingers,' said Lissak, all innocence. He gestured through the open door of the great cabin to where Vickers still sprawled unconscious on the deck.

Quested narrowed his eyes at Lissak. *He knows*, thought Lissak. *He knows I was eavesdropping . . . and he doesn't like it; not one little bit.*

'All right,' hissed Quested, after an uncomfortably long pause. 'Come on, Mr Forgan. Let's get this ship closer to the shore.'

XIII

Mrs Cafferty's Run

Scrunched up in the locker beneath the window seat, Mrs Cafferty listened as Lissak dragged Vickers out of the great cabin and closed the door behind him. On the deck above, she heard Quested order the sails unboxed and tell the helmsman to put the tiller over. She lay perfectly still, feeling the change in the rolling of the deck beneath her as the ship changed direction.

It felt like hours before she heard the anchor splash into the sea, but she had heard the ship's bell ring seven times and knew she could not have been in the locker for much more than three-quarters of an hour.

'Bring that boat in, Mr Macy!' Quested bellowed. 'You too, Mr Forgan. We're going ashore. Break out the shooting sticks and any lanterns you can find, Utumate.'

'Shooting sticks, Captain Quested?'

'Muskets, Mr Cusack. The natives on that island are only half civilised. It's less than eight years since the crews of the *Star* and the *Catherine* were massacred here. The Kunies may have accepted the presence of the mission and the two trading stations, but they may not be so friendly if they find us creeping about on their island in the wee small hours of the morning. I'll take one boat with Tavu, Inácio, Gog and Magog, and Mr Cusack; Mr Forgan will take another with Mr Pilcher and Chase, Mr Wyatt, Mr Lissak and Mr Griddha.'

In the darkness of the seat-locker, Mrs Cafferty smiled to herself in spite of everything. Obviously Quested did not trust Cusack, Wyatt, Lissak or Mangal enough to leave them on board the *Lucy Ann* while he was ashore.

'Everyone else will stay on board, and keep a close watch. You're in charge until I get back, Mr Macy.'

More footsteps on the deck above, and the plash of oars as the two boats headed for the shore. Having worked out that the *Lucy*

Ann's crew was reduced to twenty by the time it sailed from Norfolk Island, she had kept a careful tally: with Quested ashore with Cusack, Wyatt and nine others, that left Mr Macy and Mr Gardner on board with ten sailors and the two remaining convicts.

Her heart pounded in her chest as she debated what to do next. She had supposed there would be natives on the island, but it had not occurred to her they might be cannibals. She could hardly remain hidden in the locker for the rest of the voyage: it would be weeks before they reached California, and even if she kept sneaking out for food or to relieve herself, she was bound to be caught sooner or later. So she had a simple choice of pressing ahead with her plan or giving herself up to Quested and the others at once. They would be furious she had pulled the wool over their eyes, and there was no telling how the hot-tempered Wyatt might react.

Her experiences in Afghanistan had taught her that the old axiom 'better the devil you know' was not always true. When Akbar Khan had offered to take the officers' wives of the army under his protection, if she had been given any choice she would certainly have chosen to stay with the army as it retreated towards the Khyber Pass. But she had not been given any choice in the matter: the officers had taken the decision for her, and despite her conviction that the Afghans would submit all the women to a fate worse than death she had been too timid to argue in those days. In the event, the Afghans had treated herself and the other women as honourably as circumstances would permit, while the army had been wiped out at Gandamack.

Quested might claim that the natives of the Isle of Pines were cannibals, but how savage could they be if a mission and two trading stations could survive on the island? The natives were an unknowable quantity; but she knew all about Wyatt, Vickers and the other escaped convicts, and it did not take her long to decide she would prefer to take her chances with the natives than spend another day on board the *Lucy Ann*.

She waited until she heard the shore party climb down into the two whaleboats before she pushed up the seat and peered out into the great cabin. Seeing the coast was clear, she climbed out of the locker and lowered the seat back into place.

She looked around, wondering what she could take with her. She wished she had the courage to creep down to the galley to steal some food, but she had calculated that the shore party had left plenty of men on board, and she could not run the risk of running into them. There was a box of matches, but she could think of no way of taking them ashore without getting them soaked. She needed a knife: something to help her build a shelter of some kind if necessary, and to defend herself *in extremis*; but the best she could come up with was a letter-opener. There was no sheath for it, but she found a kid glove and thrust it over the blade so she would not cut herself when she tucked the knife behind her belt.

She extinguished the oil lamp and crossed to the window. It was still dark outside, but she could see the bull's-eyes and flambeaux of the men in the boats as they rowed towards the shore, now less than a hundred yards away. The lights glittered on the waters that surged through a gap in the reef, perhaps half a mile wide.

The boats reached the beach and the crews drew them up on the sand; two men stood by them while the remaining ten members of the shore party headed inland. If she could stay clear of them for long enough, perhaps they would give up the search and sail on without her. She knew she was taking a big chance, but a big chance was better than no chance at all.

She took one of the sheets off the bunk in the cabin and carried it into the day room, tied one corner of the sheet in a double knot around the frame between the two windows, and hauled on it with all her might to make sure it would take her weight. Then she tied the laces of her half-boots together, hung them around her neck, and dropped the rest of the sheet out of the window.

She climbed up to perch on the sill, taking care not to stab herself with the knife tucked behind her belt. It seemed an awfully long way from the window down to the water below, even though she knew it was no more than a few feet. Gripping the sheet firmly, she took a deep breath and eased herself out.

It was almost impossible to get a decent grip on the sheet and she slithered as much as she climbed down, but at least she did not hit the water with a splash. The water was surprisingly cold and it was all she could do to keep herself from gasping with shock. The clothes she wore weighed her down and she knew she had no time to linger. She struck out with a powerful but silent breaststroke.

A deceptively strong current ran across the beach but it only served to carry her away from where the two men waited by the boats, which suited her to a T. It carried her past a headland, but then she realised almost too late that the coast beyond angled away from her and she was in danger of being carried out to sea. A glance over her shoulder reassured her she was already a good distance from the *Lucy Ann*.

Breakers crashed whitely ahead of her in the pre-dawn light and she realised with a surge of panic she was being swept towards the reef. She fought desperately against the current, but each time she glanced to her right the jagged rocks showed closer and closer. The next wave swept her up and carried her towards the rocks. Stinging pain lacerated her left leg and she cried out, but the noise was drowned by the crash of the surf. Then she was plunging downwards, and gallons of water smashed down against her, forcing her under. She was swirled about beneath the waves and she held her breath until it seemed she could hold out no longer. With her blood roaring in her ears, she struck out in the direction she only guessed was the surface. She found only water and more water, and panicked, thinking she was diving rather than surfacing; then her head broke the waves and she found herself treading water in the calm of a lagoon.

The next wave that broke over the reef swept her in towards the shore, and her hand brushed something in the water below her. Even then she almost lost her cool, thinking it was a shark, but then she realised it was the sand. She stopped swimming and stood up in the water.

She stumbled up on to the beach, gasping for breath from her exertions and sobbing with pain. Dawn was coming fast now, and the horizon was clearly silhouetted by the lighter sky behind the *Lucy Ann*. Glancing down, she saw that the leg of her trousers was shredded: the skin beneath was in little better condition. She tore one of the sleeves off the guernsey she wore and bound it over the lacerations to stanch the bleeding. Then she collapsed on the dry sand.

The only sounds she could hear were the lapping of the surf, the cry of birds in the jungles before her, and the occasional distant shout of the shore party as they quartered the bush for her. The first thing to do was to get clear of the beach before sun-up, then find somewhere safe to hide and rest until dawn. By some miracle she had not lost her half-boots when she had been swept over the reef, although they were soaked through. She tipped the water out of them and laced them on her feet. Then she passed between two of the palm trees that fringed the beach and headed into the forest of araucaria trees beyond.

Killigrew had seen William Hodges' paintings of Captain Cook and his officers exchanging greetings with native chieftains on exotic South Sea Islands, but even after he had joined the Royal Navy he had never thought he would feature in such a scene himself. The thought lent an air of unreality as Captain Richards, who ran the trade house on Tanna, introduced Commander Robertson to Moltata, the chief of the village overlooking Port Resolution.

Named after the flagship of Cook's second voyage in the Pacific when the great navigator had touched here three-quarters of a century earlier, Port Resolution was a large cove, about a mile deep and a third of a mile wide. The barren, treeless slopes of the volcano Mount Yasur rose up about three miles inland, barely a third as high as the two mountains of about three and a half thousand feet over the southern end of the island. But the dark plume of volcanic smoke that rose from its crater gave the peak a terrible grandeur of its own.

The north-western side of the bay was dominated by jumbled piles of black volcanic rocks, and a cluster of low, open-ended native huts with palm-thatched roofs were visible beneath the coconut palms that fringed the black sand beach on the south-eastern side of the bay. A number of outrigger canoes were drawn up on the sand, and Captain Richards' small schooner, the *Vanguard*, rode at anchor a short distance from the beach. Richards' trade house, a couple of tumbledown shacks on the edge of the beach, half nestled amongst the trees close to the village. Inland, massive araucaria trees seemed to tower almost as high as the mountains that stretched up behind them. Much of the island seemed to be carpeted with jungle as thick as any Killigrew had ever seen, from Borneo to the Guinea Coast. It was like an illustration of the Garden of Eden from a child's Bible, but with colours far more vibrant than any aquatint: sand the colour of bleached bones, foliage as green as jade and a cerulean sky in which the plume from Mount Yasur was the only cloud other than the smoke from the *Tisiphone*'s funnel.

It was two days since they had parted company from the *Wanderer* off the Isle of Pines; the following day they had stopped at Paddon's main trading station off the cost of Aneiteium. Killigrew had expected to find a tumbledown shack like one of the trade houses he had seen at the Isle of Pines; instead he had found a small but bustling community with a try-works, a sawmill, a chandler's store, a saloon, a number of weatherboard cottages and pens full of cattle. Robertson had interviewed the Reverend Mr Geddie, a dour Scots-Canadian who, with the help of his wife, ran the Presbyterian mission on the opposite side of the anchorage.

As Thorpe had predicted, the reverend had nothing good to say about Captain Paddon, and had condemned the trading station as a den of iniquity. On investigating the trading station itself, they had found that while the saloon had a goodly compliment of native girls dressed up in the latest fashions from Paris, with a paint on their faces, the station also boasted its own library, and Paddon's boat builder – a sober Scotsman named Mr Henry, who was raising a family on the islet – turned out to be a Presbyterian himself, although he had as little time for Geddie as the reverend had for Paddon.

There had been no sign of Paddon himself: Henry had informed them that the captain was 'awa' picking flowers': an unprovoked piece of sarcasm, as far as Killigrew could tell. They had left Lord Hartcliffe there with two dozen bluejackets and half a dozen marines, and Robertson had instructed Hartcliffe that if the

181

elusive Captain Paddon did return, he was to be held for questioning until the *Tisiphone* returned in just over two weeks' time. One of Paddon's brigs, the *Julia Percy*, had been in the anchorage, so if the *Lucy Ann* turned up they would have the means of pursuing her if necessary.

There were about a hundred natives on the beach here at Port Resolution, brown-skinned Polynesian negroes, naked but for penis-wrappers, armed with spears, war-clubs, European-made tomahawks – a key good for exchange in the sandalwood trade – and even one or two muskets. If things had turned nasty, they could easily have slaughtered the handful of naval officers and ratings amongst them, but they seemed well disposed for now.

'You feller is welcome long Tanna,' said Moltata. His hair was grizzled and his face was wrinkled and seamed like old leather, but he stood tall and well built. He wore a pair of boar's tusks on a thong around his neck to denote his status as *yeremanu* – the village 'bigman'. 'M'be people b'long me got big *kae-kae* long honour b'long you. M'be you feller is come long shore b'long *kae-kae* too much.'

'I thought you said he spoke English?' Robertson hissed at Richards through the fixed smile on his face.

'That *was* English,' said Richards. He was in his late forties or early fifties, with greasy salt-and-pepper hair and stubble on his jaw. He wore a grimy white jacket, his barrel-chest naked beneath, and his trousers were ragged to the knees. His face was tanned brick red by the sun. 'Or at least *bêche-la-mer* – that's what we call the pidgin in these parts.'

'He says they're going to hold a feast in our honour,' explained Killigrew, who found the pidgin of these islands remarkably similar to those he had encountered on the Guinea Coast and in China.

'Tell him the honour is all ours,' Robertson instructed Richards.

Moltata spoke to Richards in his own tongue, and the trader responded in the same. 'Any idea what they're saying, Second?' asked Robertson.

'Probably trying to decide what wine to drink with white meat, sir,' Killigrew replied mischievously.

'Pay no attention to him, Strachan,' growled Robertson. As an amateur of the young science of geology, the assistant surgeon had been keen to come ashore to get a closer look at the volcano, but at Killigrew's words he looked distinctly uncomfortable.

Richards turned back to the commander. 'He's inviting you to join him in the *nakamal* to drink *kava* with him.'

'What's a *nakamal*?'

Richards clawed at his stubbled, greasy cheek. 'Sort of like the village hall, but it's *tabu* to women. The village elders gather there in the evening to drink *kava* – that's a native brew – and bore each other with long stories.'

'Sounds like the Carlton Club,' said Killigrew.

'Should we go?' asked Robertson.

'He'll be insulted if you refuse,' said Richards.

'In that case,' opined Strachan, eyeing the native warriors dubiously, 'we should definitely go.'

As they followed Richards and Moltata to the village, the seamen with the shore party looked equally uncomfortable about being surrounded by the natives. 'A feast, eh?' muttered Endicott. 'With us as the main course, I suppose!'

Richards overheard him. 'Don't worry. They ain't going to eat you. The kanakas don't look at a chap, lick their lips and say: "He looks tasty. Let's have him for supper." They usually only eat the men they kill in battle. They believe that by doing so, they take the strength of their enemies into themselves.'

'What about that missionary feller that got et on Erromanga?' asked Endicott.

'The Reverend Mr Williams broke a *tabu* – even though the kanakas on Erromanga warned him against it. He brought his death on himself.'

'What's a *tabu*?'

'It's a sort of rule – something that's forbidden. Like when you go in church, you're supposed to take your hat off. That's a *tabu*.'

'I never heard of a church where they et you for not taking your hat off,' grumbled Endicott.

'Like when we were in Singapore, sir, and the bosun went in that heathen temple, and the priests got all shirty because he'd kept his boots on?' asked Molineaux.

'I suppose so,' agreed Killigrew. 'The imam said he'd defiled the mosque.'

'If they thought his boots defiled their temple, they should see the state of his feet,' said Endicott, and the rest of them laughed.

'But how are we supposed to know what the *tabus* are?' asked Molineaux.

'The kanakas don't believe that ignorance of the law is no excuse,' Richards assured them. 'In my experience they're usually quite good about trying to warn you away from *tabu* areas.'

'All the same, I don't want any of you wandering off on your own, hoist in?' Killigrew told his men. 'And please bear in mind that while we do have firearms, the natives outnumber us; and we're on their territory, so let's remember we're guests and be on our best behaviour. It's true that these islands are renowned for the attacks of natives on traders and missionaries, but in most cases I've heard about, it was usually the white men that provoked them.'

'I don't reckon it's all the white man's fault, though, sir,' said Molineaux. 'I mean, imagine you're a native on one of these islands. Cap'n Cook or someone like that comes by on one of his ships, with fine clothes with lots of shiny buttons, and guns, and all kinds of stuff which'd seem amazing to a native who's lived his whole life in some poxy village in the back end of beyond. Of course the natives are going to want to get their fams on it, ain't they? And if they can't prig it, they'll croak you for it. That's human nature, ain't it?'

Killigrew smiled. 'I can see you're not a believer in Rousseau's theory of the noble savage, Molineaux.'

'I ain't saying the savages are any worse than us, sir; I just don't think that automatically makes them any better than us, either. Coves are coves, the world over; that's my experience, and I've seen more of this world of ours than most folks. Some of the worst savages I ever met wore inexpressibles and weskits, and spoke of God and Christian duty.'

The village was formed of a loose circle of small, open-ended huts with thatched roofs. Most of the huts had an adjoining pen where pigs rooted and squealed. The preparations for a feast seemed to be underway. Dark-skinned women in grass skirts were grating manioc to form a doughy paste, helped by children as naked as the day they were born, with great mops of curly blond hair which looked out of place above their cherubic brown faces. An old man with a wizened face was carving some kind of idol out of a log with patience and care.

Moltata led his guests to the largest of the huts, open at one end but with a closed section at the back, and invited them to sit with the village elders on mats woven from pandanus leaves. Coconut halves containing some kind of milky, mud-coloured fluid were handed out. Moltata tipped his coconut half so that a few drips fell to the packed-earth floor before taking a draught. Then he signalled for Robertson to drink next.

'You have to spill a few drops on the floor before you drink it,' Richards warned Robertson. 'It's supposed to be good luck.'

The commander looked dubious, but complied before taking a sip. There was a murmur of approval from the natives.

'How is it, sir?'

'Not bad,' allowed Robertson. 'A little earthy for my taste, but not bad at all.'

'Chin chin,' said Killigrew, and he and Strachan raised their coconut halves to their lips.

'How is it brewed?' asked Robertson.

'The village boys bring the *kava* roots to the *nakamal* each afternoon, wash them, and chew them up into a mush, spitting out the hard bits on to leaves,' explained Richards. 'Then they put the

184

mush into a bowl, add water, stir it with their hands, and filter it through coconut fibres.'

Both Killigrew and Strachan froze with their coconut halves tilted to their lips. Strachan lowered his as quickly as politeness would allow, but Killigrew drained his before smacking his lips. 'Mm! Delicious.'

'More?' asked Moltata.

'No more,' Killigrew told him.

Moltata shook his head. 'More, more!' he insisted, and before Killigrew could protest one of the other natives had refilled his coconut half. The lieutenant was forced to sip it while Strachan grinned at his discomfiture.

'All right, let's get down to business,' Robertson told Richards. 'Explain to Moltata that we understand that several villages on this island have been attacked by white men, and their young kidnapped and taken away to be used as slave labour. We're here to investigate.'

On the voyage from Aneiteium, Robertson and Killigrew had agreed they would start off with this part of their explanation, in order to win acceptance from the natives. Later on, perhaps, Killigrew would tell Richards about Mrs Cafferty and the escaped convicts; if the *Lucy Ann* showed up but then realised she was about to sail into a trap, Killigrew would need to commandeer the *Vanguard* in order to give chase. Whether or not he explained any of this to Moltata would have to wait until he was confident he could explain the situation to the *yeremanu*.

Richards translated Robertson's words, and the village elders responded with beams and nods of approval. While the natives debated amongst themselves, Robertson addressed Killigrew in a low voice.

'I'll be leaving with the *Tisiphone* in the morning. According to Yelverton's calculations, if the *Lucy Ann* is bound for Thorpetown she won't arrive before Friday – that gives us more than enough time to get there ahead of them.' Thorpetown was on the island of Éfaté, about a hundred and twenty miles north-west by north of Tanna. The *Tisiphone* would be able to steam there in less than fifteen hours. We'll wait there for two weeks. If the *Lucy Ann* doesn't show up in that time then we can safely assume that she isn't coming. We'll head back here and hope either you or Hartcliffe have had better luck, so expect us around the twenty-fourth; earlier, if the *Lucy Ann* does show her face at Thorpetown.'

'And Mrs Cafferty?'

'Then God help her, for there'll be nothing more we can do for her. Any notion of how you're going to proceed here on Tanna?'

'Yes, sir. I'll need bull's-eyes, flags, two dozen men, and plenty of arms and ammunition. Oh, and victuals. If the natives' food is prepared similarly to their drink, I can't see our lads relishing it; besides, I'd rather not have to rely on the natives for victuals if I can help it.'

'You don't trust them?'

'It's not that, sir. I know we Europeans like to think of islands like this as the garden of Eden, but the truth is that most of these natives have barely enough for their own needs. That's the mistake Cook made when he went back to Hawaii for provisions. The natives there were generous to start with, and I'm sure Moltata's people would be the same; but Cook outstayed his welcome, and in the end it cost him his life.'

'Sensible thinking,' Robertson said approvingly. 'Where will you make camp? Somewhere near the centre of the island, so that when – if – the slavers come, wherever they land you'll be able to get to them as quickly as possible?'

Killigrew shook his head. 'That was my first plan, but I had to dismiss it. It's a good twelve or thirteen miles from the middle of the island to the furthermost point. If the slavers attacked at the south end of the island, we'd have rough country to cross – it would take us too long to get there. I don't want to divide my forces, so we'll stay here at Port Resolution. I'll position a lookout on one of the mountains so we get advanced warning of the approach of any ships.'

'All right. I'll let you have Corporal Summerbee and three of his marines, and seventeen bluejackets.'

'All right.'

'Aren't you forgetting something?' asked Strachan.

'Good point,' said Robertson. 'You'll need a medical officer in case anyone gets hurt or falls ill; you won't have the same resources here on Tanna that Hartcliffe has access to on Inyeug. It sounds to me like Mr Strachan is volunteering his services.'

Killigrew suspected that Strachan might have an ulterior motive for volunteering to exchange the comforts of the *Tisiphone* for two weeks on an island full of savages and the prospect of having escaped convicts to fight, but as long as the assistant surgeon performed his duties, he would have no complaints. 'We'll be happy to have him. I just hope we don't have need of him.'

'She come this way, Cap'n.' Tavu, one of the *Lucy Ann*'s muscular young Polynesian harpooners, pushed himself to his feet with the haft of the tomahawk he carried, and indicated where the trail led up out of the trees to the arid slopes of the central plateau that rose above them.

He also had a hunting rifle slung over one shoulder, and had exchanged the trousers and guernsey he wore on board the *Lucy*

186

Ann for a kilt woven from pandanus leaves, and precious little else. As much as he looked to Lissak to be at home on the deck of the whaling ship, now he really looked in his element, a savage on a savage island. 'She pass this way half one hour, one hour, no more.'

'Good work, Tavu.' Quested stuck two fingers in his mouth and gave a shrill whistle. They had spent the hour before dawn quartering the jungle for Mrs Cafferty, but not until the sun had risen over the Isle of Pines had Tavu been able to find any traces of her passing: a freshly broken twig here, a stone overturned there to reveal its damp underside, moss scuffed from a rock a little further on.

Within a minute, the three of them had been joined by Cusack, Wyatt, Mangal, and the other six men from the *Lucy Ann*. Mangal had plucked a yam and was munching on its flesh, the juice running down his flabby jowls. *Eats like a pig as well as looking like one*, Lissak thought uncharitably. In spite of the fact that Wyatt had seen to it that his *thug* croaksman had received double rations when on Norfolk Island, Mangal had still gorged himself as soon as they had arrived on the *Lucy Ann*, as if he had starved in the penal colony.

'What's going on?' demanded Wyatt.

'You were right, Mr Forgan,' Quested told the second mate. 'Looks like she made it ashore after all.'

'She's alive?' exclaimed Cusack, evidently both astonished and delighted.

Quested nodded. 'Tavu's picked up her trail.'

'Trail!' spat Wyatt. 'It could be anyone's trail. How does that heathen know it's hers?'

Quested looked at Wyatt with dark, warning eyes. 'If Tavu says it's her trail, it's hers. He could track a ghost over the ocean, if he had to.'

Forgan took out a handkerchief and mopped sweat from the underside of his jaw. 'Looks like she's heading for the higher ground.'

Quested nodded. 'Trying to get her bearings, find her way to the mission.'

'Why follow her, then?' demanded Wyatt. 'Why not just make our way to the mission and wait for her to show up?'

Quested smiled. 'And what are we going to say to the missionaries?'

'I ain't frightened of a couple of priests.'

'Nor am I, Mr Wyatt. But if we kill them, the chances are we'll have the French Navy after us as well as the British. Besides, she won't be able to see the mission from up there: Pic N'Ga is in the way.'

'Pic N'Ga?'

187

'A peak in the south-west corner of the island. Come on. She's no more than an hour ahead of us. Rest assured, Mr Wyatt, we'll catch her.' Quested set off after Tavu, and the others followed.

Cusack fell into step beside Quested. 'You seem to know this island pretty well.'

'I should do. I've been here a few times in the past, trading sandalwood.'

'But it doesn't pay as well as whaling?'

'Nothing pays better than whaling, if you can find the whales. If you can't . . .' He shrugged. 'The income from sandalwood is steadier, if you know where to find the trees, how to deal with the kanakas, and aren't afraid of a little risk. But there's nothing to match the thrill of whaling. Six men in a boat pitted against the leviathan of the deep. Now, that's a challenge, Mr Cusack.'

As the slope above them became steeper, the trail left by Mrs Cafferty doubled back on itself several times as she searched for a way up. By the time they reached the crest of the plateau, they were all dripping with sweat beneath the tropical sun and panting from their exertions. Unlike the coastal lowlands of the island, the plateau was an arid landscape with no plants taller than clutches of bracken that grew here and there.

Tavu pointed off to the north-west. 'She go this way, Cap'n.'

'But the mission's back that way.' Forgan pointed to the south-west.

'She doesn't know that.' Quested took the telescope he had brought from the *Lucy Ann* from under his arm and extended it, raising it to one eye to survey the landscape. After a moment, he stopped the sweep of the telescope and moved it back a fraction. 'Ah-ha. There she goes. She's about four miles off, headed in the direction of Paddon's trade house. She can't know— God damn it!'

'What's wrong, Cap'n?' asked Forgan.

'There's a ship in the Bay of Crabs.'

'The *Tisiphone*?' Cusack asked in alarm.

'No. It's a schooner.'

'You don't think—' began Forgan.

'No,' Quested cut him off sharply, tapping him on the chest with his hook. 'And neither should you. Don't think, and don't talk. Just do as I tell you.' He gave Forgan a significant look, the point of which was lost on Lissak.

'If she gets to that ship . . .' warned Wyatt.

'She won't,' Quested assured him. 'Tavu, you go after her and see if you can catch her before she gets there. The rest of us will go back to the *Lucy Ann* and see if we can head her off. We'll meet you at Paddon's trade house.'

XIV

Speculation

It had been a hard climb to the crest of the plateau, but from there it was downhill in almost every direction. Mrs Cafferty had hoped she would be able to see the mission or one of the trading stations from up there, but she had been disappointed. She decided the best thing to do was to descend to the coast on the far side of the island from the *Lucy Ann*, and then follow it round until she found some semblance of civilisation. She could not help thinking that even the sanctuary of a native village would be an improvement on the *Lucy Ann*.

She was halfway across the plateau when she saw the ship about five miles away, anchored in a bay in the north-west corner of the island. Her first thought was that she had lost her bearings and it was the *Lucy Ann*, but when she glanced over her shoulder she could see the whaling ship's masts in the V of a valley which had opened up off to her right. Realising that her escape from this ordeal was less than an hour's walk away, she made straight for the unknown ship. Even though it was more than twenty-four hours since she had last slept, she forgot her exhaustion and broke into a stumbling run, terrified the ship might weigh anchor and set sail before she got there.

The land dropped gently down on the far side of the plateau and a mile further on she lost sight of the ship when she descended into the forests on the north side of the island. The sunlight lancing slantindicular through the boughs above her from the right gave her some indication which direction she was heading in.

The jungle was wild and beautiful at that time of morning, the sounds of the tropical birds crying to one another in the trees above her almost melodious. A thin mist hung between the trunks of the araucaria trees that towered high above her, picking out the beams of sunlight and making them look almost solid. Hosts of butterflies danced amongst the bracken.

And then the birdsong died.

Mrs Cafferty stopped. For all she knew, it was a perfectly natural phenomenon, the same as the crickets in India had all stopped chirping at the same time of the evening. But whereas a moment ago she had almost been enjoying the walk, now she felt uneasy. It was as if the forest hid a thousand malevolent eyes, all watching her. Not daring to move, hardly daring to breathe, she listened to the silence.

She was just being jumpy, she told herself. Hardly surprising, after the ordeal she had been through. But she was wasting time: that ship was not going to remain anchored in the bay for ever.

She took a step forward and a twig snapped beneath one of her boots. Something came whirring out of the bushes at her and she threw up her arms with a cry of alarm, but it was only a dove. She laughed out loud at her own foolishness.

Something stung her on the shoulder, and in the same instant she heard a flat crack behind her. She whirled, and saw a cloud of blue-tinged smoke drifting through the trees perhaps three hundred yards behind her. Nearby, a frond of bracken waved to and fro, although there was not a breath of wind to stir it.

Her fear returned all at once, multiplied a thousandfold. The eerie beauty of the jungle had lulled her into a false sense of security; but she was not away for slates yet, as her husband would have said. She set off walking again, more hesitantly now. Realising her shoulder felt wet, she glanced down and saw a crimson stain spreading across the upper sleeve of her guernsey.

She had been shot.

Feeling sick with the realisation, she struggled to control a rising panic. She was still standing; how bad could the wound be? She grabbed the neckline of the guernsey and pulled it aside to look at her shoulder. The bullet had creased her: the wound was not deep, but it was bleeding steadily.

She realised that was the least of her problems. Whoever had shot her was still out there somewhere, reloading his rifled musket. She knew enough about firearms to know it must have been a rifle, at that range.

She broke into a run. Another shot sounded. She heard the bullet sough past her head and saw it kick pale splinters from beneath the bark of a tree trunk ahead of her, but she did not waste time glancing over her shoulder. Tearing a strip from the bottom of her guernsey and wadding it against the wound in her shoulder, she redoubled her efforts. She dodged through the trees, stumbling over thick buttress roots and fending off fronds of bracken that lashed her face. She thought she saw another figure moving through the trees to her right, but when she looked again there was nothing.

190

Then she crashed into a tree and fell to the ground, winded, but picked herself up and ran on.

She risked a glance over her shoulder. No sign of her pursuer. Perhaps she had outrun him . . . She looked to her front once more, and that was when he stepped out in her path from behind a tree and slammed the stock of a rifle against her midriff.

She was hurled to the ground a second time. He slung the rifle from his shoulder and hefted a tomahawk. A savage figure, naked but for a kind of kilt and a cartouche box, one of the harpooners from the *Lucy Ann*.

He moved to stand over her, swinging the tomahawk back over his shoulder, aiming a blow at her head. The razor-sharp head of the weapon glinted where it caught the sunlight.

She kicked him in the kneecap. His leg crumpled and he went down on one knee, the swing of his tomahawk missing her face by barely an inch. She grabbed the haft of the tomahawk and tried to wrest it from him, but he pushed her back and pressed the haft against her throat, throttling her. She tried to knee him in the crotch, but he saw it coming and avoided the blow, before crouching over her with one knee across her legs, pinning them to the ground.

Feeling herself losing consciousness, she gave up her futile efforts to push the tomahawk back and scrabbled on the ground beside her head, searching for a rock. Her groping fingers found a dead branch: not as thick and sturdy as she might have wished, but it would have to do.

She slammed it against the side of his head with all her might. His eyes rolled up in his head and he slumped over her.

She lay there for a few seconds, sobbing for breath. Then it occurred to her he might not have been alone. She pushed his body off. Fearing she might have killed him, she felt for a pulse in his wrist, and was almost disappointed to find one. She thought about finishing him off with a blow from his tomahawk, but did not have it in her to kill a helpless man. Perhaps that was why she had balked at killing Price. Instead she took the rifle – she noticed that the harpooner had carved weird, ethnic patterns on the wooden stock – and cartouche box.

When her husband had learned his regiment had been ordered north with General Elphinstone's Army of the Indus, they had laughingly said they would be entering bandit country, and she would have to learn to defend herself. At the time, it had been nothing more than a joke, an excuse for him to snuggle close to her as he taught her how to aim a rifle; not that he had ever needed an excuse. She thought she had long forgotten what he had taught her, but now she had a rifle in her hands it all came back to her. She took a cartridge from the cartouche box, tore off the top, poured the powder down the musket, wrapped the paper cartridge around the ball so it would grip the inside of the rifled barrel tightly, and rammed it home with the ramrod. Finally she took a percussion cap from the cartouche box and primed the breech. All in all the process took her less than two minutes; her husband would have been proud of her. Thus armed, she headed on through the trees, where blue sky ahead assured her she was not far from the coast.

A hundred yards further on she saw two figures in white moving through the trees towards her. She froze, pressed herself up against the trunk of a tree, and raised the rifle to her shoulder – her wound was starting to sting furiously now, but she ignored it – and drew a bead on the nearest of the two men.

'Halt, or I fire!' she called.

They froze, searching the trees with their eyes. Both carried rifles of their own. Both were Europeans, dressed in immaculate white uniforms with a nautical look to them. Whoever they were, they weren't from the *Lucy Ann*.

Then one of them spotted her. 'It's a white woman!' he exclaimed in surprise.

She lowered the rifle and stepped out from behind the tree. 'You're English?'

One of the men nodded. 'Able Seaman Appleby, at your service, miss. This here's Able Seaman Owens.'

'Royal Navy?'

Owens shook his head. 'No, the yacht *Wanderer*, miss. Is everything all right?' Then he saw the blood on her shoulder. 'Jesus! Pardon my French, miss – but you're wounded!'

She nodded. 'It's all right, I'm not going to faint. There are men after me. They kidnapped me . . . It's a long story. You're from that ship I saw anchored near here?'

They both nodded. 'The *Wanderer*, miss,' said Appleby. 'We came ashore to fetch water . . . when we heard shots—'

'Never mind that now, Horace. Let's get her safely on board and get that wound seen to.'

'Thank you.'

Half an hour later, she was in a cabin on board the yacht. The *Wanderer* did not boast its own surgeon, but the chief mate, Irwin, knew enough about first aid to be able to swab down her bullet-graze and stitch it up. 'There, now,' he said when he had finished. 'You lie down and rest easy. You're safe now.' He left the cabin, and less than a minute later there was a knock on the door.

'Come in.'

The man who entered was the fat, jolly-looking man who had

asserted command of the situation as soon as she had been brought on board. 'Just come to make sure you're all right, miss, and there's nothing I can get you?' he offered.

'It's "ma'am", not "miss", she corrected him. 'Mrs Philippa Cafferty. And I wouldn't say no to a brandy.'

'Brandy it is.' He withdrew his head from the door. 'Yarrow? Be so good as to fetch the brandy from the saloon.' A bottle of five-star Hennessey was brought on a silver platter with a balloon glass, and she tossed back a generous measure in one, causing the fat man to arch an eyebrow.

'By the way, I have not yet introduced myself. Thaddeus Thorpe, ma'am, at your service.' She extended a hand, and he took a step inside the cabin, bowing as low as his impressive girth would allow to brush the back of her hand with his lips. 'I have the honour to be owner and captain of this vessel. Forgive me, but did you say your name was Cafferty?'

She nodded.

'Good gracious me! You're the young lady who was kidnapped on Norfolk Island by those rogues!'

'You know about me?' she asked incredulously.

'Indeed I do, m'dear. Why, it was only the day before yesterday I had the honour of entertaining Commander Robertson and Lieutenant Killigrew of HMS *Tisiphone* at tea in this very bay!'

'Kit . . . The *Tisiphone*'s been here?'

'Indeed it has, ma'am. They're looking for you even as we speak.'

'Do you know where they've gone?'

He nodded. 'Commander Robertson was good enough to confide the details of his itinerary in me. He was bound for Aneiteium when he left this bay.'

'Could you take me there?'

'Of course. But that's no good – the *Tisiphone* will have been and gone from Aneiteium by now. Let's see, by now she's probably at Port Resolution; but she'll almost certainly have gone by the time we get there. No matter – after that she was bound for Thorpetown, the very place I happen to be bound myself.'

'Thorpetown . . .' she echoed. 'You're *that* Thaddeus Thorpe?' Not that there could be two men in the whole world with that name, but she had not made the connection until he had named his trading station on Éfaté.

He beamed with pleasure at having his name recognised. 'I have that honour, ma'am. Commander Robertson thought there was a possibility the ship that took those fiends from Norfolk Island might be bound for Thorpetown; if we sail today, I'm sure the *Tisiphone* will still be there when we arrive.'

A seaman appeared in the doorway behind her and knocked

hesitantly on the open door. 'Begging your pardon, sir, but there's a ship coming round Tuurè Point.'

Thorpe rounded on him irritably. 'Damn it, Edington! Can't you see I'm busy?'

'Yes, sir. Sorry, sir. It's just . . . it's the *Lucy Ann*. Captain Irwin said you'd want to know.'

Mrs Cafferty stared at the seaman. 'Did you say the *Lucy Ann*?'

'Yes, miss.'

'That's the ship!' she stammered. 'The one that kidnapped me! That's it! They must know I'm here.'

Thorpe took her hand and patted it comfortingly. 'Now don't you worry about a thing, m'dear. Whatever roguish tricks those desperadoes may attempt, you're quite safe on board the *Wanderer*. I dare say you were in no condition to notice when you were brought on board, but my yacht carries an impressive armament. Does the *Lucy Ann* have any cannon?'

She shook her head. 'Just small arms.'

'Then there's nothing they can do against the *Wanderer*.' He looked thoughtful. 'All the same, I think I should have a word with the captain of this whaler . . .'

She shook her head. 'Mr Thorpe, I implore you to exercise extreme caution. Captain Quested is a ruthless man, if I am any judge of character; quite as dangerous as any of the convicts he freed from Norfolk Island.'

'Now don't you worry your pretty little head, m'dear. I may not look imposing, except perhaps in terms of bulk.' He chuckled. 'I dare say you might think that the only thing another man has to fear from me is the danger I might fall on him . . .'

His self-deprecating humour brought a smile to her lips.

'. . . But my career as an entrepreneur in some of the less civilised corners of the Empire has given me a great deal of experience of dealing with villains like this fellow Quested. He won't attempt anything while the *Lucy Ann* lies under the *Wanderer*'s guns; and before I step on to his ship I'll make it plain I've left orders with my chief mate that if I'm not safely back on board the *Wanderer* within half an hour, he has orders to open fire and sink the *Lucy Ann*.'

She was appalled. It was touching and at the same time pathetic: a middle-aged man risking his own life just to impress her. 'Please, Mr Thorpe. I implore you. Let's set sail now; I don't know much about ships, but I'd say this yacht could outrun that filthy tub with ease. Why not set sail for Thorpetown at once?'

'No, no, m'dear. Trust me: I know what I'm doing. A stern word from me will convince these bullies we're not to be trifled with.' And before she could protest further, he had gone from the cabin.

She slumped back down on the bunk, too exhausted to do more.

'They'll rip him to shreds,' she sighed.

A couple of minutes later she heard the *Wanderer*'s jolly boat being lowered from its davits, and by kneeling on the bunk she was able to see two seamen row Thorpe across to where the *Lucy Ann* had anchored not fifty yards from the yacht. Most of the crew and the convicts were gathered on deck: she could not miss the massive figures of Gog and Magog, and Quested's slight but oddly menacing figure standing at the entry port. She watched with her heart in her mouth as the jolly boat approached the whaler's side. Quested said something – he was too far away for her to make out what – and then Thorpe stood up in the boat and levelled a rifle at the captain. Quested just laughed at this show of defiance, but something else Thorpe said made him frown.

Then Thorpe had slung the rifle from his shoulder, and was climbing up the side ladder. Gog and Magog had to help him through the entry port; as a white knight coming to her rescue, he cut an unlikely figure. As soon as he was safely on deck, he unslung the rifle once more and levelled it at Quested, who raised his hand and his hook slowly. Then the captain headed for the after hatch, and Thorpe followed him down.

Mrs Cafferty shook her head in disbelief. Was he trying to arrest the crew of the *Lucy Ann* single-handed?

In the *Lucy Ann*'s great cabin, Quested rounded angrily on Thorpe and tapped him on the chest with his hook. 'Now would you mind telling me what in tarnation is going on?'

'I'll tell you what's going on, Captain Quested. Just as soon as you tell me what you think you're playing at, kidnapping Irish revolutionaries from Norfolk Island?'

'Irish revolutionaries? How the hell do you know about that?'

'Perfectly simple, Captain. HMS *Tisiphone* was here in this very bay not two days ago, seeking you.'

'The *Tisiphone* was here? How did they know I'd be coming this way? Hell, I didn't even know it myself until a few hours ago!'

'They had no notion. They've calculated that if you're bound for California then the swiftest route is to head through New Caledonia and the New Hebrides, and they're touching at every trading station in these islands in the hope they'll find you at one of them. This seemed like an obvious location in which to commence their search; so obvious, indeed, that they didn't trouble to leave any men here to ambush you. How fortunate for you, Captain, that you're not as clever as they seem to think you are!'

Quested stared at the carvings on the stock of the rifle Thorpe was carrying. He snatched it from him to get a better look. 'Where the hell did you get this?'

'Do you recognise it, by any chance?'

'Sure. It belongs to one of my men. He's on the island, searching for a hostage that managed to slip away from us. How did you get it?'

'Mrs Cafferty was carrying it when two of my people found her on the island.'

'Where is she now?'

'On board the *Wanderer*.'

'Then you'd better hand her over, and I can get out of here.'

'I think not, Captain.'

Smiling, Quested prodded Thorpe in the gut with the rifle. 'That woman can identify the *Lucy Ann* as the ship that rescued Devin Cusack from Norfolk Island; and me as her captain. If you think I'm going to let her go—'

'You've already been identified,' Thorpe snapped impatiently. 'Oh, yes! Commander Robertson and Lieutenant Killigrew know exactly what ship they're looking for.'

'Who the hell told them that? You?'

'Don't be preposterous. I didn't know a thing about it until the day before yesterday, when Robertson and Killigrew came on board my ship for tea. No, Quested. *You* told them.'

'Me?'

'By leaving one of your irons behind at Norfolk Island; stamped with the name of your ship, you dunderhead!'

'Damn that fool Jeffries! I told him to make sure there was nothing on that boat that could identify it as belonging to the *Lucy Ann*.' Quested sighed. 'Speaking of Killigrew, what the hell were you doing back in Hobart Town, helping one of my men to desert?'

'I had no notion that wretched kanaka was one of your men. When Killigrew brought him into the Harbour View Hotel, I saw a perfect opportunity to reassure Hobart Town society that I was anything but the brutal abuser of island labour that unpleasant business two years ago made me appear to be.'

Quested chuckled. 'People will believe anything, won't they?'

'Robertson and Killigrew believe it; which is why I'm not going to hand over Mrs Cafferty to you. So far no one has any reason to suspect that you and I are in any way connected; I'd much rather keep things that way, if it's all the same with you.'

'Aye, well, that's about your speed, isn't it? You don't like to get your hands dirty, but you've no exception to profiting from the dirty work I've done for you in the past.'

'Money has no smell, Captain Quested. You of all people should appreciate that. Your previous association with me has not exactly left you in the gutter; and it seems to me that once again we find ourselves in a position to be of assistance to one another.'

196

'Sure we are. You help me by handing over the woman, and I'll help you by not blowing your fat head off.'

Thorpe sighed. 'You still haven't grasped the nature of your predicament, have you? Pour me a libation, and I'll spell it out in words that even you can comprehend.'

'That mean you're going to stop using all those high-falutin, long-winded words you're so fond of?' Quested crossed to the sideboard and poured out a sherry, and a rye whiskey for himself, clamping each bottle in turn under his left arm so he could remove the stoppers. He handed the sherry to Thorpe, and then went back for the whiskey.

'Thank you. Now, you can dismiss all thoughts of murdering Mrs Cafferty; there are no facts she is in a position to communicate to the authorities which they are not already in possession of. It will be of no benefit to you; indeed, quite the opposite, I should say. Kill ten thousand natives, and most Royal Naval officers will shrug it off—'

'Not Killigrew,' snarled Quested. 'I know his sort. Goddamned self-righteous, nigger-loving liberal. When I catch up with him . . .'

Thorpe waved him to silence. 'As for rescuing a man like Cusack, they'll probably secretly admire you for it, no matter what their feelings about the man himself and his politics. Come to think of it, since when did you concern yourself with the fate of Young Ireland? The last time I saw you, you informed me you were going back to whaling.'

'I don't give a damn about Young Ireland. But it so happens that the Irish Directory is paying me a cool ten thousand dollars to rescue Cusack.'

Thorpe raised his eyebrows. 'Ten thousand dollars, eh? A tidy sum.'

'Half in advance, the remainder in cash when I deliver him to 'Frisco. So you can understand why I was tempted. That, and the pleasure of putting one over on the Limeys.'

'Hmm. Well, as I was saying, kill a thousand natives, and most Royal Naval officers will turn a blind eye. But kill one English woman – especially a young and attractive widow, like Mrs Cafferty – and they'll hunt you down to the ends of the earth. Especially your friend Killigrew. He didn't say as much, but from our last interview I got the distinct impression he'd like to renew his acquaintance with you every bit as much as you would with him, and for similar reasons. But if Mrs Cafferty turns up alive and relatively unscathed, there's a chance Mr Killigrew will be prepared to forget his quarrel with you.'

'Aye? Well, maybe *I'm* not prepared to forget my quarrel with *him*.'

'Will you please do me the courtesy of being silent for one

197

moment, and attend to what I have to say? I'm endeavouring to provide you with assistance here. I require you to collect a cargo of sandalwood for me.'

'By all means. Just as soon as I've taken Cusack back to 'Frisco and collected the five thousand dollars I'm owed.'

Thorpe shook his head. 'I don't mean in a few months' time. I mean *now*. Timing is absolutely crucial in this. I know that this time two years ago the bottom had dropped out of the sandalwood market: too many traders in these islands had flooded the market in Shanghai. But a great deal has occurred since then. After you left, news came through of the discovery of gold in California. A good many of our rivals also dropped out, deciding there was less risk and more profit in prospecting. The sandalwood trade's been slowed to a trickle, and I have reliable intelligence that sandalwood stocks in China are running low. If I can dispatch a cargo this month, by the time it reaches Shanghai the price should have risen to a record high. We should be able to realise a six-hundred-per-cent profit on the transaction. But it has to be now. Once the other traders realise that the price is creeping back up . . .'

'You don't get it, do you, Thorpe? I'm supposed to be taking Cusack to California. I haven't got time to swan over to China.'

'I'm not asking you to swan over to China. Captain Hawkes is presently at Thorpetown with the *Avon*. He can take the sandalwood to Shanghai. All I request is that you fetch the sandalwood from Erromanga to Thorpetown.'

'If the *Avon*'s at Thorpetown, why not get Hawkes to fetch your damned sandalwood?'

Thorpe looked uncomfortable. 'Because I haven't got any trade goods to barter with the natives. And you know what that means.'

Quested grinned broadly. 'Sure. I know exactly what that means. Hawkes wouldn't touch our old trade goods with a set of tongs. So you need me. Sorry, Thorpe. I'm going to 'Frisco.'

'I'll pay you another ten thousand dollars.'

Quested stared at him. There was no mistaking the desperation in Thorpe's voice. 'Ten thousand dollars?' he echoed sceptically. 'Oh-kay. Five thousand now, the other five thousand when I deliver the wood to Thorpetown.'

'Damn it, Quested. You know I haven't got that money on me.'

'How about at Thorpetown?'

'All my money is tied up in investments.'

'Investments my eye! You're bankrupt, if only the banks knew it. You think I didn't hear the rumours in Hobart Town? You've had one failed trading venture after another. The only reason people still think you're a millionaire is because you put on a good show; but they're getting wise to you.'

198

'That's why I need this cargo so desperately, Quested. If I can deliver one cargo to Shanghai when the price is right, it will renew the market's confidence in me. Then I'll be able to borrow the money to remunerate you.'

Quested stood up. 'Sorry, Thorpe. I'm a sea captain, not a speculator. And even if I were a speculator, shares in Thorpe and Co. would be the last place I'd invest my hard-earned dough.'

Thorpe sank to his knees. 'Please, Quested . . . Barzillai . . . I'm begging you. Look at me, blast your eyes! I'm down on my knees!'

'I'm flattered. But the answer's still no.'

Thorpe pushed himself angrily to his feet. 'I didn't want to resort to threats, Captain, but if you won't be of assistance you'll leave me no alternative but to inform the authorities of who it was who kidnapped all those natives from Tanna two years ago – and for what reason.'

Quested laughed. 'You wouldn't do that. You'd only incriminate yourself.'

'If I'm going down, I'm taking you with me.'

'What difference does it make to me? Like you said, I'm already a marked man. The authorities know I was the one who rescued Cusack from Norfolk Island.'

'It doesn't have to be that way. I can give you new ship's papers; you know I've got the facilities at Thorpetown so you can alter the *Lucy Ann*'s appearance. She'll look like a completely different ship.'

'Keep whistling.' Quested crossed to the door and opened it. 'Come on, you pathetic old fool. Much as it amuses me to have you grovelling on your knees before me like the fat sack of turds you are, you've got to get back to the *Wanderer*. Otherwise Mrs Cafferty is going to get mighty suspicious about what it was we had to discuss for so long.' He smirked. 'She might even get the notion you and I were old friends; and I fancy that would hurt you a good deal more than it would hurt me.'

Struck by a sudden inspiration, Thorpe realised he had one more card left to play; and it was a trump. 'I'll give you Killigrew.'

'What?'

'You heard me. You said you had a score to settle with him; I can tell you how to do it.'

Quested closed the door again. He was smiling. 'You know something? Maybe I could develop a taste for speculation after all.'

It was ten o'clock the following morning by the time Killigrew's shore party had unloaded sufficient provisions from the *Tisiphone* to last them two weeks. Robertson looked as though he was having misgivings about their plan when Killigrew walked him to where his gig waited on the beach to take him back to the *Tisiphone*. 'I'm well

199

aware that asking you not to take unnecessary risks is like asking a lawyer to work for free, Second, but . . . well, just try not to get yourself killed.'

Killigrew gestured to where he had set his bluejackets to work building a large marquee to serve themselves and Corporal Summerbee's marines as a barracks for the duration of their sojourn on Tanna, using canvas and spare spars from the sloop; a second, smaller tent had already been erected for the use of Killigrew, Strachan and Cavan. 'I'll wager any one of those lads against ten slavers any day. Don't worry, sir. Even with the convicts, he's still got only twenty-seven men. Twenty-five bluejackets and marines against a rag-tag mob of spouters and convicts? We'll slaughter 'em.'

'Metaphorically speaking, I hope,' Robertson reminded him sternly. 'I don't want this becoming a personal matter. If Cusack and the convicts turn up here and you can take them alive, kindly do so. I don't want my officers taking the law into their own hands. The same goes for any slavers who have the misfortune to make an appearance while you're here. Kill them if there's no other choice – I'm sure we both agree that scum like that deserve nothing better – but there are laws, even here in the South Seas, and it's part of our job to enforce those laws, not break them. Oh, and while you're here, try to give the *kava* a wide berth, there's a good chap.' He massaged his temples. 'That stuff's worse than absinthe, and you'll need a clear head if the *Lucy Ann* does turn up. I'll wish you good luck.'

'I never rely on it, sir.'

'Perhaps not, but you've had need of it in the past, nonetheless. If we're not back by the end of the month, commandeer the *Vanguard* and sail to Thorpetown. If our pursuit of these convicts leads us deeper into the Pacific, we'll try to leave word for you there.'

'I'll see you in two weeks, sir. If not before.'

Robertson nodded and climbed into his gig. 'Shove off!' he ordered the oarsmen.

Killigrew lit a cheroot and stood watching as Robertson was rowed back to the *Tisiphone*. The chief engineer already had steam up, and Killigrew watched the sloop move out of the bay until it disappeared to the left, heading north towards the northern tip of Tanna where it would turn north-west by north for Éfaté.

Killigrew strode back across the black sand to where the bluejackets were erecting the marquee next to Richards' shack. Strachan had insisted on giving each and every man a full medical examination before permitting him to go ashore with a clean bill of health. None of them had turned out to have any nasty social diseases, which Killigrew suspected was a testament to the effectiveness of

Strachan's approach of assuming that boys would be boys, and teaching them how to take precautions accordingly. Mr Westlake scoffed at the practice – his philosophy was that abstinence was the best protection – and insisted that teaching such things to seamen only encouraged them to misbehave. But Robertson approved of Strachan's approach: a seaman who could not work because he was suffering from the Haymarket gout was no use to anyone.

Not that the seamen would be permitted to sneak into the trees and get up to no good with the native girls. So far Moltata's people had shown them nothing but hospitality, but all that might change if someone tried to seduce the chief's daughter. So Killigrew watched the men like a hawk to make sure none of them tried to sneak away from the beach with carnal intentions in mind.

Between the marquee and the shack, Strachan was checking the equipment he had unloaded from the *Tisiphone*. The assistant surgeon seemed to have brought more personal belongings ashore than the rest of Killigrew's shore party put together. The lieutenant was about to ask Strachan if all this equipment was really necessary when he heard a strange twanging sound somewhere above his head. He glanced up, twisted around, and saw an apparition so alarming he took a step back, tripping over the tripod of Strachan's camera and falling on his back in the sand.

'Oh, do be careful, Killigrew!' chided Strachan. 'You almost fell on my microscope!'

Killigrew was still staring at the apparition that squatted on the roof of Richards' shack. Strachan followed his gaze. 'Jings!'

It was a man – at least, more like a man than any other creature in God's creation – a native from his physiognomy, except that his skin was a pale, ash-grey in colour, his eyes were pink, and his hair, plaited into hundreds of queues three or four inches long which stood up across his scalp, was white. He was naked but for the traditional penis-wrapper and tortoiseshell earrings. He was tattooed with raised cicatrices on his stomach and upper arms, and wore a reed through his nose. In his mouth he had a jew's-harp, and he plucked on it; unless Killigrew was very much mistaken, the tune was 'Oh, Susannah!'

Realising he was the subject of Killigrew's scrutiny, the apparition took the jew's-harp from his mouth and grinned at them, revealing a mouth full of teeth filed to sharp points, like the Krumen Killigrew had encountered on the Guinea Coast.

On the verandah in front of the shack, Richards was laughing. 'Don't mind him. That's Sharky. He's from Paama,' he added, as if that explained everything.

Killigrew picked himself up and dusted himself down. 'Parma?' he echoed, thinking of ham and grated cheese.

'It's a small island just south of Ambrym. Sharky was the head *nakaimo* on the island, until he got soft on the bigman's daughter. Unfortunately she was already betrothed to another man. When the man was killed in a shark attack, Sharky got the blame and the chief banished him.'

'He got the blame for a shark attack?' stammered Strachan. 'Because his name's Sharky?'

Richards laughed. 'Sharky's not his real name. His real name's . . .' Richards frowned. 'Hey, Sharky! What the hell is your real name, anyhow?'

'Me Sharky,' asserted the albino, jabbing a thumb at his chest before reinserting his jew's-harp in his mouth and plucking away tunelessly.

Richards shrugged. 'Sharky got blamed for the shark attack because he's a *nakaimo*.'

'A *nakaimo*?' said Killigrew. 'What's that?'

'It's a kind of witch doctor they have on Paama. *Nakaimo*s are men who can turn themselves into sharks.'

'Primitive superstitious nonsense!' snorted Strachan. 'Surely you don't believe that, Captain Richards?'

'What I believe ain't important,' said Richards. 'What matters is that he believes it. And so do the rest of the kanakas.'

'Sounds a lot like them leopard people they had on the Guinea Coast, sir,' said Molineaux, walking over from where the rest of the bluejackets were putting the finishing touches to the marquee.

Killigrew nodded. 'What mattered was that many of the natives actually believed that the leopard people could turn themselves into leopards to attack their enemies: the real weapon they used was fear.'

Sharky jumped down from the roof and picked up one of the complicated-looking scientific instruments Strachan had laid out on the sand. 'Put that down!' snapped the assistant surgeon. 'That's a very expensive piece of equipment!'

Angered by the assistant surgeon's terse tone, Sharky glowered at him. Then, without taking his eyes off Strachan's, he tossed the instrument over his shoulder. Fortunately there was nothing wrong with Richards' reflexes, and he caught it before it hit the ground. Sharky leaped into the air, flailing his arms and legs with a wild yell, and then turned his back on Strachan and bent forwards, waggling his buttocks at him. Finally he turned, ran across to the water's edge and dived into the sea.

'What extraordinary behaviour!' exclaimed Strachan.

'You made him pretty mad, Mr Strachan,' said Richards. 'I shouldn't go swimming for a while until he's had a chance to cool off.'

'What's he going to do? Bite my legs off?'

Killigrew smiled. 'With those teeth, he could probably make a fair go of it.'

Molineaux was gazing out to sea, shading his eyes with one hand. 'I'll say one thing for that witch doctor cove: he can hold his breath a long time.'

'That's the skill of being a witch doctor,' Strachan said dismissively. 'They don't have any real powers, but they give the impression of having them. It's the same as with your sleight-of-hand tricks, Molineaux. It's nothing to do with the quickness of the hand deceiving the eye. It's all about misdirection.'

'There's no misdirection in my magic tricks,' asserted Molineaux, and produced a deck of cards from inside his jacket. He fanned them and presented them to Strachan. 'Pick a card, sir.'

'All right.' Strachan took a card and glanced at it.

'Now put it back.'

Strachan complied and Molineaux shuffled the deck. 'Perhaps you'd like to shuffle the deck?'

'Aye, that I would.'

The assistant surgeon was still shuffling the cards when Molineaux said: 'Eight of hearts.'

Strachan's jaw dropped. 'How does he do that?' he demanded.

'It's magic,' said Molineaux.

Richards sniggered. Unlike Strachan, he had seen Killigrew glance over the assistant surgeon's shoulder, hold up eight fingers and tap his left breast. The lieutenant and the able seaman had worked out a code of simple signals that enabled Killigrew to describe any card in the pack without speaking, and they had been using this system to tease Strachan for several weeks.

'My granddaddy was a West Indian juju man,' Molineaux explained to an unconvinced Strachan.

'I thought you said your grandfather was Tom Molineaux, the pugilist?'

'That was my other granddaddy.'

'Hmph!' Strachan gingerly took the scientific instrument back from Richards.

'What the hell is this, anyhow?' asked the trader.

'It's a hygrometer,' explained Strachan.

'Of course it is. What does it do?'

'It measures the humidity of the air by cooling a highly polished silver cylinder and measuring the condensation point.'

'You had to ask,' Killigrew chided Richards.

'That got something to do with weather forecasting?'

'It can be used for that,' said Strachan. 'I'm planning to use it to measure the water content of the gases escaping from the fumaroles in that volcano.' He pointed to where the great plume of smoke still spiralled upwards from Mount Yasur.

Richards almost choked. 'You're *what*?'

'Oh, don't worry. I've done it plenty of times before. It's perfectly safe. As long as the volcano doesn't erupt while you're up there, or there isn't an earthquake or landslide which knocks you into the crater, or you're not overcome by noxious gases.' Strachan would have cowered before General Tom Thumb aggressively brandishing an ostrich plume, but give him a chance to further the cause of science and he lost all sense of discretion.

'You can't go up that volcano, mister,' warned Richards. 'It's *tabu*.'

'*Tabu* indeed!' snorted Strachan. 'Primitive native superstition.'

'Primitive native superstition it may be, but that volcano's sacred to the natives. How would you like it if you saw a kanaka doing a *naghol* dive from the tower of Westminster Abbey?'

'I'm sure I shouldn't care one way or the other.'

'He's an atheist,' explained Killigrew.

'Aye, well, these natives are very devout as far as their own religious convictions go,' said Richards. 'And if they catch him profaning the slopes of Mount Yasur . . . there's only one way to cleanse the desecration, and that's the Niel Ceremony.'

'What's that?' asked Killigrew.

'That's where they kill you and eat you.'

'Strachan?'

'Aye?'

'Stay away from Mount Yasur.'

'If you insist.'

XV

Thorpetown

'Where the blazes is it?' demanded Robertson. 'A little difficult to encourage trade if traders can't even find your blessèd trading station!'

'Should be around this next headland, sir,' Yelverton assured him.

With both steam and a following wind full in her sails, it had taken the *Tisiphone* eleven hours to reach the island of Éfaté, and now she steamed clockwise round the south coast in search of Thorpetown. The island was one of the largest in the New Hebrides, much of it dominated by low rolling hills carpeted with jungle which rose in the north-west corner of the island to a rugged peak over two thousand feet high. The coast off the starboard beam was a succession of headlands and bays, with numerous native villages like the one they had seen at Port Resolution, the surrounding hills cultivated into coconut planta-tions, but there was no sign of anything that could remotely be described as a trading station.

The next bay was almost triangular, with a small island in the middle, near the apex. Roughly circular in shape, the island was covered in palm trees surrounded by white sand beaches, but there were native huts amongst the trees, and a couple of mission buildings.

'According to the chart, the entrance to the harbour is somewhere behind that island,' said Yelverton.

'Very well,' sighed Robertson. 'Steer six points to port, Holcombe.'

'Six points to port it is, sir.' At a nod from the quartermaster, the helmsman spun the wheel and the *Tisiphone* turned her head to starboard, making for the back of the bay.

'You know, I'm inclined to think we're wasting our time here,' grumbled Robertson. 'If we're having such difficulty finding the place even with a chart, what chance does this fellow Quested have?'

'Could be he's been here before, sir,' said the master. 'If I had one of Ireland's most wanted revolutionaries and half a dozen convicts on board my ship and I wanted to lie low, I might think this was an ideal place to head for.'

The natives on the island had run down to the beach. Robertson saw two missionaries with them – Polynesians in clerical garb – climb into an outrigger canoe with a dozen of the dark-skinned natives. They were pushed out through the surf, and the natives began to paddle them to meet the *Tisiphone*.

Polynesian missionaries were nothing unusual in these islands. Since the death of the Reverend Mr Williams on Erromanga, the London Missionary Society had started taking young men from the islands of Polynesia, where Christianity had found more acceptance, and trained them to bring the word of God to the New Hebrides. It was hoped that, having a better understanding of the ways of the peoples of the South Seas, they would be more acceptable to the dark-skinned heathens of these islands who had reacted so violently to the incursions of the white man.

The missionaries' greeting as their pirogue approached the *Tisiphone*, however, did take Robertson by surprise. 'Are you looking for Thorpetown?' asked one, in perfect English.

The commander leaned out from the entry port. 'Yes. Is this the right way?'

'Turn back! Turn back now! The place is damned, do you hear? Damned! For Thorpetown is the Babylon of the Pacific, mother of all whores! Abandon all hope, you who enter here! Shun the Sodom and Gomorrah of the South Seas, for all who touch here are accursed!'

'Yes, yes, very good. It's this way, is it? Mad as a hatter,' he added to Yelverton, *sotto voce*.

With the missionaries' warnings still ringing in the crew's ears from astern, the *Tisiphone* steamed around the island and a channel less than a cable's length wide opened up before them.

'Looks deep enough to take the Tizzy in, sir,' said Yelverton. 'Do we go on?'

'Of course!' said Robertson. 'I think the hands would be extremely disappointed if we didn't.' There was not a seaman on board who did not know the kind of warning the missionaries had just given them usually heralded a den of vice and intemperance, and if there were two things Jack Tar could not get enough of, they were vice and intemperance. 'Pass the word to Mr Muir, Mr Woolley; ahead slow.'

'Aye, aye, sir.' The midshipman descended the after hatch to inform the chief engineer.

Beyond the bottleneck, the channel opened out into a lagoon five hundred and fifty yards wide and almost two miles long. The sloop advanced, her paddle wheels plashing at the crystal-clear turquoise waters. There was still no sign of any trading station, just thick jungles pressing in on either side of the lagoon, the mangrove trees dipping their gnarled roots into the water as if they were testing the temperature.

At the far end of the lagoon, the channel divided in two, but there was a sign at the fork, an ornately carved stone bearing the single word 'THORPETOWN', and a stylised hand pointing to the right. Robertson supposed the stone was intended to be in the form of a milestone back in England, but to his jaded eye the marble block looked more like a headstone.

'Steer two points to port, Holcombe,' he commanded. 'Leadsman to the chains. Shorten sail, Mr Darrow.'

The right-hand channel narrowed to a cable's length once more, and with the leadsman at the chains calling out the soundings as rapidly as he could take them, the *Tisiphone* nosed her way through. The channel curved to the right and grew narrower and narrower, until it was barely a hundred yards wide. Robertson was just starting to think he had made some mistake – perhaps he had missed another sign, another turning – when suddenly the jungle opened out on both sides and a second, upper lagoon was visible before them, a mile and a half long and broadening out like the head of a sperm whale to a width of over half a mile. On the south side of the lagoon was a beach of white sand where the crystal-clear waters lapped, and a thick jungle of coconut palms and banyan trees draped with vines and lianas, with rare jungle blooms adding splashes of colour to the emerald verdancy.

On the north side of the lagoon stood Thorpetown.

Compared to Paddon's main trading station at Aneiteium, it was magnificent. Paddon looked as if he intended to stay on Aneiteium until all the sandalwood was logged out of these islands. The scale of Thorpetown suggested that Thorpe intended to start a whole new civilisation. There were houses, stores, godowns, a sawmill and a try-works, even a library. Streets ran between the weatherboard houses in straight lines, as if Thorpe planned to extend the settlement inland in an orderly grid pattern; while many of the houses still looked to be under construction, more jungle had been cleared behind them to bear out the suggestion that Thorpe intended to expand this overlarge settlement. Behind the wharf there was a plaza where a bronze statue of a man stood on a marble plinth. But the focal point was a broad flight of stone steps, carved out of the rock that rose up behind the plaza, which would not have looked out of place in Rome or Paris. At the very top of these steps stood a large stone mansion, with two gleaming bronze cannon flanking the impressive portico.

But the strangest thing of all was that there was not a living soul in sight.

Robertson felt like an explorer in the jungles of Indonesia or Central America, stumbling unexpectedly across the ruins of a once-great but long-dead civilisation. Thorpe had only founded this place two years ago and everything was obviously new, and yet at the same time there was an unmistakable air of decay over it all. Despite the land clearance behind the settlement, the jungle encroached on either side of it as if it were merely biding its time. Dead leaves lay in the streets like harbingers of the inevitable invasion, and here and there lianas were already starting to creep forwards. Apart from the cries of strange jungle birds, the only sound to be heard was the splashing of the *Tisiphone*'s paddles.

It was Yelverton who broke the awed silence on deck. 'Lor'!' was all he could say.

The sloop drew level with the plaza, close to where a wooden jetty ran out from the wharf. 'Stop engine,' ordered Robertson. 'Starboard anchor . . . let go.'

In the eerie silence of the lagoon, the sound of the anchor hitting the water was like an explosion.

'What do you think happened here?' wondered Yelverton.

'Maybe they were wiped out by a plague,' suggested the helmsman.

'Belay that nonsense!' barked Robertson. 'Make ready my gig, Mr Darrow. I'm going ashore. There must be *someone* here who can tell us where everyone is.'

Petty Officer Holcombe gripped his musket tightly as he gazed up at the dark windows of the weatherboard buildings that fronted the lagoon. The empty windows seemed to stare back like dead eyes. 'Who d'you think built it, sir?' he whispered.

'Island labour, Holcombe,' replied Robertson, thinking: *slave labour*. He did not bother to whisper; it was not in his nature.

A set of hardwood rails ran the length of the jetty, with a wooden truck on them like a mine car. At the end of the jetty the tracks ascended a gentle wooden ramp up to the loft of the try-works; just before they reached the ramp, there was a set of points where a second branch cut across the wharf at an angle, ending in a set of buffers in front of the sawmill. A funnel that looked as though it had been cannibalised from a steamship projected through the shingled roof of the mill, betraying the presence of an engine to power the blade.

The commander climbed up the wooden steps to the mill and looked inside. The rails ended at a set of buffers right alongside the saw, which boasted one of the new, circular blades. The machinery gleamed, but there was enough grease on the moving parts to suggest this was a working engine, a supposition which was borne out by the sawdust on the floor and the aroma of sandalwood.

He climbed down to the wharf once more and followed the wooden tracks up the ramp to the half-loft of the try-works. The rails ended right next to the mincing horse, a kind of trestle for cutting up the ten-foot-long blanket pieces of whale blubber. Beside it was a mincing tub where the horse pieces could be chopped into skin-spined leaves of blubber known as 'bibles'. A sluice gate in the side of the mincing tub allowed the 'bibles' to be washed down a chute into the two huge try-pots which sat above a brick furnace surrounded by a low cistern of water to prevent the spread of fire. Another chute led from the platform to the furnace, so the fritters scooped off the surface of the simmering blubber could be delivered straight to the flames, and spigots allowed the blubber to be drained off into casks.

Looking down into the try-pots from the half-loft, Robertson saw they were gleaming and spotless inside, but that was nothing unusual. The captain of any whaler kept his try-pots polished inside and out: when a sperm whale was captured, the spermaceti was tryed-out first, and the pots needed to be spotless to keep the precious fluid pure. There was no disguising the traces of blood in the mincing tubs: these facilities had been used at least once.

He climbed down the ladder from the half-loft to the ground floor of the try-works. A door set in the far wall led into the next building, a large warehouse stacked high with casks. Robertson rapped on the nearest with his knuckles, and was surprised not to get a hollow knocking sound: the cask was full. He exchanged glances with Holcombe.

'Must be someone around, sir,' said the petty officer. 'I can't imagine anyone in his right mind leaving a godown full of whale oil. If all these casks are full, there must be thousands of guineas' worth of oil in here!'

Robertson grunted noncommittally. 'See if you can find a crowbar. There must be one around here somewhere.'

'Aye, aye, sir.'

It did not take the petty officer long to find what he was looking for. Robertson took it from him and pried the lid off the first cask. He lowered his face to the contents and took a sniff. Then he removed one of his gloves, dipped his fingers in the liquid, rubbed his fingers together to test its greasiness and finally dabbed a bit on the tip of his tongue. He spat it out. 'Salt water, to preserve the casks.'

The two of them left the try-works and rejoined the rest of the gig's crew in the plaza. Robertson walked across to the bronze, larger-than-life statue. Although the plaque on the plinth merely declared 'Our Benefactor', there was no mistaking the statue was a study of Thaddeus Thorpe himself; but either it had been sculpted before the trader had put on so much weight, or the sculptor had wisely judged there was no harm in pandering to Thorpe's vanity.

Robertson eyed the statue askance. 'Is there plenty of fresh water in the *Tisiphone*'s stores, Holcombe?'

'I believe so, sir.'

'Good. Because I don't want any of the men drinking the water hereabouts. First that deranged missionary, and now this Bedlam without inmates; there's obviously something in the water.'

'There's a kind of madness here, right enough, sir.'

'Sir!' exclaimed one of the seamen, and pointed.

Everyone turned to see a figure descending the steps leading up to the mansion. His descent was erratic: he meandered from side to side as if drunk, a possibility borne out by the bottle he clasped by the neck in one hand. A white man whose face had been tanned brick red by the tropical sun and was covered in several days' growth of beard. He was barefoot, wearing only trousers and a grubby shirt that was neither tucked into his trousers nor buttoned at the front.

'Welcome!' he called. 'Welcome to Thorpetown, strangers! The metropolis of the South Seas!'

'And who the blazes are you?' demanded Robertson.

'I?' The man looked puzzled while he tried to remember. 'I am Jeremiah Underwood, esquire: secretary, clerk, and general factotum to his imperial godhead, Mr Thaddeus Thorpe, may his black soul burn in hell; and the sooner, the better, says I.' The man made a sweeping, contemptuous gesture with the bottle that would have resulted in him falling flat on his face, had not Holcombe caught him and propped him up. His breath stank of rum.

'Where is everyone, Mr Underwood?'

'Everyone? Everyone's right here. Every one? Only one, because I am the only one. I am everyone. The one and only. That's me.'

'But what about the people who built this place?' Robertson demanded impatiently.

'Gone. Long gone. Gone back whence they came, back into the jungles.'

'The natives, you mean? But what about the whalers? The sandal-wood traders? Where did they go?'

'They didn't *go* anywhere. They couldn't, because they never came. You can't go, unless you come first. And they never, ever came.'

'*Someone* came,' said Robertson. 'There's sandalwood dust in the sawmill, and bloodstains in the mincing tubs in the try-works.'

'Oh, a *few* came,' admitted Underwood. 'Just a very few.' He held up thumb and forefinger, a fraction of an inch apart, as if to say that the men who had come had been no larger than ants. 'What brought them? I don't know. Curiosity, I s'pose.' He belched.

'We're wasting our time with this fellow,' snorted Robertson. 'Let's get back to the *Tisiphone*.'

'Not before time, sir,' said Holcombe. 'This place gives me the shivers.'

A look of panic appeared on Underwood's face. 'You're not going without me, are you? Don't leave me here, for God's sake!'

'We're not going far,' Robertson told him impatiently. 'We'll be staying here a couple of weeks.' If Quested knew what a ghost town the trading station was, then he would think it an ideal place to lie low until the *Tisiphone* gave up her search for him; the more he thought about it, the more convinced Robertson was that this was where the *Lucy Ann* was bound. 'If you want to come with us when we leave, well . . . I suppose we can find room for you on board,' he said grudgingly. 'We can drop you off in Auckland, after we've concluded our tour of the South Seas. But before you make your mind up, I should tell you Thorpe's coming back.'

'Thorpe?' Underwood's face twisted in a scowl of hatred. 'He's never coming back! That bastard left me here to rot!'

'To the contrary, Mr Underwood, I encountered Mr Thorpe aboard his yacht at the Isle of Pines just three days ago. He told us he was on his way here; I should say you can expect him some time tomorrow.'

A mixture of emotions crossed the drunkard's face all at once: hope, fear, hatred and despair. He seemed to drift off into a reverie.

Holcombe was gazing around at the buildings that surrounded the plaza on three sides. 'Notice anything rum about this place, sir?'

'I should say this whole place is rum, Holcombe. Did you have anything in particular in mind?'

'This place has got everything, sir: houses, stores, sawmill, try-works, hotels, taverns, a town hall . . . there's even a bloody library over there. But there's something missing, sir.'

'People?'

'Apart from people, sir. There's no church. Nowhere for the people Thorpe dreamed would be living here to worship.'

'Perhaps he thought they would be too busy working for him to worship,' Robertson said impatiently.

Underwood overheard them. 'Worship, d'you say? He expected them to worship, right enough. But not in any damned church.' He drained the last dregs from the bottle, and used the same hand to point up the steps to the house at the top with an extended index finger. 'That's the temple. That's where he wanted them to bow down. Before the palace of the god-king himself, Thaddeus

211

Thorpe!' He hurled the bottle furiously at the statue; it missed and shattered against the steps, splashing a few drops of blood-red rum on the pale stone.

'Signal from the lookouts, sir.' Midshipman Cavan gazed along the beach to where two seamen were stationed on Cook's Pyramid, a flat-topped rock on the east side of the bay where the great navigator himself had taken some sightings in 1774. The men were taking it in turns to take some sightings of their own, levelling a telescope to where Ågård was at the lookout post on Mount Melen with two ratings from the port watch; Killigrew was due to relieve them after supper.

One of the seamen had a telescope, and was reading the flags of the signaller with Ågård; as he spoke, the other was signalling to Killigrew with his own flags, relaying the message. The lieutenant had worked out a simple set of signals – using flags by day and lanterns by night – to indicate distance, direction and heading, which they had written down for the benefit of the others. That limited lookout duties to those who could read, but there were sufficient men in the shore party who were young enough to have attended the new 'ragged schools' for pauper children.

'Vessel sighted twenty miles off, bearing south-west by south, heading for the southern tip of the island,' read Killigrew. Any vessel approaching from that direction would have to sail around the southern tip to reach Port Resolution.

'It could be them, sir,' said Cavan.

Killigrew glanced to where the men of the starboard watch swam and splashed about playfully in the surf. Endicott floated on his back, pretending to be a whale by occasionally spouting up mouthfuls of seawater. One of the ships' boys, Cuddy Gamel, was making a sandcastle. Fourteen years old, Gamel was a little too old for that kind of thing, but he was simple-minded so no one worried about it. Besides, it really was a very good sandcastle; the tip of his tongue protruding from his lips in a show of concentration, Gamel was scoring lines in the walls to give them the look of masonry, and the black sand added to the effect.

One of Killigrew's principles was to let the men play hard when they were off watch, as long as they worked hard when they were on watch; and he had certainly kept them hard at it in the twenty-four hours since the *Tisiphone* had steamed away from Tanna. Once the marquee had been completed, he had divided his bluejackets and marines into two watches, starboard and port, and they continued to keep watches just as if they were still on board the *Tisiphone*. Without the business of sailing to be done, he kept his men busy with cutlass or small-arms drill when they were on watch.

Killigrew saw Sharky dive off some rocks into the water, and waited for him to surface. But there was no sign of the *nakaimo*. The lieutenant knew better than to let that worry him by now, but it still unnerved him, even though he suspected that Sharky had surfaced somewhere out of sight, and was only pretending to be able to hold his breath for an inordinately long period of time to add credence to his ludicrous claim that he could turn himself into a shark.

'It could be the SS *Great Britain* for all we know,' said Killigrew, not unkindly. 'These waters are well travelled, Mr Cavan. Whalers, sandalwood ships . . . we can't have the men beat to quarters every time we sight a strange sail. If it's the *Lucy Ann*, I don't imagine she'll get here for a good five hours. We'll wait until she gets closer and Ågård can take a better look at her; then we'll decide what to do, if anything.'

'It won't take her four hours to get here if she's a steamer, sir.'

Killigrew pulled his cap down over his eyes and lay back against the bole of the coconut palm behind him. 'If she's a steamer, Mr Cavan, then she's not the *Lucy Ann*. Is Mr Strachan keeping out of trouble?' Few men could be more feckless than Jack Tar on a run ashore, but in Killigrew's experience the unworldly assistant surgeon was one of them.

'He's sketching a *ficus prolixa*, sir,' Cavan replied heavily. He had evidently made the mistake of enquiring what Strachan was doing.

'A what?'

'Banyan tree, sir.'

'Ah. You're sure? He hasn't sneaked off to take a closer look at that volcano, has he?'

Cavan shook his head. 'I detailed Private Hawthorne to keep a discreet eye on him.'

Killigrew nodded approvingly. It seemed like only yesterday that Cavan had been a first-class volunteer on board the *Tisiphone* when she had set out on her two-year spell of duty with the West Africa Squadron, a callow boy of twelve going to sea for the first time. But that had been five years ago, and now the midshipman was a young man of seventeen. When they got back to Britain at the end of the year, he would be ready to receive the queen's commission as a mate; and rightly so, for he had proved he had the aptitude for a career as a naval officer.

'Then if everything is in order, you might as well take off your jacket, sit down and relax,' Killigrew told Cavan. 'Dawton will signal Yorath and O'Houlihan if—'

'Shark!' Endicott's unmistakable Liverpudlian accent, high-pitched with terror. 'There's a shark in the bay!'

Pandemonium. The placid scene was turned into a churning

213

tumult of fourteen seamen and marines all fighting to wade out of the surf at once. Killigrew leaped to his feet and drew his pepperbox from his belt, his eyes searching for that unmistakable fin cleaving through the waves as he ran to the water's edge, but the struggling men blocked his view. Gamel's sandcastle was trampled in the panic.

'All right, quickly now!' yelled Killigrew. 'Line up in your messes! Did everyone get out of the water? Where's Powell?'

'Here, sir.'

'Take a head count, Mr Cavan,' ordered Killigrew. While the midshipman counted heads – and limbs, for that matter – Killigrew turned back to the water, searching for the shark's fin, a slick of blood that would betray the fact that one of his men had fallen prey to the shark. But the waters of the bay had turned calm once more.

'I don't see any bloody shark,' grumbled one of the seamen.

'I saw it, I tell you!' insisted Endicott. 'Swam right past me, it did! Forty foot long if it was an inch.'

'There, sir!' called Molineaux.

Killigrew looked in the direction the seaman had indicated and saw a grey shape zooming in through the shallows: then it broke the surface and stood up. Sharky grinned, showing his pointed teeth.

Killigrew hooked his pepperbox to his belt once more. 'There's your shark, Endicott,' he said wearily.

A seaman cuffed the Liverpudlian roughly around the back of the head. 'You bloody daft lobscouser!' he snarled, and suddenly everyone was laughing at Endicott in a massive release of tension. Panic over, the seamen started to drift back into the water. Sharky climbed the trunk of a palm tree that leaned out over the beach in its search for sunlight, put his jew's-harp in his mouth and started to pluck away tunelessly.

Within a couple of minutes, only Endicott and Molineaux were left on the beach with Killigrew and Cavan. 'Not going back in the water, Endicott?' asked Killigrew.

'You're pulling my leg, ain't you, sir?' muttered the Liverpudlian. 'It *was* a shark, I *know* it was. One o' them great big white ones. What are they called?'

'A great white?' suggested Killigrew.

'Aye.'

'It was your imagination, Endicott. A trick of the light.'

'Oh aye? Well, this trick of the light had black eyes and massive fins and a great big gob full of razor-sharp teeth,' insisted the Liverpudlian. 'Sir,' he added truculently.

Killigrew sat down to supper with Strachan, Cavan and Richards at two bells in the first dog watch, as the sun was sinking below the mountains to the west of Port Resolution. While the men were content to eat their meals sitting on the beach, the officers dined nearby at a rough-and-ready but perfectly serviceable table knocked together by the carpenter's mate. A couple of bottles of hock were produced from one of three crates of wine landed from the *Tisiphone*, while in the absence of the ship's cook, the meal itself was prepared by Molineaux, who had started in the navy as a cook's mate. Unlike the cook himself, who had lost any enthusiasm for cooking after having to prepare meals for a hundred officers and men three times a day for years on end, Molineaux enjoyed the luxury of only occasionally being called upon to use his culinary skills, and he took characteristic pride in his cooking. This was their second evening at Port Resolution since the *Tisiphone* had sailed, and once again the seaman excelled himself. That morning he had borrowed Richards' hunting rifle and had procured some fresh meat with the help of a native guide, and taking a collection from his shipmates, he managed to get enough chewing tobacco to barter with the natives for fresh yams.

'This is excellent, Molineaux,' Cavan complimented him as the officers tucked into their meal. 'Tastes like chicken. What is it, *coq au vin*?'

'*Renard volant au Molineaux*,' the seaman replied, with a conspiratorial wink at Killigrew.

'*Renard volant*,' mused Cavan. 'Wait a minute! That means . . .'

'Flying fox,' said Strachan, before shovelling more into his mouth. 'Mmm! Absolutely delicious. You've excelled yourself, Molineaux. Not hungry, Mr Cavan? I'll have that if you're not eating it. Waste not, want not, as my guv'nor never tired of telling me.'

Twilight was giving way to dusk by the time they had finished eating. The men who had replaced Ågård and the other lookouts on Mount Melen reported that the approaching ship, still more than ten miles from the southern tip of the island, had lit lanterns, so they would have no difficulty following her progress in the dark. Night fell, and Killigrew watched Cavan muster the first watch before retreating to his hammock in the tent he shared with the midshipman and Strachan.

He slept fitfully, his mind troubled by anxiety for Mrs Cafferty – he knew that in all probability she was already dead, but he could not give up on her until he was certain – and when he did sleep he was tormented by nightmares. One was so violent he almost tumbled out of his hammock, and when he caught his breath and realised it had been nothing more than a bad dream – apparently flying fox agreed less well with his digestion than it did with his palate – he was glad that neither of the other two officers were in their hammocks to see the state he was in.

215

He struck a match so he could check his fob watch, and was disappointed to discover it was still only just ten o'clock. Cavan was on duty, of course, and Killigrew was not due to relieve him until midnight, but being reluctant to go back to sleep he used Strachan's absence as an excuse to get dressed.

Part of him hoped that the assistant surgeon had gone off to study the volcano. Despite the paradisiacal surroundings, even after only three days on the island Killigrew was hungry for some excitement to relieve the tedium of doing little more than waiting. But for once Strachan disappointed him: the assistant surgeon was still at the table, discussing palaeontology with Richards over a bottle of evil-looking whisky. Or rather, lecturing Richards, who had fallen asleep at the table; given that Strachan's boyish enthusiasm for science could breathe life into the driest of subjects, Richards' snores were probably a testimony to the strength of the whisky. Even Strachan, who could put whisky away with the best of them, must have been affected, for he had failed to notice the unconscious condition of his audience.

Killigrew glanced across to where he could see Cavan talking to Molineaux and Endicott, who had taken over lookout duties on Cook's Pyramid, in the light of the half-moon.

The lieutenant approached the table and touched his friend on the shoulder. Strachan blinked up at him blearily, then glanced to where Richards was slumped over the table. The assistant surgeon picked up the bottle of whisky and put on his spectacles to read the label. 'Laphroaig, it says! If this fousome stuff is Laphroaig, then I'm Lola Montez.'

'Capital!' Killigrew poured himself a glass of the putative Scotch and sat down with his feet on the table, lighting a cheroot. 'We could do with some feminine company around here. Don't you think you ought to get some sleep?'

'I'm no' sleepy. What about you? From those bags under your eyes, I'd say you've not bowed an eye in days.'

Killigrew yawned cavernously. 'I don't need much sleep.'

Strachan took off his spectacles and rubbed his eyes. 'Hullo,' he said, glancing down the beach towards Cook's Pyramid. 'Here comes Mr Cavan. Always in a hurry, that boy.'

Killigrew glanced over his shoulder. Cavan was indeed running full pelt across the sand towards the table; as he drew near, the look on his face in the light of the torches lit around their camp alerted the lieutenant that all was not well. Sloughing off his exhaustion, Killigrew stood up and turned to meet the midshipman.

'Something wrong, Mr Cavan?'

'The ship, sir. The one Ågård saw earlier. It's disappeared!'

'Ships don't just vanish into thin air, Mr Cavan. How long is it since they last saw it?'

'About a quarter of an hour, sir. The lookouts were following its lights when they disappeared behind a headland on the south side of the island. They waited for the lights to emerge on the other side, but . . . they never did.'

Killigrew frowned. It was not impossible that the lookouts on Mount Melen had made a mistake, but they were both reliable men. The moon was low in the night sky to the east, which would throw the eastern coast of the island into shadow; but the only possible explanation for the disappearance of the lights was that the ship had moored behind the headland, or her lights had been extinguished. In either case, it was damned suspicious.

'*Ågård!*' roared Killigrew.

Richards woke up abruptly at the yell, and fell backwards off his stool. He promptly fell asleep again on the sand.

Ågård emerged from the barracks-tent, naked but for a pair of woollen drawers. 'Sir?'

'Beat to quarters, Ågård. We're going for a moonlight cruise.'

XVI

Decoyed

'Heave to and lower my boat, Utumate,' ordered Quested. He spoke barely above a whisper, and instead of passing on the instructions in his usual, booming baritone, the specksnyder padded across the deck on his bare feet to order the hands to box the sails in a low voice.

Quested turned to the second mate. 'This looks like a perfect opportunity to try out your newfangled toy, Mr Forgan.'

'Aye, aye, Cap'n.' Grinning, the mate scurried below.

It was a dozen minutes or so after two bells in the middle watch – not that the *Lucy Ann*'s bell was being rung that night – and the darkness was blacker than pitch. Vickers and Lissak had been on deck during the last dog watch, and in the dying twilight they had seen the island they were approaching. Now they were somewhere off the west coast – not that Lissak could see a thing beyond the gunwale – but Quested and Macy seemed to know exactly where they were.

It was two and a half days since the *Lucy Ann* had fallen in with the *Wanderer* at the Bay of Crabs. Lissak had no idea what Quested and Thorpe had discussed for so long in the great cabin, but it had been obvious that they were old friends; at least, they had been when they gone below. When they had re-emerged Quested had ordered Macy to chart a new course, before assuring Cusack that the woman was all right, and no longer any concern of theirs. The Irishman seemed to accept that, but an argument had ensued about the change of course. Apparently it was Quested's intention that they break off their voyage for a couple of days to trade in sandalwood.

'Sandalwood!' Cusack had protested. 'We've half the Royal Navy after us, and you want to trade in sandalwood?'

'You've no need to worry about the *Tisiphone*, Mr Cusack,' Quested had replied calmly. 'She's on her way to Thorpetown –

219

where we were bound, as it happens, so we were lucky to run into the *Wanderer*, otherwise it would have been the *Tisiphone* we ran into. The deal I had with your Mr Fallon was that we would be allowed to stop and lower boats if we saw any whales on our way to California, to defray the cost of the voyage. Well, the deal Mr Thorpe has just put in my way is worth the oil of a hundred whales to me, so I don't see why the same principles shouldn't apply. Don't worry; Erromanga's practically on our way. All we've got to do is take the sandalwood to Thorpetown, and then we can resume our original course.'

'I thought you said the *Tisiphone* was at Thorpetown?'

'She is. But Mr Thorpe will see to it she's long gone by the time we get there on Sunday.'

Lissak had never heard of Erromanga until that day, but since then spouters on the *Lucy Ann* had told him all about the island; or, to be more precise, the cannibalistic savages that inhabited it. 'Is that Erromanga?' he asked Pilcher nervously, jerking his head in the direction he guessed the coast lay.

'No, that's Tanna,' snorted the boatsteerer.

'But I thought we were going to Erromanga.'

'We are,' Pilcher promised them. 'But first we've got to pick up trade goods from Tanna. The Erromangoans won't welcome us with open arms if we turn up empty-handed. Or at least, if they do, it will be as their supper.'

'What sort o' trade goods are we picking up?'

'Hist!' Pilcher winked. 'You'll see.'

'Belay that gassing!' snarled Macy.

A boat had been lowered from the starboard quarter by the time Forgan came up on deck carrying something Lissak could hardly make out in the darkness, even with eyes attuned to seeing in the dark. It looked like a harpoon gun of some kind. Quested and Forgan climbed down into the boat with four oarsmen. They pushed off and rowed away with barely a sound, the oars muffled in the rowlocks. A moment or two later the darkness had swallowed up the boat.

Then all was silent but for the gentle lapping of the waves against the *Lucy Ann*'s hull. The hands on deck crowded the starboard gunwale, staring into the darkness expectantly; Lissak could not even begin to guess what they were waiting for.

When it came, it was such a shock after the silence on board that Lissak almost jumped out of his shoes: a flat crack, a white flash reflected on the water, and then a brighter flash, further off, followed less than a second later by a loud crack. In the split second of the flash, an image of trees and native huts was burned into Lissak's eyes, only a couple of hundred yards distant: the *Lucy Ann* was closer to the shore than he had realised.

The seconds ticked by. Perhaps a minute later the twin bangs and flashes were repeated, and this time the second flash silhouetted illuminated Quested's boat, with a figure standing in the bows.

Now there were yells drifting faintly from the shore, and voices crying out in a heathenish jabber Lissak could not understand. The next flash set fire to a native hut that turned into a roaring inferno in seconds, and in its light Lissak could see the naked figures of savages running back and forth.

Awoken by the noise, Wyatt, Mangal and Jarrett joined Lissak and Vickers on deck to watch the fireworks display. Then Cusack emerged from the after hatch, wearing a tasselled nightcap and nightshirt. 'What's going on?' demanded the Irishman.

'Damned if I know,' said Wyatt. 'Quested and some of his crewmen climbed into a boat and rowed towards the island; now they're shooting bombs at a native village ashore.'

'What!' Cusack turned to where Macy was watching the attack on the village through a telescope; he snatched the telescope from the chief mate to look for himself.

With the village in flames, Lissak could see things more clearly now. In the boat's bows, Forgan was firing bombs from the harpoon gun as quickly as he could ram the projectiles into the barrel and prime the breech. The light from the flames gave him something to aim at now, and each shot found its mark, setting another hut ablaze. One native running through the huts was caught by a blast, and was picked up off his feet and thrown into a somersault. His screams reached the *Lucy Ann* clearly; so did another sound, a manic laughter coming from the boat.

'Jaysus Christ!' Cusack exclaimed in horror, and turned to Macy. 'For pity's sake, man! What's he doing? It's cold-blooded murder!'

'Calm down, Cusack,' snapped Macy. 'They're only kanakas.'

'Only kanakas!' spluttered the Irishman. 'Jaysus Christ! Are they not God's children, the same as the rest of us?'

'God?' spat Macy. 'Those heathen devils know nothing of God, Mr Cusack. Those savages would as soon run you through with a spear or bury the head of a tomahawk in your skull as look at you, so don't go wasting your pity on them.'

Forgan sat down again and the oarsmen rowed the boat back to the *Lucy Ann*. Cusack was waiting for them at the gangway by the time they climbed back on board, laughing and slapping one another on the back as if they had been enjoying a good joke.

'Captain Quested!' snapped Cusack. 'I demand an explanation!'

At first the captain ignored him, turning to his crew. 'Bring the ship to the wind, there! Brace up the fore and mizzen tops'ls and haul aback the main yard!'

'Cheerly does it, bullies!' said Macy. 'Let's get underway, before those kanakas rally and start chasing us in their canoes!'

Quested slapped his second mate on the back. 'Good work, Mr Forgan.'

Forgan grinned. 'My pleasure, Cap'n.'

'Captain Quested!' insisted Cusack.

The master finally turned to meet the Irishman's glare. 'What seems to be the trouble, Mr Cusack?'

'Captain Quested, I demand to know what's going on!'

Quested gestured dismissively. 'Just a little diversion, that's all.'

'A diversion! Diverting *whom* from *what*, may I ask?'

'My agreement with you is that I'll deliver you in one piece to your friends in 'Frisco,' Quested said coolly. 'How I conduct my voyage on the way is no concern of yours.'

'It's my charter!'

'Correction, Mr Cusack. It's the Irish Directory's charter. If you have any complaints about the way I do business, I suggest you discuss it with them when you get to New York.' The captain seemed to soften. 'Look, calm yourself, Mr Cusack. We were just making a lot of fire and noise, that's all. Those bombs are deadly when they penetrate a whale's blubber, but otherwise they're no more dangerous than firecrackers.'

'Then account for all that screaming, damn your eyes!'

'Kanakas have a low pain threshold, Mr Cusack. That's a well-known fact. You've only got to slap them about a bit, and they blubber like weenies. Isn't that right, Mr Macy?'

The chief mate nodded.

'I told Mr Forgan to try to avoid hitting anyone; if any of them got hurt, it was an accident.'

'One of them ran in front of my bomb-gun,' explained Forgan, grinning. Macy cuffed Forgan around the back of the head, but Cusack did not see: he was too busy glaring at Quested.

'There's no real harm done, Mr Cusack,' insisted the captain. 'You have my word on it.'

'No harm done,' Cusack said dully. 'You set their entire village alight, and you tell me there's no harm done?'

'You think the kanakas build their huts out of palm-thatch and pandanus leaves because they don't know any better? These island are often ravaged by cyclones, Mr Cusack. The kanakas build their homes out of such materials because they're easy to replace.'

'But . . . why?'

'I can't explain now; but rest assured, it had to be done. In a few days I'll be able to explain it all to you; and I hope then you'll see I had no choice. What do you take me for? The kind of man who takes pleasure in the suffering of others?' Butter would not have

222

melted in his mouth. 'Trust me, Mr Cusack. That's all I ask.'

'I'd sooner trust an Englishman, Captain Quested.' Cusack turned on his heel and stalked back down the after hatch.

'He's going to be trouble, Cap'n,' opined Macy.

'Aye,' agreed Quested, rubbing his jaw thoughtfully. 'Who'd've thought a Paddy revolutionary would get so sentimental over a bunch of goddamned kanakas?'

'That's the least of it,' said Macy. 'What's he going to say when the trade goods are brought on board?'

'You're right,' said Quested. Then he shrugged. 'Ah, what does it matter? If he tries to make trouble, we can just hand him over to Kowiowi with the trade goods. It'll mean kissing goodbye to the balance of that ten thousand dollars; but Thorpe's offered me twice that. Besides, if I have to choose between collecting that five thousand dollars and avenging my nephew's death, it's no choice at all. There are some things you can't put a price on. Killigrew's head is one of them.'

'Now just hold on a minute!' protested Gardner. 'Don't we get a say in this? We've all got lays in the profits of the voyage, too . . .'

'Stow it, Mr Gardner. I'm captain of the *Lucy Ann*; you knew that when you shipped with me; and you agreed to abide by my orders. Well, those are my orders.'

'I shipped with you because I was told that no voyage with Captain Quested at the helm failed to turn a good profit; but I never shipped to take part in some quest for personal vengeance.'

Quested put his hand on the revolver holstered at his hip. 'Are you saying you want to break your contract with me, Mr Gardner? Is that it?'

The third mate blanched. 'No, sir! That ain't what I meant at all . . .'

'Easy, *amigos*!' said Forgan. 'No need to part brass rags. The way I figure it, there's a way Thorpe can have his sandalwood, the cap'n can have his vengeance and we can all share in the profits of this voyage.'

'Go on, Mr Forgan.'

The second mate lowered his voice. 'We'll get the doc to put pipe ash in Cusack's vittles.'

'Pipe ash?'

'It's an old trick for swinging the lead when there's dirty work to be done; I used to know a sailor who'd put ash in his own coffee rather than pick the stink out of the casks, until the old man got wise to his tricks. It made him sick as a dog for a few hours, and after that he was right as a trivet. If the doc puts pipe ash in Cusack's dinner tomorrow, he'll be so sick by the time the cap'n gets back from Port Resolution, he won't know what's going on. By the time he's recovered, Erromanga will be behind us, and he'll be none the wiser to anything that happened.'

Macy and Gardner exchanged hopeful glances. Quested was silent, and then a smile spread across his face. 'I'm obliged to you, Mr Forgan. That's as neat and tidy a solution as any. Cigar ash seasoning with dinner it is. We'd better get smoking, gentlemen.'

'What about them?' Macy jerked his head to where Lissak stood with the other convicts.

'I'm sure we don't need to worry about them.' Quested turned to Wyatt. 'What do you say? You and your friends aren't squeamish about what happens to a few kanakas, are you, Mr Wyatt?'

'You can sell a thousand of the heathen bastards into slavery for all we care, Captain Quested.' As usual, Wyatt took it upon himself to speak for all the convicts. 'As long as you deliver us safely to California, you'll have our thanks.'

'Now that's what I like to hear, Mr Wyatt – a little appreciation when one man does a favour for another. As it happens, I'm glad you feel that way: I'll be in need of a man of your talents and disposition tomorrow. Help me out, and I might just cut you and your friends in for a share of the profits.'

'What do you want us to do?'

'Whatever it was, it's stopped now.' Molineaux picked his way over the bodies of the men who lay cramped on the deck of the *Vanguard* to where Killigrew stood at the helm. With Ågård acting as boatswain, Endicott and three other seamen worked the sails, while the remaining sixteen bluejackets sat on the deck with Summerbee and his three marines; those seamen who had muskets checked and rechecked them; while the rest clutched cutlasses, tomahawks and boarding pikes.

The schooner was a small vessel, barely thirty-five feet from stem to stern; small enough for Richards to make short voyages between the islands of the New Hebrides solo, if the need arose, although he usually employed the services of Sharky and a couple of other friendly natives to help him.

It was not often that the lieutenant had the chance to get his hands on the tiller of a ship. On board the *Tisiphone*, that task was usually given to one of the hands, rotated amongst the crew so that sooner or later every seaman got a chance to learn how to steer, under the close supervision of an experienced quartermaster. But as much as he enjoyed being at the helm, he was in no mood to appreciate it now.

'What was it?' he asked Molineaux. 'Musket fire?'

'I don't think so, sir.'

The *Vanguard* was still off the south-east coast of Tanna. The shore party had responded with impressive efficiency to Killigrew's order to board the schooner, but it had taken more than three hours to get the *Vanguard* out of Port Resolution in the dark, tack around Yewao Point against the south-easterly winds and sail with the wind two points before the port beam to a position four miles from where the mysterious ship had last been seen. Killigrew had been hoping they would encounter the ship sailing in the opposite direction, but so far they had seen no sign of her; if she had changed course and was sailing clockwise round the island, she had had enough time to get more than a dozen miles away by now.

The sound of distant bangs had come from somewhere off to landward, but it had echoed off the sides of the two mountains ashore, making it impossible to pinpoint precisely. To leeward, all Killigrew could make out was the faint white gleam of the surf crashing against the shore in the weak moonlight, but he was aware that Mount Melen towered above them in the blackness somewhere off the starboard bow.

'Grab that bull's-eye and see if you can signal the lookouts, Molineaux,' ordered Killigrew. 'Send that this is Killigrew on board the *Vanguard*, and ask them to acknowledge. Cavan, you take the telescope from the binnacle and look for a response.'

'Aye, aye, sir.'

Molineaux sent the signal, passing his sennit hat before the beam to break it up, while Cavan levelled the telescope in the direction Killigrew indicated.

'No reply, sir,' said the midshipman, when Molineaux had finished signalling.

'Send again, Molineaux . . .'

'Wait a minute, sir!' said Cavan 'I'm getting a response.'

'Good. Molineaux, send this: "What?"' The signals he had worked out did not include the word 'bangs', but the lookouts must have heard the reports too. Killigrew hoped they would understand his own bewilderment, and find some way of signalling an answer, if they had one.

The seaman sent the signal, and before long the reply came back. ' "Lights, west by north-west, twelve miles." '

'Take the tiller, Ågård.' Killigrew descended to the *Vanguard*'s cramped cabin, where Strachan was stretched out on the window seat, sleeping off the whisky. If the ship did turn out to be slavers and there was a fight, then Killigrew knew that if anyone was badly wounded then Strachan's best chance of saving them lay in getting to them as quickly as possible. But first they would have to catch the slavers, and if this hunt turned into a stern chase, that could take hours: there was plenty of time for Strachan to sleep.

Killigrew lit an oil-lamp and searched through the drawers in the cabin until he found a rough chart of Tanna that, from the look of it, had probably been drawn by Richards himself. Spreading it on the table, Killigrew took a ruler and pencil and drew a line running west by north-west from the lookouts' position; then he took a compass and measured off twelve miles. The location this pinpointed was approximately halfway up the west coast: whatever the bangs had signified, it was almost certainly the handiwork of the ship that had vanished. But it would take the *Vanguard* the best part of six hours to get there.

Strachan stirred and blinked at Killigrew, without trying to get up. 'What's going on?' he murmured sleepily.

'I wish I knew,' Killigrew replied grimly.

'Stand clear of the chain!' ordered Quested. 'All hands bring ship to anchor!'

One of the bower anchors was dropped from the cathead and the chain rattled noisily through the hawsehole as the anchor splashed into the waters a hundred yards out from the north coast of Tanna. The northern end of the island was relatively flat, a broad expanse of scrub and grassland, and in the early morning light the mountains which dominated the southern end of the island were visible about fifteen miles off.

One thing was obvious to Lissak as he stood on deck and watched the captain and his shore party get ready to leave the ship: Captain Quested was insane. If he wanted to kidnap natives from that island, that was no skin off the old lag's nose; but he could easily have taken them from the village they had attacked last night. Yet clearly that was not enough for Quested. He wanted to take them from Port Resolution, right from under Killigrew's nose, just as he had taken Cusack from Norfolk Island right under the nose of the *Tisiphone*.

And he wanted Killigrew. Lissak had heard from some of the hands on board the *Lucy Ann* about how the lieutenant had killed Quested's nephew in Hobart Town. Whatever it cost Quested, no matter how long it took, he hungered for Killigrew's death with an intensity that glittered feverishly in his eyes. Lissak shuddered: he was glad he was not the lieutenant.

Forgan came up on deck. 'Cusack?' Quested asked him.

The second mate grinned. 'Fast asleep in his cabin, Cap'n.'

'Good! Let's leave it that way for now.' Quested turned to Macy. 'Make sure doc puts the ashes in his dinner. I want him in his bunk when I come back aboard this evening. You'll have the larboard side to shoreward when you get to Judgement Point; make sure you keep it that way when you anchor. I don't want Cusack glancing out of his cabin porthole and seeing me bringing the trade goods on board.'

'And what if we run into Killigrew sailing in the opposite direction on our way to Judgement Point?' demanded Macy.

'You won't. By now Killigrew will have heard there was an attack on that village last night. Word travels fast on an island like Tanna: if there's an attack on one village, word goes out to warn the others by the bush telegraph. Richards understands the jungle drums; he'll have told Killigrew, and Killigrew will have commandeered the *Vanguard* to investigate. If he left Port Resolution within an hour of our attack on the village, he'll reach it some time later this morning; when he gets there, it won't take him long to realise it was a diversion. He'll ask himself what he was being diverted from; he may not guess what, but as to where, there's only one possible answer.'

Macy smiled. 'Port Resolution.'

'And the quickest way from that village to Port Resolution by sea is around the south coast,' concluded Quested. 'He'll know we've got several hours' head start on him; but he'll also know that if we're sailing around the north side of the island, we'll have to tack down the east coast; so he'll think he's got a chance of getting there before us.'

'And supposing he guesses that we're going overland?' demanded Wyatt. 'Supposing he heads overland himself? He could be back at Port Resolution before we get there.'

'He could,' allowed Quested. 'We'll find out soon enough. We'll approach the village carefully, find out who's there before we attack. If Killigrew gets back before us, or if he never left, we'll just have to improvise, that's all.'

'I don't like it,' grumbled Wyatt. 'Going overland. It's got to be about twenty miles – some of that through thick bush and rough country. What if we run into any natives?'

'That's why we're taking precautions,' said Quested. 'Mr Forgan? Pass out the precautions.'

The 'precautions' were a veritable arsenal of firearms: a musket and two revolvers for each of the eleven men who would go ashore with Quested: Forgan, Wyatt, Mangal, Vickers, and seven of the spouters from the *Lucy Ann*, including the massive Lawless Twins.

Wyatt checked his revolvers. 'They're primed and loaded, Mr Wyatt,' Quested assured him. 'I'm trusting you and your two friends. I'd advise you not to disappoint me.'

'Do all whalers carry this many guns on board, Captain Quested?'

'Most carry a few. But I learned the advantage of being well armed when I was a sandalwood trader; I thought this little lot might come in handy when Mr Fallon asked me to rescue Cusack from Norfolk Island. If we do run into any kanakas, they'll outnumber us ten to one; the only thing that will save us will be firepower. And we'll need it when we get to Port Resolution. Don't underestimate the kanakas, Mr Wyatt. They use their bows for hunting, not for war; but I've seen one of them throw a spear clean through six inches of solid wood from a distance of fifty yards. Firearms won't save us if they attack us in the bush: they'll appear out of the trees with their clubs and tomahawks, and strike before any of us gets a chance to shoot, so keep your eyes and ears open as soon as we get in the trees. Oh, and another thing: some of them will have muskets. They may even know how to use them.'

'This just gets better and better,' Wyatt said sourly.

'Scared, Mr Wyatt? I can leave you behind on the *Lucy Ann*, if you prefer. Someone else can go in your place.'

Wyatt shouldered his musket. 'I fear no man.'

'Glad to hear it.' Quested picked up a brown-paper package, looping his hook under the string which held it together, and handed it to Mangal. 'You take this.'

'What is it?' asked Mangal. Stuffing his face as usual – he had a hunk of stale bread in one hand – he spoke with his mouth full and had no qualms about letting everyone see the half-masticated food on his tongue.

Quested grinned. 'A little present for Killigrew. Something to make sure he comes dashing to Mrs Cafferty's rescue after he gets back to Port Resolution.'

'But we do not have Mrs Cafferty on board!'

'He doesn't know that; and what's in that package will convince him we do. Gog? Magog? You two take a couple of coils of rope each. We'll need them when we get to Port Resolution. All right, let's go.'

'This must be the place.' From the deck of the *Vanguard*, Killigrew studied the village ashore through the telescope. Many of the native huts had been burned to cinders, and there were several bodies sprawled on the sand, including one or two small children. Killigrew was close enough to make out the silvery tracks of tears on the cheeks of the brown-skinned women in grass skirts.

It was ten past seven in the morning, and already the sun was high in the sky. As soon as the *Vanguard* hove into sight, there was much activity ashore as the men of the village ran to and fro amongst the huts which still stood.

'Butchery,' snorted Strachan. He looked pale and ashen from the previous night's excesses. 'But why?'

'Slaves, Mr Strachan.' Killigrew snapped the telescope shut and handed it to Cavan. 'It seems Mr Thorpe was right: the scourge of blackbirding really has reached the South Seas.'

228

'It looks like there are wounded people over there,' said Strachan. 'We have to go ashore and do what we can to help.'

'Agreed,' said Killigrew. 'Get your medicine chest, Strachan. We're going ashore. Ready the jolly boat, Ågård.'

'Are you sure about that, sir? Looks as if they're coming out to meet us.' He pointed to where the warriors of the village, having collected their spears, war clubs and tomahawks, were converging on the three outrigger canoes drawn up on the beach.

'They don't look pleased to see us, do they?' observed Endicott.

'Can you blame them?' asked Killigrew. 'It was dark last night. They probably think this is the ship that attacked their village. Besides, the natives of these islands have a policy of communal responsibility. If a man from one tribe commits a transgression against another, then it is the duty of all members of his tribe to make reparations, or be punished. To the natives, all white men belong to the same tribe.'

The natives had pushed their canoes out through the surf and were now paddling furiously towards the *Vanguard*. 'With all due respect, sir, they don't look as if they're going to ask for reparations,' said Cavan. 'Might I suggest that discretion is the better part of valour?'

'Quite right, Mr Cavan,' agreed Killigrew. 'Yorath, Endicott! Brace up those sails, chop chop.'

The *Vanguard* could have stayed and made a fight of it: the Tisiphones on board might even have beaten the natives, although there were no guarantees. But Killigrew did not want to kill any natives simply because they knew no better, no more than he wanted to risk the lives of his own men for no good reason.

'We're leaving?' stammered Strachan. 'But there are injured people ashore! They need our help!'

'Need it they may, Mr Strachan. Want it they certainly do not. You can't do anything for them if you're skewered on one of those spears.'

Killigrew spun the helm, bringing the bow round to port. He pointed the *Vanguard* north-west, so they would have the wind full behind them; but the three canoes continued to overhaul them. Seeing that the ship was turning tail, a few of the natives launched spears that whirred through the air and landed all around the schooner. A few buried themselves in the deck, and Endicott scrambled out of the way with a yelp when one missed him by a few feet.

'Fire a couple of shots over their heads, Hawthorne,' ordered Killigrew. The marine was a crack shot, and if any man could be relied upon not to hit any of the natives, it was him. 'Perhaps that will discourage them.'

'Or encourage them, by making them think we're rotten shots,' muttered Corporal Summerbee.

At the stern, Hawthorne fired, reloaded, and fired again. The natives paid no attention to the bullets that whizzed over them.

'They're going to catch us, sir,' said Summerbee. 'For God's sake, let's shoot a couple of them. That'll make the rest think twice.'

'Belay that, Corporal. I refuse to be party to any further butchery of innocent natives.'

'Innocent! Attempted murder is a crime in any country the last time I heard, sir. And those kanakas have got murder in their hearts, or I'm a Dutchman. I've done enough killing to know I'm not overfond of it, sir, but there is such a thing as self-defence.'

Killigrew ignored him. 'Take the helm, Ågård.' He ran to the stern and leaped on the gunwale, balancing there as he waved his hands over his head and motioned for the canoes to keep their distance. 'Go back! Go back, damn you! We don't want to hurt you . . .'

The natives at once started to hurl spears at him. They whirled down around him, one narrowly missing his head.

'That's as good a way to commit suicide as any,' remarked Molineaux. He sauntered over to the stern, keeping his head down. 'Good idea, sir. You draw their fire.'

'I'm trying to make them stand off!'

'Yes, sir. Pity they don't understand English.' Molineaux unslung Richards' hunting rifle from his shoulder, took careful aim, and fired. The native sitting in the bow of the foremost canoe dropped his paddle and fell back, clutching a bloody wound in his arm.

''Vast shooting, Molineaux! Damn your eyes, didn't you hear me say I didn't want to kill any of them?'

'He'll live.' Molineaux took another cartridge from his pocket and tore the top off with his teeth, pouring the powder down the barrel of the rifle. 'Sir, much as I admire your principled stand on the issue, the only way we're going to get them to back off is if we convince them we're in deadly earnest.' He inserted another ball in the muzzle, and then rammed it home expertly with the ramrod. 'If you want to get yourself killed, sir, don't let me stop you. But the rest of us would like to see England again.' He primed the rifle with a percussion cap, and raised the stock to his shoulder. 'Don't worry, sir. I don't much like the idea of killing them either. I'll aim to wound.'

'And if you miss? If you kill him?'

'See the cove sitting at the front of the canoe on the left, sir?'

'What about him?'

'Right shoulder.' Molineaux fired. The native clapped an arm to his shoulder. 'I never miss,' the seaman asserted proudly.

230

Molineaux worked methodically, reloading, aiming, firing, and managing an impressive rate of three shots a minute; good enough to rival a trained rifleman. Each wound he delivered was painful enough to render the victim unable to paddle, without being life-threatening. Each wounded native took a fraction off the speed of the canoe he was in. After five shots, the canoes were starting to fall behind; finally realising they were on a hiding to nothing, they gave up and started to paddle back to the shore.

Killigrew rounded on Molineaux. 'You disobeyed an order, damn you!'

'That's all right, sir,' the seaman replied coolly. 'No need to thank me.' He lowered his voice. 'With all due respect, sir, you may have lost the will to live back in Hong Kong, but some of us still value our hides. And there's a chance – just a chance – that Mrs Cafferty is still alive. We can't do anything for her if we get slaughtered by the natives now, can we?'

Killigrew did not know whether to damn the seaman for his impertinence or thank him for his common sense. He sighed. 'Good shooting, Molineaux.'

'Thank you, sir,' the seaman replied breezily.

Killigrew turned back to where Cavan and Strachan stood by the binnacle. 'Want me to hold this course, sir?' asked Ågård.

'For now.' The lieutenant cast his eyes about the sea. 'Whatever ship attacked that village, it's long gone by now. Damn it! We were here waiting for those blackbirders, and they still managed to land and take slaves before we could get there.'

'They must've worked quickly,' said Molineaux, slinging the rifle from his shoulder. 'Remember on the Guinea Coast, sir? How the slavers used to take their time? Attack one village, and then use it as a base camp to seize the natives from as many neighbouring villages as possible? That way they got their pick of the bucks: good, strong labourers. But the coves who attacked that village last night, they didn't want to linger. Almost as if they knew we were coming.'

'Commander Robertson and I didn't exactly make a secret of our itinerary and our plans on our way here,' Killigrew said ruefully. 'I'll lay odds that word of mouth spreads surprisingly swiftly through these islands. The blackbirders must've heard we were on Tanna.'

'Then why the devil did they seize natives from Tanna at all, sir, if they knew we were here?' demanded Cavan. 'If they knew that much, they must've known Hartcliffe and his party are at Aneiteium and that the Old Man's gone on to Éfaté. Why not seize natives from some of the islands where they know we aren't, so they could take their time?'

'And another thing, sir,' said Molineaux. 'Doesn't it strike you as a little bit odd? The last raids took place two years ago. Then nothing. And then, when there's a party of British seamen on Tanna, all of a sudden the raids start all over again. Bloody bad timing on the part of the blackbirders, wouldn't you say?'

Killigrew smiled wanly. 'Our presence doesn't seem to have incommoded them in any way.'

'Yur: because they just happened to pick the village furthest to reach by sea from Port Resolution.'

'What are you trying to say, Molineaux?'

'I don't know, sir,' admitted the seaman. 'I'm just saying, there's something rum about this whole business.'

Killigrew was inclined to agree, but he could not put his finger on—

'Oh, Christ! Put us about, Ågård. Hard a-starboard. Bring us about until we're as close to the wind as you can get her. Luff and touch her.'

'Aye, aye, sir.' The petty officer spun the helm.

Killigrew turned to Strachan. 'How many men would you say live in each village that we've seen in these islands? Grown men, I mean.'

The assistant surgeon shrugged. 'I don't know. A hundred?'

'There were forty men in each of those canoes. A hundred and twenty in total. Even if it was a large village, the blackbirders didn't get many, did they? If they got any at all.'

'What are you saying, sir?' asked Cavan.

'We've got so caught up in the notion of slavers raiding this island . . . we don't know for a fact that it *was* slavers who attacked that village. We don't even know that any natives were kidnapped there last night. We only assume they were.'

'Who else would attack a native village but blackbirders, sir? Who else would have reason to?'

'*Who*, I don't know,' admitted Killigrew. 'But I think I can guess *why*. Think about it. What benefit might someone have from attacking a village on the west coast of the island?'

'I don't know, sir. There are some deuced rum fellows in the world. Maybe the captain of that ship enjoys slaughtering natives the way some people enjoy hunting foxes. It's twisted, I know, but . . .'

'I suspect you're right, Cavan. It wouldn't surprise me in the least to learn that the captain of our mysterious ship took some kind of warped pleasure from attacking that village. But perhaps it was not a senseless attack; not in his eyes, at least.'

'I don't follow you, sir.'

'Cause and effect, lad,' said Strachan. From the expression on his face, he had seen what Killigrew was driving at. 'That village was attacked last night to achieve something. What did it achieve?'

'It got me out of my hammock in the middle of the night,' grumbled Endicott.

'Stow it!' growled Ågård. 'No one asked you your opinion.'

'No, Ågård,' said Killigrew. 'I fear Endicott's hit the nail on the head: the attack on the village got us out of Port Resolution, didn't it? Gentlemen, I put it to you that's exactly what the intention was. To draw us away.'

'But *why*?' asked Cavan.

'I don't know,' admitted Killigrew. 'But I've an unpleasant feeling that all will be revealed when we get back there.'

XVII

A Leap in the Dark

'Damn it, how much longer must we wait here?' Cusack asked Macy on the quarterdeck of the *Lucy Ann*.

'I told you. My orders are to wait here until seven o'clock. If Cap'n Quested and the others aren't back by then, my orders are to take over and deliver you directly to your friends in 'Frisco.'

The whaler was anchored off the west coast of the island, six or seven miles up the coast from the island they had attacked during the night. It was one o'clock in the afternoon – five and a half hours since the *Lucy Ann* had anchored – and Cusack had just come up after dining in the great cabin with Macy and Gardner. The ship's lookouts had been ordered to keep a sharp watch for any natives seeking vengeance for the attack on the village. But there were no natives in sight, either by land or sea. There was no jungle ashore at this part of the coast, just a beach of black sand, some dark dunes, and behind that a broad plain of yellow elephant grass.

'Does that satisfy you, Mr Cusack?' concluded Macy.

'Frankly, it does not. If Quested's gone to collect trade goods from Port Resolution, why are we here? Won't he have to carry the goods overland? Why not sail this ship into Port Resolution itself?'

'For all we know, the *Tisiphone* is anchored at Port Resolution even as we speak,' Jarrett said smoothly. 'Quested learned from Thorpe that the *Tisiphone* is somewhere in these islands, looking for us. This way, he can make sure the coast is clear before he enters the harbour.'

Cusack shook his head. 'I don't believe I've heard a word of truth from you or Quested from the moment we left the Isles of Pines,' he said. 'In fact, I'm starting to wonder if I've heard one word of truth from you—' He broke off, and clutched at his stomach. 'Oh God!'

'Everything all right, Mr Cusack?' asked Macy, an amused smile playing on his face.

In the blink of an eye, all the colour had drained from the

235

Irishman's face. 'I don't feel well . . . I . . . oh, God!' He staggered across to the entry port and vomited over the side.

Macy turned to two of the spouters. 'Mr Cusack has been taken sick. Help him down to his cabin and put him in his bunk.'

'I'm fine!' protested Cusack. 'Just a little . . . oh, dear God!' He doubled up again, retching drily, but there was nothing left for him to bring up.

'Come along now, sir,' said one of the spouters, helping him up. 'You have a lie down and you'll feel right as rain soon enough.'

'I'll send the doc along to take a look at you, see if he can give you something to soothe your stomach,' said Macy. If Cusack heard him as he was helped down the after hatch by the two spouters, he gave no indication of it.

Laughing, Macy turned to Lissak and Jarrett. 'Must've been something he ate.'

The sun had set and the sky was turning from a fiery crimson to a velvety purple by the time the *Vanguard* sailed back into Port Resolution, so the damage to the village was not obvious at first. Killigrew left Cavan to see to it that the schooner was securely anchored for the night, and went ashore in the jolly boat with Ågård, Molineaux, Endicott and Yorath. All four ratings carried muskets, except for Molineaux, who still had Richards' rifle slung from one shoulder. As the men dragged the boat up through the surf, Killigrew waded ashore and ran up the beach with a pepper-box in one hand.

'Richards! Moltata! Hullo?'

Except on nights when they were holding feasts, when they lit flambeaux and gathered round a bonfire, the natives tended to rise with the dawn and go to bed with the sunset; but even at this hour there was usually more evidence of life than Killigrew found. His cries failed to bring anyone to greet him, and there was an eerie silence over the whole village. He made his way to the *nakamal*; even at that hour, Moltata would usually have been there drinking *kava* with the village elders.

Except the *nakamal* was no longer there. Just a pile of ashes, still warm.

Ågård came running up with the bull's-eye and shone the beam about, revealing more burned-out huts. 'Looks like the slavers got here first, sir,' he said grimly.

'If slavers they were,' agreed Killigrew.

The three seamen caught up with them. 'What happened?' asked Endicott. 'Did the slavers kidnap the entire village?'

'No bodies,' remarked Molineaux. 'That's some good news, at least.'

236

'It's early yet,' said Ågård. 'Keep looking.'

A few huts still stood, and the five men carried out a quick search, glancing inside each of them, but found no one cowering inside. 'Let's try the trade house,' suggested Killigrew.

They hurried across to Richards' shack and paused on the verandah in front. 'Captain Richards?' called Killigrew. It occurred to him that whoever had attacked the village might still be around.

'*But answer came there none*,' said Molineaux.

'Give me the bull's-eye, Ågård. Stand back, all of you.' With the pepperbox in his right hand and the bull's-eye in his left, Killigrew braced himself. 'Richards?' he called one last time. 'It's me, Killigrew. I'm coming in!' He kicked the door open and jumped to one side, holding the bull's-eye at arm's length so that it would seem to anyone on the other side that someone was standing in the doorway, holding a torch.

When seconds passed without any answering fusillade of shots, he edged through the door, flashing the beam of the bull's-eye around and following it with his pepperbox. It did not take long to establish that the shack was every bit as deserted as the village. 'It's clear,' he called to the others.

While they shuffled in through the door, he hooked his pepperbox to his belt and set the bull's-eye down on the counter. He found an oil lamp and lit it with a match. As its warm yellow glow spread through the dark room, Endicott gasped. Killigrew turned to look at him, and saw the seaman was staring at the back wall. Following his gaze, he saw a large piece of blue cloth nailed to the wall, and something written in what looked like dripping blood on the weatherboards beside it:

> Killigrew –
> Judgement Point
> Midnight
> Come alone or she dies

Ågård crossed to the wall and dabbed a fingertip against the writing. 'It's still tacky,' he remarked. He touched a fingertip to his tongue.

'Is it . . .?' Endicott asked hesitantly.

Ågård spat. 'Paint,' he said.

'Someone has an overdeveloped sense of the melodramatic,' Killigrew said drily. He touched the blue cloth and rubbed it between his fingers: it was the evening dress Mrs Cafferty had been wearing the night she had been kidnapped. He tore it down and screwed it into a ball in his fists.

'Where's Judgement Point?' Endicott wondered out loud.

237

'I don't know,' Killigrew snapped back tersely. 'Take the jolly boat back to the *Vanguard* and fetch the chart.'

'Aye, aye, sir.' Endicott turned to leave, and then let out a yell of alarm.

Killigrew whirled, pulling the pepperbox from his belt, and levelled it at the doorway where he saw a savage figure brandishing a spear threateningly. Recognising him, he relaxed. 'Sharky! Christ! You scared the living daylights out of me.'

Sharky lowered his spear. '*Ale!*' he growled. 'You come too much back again. White men come finish. Attack village, take man finish. No good.'

'Man? Which man?'

'Two man and ten. Moltata, Guevu, Kateingo . . . white man take all.'

'What about Captain Richards? Is he alive? Did they take him?'

'Him too much sore. White man attack him, beat him long time finish. But him too much strong, m'be him live.'

'Where is he?'

'In tree. When white man come finish, woman and pikanini hidem in tree. Back again, we see *Vanguard* come long place here, we ting maybe bad white man come back again. We hidem again. Sharky come long hut long look-see.'

'How far away?'

'Two, maybe t'ree hunnerd yard through tree.'

'Can you take me to him?'

'*Ale!*'

'Go and get that chart, Endicott, and meet me back here in fifteen minutes.'

'Aye, aye, sir.'

As Endicott headed back to where they had left the jolly boat, Killigrew and the others followed Sharky into the trees, using the bull's-eye and the oil-lamp to light their way.

'I don't get it, sir,' said Molineaux. 'Was it slavers who attacked this village, or Quested and his men?'

'Both,' explained Killigrew. 'You were right about the *Lucy Ann* making for these islands, but for the wrong reasons; or at least, you didn't know all his reasons for coming here. I'll lay odds Quested knows these islands like the back of his hand.'

'You think he's the slaver that kidnapped all those natives two years ago?'

'I'll stake my life on it.'

'It still don't make any sense, sir,' said Ågård. 'Why stop here to pick up slaves? Hasn't he got his hands full getting Cusack to California? Maybe if he thought he'd given us the slip, he could turn a tidy profit on the way somehow; but he knows he hasn't given us

238

the slip: the writing on the wall tells us that.'

'Quested didn't come here for slaves, Ågård. He's got a score to settle with me, don't forget. The slaves were just the icing on the cake. He knows how I feel about slavery: kidnapping natives right from under my nose would appeal to his twisted sense of humour.'

'It also gives you an added incentive to go after him, in case you weren't gammoned by that dress into thinking that Mrs Cafferty might still be alive,' said Molineaux. 'He's no fool, that Quested: the dress, the slaves . . . all of it carefully judged to get you all worked up so that you go charging off to Judgement Point on your own, just like the message said . . . and walk slap-bang straight into a trap.'

'The thought had occurred to me.'

'But you're going anyway,' Molineaux said heavily.

'Unless you have a better suggestion? Mrs Cafferty may yet be alive; we don't know for sure. And even if she *is* dead, Moltata and the other eleven natives who were kidnapped only got caught up in this because of me. I owe it to them to rescue them.'

Sharky called out in his own language, a warning to the people hiding in the jungle that they were approaching. Suddenly the five seamen were surrounded by natives who materialised out of the trees into the light of the oil-lamp. But they let the seamen pass, and Sharky conducted Killigrew to a grove where several native women were tending a prone figure that lay on a bed of leaves. As the women parted to let Killigrew approach, he gasped.

'I guess I look a precious sight, eh?' said Richards.

Killigrew only recognised him because of the voice. The trader was covered in head to toe in some kind of mud. 'It's a poultice Sharky made for me,' explained Richards. 'For the bruises.'

Killigrew crouched over him. 'What happened to you?'

'A couple of walking mountains called Gog and Magog, would you believe? Twins, at that. Quested told them to work me over. I think they enjoyed it.' He grinned weakly. 'It don't seem so bad when I think that at least someone got pleasure from it.'

'You're certain it was Quested?'

'Oh, aye. He tapped me on the chest with his hook, and made me repeat his name so he could be sure I'd got it right.'

'Do you want me to ask Mr Strachan to come and take a look at you?'

'No. Sharky's a pretty good doctor. Oh, his methods might raise some eyebrows at the Royal College of Surgeons, but I've seen him cure sick men that most Western physicians wouldn't even bother to look at, for fear of losing their fee.'

'I'm sorry this had to happen to you . . . It's my fault . . .'

'Hey, stop trying to carry the weight of the world on your

shoulders, Killigrew. If anyone's responsible for this, it's that bastard Quested. If you want to do me a favour, just make sure you take your time killing him.'

Killigrew made his way back to the trade house with Sharky and the three seamen. When they got there, Cavan and Strachan were waiting for them with Endicott by the light of a second oil-lamp. 'Got the map?' Killigrew asked Endicott.

The Liverpudlian nodded and spread the chart on the table. 'You're not going to like this, sir. Here's where we are, at Port Resolution; and here's Judgement Point – way over here on the other side of the island.'

'Lumme!' exclaimed Molineaux. 'Begging your pardon, sir. But that's got to be at least twenty miles!'

'Probably nearer seventeen,' Killigrew said mildly.

Strachan checked his fob watch. 'It's quarter past seven now. How long will it take the *Vanguard* to get there?'

'She couldn't do it in less than seven hours,' said Cavan. 'Even that's asking a lot.'

'Yes, and Quested knows it,' said Killigrew. 'He wants me to go alone, remember?'

'And you're going?' Strachan demanded incredulously.

'Seventeen miles in four and three-quarter hours. That's only . . .' Killigrew started counting on his fingers.

Cavan coughed with embarrassment. 'Four miles an hour, sir?' he suggested helpfully.

'A brisk walk should do it,' said Killigrew.

'Seventeen miles as the crow flies, sir,' Molineaux pointed out. 'Probably nearer twenty on foot. Over rough country. In the dark.'

'I'll take Sharky here part of the way to guide me,' said Killigrew. 'If that's all right with you, Sharky?'

'*Ale!*' responded the *nakaimo*.

'You'll never make it, sir,' said Molineaux. 'And even if you do, they'll kill you when you get there.'

'Maybe,' allowed Killigrew, checking he had his cutlass and that both his pepperboxes were primed and loaded. 'Cavan, get the men back on board the *Vanguard* and set out at once for Judgement Point. You said just now it would take her seven hours to get there; cut it down to six, and I'll see to it they make you an admiral. I'll set out overland with Sharky; when I get there I'll try to delay them from sailing before you get there.'

'I'm coming with you, sir,' said Molineaux.

'The devil you are.'

The seaman unslung his rifle. 'I'm coming with you, sir; otherwise you don't walk out of that door.'

Killigrew turned and faced him. It was obvious the seaman was

240

in deadly earnest: he would not shoot the lieutenant dead, but he might wound him the way he had wounded one of the natives on the west coast earlier that day. 'Ågård, place Able Seaman Molineaux under arrest for mutiny. I'll decide what's to be done with him when I get back.'

'If you get back,' said Strachan.

Uncertainly, Ågård took a step towards Molineaux. 'Sorry, Wes . . .'

Molineaux turned the rifle on him. 'Stay back, Ollie. I'm serious.'

It was Cavan of all people who broke the standoff. 'All right, Ågård, stand down. If you're going to arrest anyone, arrest Mr Killigrew.'

'You don't have the authority, Mr Cavan,' warned the lieutenant.

'As the second-ranking executive officer present I do, sir, if the senior medical officer rules you unfit for command by reason of insanity. What do you say, Mr Strachan?'

'Hmm?' Apparently it was news to Strachan that he was the senior medical officer present. 'Oh, yes. Mad as a March hare.'

'Are you going to put that in writing, Strachan?' Killigrew asked softly.

'I'm sorry, sir. If it was up to me neither you nor Molineaux here would go anywhere near Judgement Point tonight. But I can see I'm going to have no more luck persuading him to stay than I am you. At least if you both go, there's a chance one of you might live long enough to tell us what happened to the other.'

Molineaux shouldered his rifle. 'We're wasting time, sir.' He pushed past the lieutenant and stepped outside.

'Damn it!' said Killigrew. 'You're supposed to obey superior officers, Mr Cavan!'

'You can court-martial me when I get to Judgement Point with the *Vanguard*, sir. Good luck.'

The first ten miles were the worst. Sharky led the way, setting a punishing pace; he had to stop every few hundred yards and wait for Killigrew and Molineaux to catch up. The path led inland, around the south and western slopes of Mount Yasur, which rumbled ominously above them. To the north-west of the volcano was a barren plain covered in ash where nothing grew: in the orange glow of the volcano, the plain looked eerie.

They hurried across the shore of a lake, and then they were moving along a trail through thick jungle. As he struggled to keep pace with Sharky, Killigrew's one consolation was that at least the nights were temperate on Tanna; he was soon dripping with sweat from the exertion, and had the climate been more sultry the humid air might have overcome his European constitution.

Sharky seemed to have no difficulty following the trail, such as it was, and when Killigrew lost sight of his pale figure flitting through the darkness he could usually be counted on to be waiting for them up ahead. The path grew steeper, emerging from the trees and twisting and turning its way up the side of a high ridge as they entered the mountains of the central range. It was hard going, and a couple of miles further on Killigrew had to stop and clutch at a stitch in his side.

'It's all them cheroots you smoke, sir,' said Molineaux, who had lost none of his bounce. Even as he waited for Killigrew to get his wind back, the seaman ran on the spot, as if to taunt him. 'They take the wind from a man's lungs.'

Killigrew looked the seaman up and down. 'Damn your eyes, Molineaux! Don't you ever break into a sweat?'

'Not me, sir. "Cowcumber Henson" they used to call me back in London.'

'Why did they call you that?'

'Partly on account of how I never sweat, no matter how hot things get.'

'Partly?'

Molineaux grinned. 'You don't want to know the other reason, sir.'

'I think I can guess. But what I wanted to know is why they called you "Henson"?'

'That's my mum's maiden name, sir. After my dad walked out on us for the last time, she changed her name back. We all did – didn't want to be associated with that sonuvabitch any longer. Then, when I was on the run and I signed on board HMS *Powerful*, well . . . I couldn't give them my real tally with the peelers after me, could I? Molineaux was the first tally that popped into my noggin.'

'You never told me what it was you were on the run for.'

'Stealing, sir. Same as some of those coves we've been chasing ever since Norfolk Island,' he added significantly.

'You've no need to feel guilty, Molineaux. Whatever you stole, I think you can say you've redeemed yourself by now, after the work you did on the Guinea Coast and in China.'

'Maybe,' Molineaux said dubiously. 'What about Sol . . . about Wyatt and them other coves? Do they get a chance to redeem themselves?'

'They've had their second chance. That's why they were transported to the Australias. But they proved themselves incorrigible; that's why they were sent to Norfolk Island.'

'Easy for a cove like you to condemn them, sir. You don't know the full story. There might be mitigating circumstances.'

'It's not my job to condemn them. That's up to the courts. Our job is to take them back to Norfolk Island.'

'Dead or alive?'

'That's entirely up to them.' Seeing Sharky gesture impatiently and, mindful that time was running out, Killigrew started running again – a shambolic, stumbling run, but it covered the ground. At length the terrain levelled out as they hurried through a pass between two peaks. At one point they ran through a patch of yam vines and Killigrew tripped and fell flat on his face.

Molineaux helped him up. 'You oh-kay, sir?'

'I'm fine.' Killigrew dusted himself off with stinging palms, feeling foolish. 'Come on, let's keep moving.'

Killigrew paused and peered at his fob watch in the faint moonlight. 'What time is it, sir?' gasped Molineaux; even he had the decency to be out of breath by now.

A cloud moved across the face of the moon, and Killigrew had to light a match to see the watch face. 'Just coming up to ten. How much further, Sharky?'

The *nakaimo* pointed off into the darkness. 'Judgement Point – four mile.'

'Only four miles!' exclaimed Killigrew. The thought gave him renewed strength. 'Come on, we're almost there!' He broke into a sprint, but before he had taken a couple of paces Sharky had caught him by the collar and hoiked him back. Killigrew sprawled on his back. 'What the devil—'

Sharky picked up a rock. Killigrew thought he was going to hit him with it, but the *nakaimo* stretched out his arm and let go of it. A second or two passed before the sound of it hitting the ground a hundred feet or so below carried back to them.

'Jesus!' Killigrew felt cold when he realised how close he had come to stepping over the precipice in the darkness.

'Four mile as bird fly. We walk . . .' He gestured off to their right. 'Nine, maybe ten mile.'

'Ten miles!' groaned Molineaux. 'We'll never make it. Not in two hours.'

'Is there no quicker route down?' Killigrew asked Sharky urgently.

The *nakaimo* grinned. '*Ale!* You step out – you get down too much quick. Then just little bit walkem, flat ground all way. But you no walkem again.'

Molineaux crawled to the lip of the precipice and peered down. 'What do you think, Molineaux?' asked Killigrew. 'Can we climb down?'

'Not in this light, sir. Looks like a sheer drop to me. I dunno – maybe I could make it in the daytime. But it could take longer climbing than walking. We could get halfway down and run out of handholds, find we've come to a dead end and then have to climb back up and start all over again. Now, if we had some rope, it would be a different matter . . .'

Killigrew snapped his fingers. 'What about those vines we passed a couple of hundred yards back?'

Molineaux grinned. 'Now, they might just do the trick.'

The three of them hurried back to where they had seen the vines. Molineaux pulled up a length, cutting it with the Bowie knife he carried in a sheath in the small of his back, and measured it in his outstretched arms. 'Twelve fathoms. Not long enough.'

'So we'll pull up another and tie them together.'

Molineaux ripped up the second largest vine he could find. When he measured it between his arms it was only half as long as the first, but in combination they would be long enough. He tied them together and tugged on the knot to make sure it would hold.

The two vines came apart.

'Damn it, Molineaux!' exclaimed Killigrew. 'What kind of a snowball hitch was that? Do it properly. Our lives are going to depend on that rope.'

Scowling, the seaman tried again.

'Rabbit goes into the hole, round the tree . . .' Killigrew reminded him helpfully.

'Hey, I do know how to tie a knot, sir.' Molineaux pulled the knot tight, and then tested the rope again. Again it came apart.

'You're supposed to be an able seaman, damn your eyes!' snapped Killigrew. 'Here, give them to me. Little rabbit goes into the hole, round the back of the tree, across the boughs, round the back of the tree again, and back out through the hole, *thus*.' He pulled on the vines, and his own knot came asunder.

'See?' Molineaux demanded truculently. 'There's no way them vines are going to hold. They keep bloody stretching!'

Killigrew took the longer of the two vines and pulled on it with all his might. The length between his fists stretched to half its length again, without coming close to snapping. 'That's it!' he exclaimed.

'What is?'

'How we can get down the cliff quickly.' He started coiling up the seventy-foot length of vine. 'Come on, back to the cliff.'

'Sir, I ain't got a notion what you're talking about.' Molineaux followed Killigrew back to the precipice. The lieutenant tore a few pages out of his pocket book, wrapped them round a small stone, then set fire to them with a match and dropped the burning paper over the cliff. The three of them watched the flame plummet into the darkness before it hit the ground far below.

'How far, would you say?'

'About a hundred feet. That leaves us thirty feet short – prob'ly nearer forty once we've tied the end of the vine to that rock there. And we know the knot will come apart as soon as we put any weight on the rope.'

Killigrew shook his head. 'We'll tie it in a double Cornish bowline hitch – that should hold long enough for my purposes.'

'Long enough for us to climb all the way down?'

'The knot won't come apart until the full weight of my body is on it,' explained Killigrew. 'All I have to do is make sure that the full weight of my body doesn't come to bear until I'm at the end of the rope.'

'And how the hell are you going to do that?'

'By tying the rope around my chest and jumping off the cliff.'

'*What?*'

'It's a trick the natives on Pentecost Island use in one of their ceremonies.' Killigrew secured one end of the vine to the rock as he spoke. 'When there's no more slack, the rope will start to stretch, slowing my descent. I should come to a halt before the knot starts to come apart – if I tie an ordinary knot around my chest, that will come apart first. If I use ten fathoms of vine, that should stretch to about fifteen fathoms. I'll be motionless when the knot comes apart, and only have ten feet to drop.'

'You're crazy, sir,' said Molineaux.

'I'm not asking you to do it. When I get to the bottom, I'll strike a match to let you know I'm all right. You can go down the long way and meet me at Judgement Point as soon as you can.'

'What if you've miscalculated? What if the knot comes apart before the vine stretches to the full extent? What if it stretches too much before it's slowed your fall enough? What if you hit a tree or a spur of rock or something on the way down? You'll be killed for sure!'

'Maybe,' admitted Killigrew, and grinned in the darkness as he knotted the vine around his chest. 'But what a way to go, eh!'

Before Molineaux could protest further, he stepped backwards off the cliff and plummeted into the darkness.

XVIII

Midnight At Judgement Point

As Killigrew fell, a feeling of peace descended over him. He had tied the vine as swiftly as caution would allow, and jumped off the precipice without thinking about it because he knew that if he stopped to think he would never have the courage to do it. He could not see the cliff face rushing past beside him, but he was aware of it: six feet away or an inch, he had no way of telling. The wind rushing past him gave him a curious sense of exhilaration, and for the first time in fifteen months it felt good to be alive; in fact, he felt more alive than he had ever felt before in his life.

Except that somewhere far below him the unforgiving ground was rushing up to meet him.

A sense of panic seized him – to die just when he had regained the pleasure of living would be too ironic – but it was only fleeting. Either this was going to work, or it was not. There was nothing he could do about it, except relax and enjoy the ride.

The vine grew taut above him. He braced himself for the sudden jerk, but it never came: the creeper just stretched and stretched, slowing him to a gentle halt . . .

And then the knot against his chest came apart.

He was falling again, dropping into the unknown, but it lasted less than a second: then he hit the ground, his knees slightly bent to absorb the shock, and rolled over.

The ground was not flat, however, but sloping, and he fell head over heels and rolled down the scree-strewn gradient in a small avalanche, carried down on a bed of tiny, rolling pebbles. At last he slid to a halt, winded, dazed, covered in bruises and scratches, and feeling elated.

He was alive!

He lay there for several seconds, simply revelling in the joy of being alive as a man waking up in bed on a cold and frosty morning might revel in a lie-in. Then, remembering why he had taken such an insane risk, he picked himself up and dusted himself down. There was work to be done.

The moon had come out from behind its cloud and he could see the landscape before him silhouetted vaguely in the darkness against the purple night sky. The terrain before him seemed to slope away gently, and in the distance he could hear breakers somewhere off to his left. Taking out a pocket compass, he struck a match to signal Molineaux and Sharky on the cliff top that he was all right, and then used the light to get his bearings. If he struck out north-west until he reached the coast, and then followed it north, sooner or later he must get to Judgement Point.

He heard a noise high above him: half whoop of exultation, half scream of terror. The cry grew louder and louder, and then stopped with a gasp, followed a split second later by a thud and a grunt. Then there was a rustling sound, pebbles bounced in all directions around him, and a moment later Molineaux pitched up a couple of feet from where he stood.

'Glad you could join me,' Killigrew told the seaman cheerfully. 'Capital lark, isn't it? We'll have to try that again some time, when this is all over. In daylight, perhaps.'

Molineaux glowered up at him. 'No thanks, sir. It was bad enough when I couldn't see what I was doing.'

'You know, the natives of Pentecost Island do it with the vine tied to their ankles. Now that must really be a lark – plummeting headfirst, down and down, watching the ground rushing up towards you . . .'

'You're nuts, sir.'

'Come on.' Killigrew checked he had not lost his cutlass or his pepperboxes in the fall. 'Got your rifle and your knife? Good man. Let's look lively.'

They set off walking, wading through shoulder-high elephant grass. 'What time is it, sir?'

Killigrew checked his watch. 'Twenty past ten. No need to run. We should make it with the best part of an hour to spare, thanks to my short cut.'

'And then what?'

'Let's take a look at the lie of the land before we decide that.'

But Killigrew could not help thinking that getting there early might just work in their favour. Quested had timed it perfectly, or so he had thought. Until then he had been one step ahead of Killigrew all the way. He had known roughly what time the *Vanguard* would get back to Port Resolution. By choosing midnight as the time for Killigrew to meet him at Judgement Point he had known the lieutenant would barely have time to get there on foot. He was expecting Killigrew to turn up there alone and out of breath at midnight. But if Killigrew arrived with Molineaux, both of them in fighting trim, at a quarter past eleven . . . it would give him the chance to turn the tables on Quested.

They reached the sea, where the surf washed gently against the black sand in the moonlight, and followed it north. As they reached the next headland, Molineaux suddenly grabbed Killigrew by the shoulder and pulled him back. 'Wait, sir. There: d'you see her? A ship.' He pointed off the coast ahead of him.

Killigrew could not see a thing in the darkness. 'Damn it, Molineaux, you must have eyes like a bat.'

'Her lights are out, but she's there right enough: just beyond that next headland, half a mile away.' He unslung the rifle. 'Come on.'

Killigrew unhooked one of his pepperboxes from his belt and the two of them crept forward more cautiously, sticking to the shadows at the back of the beach. As they neared the headland Molineaux lost sight of the ship, but once they started to crest the rise in the ground above even Killigrew could make it out: the *Lucy Ann*.

The two of them ducked down, and the lieutenant took a miniature telescope from his pocket to survey the scene. A harpoon had been thrust into the sand atop a dune about two hundred yards away, and a lantern hung from the top of its wooden shaft. Three men stood in the circle of light below it, and Killigrew recognised one of them as Quested by his hook-handed silhouette. A boat had been drawn up on the beach behind them, and two more men, both armed with muskets, stood on guard over it.

'How many can you see, sir?' whispered Molineaux.

'Five.'

'There'll be more,' the seaman assured him. 'Someone hidden in the long grass with a rifle, waiting to put a bullet in your head the moment you step into view.'

'No sign of Mrs Cafferty. I suppose she's still on board the *Lucy Ann*.'

'If she's still alive.' Killigrew looked at him. The seaman shrugged. 'Got to face the facts, sir. Quested doesn't need her any more. You think he's the sort of cove who'd keep her alive when he don't need her?'

'Either way, Moltata and his people still need to be rescued.'

Molineaux glanced behind them. 'Still no sign of the *Vanguard*.'

Killigrew checked his watch. 'It's only a quarter past eleven. We can't expect Mr Cavan with the *Vanguard* for another three hours. Until then, it's just you and I.'

'Against maybe three dozen of them.'

'That's only eighteen each.'

'Easy as caz,' Molineaux commented ruefully. 'Got any ideas, sir?'

Killigrew nodded. 'Quested isn't expecting me for another

249

three-quarters of an hour. That gives me all the time in the world to swim out to the *Lucy Ann*, find out if Mrs Cafferty's on board, and free Moltata and his people.'

'And then what? Instigate a slave revolt and take over the ship?' Molineaux asked sardonically.

'That might work in one of M'sieur Dumas' novels, Molineaux; I'm going to have a hard enough time as it is getting our friends off the *Lucy Ann* alive. Arresting Cusack and Quested will have to wait for another day, if it happens at all. Our first priority has to be to protect the innocent.'

'Now you're talking sense. What do you want me to do? Come with you?'

Killigrew shook his head. 'You can do more good ashore. Try not to precipitate things: the longer we can keep them here, the better. Until midnight they'll be content to wait; after that they're going to start getting restless. As soon as they head back to the boat, start shooting: try to keep them pinned down. No heroics: keep your head down, hoist in?'

'That's rich, coming from you, sir!'

'I get paid more than you, Molineaux. Taking risks is my job. They'll be able to pinpoint you from your muzzle-flashes, so keep moving. And if you get the chance to kill any of those bastards . . . don't waste it. I've a feeling that if we don't get them tonight, we never shall.'

'How will I know when you're safely off the ship?'

'Because I'll set her on fire before I jump over the side. That should stop the bastards from trying to sail away.' Killigrew unhooked his pepperboxes from his belt and handed them to Molineaux. 'You'd better take these: there's no way I can take them on board without getting the powder soaked.'

'Good luck, sir.'

'You too.'

Killigrew nodded curtly, crawled across the beach and dragged himself out through the surf before striking out for the *Lucy Ann*.

Molineaux watched Killigrew swim out into the darkness before turning back to where Quested and his men waited on one of the dunes. Holding his rifle before him, he squirmed on his belly through the sand, trying to work his way through the dunes until he was to the north of Quested and the others, the one direction they would not expect anyone to come from.

He moved silently, a shadow amongst the shadows. When it came to creeping around in the dark, no one had been more at home than Cowcumber Henson moving silently through the rooms of a town house in London while the owners and servants slept. Every so often, he would pause and become one with the shadows, listening intently. Patience was the real virtue that lent a man stealth: the patience to outwait the peelers lurking to trap you. Sooner or later one of them gave himself away with a sniff of a nose made runny by the damp London air. *When that happens*, Foxy had always taught him, *get out. Don't stop to prig the gob-sticks from the dresser; just mizzle and don't look back over your shoulder. There's many a dab snakesman that got lagged because he got greedy. Know when to walk away from a job: you mayn't die a blunted cove, but at least you'll die a free one.*

But this was one job Molineaux could not walk away from, not now that Killigrew had swum out to the *Lucy Ann*.

It was his nose rather than his eyes and ears that saved him, however: a whiff of tobacco carried on the breeze, when he knew that neither Quested nor the two men with him had been smoking. He glanced upwind, and saw the glow of a pipe amongst the reeds to his right, overlooking the patch of exposed ground he had been about to crawl across. Molineaux changed direction, crawling around to approach the man from behind.

The man lay on his stomach amongst the reeds, a musket cradled to his shoulder, a clay pipe stuck in one corner of his mouth. Clearly he had never been duck hunting: a man stupid enough to smoke when lying in ambush did not deserve a chance, and Molineaux did not give him one. The man never knew what hit him. Molineaux was all over him in the blink of an eye, his left hand clamping over the man's mouth as his right drove the blade of his Bowie knife between his ribs in search of his heart. The man gave a single spasm, and was still.

Molineaux lay motionless on top of the man's corpse, listening to make sure the scuffle had not been overheard. The only sound that had been made was the man's toecaps scraping against the sand, and even that had only been momentary, but Molineaux lay still nonetheless, in case someone more skilled at ambushes was nearby, waiting for him to make a move. Five minutes, ten minutes, Molineaux had the patience of a spider.

Nothing. At last Molineaux took the man's musket and slung it from one shoulder, and retrieved the rifle he had left at the foot of the dune, carrying it so it was ready and it would not knock against the musket, giving away his position. He crawled around the back of a couple of dunes, climbed to the top of the furthest and peered through the reeds on the crest to where Quested and the two men waited beneath the lantern. Now he was in position, there was nothing to do but wait until midnight. He had no watch, which was just as well: a man waiting with a watch was forever looking at it, making the time pass more slowly; but he did not need one. He would know when it was midnight, because all hell was going to break loose.

The water was perfect: a gentle chop stirred up the sea into waves which slopped against the *Lucy Ann*'s hull, the sound masking any noise Killigrew might have made, but not too choppy to prevent him from employing a strong, silent breaststroke to take him out to the whaler. He duck-tailed beneath the water, swam under the keel and surfaced on the far side of the hull, in the shadows of one of the boats suspended over the side.

Treading water, he glanced up and saw a man on sentry-go at the starboard entry port a few feet above him, armed with a musket. Slow, steady footsteps sounded on the deck as another man, presumably also on watch, paced back and forth. At least two guards, then: he had been hoping against it, but expecting it nonetheless. It was no good climbing the anchor chain and hauling himself up on to the head: he needed to get to the accommodation aft, but he could not sneak down the fore hatch and through the forecastle: that would be crowded with men, and on a night like this he did not imagine many of them would be sleeping. Nor could he cross the deck with at least two men on guard: there was no way of dealing with one without giving the other a chance to raise the alarm.

He swam around to the stern and studied the rudder, looking for a way up. There was a gap between the mainpiece and the sternpost where the rudder was hinged, wide enough for him to get his fingers through. He gripped the mainpiece and braced his feet against the planks of the sternpost, on either side of the rudder. Then, pulling back against the mainpiece with his hands and pressing the soles of his feet against the sternpost, he edged up, hand over hand, until he could hang from the rudder hole. There was an overhang immediately above him. He groped for a handhold, found one, and swung himself out. He dangled by one arm, then reached up with the other and hauled himself up until he was peering through the stern window. The great cabin behind the window was dark, but one of the windows was ajar. He managed to pull it open, hauled himself through and sprawled on the seat on the other side.

'Good evening,' an urbane voice said in the darkness.

Killigrew froze as someone struck a match. The flame was applied to the wick of an oil-lamp, and the guttering flame illuminated the great cabin to reveal Jarrett standing over the lamp while one of the other incorrigibles stood with his back to the door, thrusting each of his fingers into his mouth in turn as if sucking grease from them. Jarrett picked up a pistol and levelled it at Killigrew's chest.

252

'Silas Jarrett,' said Killigrew.

'Call me Speeler,' Jarrett said jocularly. 'Come to drag us back to Norfolk Island in chains, have you? Sorry to disappoint you, Lieutenant.' He chuckled. 'You're pathetic, do you know that? Trying to sneak on board this ship, rescue the damsel in distress and save the day. You're so predictable. Did you think Captain Quested wouldn't anticipate you might get here a few minutes early and swim out to the ship while he was waiting on the point?'

Killigrew shrugged. 'Hope springs eternal.'

'Put your hands up.'

Killigrew raised his hands as high as the low deck head would allow. His knuckles brushed a metal catch, but he was careful enough not to glance up and draw Jarrett's attention to it. He was familiar enough with that kind of catch, designed to hold in place the partition that folded up against the deck head when not in use.

'Get his cutlass, Fingers. And make sure he isn't carrying any other weapons.'

Vickers crossed the deck and dragged the cutlass from its scabbard, laying it out of Killigrew's reach before turning back to check Killigrew's pockets.

'Check his sleeves,' ordered Jarrett.

Vickers pulled down Killigrew's arms, one after the other, and pushed his sleeves back to make sure the lieutenant had no knives strapped to his forearms.

'And the small of his back.'

Vickers moved around behind Killigrew and lifted the hem of his pea jacket. 'Nothing.'

'And his ankles.'

'Thorough, ain't he?' remarked Killigrew, surreptitiously unfastening the catch above his head so that the partition was held up only by his raised hands.

Vickers scowled at him, and got down on his knees to pat down the lieutenant's pantaloons. Killigrew kneed him in the face and swung the partition down against Jarrett's head with all his might. The swindler never even got a chance to cry out, let alone squeeze off a shot: he staggered back against the forward bulkhead, cracked his head against the panels, and slumped to the deck.

Killigrew checked that Vickers was equally unconscious – the convict would have an impressive black eye in the morning – before cupping a hand behind the glass flue of the oil-lamp and blowing it out. He crossed to the window and tried to peer out. He could not see where Quested and his men waited on Judgement Point, which meant they could not have seen what had taken place in the cabin. He glanced up and checked that the blinds had been drawn beneath the skylight. Nor were there any sounds to indicate that anyone else on board the whaler was aware that anything was amiss.

He glanced inside the stateroom, pulled one of the sheets off the bunk and cut it into strips with which he tied up and gagged the two unconscious convicts. Then he slotted his cutlass back into its scabbard, picked up Jarrett's pistol and crossed to the door. He listened and, hearing nothing, eased it open a crack to peer out. The corridor beyond, illuminated by an oil-lamp, was deserted. He slipped through the door and closed it softly behind him.

Listening at the first door he came to, he heard a man groaning. Not quite sure what to expect, he opened the door and let the pistol in his hand precede him through. Cusack lay on the bunk, tossing and turning, his face deathly pale. He was neither asleep nor awake, but trapped in a fevered limbo between the two. In any event, he was quite oblivious of Killigrew, and in no condition to present a threat to anyone. Killigrew left him where he was and slipped back out into the corridor; Cusack could wait.

He was about to try the door to the next cabin when he heard ponderous footsteps descending the companion ladder up ahead. He turned, levelling the pistol, and saw the biggest, ugliest man he had ever had the misfortune to clap eyes on The behemoth was followed by its mirror image. They both stopped when they saw him.

'You two *must* be Gog and Magog,' Killigrew said wryly.

The two giants exchanged glances, and then one of them reached into his trouser pocket.

'Hey! Belay that. Whatever you've got in there, bring it out handsomely.'

The twin drew his hand from his pocket and held up a coin for Killigrew to see. Then he flipped it, caught it out of the air and slapped it against the back of one of his massive, hairy paws.

'Heads,' said the other.

They both consulted the coin. The one who had spoken looked delighted. 'I win, Magog,' he told his brother.

'Excuse me?' said Killigrew. 'Do you mind not ignoring me when I'm holding you both at gunpoint—'

Gog advanced on Killigrew. The lieutenant menaced him with the pistol. 'One more step, my bucko . . .'

Gog clapped a massive hand over Killigrew's wrist and forced the pistol aside. Then, with his other hand on the back of Killigrew's neck, he slammed the lieutenant against the bulkhead to his left and twisted his arm up into the small of his back. Even if Killigrew had not had that shoulder dislocated eleven months earlier, it would still have been agonising. He cried out and dropped the pistol. Gog kicked the gun with his heel so that it slithered across the deck and came to rest by his brother's feet. He released the lieutenant, allowing Killigrew to see Magog stoop and pick up the pistol. He tucked it in his belt, and stood with his arms folded.

'Now it's a fair fight,' said Gog.

Squared up to Gog, Killigrew looked him up and down. Even with their knees bent, like a couple of overgrown orang-utans, both twins had to hold their heads at an angle to avoid banging them against the beams on the low deck head. 'You against me?' Killigrew spluttered incredulously. 'That's not my idea of . . . *fair!*' On the last word, he threw his fist at Gog's jaw in a powerhouse right cross. It looked pretty hopeless, but it was worth a try: sometimes the bigger they were, the harder they fell.

Gog's head was snapped round by the blow. He turned his face back to Killigrew with a contemptuous snort.

Killigrew wasted no time in self-recrimination, but at once launched into an all-out attack, the pugilistic set piece he thought of as the Killigrew special: right jab, right jab, left uppercut, right cross and then the *coup de grâce* – that old left hook that came out of nowhere when they were too dazed to see it coming. It almost never failed to floor an opponent.

Almost never.

'Finished?' asked Gog.

'I think so,' Killigrew said with a sinking feeling.

'Good.' Gog reached forward and seized a fistful of Killigrew's shirt in his massive paw. Then, with one arm only, he lifted the lieutenant bodily off his feet and smashed his skull against the deck head above. When he released him, Killigrew staggered on watery legs and had to grab hold of one of the handrails to stop himself from crumpling.

Gog punched him. Before Killigrew lost consciousness, the last thing he was aware of was the door at the far end of the corridor splintering under his weight.

Molineaux guessed there were still thirty minutes until midnight when he saw a lantern being raised to the masthead of the *Lucy Ann*. He was still trying to work out what it could signify when one of the men with Quested saw it too, and pointed it out to the captain. Quested said something which made his companions laugh, and then stuck two fingers in his mouth, blowing a piercing whistle and motioning for someone unseen to join him from out of the dunes.

He's wasting his time, Molineaux thought to himself with a grim smile.

Five men stood up from various positions where they had been concealed amongst the dunes; but if Molineaux had failed to spot them, then at least they too had failed to spot him.

Six men waiting in ambush: Quested had certainly intended to make sure of Killigrew when he arrived. But in that case, why was he leaving now?

Molineaux's heart sank when he realised what the lantern at the *Lucy Ann*'s masthead signalled. And now the *Lucy Ann* was leaving, and the *Vanguard* was not due for another two and a half hours.

Wondering what the hell he should do next, Molineaux remembered Killigrew's orders: *if you get the chance to kill any of those bastards . . . don't waste it.* That was one order the seaman had every intention of obeying.

One of the men converging on the dune where Quested stood was walking straight for the clump of reeds where Molineaux was concealed, oblivious of the seaman's presence. Molineaux waited until the man had almost stepped on him, and then slashed him across the knees with the rifle. The man went down, and Molineaux pushed himself to his feet and smashed the man in the face with the musket.

The other four men heading back to the beach had no idea that their numbers had been reduced by a third. One of the men with Quested pulled the harpoon out of the sand and took down the lantern. Quested had already set out down the far side of the dune and would be hidden from view in a few more seconds.

Molineaux raised the stock of the rifle to his shoulder, took aim, and fired.

It was impossible to say if the other man stepped in the way of the shot before or after Molineaux pulled the trigger; but the effect was the same. The man went down; Quested and his other companion stared at his body for a split second. Molineaux threw aside the rifle and unslung the musket, but by the time he had levelled it Quested had ducked back out of sight.

But the other four men were now staring at him. One of them unslung his own musket. Molineaux swung the barrel of his weapon round and fired, then jumped down behind the dune as the other three sent bullets winging his way. He rolled over on the black sand at the bottom, then picked himself up. He started running, knowing that the three men would come looking for him where they had last seen him. He weaved his way through the dunes, trying to outflank them.

As he rounded one dune, he came face to face with another man less than thirty feet away. The man was in the process of reloading his musket. Molineaux knew this was no time for being chivalrous: the man's two friends were probably not far off. He dropped the empty rifle, and pulled one of Killigrew's pepperboxes from his belt. The handgun had no sights, so all Molineaux could do was point it

256

in his general direction and squeeze off six shots – the double-action was a bugger; Killigrew must have had fingers like bananas to be able to pull the heavy trigger – in the hope that at least one would find its mark. The theory proved sound: the man was thrown on his back and lay still.

'Capital shooting, Summerbee!' he called, in a fair imitation of Lord Hartcliffe's clipped tones, an impersonation that never failed to amuse his shipmates on the lower deck. 'You take your men around to their left, I'll take the rest to their right, and we'll round up the rest of these swine.'

'Very good, sah!' – this in mimicry of the corporal's voice.

'Come on, men!' Hartcliffe again. 'This way!' Molineaux ran around the next dune and collided with another man running in the opposite direction. Both fell back to the sand, but Molineaux recovered first, pulling Killigrew's other pepperbox from his belt and shooting the man twice in the chest.

Quite aside from the benefit of reducing his enemies' ranks by one, this had all the effect Molineaux could possibly have desired. To Quested and the remaining five men on the beach and amongst the dunes, it must have sounded as if there was gunfire all around them.

'Let's vamoose, *amigos, pronto!*' a panicky voice with a Carolina accent yelled off to Molineaux's right. 'The whole goddamned Royal Navy's here!'

'Don't be a half-wit, Forgan,' Quested snapped back from another direction. 'There's one man out there!'

'Oh? Well, your one man's killed Andy and Obed, and I can't find Ike or Eber anywhere! Where's that consarned Utumate gotten himself to?'

'Never mind Utumate!' snapped Quested. 'Find whoever it is that's taking pot shots at us, and kill him!'

Molineaux decided that Quested was getting just a little bit too clever for his own good. There were four shots left in the pepperbox in the seaman's hand; the next one was for the whaling captain.

He was following the sound of Quested's voice when he heard a sound above him and looked up in time to see a muscular figure leap at him from the dune above. Molineaux managed to squeeze off a wild shot, and then the man had crashed into his shoulder and the two of them went down. The gun flew from Molineaux's hand. Before he could even think about retrieving it, the man – a Polynesian, naked but for a pandanus kilt – came at him with a dagger every bit as large and wicked-looking as the Bowie knife in the small of Molineaux's back.

The seaman managed to grab the Polynesian's knife-wrist in one hand and caught his stomach against the soles of his feet. Rolling

257

on his back, he flipped the Polynesian over his head. The Polynesian landed heavily on his back, and Molineaux was astride his chest in an instant, trying to wrest the dagger from his hand.

'You kill Andy,' hissed the Polynesian. 'Him friend of Utumate. Utumate sing out for help, can. But Utumate no sing out for help. You know why?'

'I've a feeling you're going to tell me anyway,' grunted Molineaux, who preferred his brawls without banter.

Utumate threw him off and rolled on top, pushing the point of his dagger down towards Molineaux's chest. 'Utumate want pleasure in kill you for self.'

The seaman managed to push the dagger aside, and butted Utumate on the bridge of the nose. Blood gushed from Utumate's nostrils, and his eyes rolled up in his head. Molineaux pushed him off. 'The pleasure was all mine, covey.'

Almost as dazed by the head-butt as the Polynesian, Molineaux shook his head muzzily to clear it, and then retrieved the pepper-box. He crawled over the next dune and glanced across the beach to where the *Lucy Ann*'s boat was still drawn up beyond the reach of the surf. There was no sign of Quested, or of either of the two men who had been guarding the boat earlier. He cast a glance back over the dunes behind him, but Quested and his men were keeping their heads down now. Only the occasional cry carried back to where Molineaux was, as Quested and Forgan tried to co-ordinate their search for the seaman. Smiling to himself, Molineaux slithered back down the dune on his hands and knees.

Behind him, the hammer of a musket clicked as someone cocked it. 'Don't move a muscle, shipmate. Drop the barker, put your fams above your noggin, and turn around slowly.'

Molineaux complied. 'Hullo, Foxy.'

Solomon Lissak narrowed his eyes. 'I ain't been called Foxy in years . . . Do I know you?'

'You used to. Back in the days when they called me Cowcumber Henson.'

'Cowcu—' Lissak stared. '*Wes?* Wes Henson? Is it you?'

Molineaux grinned. 'It was the last time I looked in a mirror.'

'. . . and you been fighting against seven years' bad luck ever since,' Lissak concluded the old, private joke for him. Then he threw aside his musket and seized Molineaux in an embrace. 'Wes, my boy! I can't believe it. Let me look at you!' He held the seaman at arm's length. 'My, but you've grown. Filled out a bit in the chest and shoulders, I should say. Not much good for climbing through skylights and down chimbleys, though.'

'I don't do that kind of thing any more.'

'What are you doing here?' He took in the pusser's slops Molineaux wore. 'A lagger now, is it?' Then realisation struck him. 'You're one of the seamen from that navy sloop that's been chasing us!' He lunged for the musket he had thrown aside, but Molineaux was younger and faster. Even as Lissak grabbed the musket, the seaman put his foot on the barrel and pinned it to the sand.

Lissak looked up at him pleadingly. 'You wouldn't . . .?'

Molineaux picked up the musket and levelled it at him.

'Wes! You was living in the gutter when I found you! You wouldn't send me back, would you? After all I done for you?'

Molineaux sighed. 'Aw, hellfire! Course not. Go on, you old rascal. Nommus, before my shipmates get here. Whatever happens here tonight, the others won't be staying long. Stay in lavender for a couple of days, then pad the hoof to Port Resolution. A ship's bound to call in there sooner or later. Maybe we'll meet again. In the next life.'

'God bless you, Wes! You're a fine boy!' Lissak took a couple of halting steps away from the beach, and then stopped and turned back. 'It's brown shirt, Wes. I can't!'

'You daft old flat! I'm giving you the cokum to make leg bail, damn it!'

'I can't leave 'em, Wes. Don't you see? If it wasn't for them, I'd still be rotting on the Isle of Mis'ry!'

'What? That bludger Wyatt and his pals? What do you care about them? They're just the kind of coves you always taught me to steer clear of back in the Big Huey.'

'Since when did you start listening to my advice?'

'Just about my whole life.'

'Then you'll remember another piece of wisdom I taught you. You never play booty on your pals. Not ever.'

'I'm not asking you to peach on them, Foxy!' Molineaux protested in exasperation. 'Just get away from here, while you still can.'

'I never played booty on you, Wes. After I got nabbed for the Haymarket job, they kept asking me who my accomplice was. Said they'd give me a reduced sentence too. But I never told.'

'You might as well've done. After I mizzled from that prad-ken where they caught us, the traps were waiting for me at the Rat's Castle, my mum's drum, the gathering where Luther works . . . Someone gave 'em my tally, Foxy.'

'It weren't me, Wes! I swear it!'

'I know it weren't, Foxy. You think we'd be standing here talking if I thought it was you that peached? My money's on Sammy the Swell. Who else d'you think planted that monogrammed sneeze-box in my gropus so the peelers would have something to connect us with the Haymarket job?'

Lissak nodded thoughtfully. 'Sammy the Swell. He was planning to play booty on us from the beginning, weren't he?' He gave a high-pitched, hooting chuckle. 'I had the last laugh on him, though.' Lissak raised a finger to his lips enjoining secrecy, looked about surreptitiously, and winked at Molineaux. 'That bosh I passed to Deadly Nightshade through the window of that cross rattler? It weren't the one we'd prigged.'

Molineaux stared at him in amazement. 'You switched the boshes? You foxy old rascal! Sammy the Swell must've been in a right wax when he realised we'd skinned him.'

'You know what the funny thing is? I never meant to diddle him. I only did it to be on the safe side, just in case he tried to play booty on us.'

'Can't think what made you reckon he might try something like that,' Molineaux said drily.

'You know me, Wes. Fair's fair. Even though he gammoned us about how much that bosh was worth, I'd agreed a price for us to prig it; I was ready to stand by my side of the agreement. He'd've had his tol if he hadn't got greedy and decided not to pay us our fair share . . .'

'Fair share of what?' a voice demanded behind him.

Molineaux whirled in time to see Quested descend the dune behind him with Wyatt, Utumate, and a spouter and an officer – Forgan, Molineaux supposed – from the *Lucy Ann*. Quested had a revolver in his hand, levelled at Molineaux. 'Nice work, Solly,' said Wyatt. 'Keep him talking while the rest of us creep up on him from behind.'

His jaw hanging, Lissak shook his head helplessly. 'You don't understand, Ned. He's an old pal of mine. Used to be my partner.'

'Aye?' snorted Quested. 'Well, Mr Lissak, your old partner just killed five of my best men.'

'Put the musket down, boy,' ordered Forgan.

'I'm twenty-eight,' said the seaman.

Forgan was thrown off guard by the response. 'What?'

'I ain't no boy, mister.'

Forgan looked amused. 'Well, I'll be doggone! A nigger with a bad attitude. You got a lot of sass for a nigger with a gun at his head, boy.'

'The name's Molineaux. *Able Seaman* Wes Molineaux.' He raised the musket to his shoulder, keeping the muzzle in the captain's face. 'And I ain't the only one with a gun at his head, Quested.'

'What are you talking about, Wes?' asked Lissak, confused. 'Don't pay no attention to him, Cap'n. His name's Henson, not Molineaux.'

260

'I reckon I've got time for one shot before you coves croak me,' Molineaux told Forgan. 'I've been trying to make my mind up who gets it: you, Quested or Wyatt. You just made my mind up for me, mister.' He levelled the muzzle at the third mate's forehead.

'Wes?'

'Not now, Foxy.'

'Wes, there's something I think you ought to know . . .'

Ignoring his old mentor, Molineaux pulled the trigger. Forgan flinched. But there was no percussion cap under the hammer.

'What were you trying to tell me, Foxy?' asked Molineaux. 'No, wait: let me guess. The barker ain't loaded?'

'Sorry, Wes.'

Utumate snatched the musket from Molineaux and smashed the stock into his face. A twenty-one-gun salute went off in the seaman's head, but he managed to cling on to consciousness as he crumpled to the sand with blood running from his nostrils.

'Utumate payim you back, black man.'

'That's for what you did to Utumate,' said Quested, levelling his revolver at Molineaux's face. 'And this is for Eber, Ike, Andy, Jeff, and Obed . . .'

Lissak moved between Molineaux and the muzzle. 'If you're going to shoot him, Cap'n Quested, you're going to have to shoot me first.'

'Oh-kay. I got plenty of bullets, Mr Lissak.'

The old lag moved hastily aside, but continued to plead for his protégé. 'Don't you see? He ain't one of them. Oh, he might be togged up like a lagger; but he's one of us at heart. Ain't that right, Wes?'

When Molineaux said nothing, reluctant to confirm or deny the accusation, Lissak turned to Wyatt as if the coiner might give a one-time snakesman a more sympathetic hearing. 'He's a flash cove, Ned! A snakesman! Me and Wes were partners, I tell you. He . . . why, he's Cowcumber Henson, damn it!'

'Cowcumber Henson?' said Wyatt. 'Didn't there used to be a darky snakesman called that in London about ten, fifteen years ago?'

'Guilty as charged,' admitted Molineaux.

'I don't care if his name's Banana Benson,' snarled Quested. 'I'm going to kill this sonuvabitch.'

'Wait a minute, Captain.' Wyatt leaned over Molineaux. 'If you're Cowcumber Henson, you'll know Slack Jack.'

'Nice try, Wyatt. You know as well as I Slack Jack Barrett was cramped years before I was born.'

'Voker romeny?'

Molineaux was still dazed from the blow in the face Utumate had

261

given him; the incongruity of hearing thieves' cant spoken on an island in the South Seas only added to his confusion. But eleven years ago it had been a language he had spoken as fluently as his native English. 'I granny the flash patter dab enough, bit-faker. I'm down as a hammer.'

Wyatt laughed, and pushed aside Quested's revolver. 'He's down, all right. Put the barker away, Captain. We can trust him.'

'Maybe *you* can . . .'

'You don't understand, skipper. That there's Cowcumber Henson, the cleanest snakesman that ever cracked a crib. He's one of us. And I ain't going to stand by and let you burke him.'

'He may have been one of you, Mr Wyatt. But you've only got to take one look at those navy pusser's slops he's wearing to see that now he's one of them.'

Wyatt shook his head. 'Once a prig, always a prig, Captain Quested. Right, Solly? Henson ain't going to cross us.'

Quested sighed, and put away his revolver so he could take out his fob watch and glance at it. 'It's now just coming up to midnight. We can expect the *Vanguard* here within the next two hours, brim to the gunnels with bluejackets looking for a fight. I want the *Lucy Ann* to be as far from here as possible when she arrives, which means I haven't got time to argue. However, since I'm short-handed thanks to this nigger . . . I suppose we could take him along as ballast. But I'm holding you responsible if he tries to cross us, Mr Wyatt.' Quested turned to Utumate. 'And you keep an eye on our newest recruit. If he looks like he's even thinking about ratting on us, kill him. Slow as you like.'

'When Utumate kill enemy, him take long time to die,' the Polynesian said with relish. But Quested was already striding back across the black sand to where the boat waited.

Utumate leaned over Molineaux. 'You fool Wyatt. Maybe you fool Cap'n Quested, too. But you not fool Utumate.'

Molineaux could see that his enmity with Utumate was going to be a problem. He had two choices: either he could try to ingratiate himself with the Polynesian and win his confidence, or he could just accept he had an enemy. For a man like Molineaux, that was no choice at all. 'If you're going to speak English, speak it properly, you skirt-wearing fat-head,' he sneered.

Utumate looked as if he might dash the stock of the musket into Molineaux's face a second time, but Wyatt caught the musket by the barrel and gestured for the Polynesian to follow Quested. Utumate gave Wyatt and Molineaux a glance that suggested that both of them put together were not worth the effort, and turned away.

Wyatt clasped Molineaux by the hand and hauled him to his feet. 'Come on, Wes. Don't mind Utumate. He ain't so bad – for a heathen – once you get to know him.'

They pushed the boat out from the beach and Molineaux climbed aboard, unsure if he had tricked his way into the crew of the *Lucy Ann* or if Lissak and Wyatt had inveigled him into joining them. It felt more like the latter.

XIX

Robbery With Violins

They climbed on to the deck of the *Lucy Ann* and Quested ordered the boat hoisted into the davits before turning to the chief mate. 'Well, Mr Macy? I saw you raise the lantern to the masthead. I take it you have something for me?'

Macy nodded and turned to Doc, the chunky negro cook. 'Tell Gog and Magog to bring him up on deck.'

'Aye, aye, sir.' Doc disappeared down the after hatch.

'All right, heave up the anchor,' Quested told Utumate while they waited.

'Hold your horses,' said Macy. 'What about the others?'

'They won't be joining us, Mr Macy. He killed them.' Quested indicated Molineaux.

'And who's he?'

'Cowcumber Henson,' Quested said with a faint smile. 'The cleanest snakesman that ever cracked a crib, whatever that may mean.'

'And you're going to let him join the crew? Just like that?'

'Maybe. For now. Both Mr Wyatt and Mr Lissak seem to have a high opinion of him.'

'That's hardly a recommendation!'

'No. But the fact he managed to kill five of my best men is. I can use a man like that . . .'

The after hatch opened and one of the biggest, ugliest men Molineaux had ever seen emerged. He turned back, and dragged something out after him. It took Molineaux a moment to recognise the bundle of rags as a human being; even longer to recognise the human being as Killigrew. The lieutenant's lip was swollen and split, his left eye had swollen up so much it had closed entirely, and his cheek was covered in dried blood from a cut over his eye. At first glance, Molineaux could not tell if the lieutenant was dead or alive.

Once Killigrew had been dragged out of the after hatch, a third man followed him up: the spitting image of the first. Molineaux remembered what Richards had said about a gigantic pair of twins. Gog and Magog, presumably named after the two titanic statues outside Guildhall in London.

Quested's conversation with Macy had made it clear to Molineaux that if he was going to live through the next twenty-four hours, he was going to have to convince them his conversion was genuine, and he could see only one way to do it. He glared across to where Killigrew was slumped between the twins.

'You sonuvabitch!' he snarled. 'You lousy, stinking sonuvabitch!' He abruptly charged across the deck and kicked Killigrew savagely in the side; he had to make this look good. 'Boot's on the other foot now, ain't it, you stuck-up bastard. Put me in the lazaretto on six-upon-four, will you? I'll learn you!'

Killigrew managed to raise his head. 'Molineaux?' he croaked.

Molineaux kicked him again, and waited for someone to drag him away, but he had misjudged his audience: they just stood around laughing. He kicked Killigrew again, and again, and finally Quested intervened.

'Oh-kay, that's enough for now, Molineaux . . . Henson . . . whatever the hell your name is. If anyone's going to kill Mr Killigrew there, it's going to be me. But I've got other plans for the lieutenant . . .'

Something whistled across the deck. With a bewildered expression on his face, Macy glanced down and saw the bloodstained head of a spear protruding from his chest. He opened his mouth to say something, but only vomited blood. Then his legs crumpled beneath him. He sank to his knees, and measured his length on the deck, the spear in his back sticking up like a flagpole.

Dripping with water, Sharky had already jumped down from the bulwark. He swung his war club and one of the spouters fell with a crushed skull without even knowing what had hit him. With a wild, savage cry, Sharky ran across the deck to where Quested stood. Another spouter rushed to intercept him, and fell victim to the *nakaimo*'s club. Sharky was only a few feet from Quested, aiming a blow at his head, when the captain managed to draw his revolver and shoot the *nakaimo* in the stomach. Sharky dropped his war club, and staggered.

'You!' gasped Quested.

The *nakaimo* did not seem to hear him. He staggered back against the bulwark, and then managed to pull himself over the side and fell into the water with a splash. Quested ran to the side and emptied the remaining five shots of his revolver into the water.

The rest of the men on deck joined him at the bulwark, peering over at the black waters below. 'Don't just stand there!' snarled

266

Quested. 'Make sure he's dead this time!'

'Reckon you got him, Cap'n,' said one spouter.

Another pointed. 'Look! A shark!'

'Jesus!' Ashen-faced, Quested snatched a musket from one of his men and fired it over the side.

'Easy, Cap'n,' said the third mate. 'Sharks got him.'

'You goddamned half-wit, Gardner!' snarled Quested. 'That's no shark. That was *him*.' He snatched up a harpoon and flung it into the water, but whatever it was that was swimming there – man or shark – it had dived beneath the surface.

Quested was white-faced and trembling. 'Did you see, Forgan? It was *him*.'

'Couldn't've been *him*, Cap'n. You killed him two years ago, remember? Shot him in the chest.'

'Did you see the star-shaped scar on him, here?' Quested tapped his own chest with his hook. 'That's where I shot him two years ago!'

'Coincidence, Cap'n. Albinos are common enough amongst the savages in these islands. And they're always a-cutting of themselves, decorating their bodies with tattoos and cicatrices. It was just a decoration, that's all.'

'That was no tattoo, Mr Forgan! That was a bullet scar! *My* bullet scar!'

'Well, he's dead now,' said the second mate, patting the captain consolingly on the shoulder.

Quested threw off his hand and rounded on him. 'Dead? You damned fool! You can't kill a ghost!' He slumped his shoulders and stalked off towards the after hatch. 'Time's a-wasting, Mr Forgan. Let's get this tub under way.'

'Can't kill a ghost!' the third mate snorted as soon as Quested had gone below decks. 'That was no ghost, and it sure as hell weren't no shark! That was a man, plain and simple. Cap'n's going crazy, if you ask me . . .'

Forgan whirled and seized the third mate by the lapels, slamming him viciously against the bulwark. 'He's still captain of this ship, Mr Gardner,' he snarled, evidently as shaken by what he had just seen as the rest of them. 'Don't you forget it.'

So Quested's frightened of native superstitions, is he? mused Molineaux. He wondered if there was some way he could turn that to his advantage. But the fact that the captain was clearly going insane was worrying: lunatics were unpredictable, and an unpredictable man could be dangerous.

'Oh-kay, let's get this ship under way,' ordered Gardner. 'All hands to the capstan bars! Weigh anchor!'

'Pilcher!' Forgan indicated the bodies of the three men Sharky had slain. 'I want those bodies in shrouds by dawn, and this deck scrubbed clean, d'you hear? We'll give them a decent burial ashore when we get to Thorpetown the day after tomorrow. I don't want them providing vittles for the sharks.'

There was no sign of the *Lucy Ann* by the time the *Vanguard* reached Judgement Point shortly before four bells in the middle watch. Cavan went ashore in the jolly boat with Ågård and three seamen to see if there was any trace that Killigrew and Molineaux had been there. What they found was five corpses.

'Anyone we know?' Strachan asked Cavan when the shore party came back on board the *Vanguard*.

Cavan shook his head. 'They must've been members of the *Lucy Ann*'s crew.'

'Are you certain? They might have been incorrigibles.'

'No, Mr Strachan. I checked their wrists and ankles: no sign of the chafing one would associate with men who've been in irons for the past few years.'

'What about Killigrew and Strachan?'

'I have to assume they're alive, but prisoners on board the *Lucy Ann*.'

'You seem pretty sure of yourself.'

Cavan smiled wanly. 'If they're dead, why aren't their bodies here with the others? If they're still alive, why aren't they waiting for us here?'

'Maybe they couldn't stay here, sir,' suggested Ågård. 'Maybe they was being chased by Quested and his men. Mr Killigrew's hell on wheels when he's got his dander up, and Wes Molineaux's a ringer in a scrap; but even they couldn't beat all of Quested's crew plus the seven incorrigibles.'

'If Killigrew and Molineaux are headed back to Port Resolution with Quested on their trail, then they're on foot. In that case, where's the *Lucy Ann*?'

'Think about it, sir. They must've known the *Vanguard* was coming here. If you were a spouter skipper with escaped convicts and kidnapped natives on your ship, would you wait around for a schooner with two dozen bluejackets and marines on board to turn up? Besides, if Quested's ashore and after Molineaux and the lieutenant, he's got a pretty good notion of where they're headed. What would you do in Quested's shoes?'

Cavan nodded. 'Send the *Lucy Ann* to try to head them off at Port Resolution, or at least to pick him up when he gets there. We didn't pass them on the way here; if the *Lucy Ann* is on her way to Resolution, she's sailing around the northern end of the island. We'll sail after them: with the wind coming from the south-east, we'll get back quicker that way; and there's a chance we might overhaul the *Lucy Ann* on the east coast. She'll be tacking against the wind, and a square-rigged ship like the *Lucy Ann* can't sail as close to the wind as a schooner.'

'And if you're wrong?' asked Strachan. 'If Killigrew and Molineaux are already prisoners on board the *Lucy Ann*? Every minute we waste sailing back to Resolution, they'll be getting further and further away from this island.'

'If that's the case, Mr Strachan, then God help them; for there'll be nothing more we can do for them. We've no notion where they might be bound. If we get back to Resolution and they're not there, we'll just have to sail to Thorpetown and report to the Old Man on board the *Tisiphone*.'

With only eleven men left in the *Lucy Ann*'s crew, everyone was busy on deck, and it was not long before Molineaux had the opportunity to slip down the forward hatch into the forecastle. Apart from Cusack, who was still as sick as a dog in his cabin, the rest of the incorrigibles were topsides, holystoning the deck in an effort to remove the traces of blood from the three men Sharky had killed the previous night. There was no one to challenge Molineaux as he made his way down to the orlop deck.

He helped himself to a lantern, and a couple of needles from the sailmaker's stores, and after glancing left and right he crouched before the lock on the door of the lazaretto. It took him about two minutes to open, a testament to the poor quality of the mechanism as much as it was to Molineaux's skill. He opened the door, slipped inside and closed it behind him.

Killigrew sat on the deck with his back to the bulkhead, with his ankles fettered and his hands manacled behind his back. If anything, his bruises looked even worse than they had done the night before. Molineaux squatted on his haunches to address him. 'You oh-kay, sir?'

'Oh, nothing a glass of Dr James' Powders wouldn't cure.' The lieutenant tried to sound airy, but his rasping voice belied him. Still, at least he had the strength to make light of his injuries. 'Did you have to kick me quite so forcefully?'

'Sorry, sir. Had to make it look good, to convince Quested.'

'Convince Quested! You had *me* convinced; until you started going on about me having you thrown in the lazaretto on six-upon-four. Where are we?'

'You tell me, sir. It's coming up to seven bells, and according to the log board we've averaged four and a half knots since we sailed from Judgement Point.'

'What heading?'

'North by north-west.'

Killigrew frowned. 'You're quite certain? The only islands in that direction are Erromanga and Éfaté. I can't see why Quested should want to head for either of those.'

'I can, sir. I've just been speaking to the cook. Lucky for us he's got a big mouth. Guess who owns this ship.'

'Not . . . Thorpe?'

'Got it in one. It was Quested who was behind the kidnappings two years ago and Thorpe took his cut of the profits.'

'That explains how Quested knew where to find me.'

'That's not all I found out. Foxy told me one of the incorrigibles is already dead.'

'Which one?'

'Swaddy Blake. He fell asleep when he was supposed to be on look-out, and Wyatt lost his temper with him.'

'That's one less to worry about, at any rate.'

'And Mrs Cafferty ain't on board this ship any more. She's on board the *Wanderer*.'

'At least she's still alive, then.' The relief was evident on Killigrew's face. 'If we can rescue her, she can prove there's a connection between Thorpe and Quested.'

'Not necessarily, sir. Apparently she escaped from the *Lucy Ann* as it was passing the Isle of Pines and made her own way to where the *Wanderer* was moored at the Bay of Crabs. It could be she's a prisoner and she doesn't even know it. Want me to pick the locks on your clinkers, sir?'

'What would be the point?'

'Moltata's chained up in the hold with eleven of his people. We could set them free in a brace of shakes. There's only eleven men left in Quested's crew, including the cook, who we might just be able to rely on to stay neutral at the very least. As for the convicts, well – Cusack's sick in bed . . .'

'I know. I saw him last night.'

'I think they slipped him something so he wouldn't see the captives being brought on board yesterday. So I don't think we need to worry about him. Then there's Foxy – Solly Lissak, I mean. He ain't a violent man, sir. If there's a scrap, he'll have sense enough to keep well out of it.'

'Yes, I noticed you seemed pretty thick with him when you came on board last night.' Even with one eye closed by massive bruising, the lieutenant did not miss much. 'I don't suppose you'd care to tell me what your relationship with him is, would you?'

'Some other time, maybe, sir. So do the sums: the way I see it, at worst it comes to fourteen of us – the natives they kidnapped from

Tanna are all big, strong lads; I think we can depend on them in a scrap – against sixteen of them.'

'Mental arithmetic isn't my forte, Molineaux. If we can discount the cook and Mr Lissak, perhaps you'd be so good as to explain how you make it sixteen rather than fourteen?'

'I'm counting Gog and Magog as two each.'

Killigrew thought about it. 'Better make it three each,' he decided.

'Oh-kay, eighteen of them. Fourteen of us against eighteen of them: I'm game if you are, sir.'

'Isn't there something you're forgetting?'

'Sir?' Molineaux thought for a moment, and nodded. 'Even if we do overpower the others, there's no way we can sail this tub to Thorpetown without their help.'

'And why bother, when that must be where Quested's taking us anyhow?'

Molineaux grinned. 'Right to where the *Tisiphone*'s waiting for him!'

Killigrew returned his grin, but his smile was quickly replaced by a frown. 'That can't be it, Molineaux. We're missing something here.'

'Sir?'

'If Thorpe told Quested we were at Port Resolution, surely he would also have mentioned that the *Tisiphone* would be at Thorpetown for the next couple of weeks.'

The seaman swore. 'I didn't think of that, sir.'

'I don't know, Molineaux. There's something about this whole business that doesn't make sense. Either Thorpe and Quested are being very, very clever or very, very stupid. The way they've handled things so far would seem to indicate the former. You'd better leave me here for now: as long as one of us is loose, we've got a chance. Have a nose around, see if you can learn anything more. If we're bound for Thorpetown, we won't get there until some time tomorrow morning. We can decide what we're going to do then. In the meantime, you'd better get back on deck before you become noticeable by your absence.'

'Aye, aye, sir.' Molineaux straightened and stepped out of the lazaretto.

To find Utumate waiting for him with Gog and Magog.

'Utumate know not trust you.'

'You don't understand,' said Molineaux. 'I was just . . . er . . .'

'Hit him,' ordered Utumate.

Magog hit him.

'Proper botched things up, ain't I, sir?' Molineaux remarked ruefully, studying his irons. With his picks, he could have sprung the padlocks in seconds; but Lissak had made sure he did not have his picks. Like Killigrew, Molineaux too now sported one eye that was half-closed with swelling.

'If it's any consolation, we both did.' Killigrew had made himself as comfortable as his irons and the hard deck would allow. As a further precaution, Quested had had them both brought up from the lazaretto and was keeping them in irons in the lee waist, where he and his men could keep an eye on them while they worked the sails.

The incorrigibles had finished holystoning the deck – there was still a ghost of a bloodstain where Macy had died, but no amount of holystoning was going to get that out – and Lissak was free to do as he pleased, until the end of the forenoon watch. He stood over the two prisoners and regarded Molineaux with a mixture of disappointment and contempt.

'Eleven years, Wes,' he said bitterly.

'I'm sorry, Foxy. I wanted to break you out of that prison hulk in Gallions' Reach before you got lagged, but with the peelers after me—'

'I ain't talking about the eleven years I spent in the colonies, Wes. I'm talking about the eleven years you were my apprentice. I looked after you, I taught you everything I knew . . . I raised you like you was my own son! And this is how you repay me. You betrayed your own kind!'

'They ain't my kind, Foxy. Not any more.'

'And who is, now?' Lissak pointed at Killigrew. 'Gentry coves like him? Coves what makes you eat filth and crams you into a cramped fo'c'sle while he swells it up in the wardroom with his gentry vittles and flunkeys to pander to his ev'ry whim; and then expects you to risk your neck for queen and country, while they keep their heads down? All for one pound and fourteen shillings a month?'

Molineaux shrugged. 'There's worse ways of making a living than being a seaman, Foxy. The money may not pay as well as prigging; but it's regular, I get respect from coves, and I get to see a damned sight more of the world than I would've done if I'd stayed in the Holy Land.'

'You used to get respect from coves when you was a prig.'

'Respectable folk, I mean.'

'Prime flats,' snorted Lissak.

'Folks like my family. I may not see them as often as I used to, but at least now they're pleased to see me, instead of ashamed.'

'The Wes Henson I used to know would never have said a thing like that.'

'Yur, well . . . coves change, Foxy.'

272

'Not you, Wes. Once a prig, always a prig.' Molineaux looked inclined to protest, but Lissak continued, cutting him off. 'Family! You of all people should know better than to talk to me about family. Wasn't *I* your family, after your guv'nor left you and your family to starve? Wasn't it me that taught you how to put bread on your mother's table?'

'My mum wouldn't touch a penny of the money we made together, Foxy. You know that. She said it was dirty money. How do you think that made me feel? My own mum, ashamed of me?'

'And what about loyalty?'

'Loyalty? The kind of loyalty we got from Sammy the Swell, you mean? Jesus, Foxy! Didn't that business with the bosh teach you anything? Eleven years a lag in the colonies, I'd've thought even you could have worked it out by now.'

'I accepted my sentence. Didn't I always teach you: if you can't do the lag, don't take the swag? And didn't I also teach you never to trust anyone?'

'The only reason you could never trust anyone was because you never chose the kind of pals you *could* trust. Well, I had enough of that, Foxy. I had time to do some thinking when I was cook's mate on board the *Powerful*. If not being able to trust anyone is the price you pay for being the toast of the swell mob, I'd rather be a poor but honest seaman. Because that way when I'm hard up in a clinch, at least I've got shipmates I can trust to see me through.'

Lissak gave one of his high-pitched, hooting chuckles. 'Hark at you, Mr Virtuous! Having pals you can trust has done you a lot of good, ain't it?' He turned abruptly on his heel and walked away to join the other convicts on the forecastle.

'Incorrigible,' said Killigrew.

'Stow it, sir,' Molineaux replied angrily. 'You ain't got no right to judge him. What do you know about him? You know what he was lagged for?'

'Grand larceny, according to his file. Something about goods valued at five hundred guineas, I seem to recall.'

'It was a bosh,' said Molineaux.

'Pardon?'

'A bosh – you know, a fiddle? Sammy the Swell put us up to it. He was the arch-rogue of the Mayfair Crew, until he got cramped at Newgate a couple of years ago. He told us where the bosh could be found and how to get it; Foxy and me done the job; and Sam had a buyer for the bosh.'

'Sounds to me as though this fellow Sammy the Swell had the lighter end of the bargain.'

'Yur, well, it ain't easy to fence a bosh when it's listed in the *Hue and Cry* as prigged. This was a specialist job. We used to do a lot of

273

stuff like that: paintings, rare books, statues even. There's no point stealing stuff like that unless you've got a buyer lined up. But a bosh – that was a new one to me. Still, Sam was offering us a hundred shiners for stealing it. And it was one of the clushest jobs I've ever done: coves was coming and going from that theatre all the time, Foxy and me just dressed ourselves as workmen, walked right in as if we had every right to be in there, and walked out again with the bosh. Money for old rope. Easiest fifty shiners I ever made.'

'Except that you never saw a penny of it.'

Molineaux shook his head. 'Foxy warned me, but I got greedy. I was green and cocky. Thought I could handle Sammy the Swell and the Mayfair Crew, didn't I? For a hundred shiners, I thought it was worth the risk. So I talked Foxy round. Sammy double-crossed us, Foxy got nabbed and I made my lucky by the skin of my teeth. So if anything, should have been me that got lagged, not Foxy.'

'One hundred guineas is not half of five hundred, Molineaux.'

The seaman grinned ruefully. 'Yur, I know that now. First I heard about it was when I read about it in the papers; they were full of it. I mean, I know they always bump these things up for the insurance, but five hundred shiners? For a bosh? Even I was amazed. Turns out it was a *Grande Amati*.'

'A what?'

'A *Grande Amati*. Made by Niccolò Amati – the cove that taught Stradivarius how to make boshes. Apparently they're worth a lot of blunt.'

'How did you get involved with a fellow like Solomon Lissak, anyhow?'

Molineaux shrugged. 'How does anyone get dragged into the swell mob? Things were difficult after my guv'nor walked out. There were four of us – Luther, Calvin, me and Mary, and our mum – with only a job as a laundress to put food on the table.'

'Luther, Calvin, Wesley,' mused Killigrew. 'Your mother: religious, is she?'

Molineaux grinned. 'Does a fish swim? She tried to bring us up to be good, God-fearing Christian children.'

'Where did she go wrong with you?'

'I'll come to that. After my guv'nor walked out, we all had to go out to work. Luther got a job as a pot-boy, Calvin as a flunkey in a grand house in Mayfair, and I became a mudlark, scavenging on the mud flats of the Thames at low tide, looking for copper nails, lumps of coal, anything of value. You'd be amazed what you can turn up – it all adds up. Anyway, one night Mary catches sick. Mum goes to see the apothecary; she can't afford to pay for no medicines, but he's a kindly old soul so he gives her advice for free. Tells her to keep the baby warm. Warm! That was a right cold winter, that was – I'll

274

never forget it. We couldn't keep *ourselves* warm, let alone the baby. The next day I'm out mudlarking with the other lads and I hear some of 'em chaffing about how they're going to go shake a barge for coal that night. That sounded like just the job, so I asked if I could go with them. Oh, I had to put up with the usual chaffing – about how my skin will make me difficult to spot against the coal in the dark – but they agreed.

'What we didn't know was there was a charley on the barge we picked. One minute we're stuffing the coals in our sacks, the next he's shouting and waving his rattle. The others all jumped over- board and swam for it, but I couldn't swim, so the charley nabs me and hands me over to the river police. They puts me in the clink with all these grown-up criminals, reckoning it will scare me out of prigging again.'

'It didn't, of course.'

Molineaux shook his head. 'That's where I met Foxy – Solomon Lissak. He'd been cracking a peter on one of John Company's ships in the Pool, got stopped by the river peelers on his way home. Of course, he'd already passed the swag on to a pal by then, so he gammoned lushy to lull their suspicions and they put him in the clink to sober up. We gets to talking, the next thing I know he's offering me a job. I declined politely; he told me if I changed my mind, I could find him at the Rat's Castle – that's a flash crib in the Holy Land where the swell mob go. Our mum always told us to stay away from that gaff, said they were bad people that went there, and that crime didn't pay. But I used to look at the prigs, pimps and frows that used to come and go from there, and it didn't look like crime wasn't paying for them. Oh, I 'spect a gentry-cove like you could spot 'em as coming from the lower orders straight off, but to us they looked right conish. Heroes round the Holy Land, they were, like Robin Hood. Stealing from the rich to give to the poor.'

'Meaning themselves.'

'There's a precious lot of poor folk in the Holy Land.' Molineaux grinned. 'You've got to start somewhere, ain't you? Anyhow, when I got out of the clink the next morning, I went back to our drum and found out that Mary had died during the night, and me mum gave me a right bashing. Later I grannied that she'd only been worried about me, but at the time I was resentful, you know? I'd only gone prigging to get some coal to keep Mary warm; 'tweren't my fault she'd died during the night.'

'So you went straight to the Rat's Castle?'

Molineaux nodded. 'Foxy introduced me to his pals in the swell mob, gave me a drain of diddle and a smoke of a cigar. I threw up after, but I felt grown up at the time. Foxy and his mates made me feel at home; which was more than I'd ever done at home.'

'Just like Fagin in *Oliver Twist*.'

'Yur. I've heard folks say Mr Dickens based Fagin on Foxy, but if he did then he didn't know Foxy very well. I read that *Oliver Twist*, by the way, and it's a load of old hogwash. I mean, Bill Sikes is s'posed to be a dab cracksman, right? Well, let me tell you that no self-respecting cracksman would take a greenhorn like Oliver to crack a crib, not without knowing whether or not he could trust him.'

'I'll tell Mr Dickens you said that.'

'You know Charlie Dickens?'

'We've met a couple of times, at Baroness Burdett-Coutts' charity balls. Just between the two of us, he's a bit of a pompous ass, but his heart's in the right place. So, Mr Lissak took you in and taught you all the tricks of his trade?'

'Not just thieving, sir. He taught me how to read and write, how to play the guitar, how to romance the ladies. You prob'ly think he was taking advantage of my greenness, getting me to help him crack cribs; but that ain't the way he saw it, and it ain't the way I saw it, either. It still ain't. He was teaching me a trade – a lucrative trade – and that's more'n anyone else was prepared to do. Foxy was more of a father to me than my own guv'nor ever was.

'Foxy and me, we was cracking coves: I'd climb in through a skylight and let him in the back door, he'd crack the peter if there was one. We always planned ahead, got the servants to talk – got them drunk if they was coves, or bedded them if they was dolly-mops – tell us what there was worth prigging, where it was kept, and if there were any nights when the family were going out for the evening and the servants would be given the night off. That way there was never any rough stuff – no one got hurt.'

'Except for the people whose hard-earned property you stole.'

'Hard-earned my eye!' sneered Molineaux. 'Most of the flats whose cribs we cracked was stockbrokers who'd made their pot in commercial speculation, without doing a hard day's work in their lives. No one ever got rich from honest graft: either they were born rich, or cheated it out of other folks. The paupers' graveyards are full of flats who worked hard all their lives.'

'And you had the right to judge them for it? To decide that they had too much money, and some of it should be yours?'

'As much right as any man. Get fly, sir. We make judgements every day of our lives. It's up to our consciences whether they're good judgements or wrong 'uns.'

'Did it ever occur to you to get an honest job?'

'That's easy for you to say, sir. With your blunted admiral of a grandfather and a big crib in Falmouth. You've never wanted for anything in your life.'

'For your information, I've made my own way in life. I haven't asked my grandfather for a penny since I was thirteen. The only money I have is what I earn on a lieutenant's paltry pay.'

'What's that? A hundred and eighty a year? Paltry by your standards, maybe, but there's no shortage of coves in London who dream of earning a fraction of that. And still you left creditors and bill-brokers crowding the dockside when the *Tisiphone* sailed from Portsmouth. But when you're a gentry cove, they call you a bank-rupt and let you go. The rest of us are called debtors and thrown into the stone jug until we can stump up . . . and when we get charged for the privilege of being in the clink, that ain't likely to happen now, is it? Most of us are judged against from the day we're born into this world; but we try to make the best of it anyhow. So don't talk to me about judging my fellow man: he's quick enough to judge me. If you want me to repent the sinful ways of my youth, sir, you can forget about it . . .' He trailed off and looked up.

Following his glance, Killigrew saw Ned Wyatt standing over them.

XX

Martyrs' Island

'And how are you this morning, Dick Champion?' sneered Wyatt. 'The man who was going to hunt me down and arrest me. What were you going to do when you caught me, Lieutenant?'

'My duty.'

'Your duty. And what was that? To drag me back to Norfolk Island in chains? Or just shoot me in the back and say I died resisting arrest? Save the British taxpayer the expense of a trial. Don't worry, I won't hold that against you. Death from a bullet would have been more merciful than going back to Norfolk Island.'

'You broke the law. You have to be punished. It's as simple as that.'

'The law!' spat Wyatt. 'Oh, you bastards in authority are always quick to hide behind that particular petticoat when it suits you. Do you mean to tell me you never cut any legal corners in your pursuit of slavers and pirates? You never need to worry about the law, do you? That uniform you wear makes it all nice and legal, and if you say you kill the men you murder in self-defence, who's going to question the word of an officer and a gentleman? And that gives bastards like you the right to judge me. A great man once said: "He that is without sin among you, let him first cast a stone".'

'Since we seem to be quoting the Bible, isn't there also one about not trying to remove a mote from your brother's eye when you've got a beam in your own?'

'Think you're precious clever, don't you? With your fine clothes and your school education . . .'

'Actually, I had a private tutor.'

Wyatt smiled. 'Ah. Now you're deliberately being provocative, aren't you? Make the other cove angry in the hope he'll make a mistake.' He straightened. 'You want to know something? You've succeeded.' He kicked Killigrew in the head, and stalked back to the quarterdeck.

Devin Cusack emerged from the after hatch. Gone was the deathly sick man of the previous night. Now his cheeks were ruddy, and he looked to be in the prime of health.

'Hullo,' Molineaux murmured under his breath. 'It's Young Ireland!'

Quested and Forgan exchanged glances, and the second mate hurried to intercept the Irishman. 'You oh-kay this morning, *amigo*? You sure you shouldn't still be lying down? You might have a relapse if you push yourself too hard so soon after being taken poorly . . .'

'Never felt better, Mr Forgan,' Cusack replied, gazing about the deck. 'I don't know what—' Then his eyes fell on Killigrew and Molineaux. 'When did they come on board?'

'Last night,' explained Forgan. 'They were on Tanna; tried to stop us from sailing; but fortunately we were able to overpower them.'

'Then why bring them? Why not leave them on Tanna?'

Forgan glanced helplessly towards Quested.

'Thought we could do with a couple of hostages, now that Mrs Cafferty's gone,' the captain explained. 'The *Tisiphone*'s tracked us this far – there's a danger she may catch up with us yet. If we've got her first lieutenant and one of their seamen on board, that might make them think twice about blowing us out of the water.'

Cusack seemed to accept that, and started across the deck to where Killigrew and Molineaux were chained. Forgan caught him by the arm. 'You don't want to speak to them, *amigo*. They'll only rile you up.'

Cusack looked at Forgan, then at the two captives, then at Forgan again. He shrugged off Forgan's arm with deliberation, and moved off. The second mate looked as though he might make another attempt to stop Cusack from talking to the prisoners, but Quested laid his hand on his shoulder and held him back. When Forgan glanced quizzically at the captain, Quested just shook his head and raised his hook to his lips.

Cusack stood over Killigrew and Molineaux. 'So tell me, Admiral. How do you like being a prisoner?'

Killigrew shrugged. 'After being in a Turkish prison and a Chinese gaol, this is the lap of luxury.'

'Too soft for you, is it now?' remarked Cusack. 'Perhaps I should have Quested cut your rations for a few days, let you find out what it's like to go hungry. Maybe then you'll understand why I had to take up arms in the first place.'

'I'm sure you're the expert. I don't suppose there was much food in your family's big town house in Dublin during the famine, not after you'd finished feeding all your servants.'

Cusack bent down, seized him by the jacket and hoisted him to his feet, before slamming him against the bulwark, half-teetering over the sea.

'You filthy English bastard! Don't you dare try to lecture me about Ireland! You weren't there. You didn't see what I saw. You didn't see the heaps of corpses lying in every village, where the dogs and rats gnawed at their bones, because the dead outnumbered the living. You didn't see men like walking skeletons, their skin black with scurvy. You didn't see women going out of their heads with the hunger. You didn't see the children so starved they had not the strength to speak, with the hair falling from their scalps in clumps. You weren't there, you didn't see the dysentery, the typhus fever, the people living like animals: reduced to eating roots, grass, seaweed, twigs. And all the while your bloody British government exported food to England and passed laws to evict the poorest from their land!'

Profoundly aware that Cusack had only to loosen his grip and he would drop into the sea, weighted down with his irons, Killigrew refused to be cowed. 'What happened in Ireland was terrible, Cusack; no one would disagree with that. But it didn't give you the right to take up arms against your sovereign.'

'I didn't take up arms against my sovereign!' snarled Cusack. 'I took up arms against your bloody government; the government that stood by and allowed my people to starve, saying it was an act of God and 'twasn't their duty to interfere with God's will! If that doesn't give me the right to take up arms in rebellion, then what does? If the British government had sent its army into Ireland in force with orders to shoot the peasants at random, would that have given me the right? For that's what they might as well have done; except that a bullet would have given many of them a cleaner death than the famine allowed. How far must a people be pushed before rebellion is justified, Admiral? I looked into the lifeless eyes of dying children in Limerick and Tipperary and saw all the justification I would ever need for a thousand rebellions!'

'Rebellion against tyranny is one thing, Cusack. But trying to coerce a democratically elected government by force of arms is another. That doesn't cure tyranny, Cusack: it creates it.'

The Irishman laughed bitterly. 'Democratically elected, he says! Did I vote for your government? Did you, for that matter? More to the point, did the thousands who died in Ireland?' He hauled Killigrew off the bulwark and threw him roughly back to the deck, before kicking him viciously in the side.

'You can't win, Cusack,' Killigrew hissed through the pain. 'In Ireland, I mean. The British government will never bow to force of arms.'

'Sometimes it's the fights we cannot win that are most in need of fighting—'

'Land ho!' roared Vickers, taking his turn as lookout at the maintop.

'Where away?' demanded Quested.

Vickers pointed, almost dead ahead.

Quested nodded. 'Erromanga.'

'The Martyrs' Island,' said Forgan.

And suddenly Killigrew understood. Part of him cursed himself for not having realised what Quested was up to earlier; and yet at the same time part of him was horrified even to consider that mankind could be capable of conceiving such inhumanity. For a savage to feast on the flesh of his enemies . . . well, that was a crime born of ignorance of the laws of God, and one that the natives of this island might, in time, be cured. But for a white man to exploit that hideous craving for flesh by turning it to his profit . . . for that there could be no forgiveness.

He realised he had one last trump card to play before it was too late. 'For a man who talks about freedom, you keep some damned rum company, Cusack.'

The Irishman had been turning away, but at Killigrew's words he turned back. 'And what's that supposed to mean, pray tell?'

'Blackbirders,' said Killigrew. 'Slavers.'

Cusack laughed. 'Nice try, Admiral. You expect me to believe that? You'd say anything to save your own hide.'

'If you don't believe me, go down to the hold and see for yourself. You'll find a dozen natives from Tanna chained up down there.'

'Shut your mouth!' Forgan strode across the deck and kicked Killigrew in the side of the face.

'Better go below, Mr Cusack,' said Quested.

The Irishman stared at him. 'Is this true, Captain?'

'I'm not a slaver, Mr Cusack. You have my word of honour on it.'

Forgan's foot had only caught Killigrew a glancing blow on the jaw, but that had been painful enough; it felt as though it had been dislocated, but when he tried to talk he found he still could, so it probably felt worse than it was. 'He's right there,' he said thickly, licking blood from his lips. 'I'm doing the captain a gross injustice when I accuse him of slavery. He intends to sell those natives to the Erromangoans, but not as slaves.'

'I said *shut up*.' Forgan was about to kick Killigrew again, but Cusack pushed him away.

'Go on, Admiral.'

'The natives of Tanna and Erromanga have been at war for generations, Cusack. What do you think the Erromangoans intend to do with the Tannese when Quested sells them to them in

282

exchange for sandalwood? The same thing the Erromangoans always do to their enemies when they kill them or capture them. They're cannibals, Cusack.'

The colour drained from Cusack's face. 'Is this true?'

Quested shrugged. 'This is the South Seas, Mr Cusack. It's a different world. You can't apply the same rules of morality here that you do in Europe.'

'You bastard!' hissed Cusack. 'You inhuman, murdering bastard!' He strode across to where Quested stood with murder in his eyes, but Magog caught him before he got there, holding him fast. A big man, Cusack struggled furiously, but Magog did not even break into a sweat. Gog looked at Quested, who nodded once. Gog crossed to where his brother held Cusack, and drove a massive fist into the Irishman's stomach. Magog released Cusack, and he crumpled to the deck, retching.

Quested hunkered down beside the writhing Irishman. 'The only reason I'm not going to have you killed is that you're worth too much money to me, Paddy. I'll fulfil my side of the bargain and take you to California. I still intend to collect on that five thousand dollars when we get to 'Frisco.'

'You twisted fiend!' gasped Cusack. 'I'll see to it you never collect one red cent of that money!'

'Oh, I'll collect, right enough.' Quested straightened, and kicked Cusack savagely in the stomach. 'They'll pay me, because if they don't no one will ever see Devin Cusack again.'

'You're making an enemy of the wrong people, Quested. The Irish Directory has friends all over the world. When this is over, I'll be coming after you. No matter where you go, I'll find you. I'll hunt you down and when I catch you—'

'Good point,' said Quested. 'Maybe it would be safer for me to kill you now, and have done with it. On the other hand, five thousand dollars is a lot of money. And should I really be scared of a bunch of overfed Paddies who couldn't organise an orgy in a brothel, never mind a revolution to kick the British out of Ireland? Put him in the lazaretto,' he told Gog and Magog. 'I'll decide what's to be done with him later. First we've got business to attend to. Once Mr Cusack here is safely locked away, start bringing the kanakas up from the hold.'

Moltata and the other natives kidnapped on Tanna were being paraded on deck by the time the *Lucy Ann* anchored in Dillon's Bay on the west side of Erromanga. The island was much like Aneiteium and Tanna in appearance: palm-fringed beaches, rocky headlands and jungle-covered mountains. Killigrew could see a native village ashore, and a host of outrigger canoes was paddled out to crowd around the *Lucy Ann*. The natives were much the same as Moltata's people, naked but for penis-wrappers and crude ornaments, all of them armed to the teeth with war clubs and spears.

Forgan stood at the entry-port to greet their visitors, holding a blunderbuss. 'Just you, Kowiowi!' he called down, and lifted an index finger for emphasis. 'One! One only, *amigo!*'

Quested and Forgan clearly did not trust the Erromangoans. Killigrew could not blame them; when Kowiowi climbed up the side ladder on to the deck, the lieutenant did not care much for the cut of his jib: a fat, stocky man whose big belly almost concealed the penis-wrapper beneath, and whose flabby breasts would have been the envy of the most buxom Haymarket whore.

Kowiowi embraced the captain warmly. 'Hullo old feller Quested! All same with you today here?'

'I all right,' replied Quested. 'All same with you?'

'Me good,' replied Kowiowi. Then he saw Molineaux in irons in the lee waist next to Killigrew. Judging from his reaction, it was the first time he had ever seen a black man in white man's clothes. 'Why him there? Him is dressim long fashion b'long white man!'

'Him is black man b'long England. Him is warrior, too much brave. Too much *mana*.'

Kowiowi glanced at Quested with one eyebrow arched sceptically. 'Him is warrior?' he asked, and then roared with laughter. 'My pikanini too much small savvy stikim him!'

'Let Quested take these clinkers off me, and I'll show you who's a warrior, you greasy tub of lard!' snarled Molineaux.

'Quiet!' snarled Utumate, smashing the handle of a gaff-hook across the backs of Molineaux's knees. The seaman sank to the deck with a sob of pain, and Kowiowi laughed. He indicated Killigrew and Molineaux with a hopeful expression.

Quested shook his head. 'Sorry, Kowiowi. No savvy. They're mine. Two feller there is b'long me.' He led the bigman across to where the Tannese were paraded under guard. 'Here you go, Kowiowi, you heathen black bastard. A dozen number-one Tanna warriors. Too much strong, too much brave.'

When Kowiowi saw the Tannese chief, his eyes widened with delight. 'Moltata!'

Moltata replied in his own language. Killigrew did not understand a word of it, but the tone did not sound complimentary.

Kowiowi scowled, and then grinned when he realised he had nothing further to fear from his enemy. 'How much?' he asked Quested.

'Five wood per head.' The captain held up a hand with all five fingers splayed. 'One hundred more twenty wood.'

'Is too much.'

'Is no too much. Straight price. One hundred more twenty wood, or I'll take 'em back to Tanna and you can sing for your supper.'

'One hundred. No more.'

'One hundred more fifteen.'

'One hundred more five.'

'One hundred more ten.'

'*Ale!* Is good. One hundred more ten. M'be you feller is tekkim all long sand beach, more m'be me-feller is leggo wood long beach.'

Quested was sweating as he returned Kowiowi's grin. 'So you can try to overturn my longboat as we row ashore like you did last time, you treacherous sonuvabitch? No savvy. M'be you-feller tekkim wood long ship here, m'be me-feller is givim *kaekae*-man place here.'

'*Ale, ale!* You no *makas*, old feller Quested! M'be me-feller is fetchim wood long ship.' He crossed back to the entry port and called out to his men waiting in their canoes, shouting out to them in his own language. A great cheer went up from them, and several of the canoes were rowed back to the beach, where a great pile of sandalwood logs had already been stacked in readiness.

The Erromangoans carried the bundles of slender sandalwood logs into the sea and floated them out to where the *Lucy Ann* was anchored. As soon as the spouters had finished bringing the logs on board and Quested had checked the quality of the heartwood, they let half a dozen more Erromangoans on deck – Forgan and Gardner keeping a watchful eye on them and one hand on their guns – to herd the Tannese warriors towards the entry port. Moltata went with quiet dignity, but as they were pushed down the side ladder to a waiting canoe, one of the Tannese tried to put up a fight. It was useless without weapons and with his legs hobbled and his hands manacled, however. One of the Erromangoans clubbed him down, and the Tannese fell into the bottom of the canoe and lay motionless. Chanting the New Hebridean equivalent of a shanty, the Erromangoans started to paddle the canoes back towards the beach.

'Get this lumber stacked up in the hold, Utumate,' ordered Quested. 'Loose all sails. Sheet home and hoist tops'ls, t'gallants'ls and royals. Heave up the anchor.'

'Anchor's aweigh, sir,' Gardner reported from the forecastle.

'Hoist the jib and cat the anchor.' Quested watched to see that all canvas was drawing, and once the *Lucy Ann* was under way again he turned to Forgan. 'Set course for Traitors' Head.'

'Aye, aye, sir.'

Quested crossed the deck to where Killigrew and Molineaux were chained. 'I suppose you're wondering why I didn't sell you to

Kowiowi along with those captives,' he said. 'That was my original plan. But as Mr Wyatt here was good enough to point out to me, that would be much too easy. He's come up with a peach of a notion.'

'We're going to give you two a chance,' explained Wyatt, grinning. 'The same chance you would have given us, if you'd taken us back to Norfolk Island.'

'The same chance you gave my nephew,' put in Quested.

'By which I suppose you mean no chance at all?' asked Killigrew.

'That's about the long and the short of it. You see, the kanakas on the west side of the island, well . . . they pretty civilised, compared to the bastards on the east side of the island. The kanakas around Traitors' Head: now they're just plumb mean. So that's where we're going to put you ashore.'

'I want you to know what it's like,' explained Wyatt, 'to be hunted like an animal, the way you've hunted us these past nine days. Who knows? You may yet live to a ripe old age. Shall I tell you how to avoid ending up as the course of honour at a cannibal feast? You've just got to keep running.' He chuckled. 'For the rest of your life.'

'Don't worry,' added Quested. 'That won't be for too long.'

'Sail ho!'

For Robertson, the cry from the masthead was a welcome relief. He was in his cabin with his clerk, keeping the ship's paperwork up to date. One of the luxuries of being the captain of a ship, be it a first-rate ship of the line or a paddle-sloop (third class), was that one usually had lieutenants to take care of the huge amount of paperwork that the navy insisted upon. In the absence of Hartcliffe and Killigrew, the wearisome job fell to Robertson. Not that there was much else to do, while the *Tisiphone* waited at Thorpetown in the increasingly vain hope that the *Lucy Ann* might show up there.

'Carry on,' he told the clerk, before hurrying up on deck.

There was no need to ask Yelverton if he had established 'where away?': the only place for a newly arrived vessel to appear in the lagoon before the deserted settlement was the channel five and a half cables astern. Glancing past the taffrail, he saw the *Wanderer* approaching. The yacht came within a hundred yards of the *Tisiphone*, and dropped anchor. Robertson saw Thorpe on deck, and the two of them exchanged waves. The *Wanderer*'s jolly boat was lowered from its davits, and Thorpe climbed down the side ladder and was rowed across to the *Tisiphone*.

Robertson greeted him at the entry port. The trader looked flushed. 'Thank heavens I've found you here, Commander Robertson!' he said without preamble. 'I'm afraid I've received some most disturbing news from a sandalwood barque I fell in with on my way here. Apparently the *Lucy Ann* turned up at Paddon's trading station at Aneiteium, and there was a fight.'

'What happened?' Robertson demanded curtly.

'Lord Hartcliffe's men were successful in overpowering the crew of the *Lucy Ann* and arresting some of the escaped convicts, but . . . well, I'm afraid some people were grievously injured in the encounter. Including his lordship, I'm sorry to say.'

'How badly hurt is he?'

'The man I spoke to did not know for certain; but it seems his lordship is greatly in need of medical attention.'

'Damn it! What about Mrs Cafferty? Is there news of her?'

'I fear not.'

Robertson turned to the master. 'How long to get back to Aneiteium, Mr Yelverton?'

'A couple of hours to get pressure up in the boilers, a day to get there.'

'We'll proceed under sail until we've got steam up,' Robertson decided promptly. He turned back to Thorpe. 'My apologies, sir – and my thanks for bringing us this intelligence – but you'll understand if I do not stay for dinner.'

'I quite understand,' Thorpe assured him, and smiled broadly. 'Please do not delay on my account.'

'Bring them.' Quested indicated Killigrew and Molineaux.

Forgan kept the two prisoners covered with his blunderbuss while they were unchained from the ringbolt in the bulwark. Molineaux glanced across to where Lissak stood. 'You just going to let them feed us to the cannibals, Foxy?'

'Why? Do you deserve better?'

Molineaux had no answer to that.

'Remember that time you peached on me after the Castle Street East job?' asked Lissak, strolling across towards him. 'Think of this as payment in kind!'

Molineaux hobbled forwards suddenly and seized the old lag by his scrawny neck, his face twisted with rage. The two of them went down, rolling over on the deck, while the crew and Lissak's fellow incorrigibles stood around laughing and cheering. It was an even match, for while Molineaux had youth and strength on his side, his hands and feet were restrained.

'Oh-kay, that's enough,' said Quested, cuffing tears of laughter from his cheeks. 'We haven't got all day. We've got to get to Thorpetown before sunset tomorrow. Separate them.'

Gog and Magog pulled Molineaux and Lissak apart. 'Be still!'

ordered Utumate, emphasising the exclamation mark with a powerhouse punch to Molineaux's stomach which doubled him up and drove the wind from him.

Killigrew glanced to the headland two hundred yards off the *Lucy Ann*'s starboard beam. There was no sign of any natives amongst the trees ashore, but he had the feeling they were there, watching, wondering what the white men were up to.

The crew lowered one of the whaleboats from its davits and two of the spouters climbed down the lifelines. A tackle was secured to one yard-arm end, and the lower block lowered to about six feet above the deck.

'Raise your arms above your head,' Lissak told Molineaux. The seaman was uncharacteristically silent as Lissak looped the chain of his manacles over the hook at the bottom of the block and tackle. He stared at Lissak in astonishment, perhaps surprised that his old mentor could so easily turn against him and leave him to his death. Killigrew was less surprised, because he knew something Molineaux seemed to have forgotten: there was no honour amongst thieves.

Lissak backed away from Molineaux. 'All right, boys, haul away!'

Magog hauled hand-over-hand on one rope, raising Molineaux about six feet off the deck. The seaman winced as his shoulders took the weight of his body. Utumate pulled on a brace, swinging Molineaux out over the bulwark, and then Magog lowered him to where the two spouters waited in the boat below.

Killigrew was hoisted out next by the same method. As he was swung over the bulwark, he saw Quested toss a set of keys at Gardner. 'Leave them with these once you've got them ashore. We don't want to make it too easy for the savages.' He crossed to the entry port and grinned down at where Killigrew was being lowered into the boat. Gardner unlooped Killigrew's manacles from the rope and sat him down next to Molineaux in the stern, keeping them both covered with a musket.

'*Adiós, amigos!*' called Forgan.

'Remember what I told you, Killigrew,' jeered Wyatt. 'Just keep running!'

'I'm finished with running, Wyatt!' Killigrew shouted back. 'From now on, the only running I'll be doing will be to come after you!'

'Glad to see you haven't lost your sense of humour. You'll need it, when the cannibals put you in one of their cooking pots tonight.'

'It won't be the first time I've found myself in hot water.'

Wyatt just smirked. 'Tell the cannibals I said "*Bon appétit!*" '

The two spouters cast off the boat and rowed them through the surf to a white sand beach fringed with coconut palms. When the boat's keel touched sand, Gardner gestured with the musket at Killigrew and Molineaux. 'Out.'

Hampered by their irons, the lieutenant and the able seaman climbed awkwardly out of the boat. They hobbled up on to the sand, and Gardner followed them with the musket. 'Keep walking,' he told them.

Killigrew wondered if he was going to shoot them in the back. It seemed unlikely: with only one bullet in his musket, he would not have time to reload before the other tackled him; and neither of the two spouters seemed to be armed.

'That's far enough,' said Gardner. They turned back to face him, and saw him cradling his musket under one arm while he fished in a pocket with his free hand. He produced the keys, held them up for them to see, and then threw them into the foliage beneath the palm trees. 'Fetch!'

Killigrew hesitated; Molineaux just smiled. 'I don't need the keys,' he told Gardner.

'No?'

Molineaux raised his hands, and his manacles fell away. 'Because my irons are already unlocked.' He lunged forwards and grabbed the musket, pushing the barrel aside and trying to wrestle it from Gardner's grip. As the two of them struggled chest-to-chest, the two spouters leaped out of the boat and ran up the sand to help the third mate.

Molineaux swung Gardner around so that his back was to Killigrew: the lieutenant looped the chain linking his shackles over the mate's head and pulled it tight against his throat. As Gardner choked, Molineaux pulled the musket free, raised it to his shoulder, and drilled one of the spouters between the eyes at almost point-blank range. Then the other spouter caught him around the waist and the two of them went down, rolling over and over on the sand.

Killigrew forced Gardner face-down on the sand, getting one knee in the small of his back to increase his purchase as he hauled on the chain around the mate's neck. Gardner struggled futilely for a moment, and then went limp, but Killigrew was not fooled: he just kept on pulling the chain tighter and tighter until he heard the unmistakable death rattle in the mate's throat.

He looked across to where Molineaux fought the remaining spouter. The two of them had separated and faced one another across the sand. The spouter had the musket, but now Molineaux had his Bowie knife in his hand. The musket was unloaded, so the spouter swung it like a club. Molineaux was too fast to let any of the blows connect with his head, but the spouter was successfully keeping him at bay.

Killigrew picked himself up and hobbled across to help him, the fetters on his ankles impeding his every step. The spouter lunged forwards and swung the musket at Molineaux's head. The seaman ducked beneath the blow, and the spouter lost his balance on the follow-through. It was a fatal mistake: before the spouter could recover his poise, Molineaux had moved in close and buried the knife to the hilt in his adversary's side. The spouter gasped as his blood spilled on the white sand, and dropped the musket. Molineaux withdrew the blade and stabbed him again, in the heart this time.

By the time Killigrew reached him, Molineaux was wiping the blade of his knife on the spouter's guernsey. 'Where'd you get that?' he panted.

'Foxy,' Molineaux replied, returning the Bowie knife to the sheath in the small of his back. Before he could explain further, they heard a crack from the *Lucy Ann*, and a bullet soughed over their heads to rip through the foliage behind them.

'Into the trees, quick!' Killigrew hobbled the remaining few yards up the beach and plunged into the bushes, collapsing behind the trunk of a tree. Realising that Molineaux was no longer with him, he glanced under a bush and saw that the seaman had gone back for the musket and Gardner's cartouche box. As Molineaux ran back up the sand, musket-shots from the *Lucy Ann* whistled all around him. The ship was about two hundred yards out and at that range the musket was an erratic weapon at the best of times but, even so, the law of averages said that one of the bullets had to hit him sooner or later.

But Molineaux made it to the trees a few yards to Killigrew's right. 'Over here!'

With Molineaux out of sight from the ship, the shooting ceased. Molineaux made his way to where Killigrew lay and sank to his knees beside him, holding the musket in one hand and the cartouche box in the other. 'Thought we might need these,' he explained breathlessly.

Killigrew looked down at his irons and glanced about. 'I don't suppose you saw where those keys fell by any chance?'

'Don't need 'em.' Molineaux produced his picklocks and went to work on Killigrew's padlocks.

'Where did you get those? Lissak?'

Molineaux nodded. 'He slipped me the knife when we were fighting, then put the picks in my pocket when he was hooking me up to that hoist.'

'Then I hope for his sake Wyatt doesn't work out how you managed to get free so quickly.'

More shots sounded from the *Lucy Ann*. Both Killigrew and Molineaux hunkered down instinctively, but none of the bullets came close. Killigrew soon realised why: the shots were aimed at the boat in the surf. A whaleboat was a far larger target than a man, and a stationary one. While some shots still went wide, it was not long before it looked like a giant wooden colander.

While the boat was being shot to pieces, Molineaux checked in the cartouche box. 'How many rounds?' Killigrew asked him.

'Three.'

'Capital,' Killigrew said wryly.

Molineaux took out a cartridge and ball and reloaded the musket quickly and expertly. He jerked his head towards the *Lucy Ann*. 'Want me to take a pot-shot at them?'

Killigrew shook his head. 'The smoke will give away where we're hiding. Better save the ammunition for the savages.'

The men on the deck of the *Lucy Ann* stopped shooting; then she hoisted her anchor and braced her sails to the wind, heading away from the island.

After the shooting, the jungle was eerily quiet. 'Now what?' whispered Molineaux, as if fearing that the slightest sound would bring the natives running from every direction; as if the gunfire had not made enough noise already.

'Buck up, man,' said Killigrew. 'At least we're not unarmed. Things could be a good deal worse.'

Molineaux cocked his head as if listening. 'Things just got worse. Hear it?'

Killigrew listened. Somewhere far off in the jungle, he could hear the distant throb of the tam-tams. The refrain was taken up by another set, closer to, and then yet another set, closer still.

'The bush telegraph,' Killigrew said grimly. 'I wonder what they're saying.'

'Probably sending out the invitations for dinner.'

XXI

Guess Who's Coming To Dinner

'The first thing to do is get as far from here as possible,' decided Killigrew. 'The natives must have heard the shooting – that's what will bring them.' He gestured out of the trees to where the bodies of Gardner and the two spouters were sprawled on the sand. 'With any luck they'll think those three were the only ones left ashore.'

Molineaux followed Killigrew deeper into the jungle. 'I agree with you about getting as far away from here as possible, but isn't that going to be kind of awkward? I mean, bearing in mind we're on an island?'

'Don't worry; it's a big island.' Killigrew had taken the precaution of studying a chart of the New Hebrides on the voyage from Norfolk Island. As a midshipman his attempts at navigation had been the butt of many a joke – geometry and trigonometry never had been, and never would be, his strong points – and he always bowed to Mr Yelverton in matters of navigation. But his photographic memory for charts, allied with an unerring sense of direction, enabled him to match any landscape he stood in to the marks on a map in his head. 'We'll head inland to start with. Most of the villages on these islands are situated on the coast. Then we'll make for Kowiowi's village at Dillon's Bay.'

'Kowiowi? That's the fat bastard Quested sold Moltata and the others to, right? Any reason to expect he'll be any less fond of white meat than he is of dark, sir? Not that it makes any difference in my case. He seemed quite taken with the idea of *matelot noir* dressed *à l'anglais*.'

'There were canoes at Dillon's Bay, remember? It can't be more than forty miles from there to Tanna. We'll wait until dark and then borrow one from the natives.'

'Paddling across forty miles of open sea ain't going to be easy.'

'Would you prefer to wait here until the natives catch us? In any case, I think we can count on Moltata and the others to help us.'

293

'And there was me thinking we were going to prig a canoe without marching into the village itself beforehand and riling the natives by nabbing their supper.'

'It's my fault as much as anyone's they're in their current predicament. I'm not leaving without them.'

Instead of replying, Molineaux suddenly grabbed Killigrew by the arm and jerked him down amongst the ferns to their right. 'Quiet, sir!' he hissed. 'Stay down!'

They lay motionless for a few seconds. A party of a dozen natives, naked but for penis-wrappers and armed to the teeth with spears and war clubs, trotted past almost silently on bare feet, heading in the direction from which Killigrew and Molineaux had just come.

The two Britons lay still for a minute more, until they were sure the natives had passed. Then Killigrew picked himself up and dusted himself down. 'Well spotted, Molineaux. Much obliged.'

'You're welcome, sir.' Molineaux handed Killigrew the musket and the cartouche box. 'You'd better take this.'

'What about you?'

'I got my chiv, sir.' Molineaux patted his Bowie knife through the fabric of his jacket. 'We must be on some kind of native trail. Better if we give any trails a wide berth.'

Killigrew nodded and shouldered the musket. The two of them plunged into the thickest part of the jungle, moving stealthily through the undergrowth. They paused every minute to listen: the only sound they could hear was the relentless drumming of the tam-tams.

They spent the next two hours moving through the jungle, following the slope beneath the trees ever upwards, while the sun reached its zenith somewhere above the trees. Without the sea breezes to cool him, Killigrew was soon dripping with sweat; Molineaux, infuriatingly, remained as dry as a bone. At length they broke out of the trees and saw a swathe of open ground before them, rising up to a pass between two hills. They hurried up to the crest, and on the other side of the pass they could see a good part of the west coast of the island laid out beneath them. Far below them, a small, gleaming white sailing cutter was anchored in a bay. 'Saved!' exclaimed Molineaux.

'Assuming the master proves to be friendly,' said Killigrew. 'We're not going without Moltata and the others, Molineaux.'

'I know, sir. But it's going to be easier sailing to Tanna in a cutter than paddling in an open canoe. And it's a foolhardy sailor that travels these islands unarmed. I'll bet he's got at least one gun on board; we're not going to have much luck trying to rescue the Tannese with only one musket and three bullets . . .'

Killigrew heard a shout behind him. He turned and saw a native emerge from the trees on the slope below them, perhaps two hundred yards away. Several more appeared on either side of him, and within seconds there were about three dozen natives charging up the hill towards them.

Killigrew raised the musket to his shoulder, took aim, and fired. It was too much to hope he might hit one at that range, but the shot had the desired effect: the natives either dropped to the ground, or turned and fled back into the trees. He reloaded the musket, but by the time he was ready to take another shot the natives had rallied and were coming on. They were not as afraid of firearms as he had hoped.

'Come on, sir,' said Molineaux. 'They're just trying to draw your fire, get you to waste your shots at an impossible range; and I don't much fancy the notion of us waiting around until they get closer.'

'Agreed.'

The two of them turned and ran down the slope towards the cutter in the bay, but the natives came on relentlessly, tirelessly. Before Killigrew and Molineaux had covered a couple of hundred yards, their pursuers were close enough to start hurling spears in their direction. The swathe of jungle before them offered Killigrew and Molineaux some hope of respite, and they redoubled their efforts. A spear buried itself in a tree just ahead, the shaft quivering. Then they were running between the trunks, with fronds of bracken and dangling creepers lashing at their faces. They wove in and out of the trunks, Killigrew hoping that if they followed the line of the valley down it would take them to the bay where they had seen the cutter.

He glanced over his shoulder: he could see the natives behind them moving through the trees on either side, seeking to encircle them. Then he found himself crashing through a wall of foliage, and broke out on the other side to run straight into a brown-skinned figure.

The two of them went down. Killigrew barely had time to see another two dozen or so natives standing around, and then one of them had hefted a war club to aim a blow at his skull.

It never landed. A spear whipped through the trees to bury itself in the native's chest. He fell with flecks of blood spraying from his lips, and suddenly the jungle was full of war-whoops, screams of agony and the sound of bones crunching as clubs smashed against skulls. Dazed, Killigrew still sprawled on the ground, and was aware only of the brown feet stamping on the ground all around him when the native he had bumped into launched himself at him with a wooden dagger. Killigrew managed to smash him in the face with the stock of the musket, and then Molineaux grabbed him by the arm and dragged him to one side before a blow from another native could crush his skull.

There was nothing to distinguish the natives of the first tribe from the second as far as Killigrew could tell, but they certainly knew the difference as they set about one another with appalling savagery. 'It's like Parliament Square on election night!' he gasped.

'Yur, well, I don't want to wait around until the result's declared,' said Molineaux. 'Do you?'

Killigrew shook his head and the two of them took advantage of the confusion to disappear through the bushes once more. As soon as they were clear, they broke into a run, dashing off through the trees. They could not be more than a couple of miles from the coast now. Seeing sunlight dappling the ground in a glade, Killigrew headed for it, where the gap in the trees offered an easy passage. Molineaux followed him, and a moment later the two of them sank up to their chests in a quagmire.

Molineaux swore. 'If it ain't one thing, it's another.'

Killigrew kept very still, knowing full well that if he moved about too much it would only hasten things. 'Try to stay calm,' he said, holding the musket above his head so that the filthy ooze would not get in its workings.

'I am calm!' Molineaux snapped back. 'Cowcumber Henson, that's me.'

'Buck up, man. Things could be worse.'

'Worse? *Worse!* We're marooned on a cannibal-infested island and up to our necks in a swamp! How could things possibly be any worse, sir?'

Killigrew thought for a moment. 'Well, it could be rai—'

'Don't say it!' hissed Molineaux. 'Don't even think it. Christ, sir! You've got a lot to learn about not tempting fate.'

With the leaves carpeting the forest floor, it was difficult to tell where the quagmire ended and more solid ground began, but the gnarled roots of trees about ten feet ahead offered some purchase. Killigrew tried to move through the morass towards them, but the ooze held him fast and sucked him down remorselessly. Already he was up to his shoulders, and behind him Molineaux was little better off.

'Got any notion as to how we're going to get out of this one, sir?'

'I'm working on it.'

'Well, look lively, sir.'

'You might try to come up with a suggestion, instead of complaining.'

'As soon as I think of anything, I'll let you know.'

The morass was over their shoulders and up to their chins now. Killigrew stared at those gnarled roots. Ten feet away – it might as well have been ten thousand miles. He glanced about, looking for inspiration, and saw a strand of creeper stretching from one tree to the next about twenty feet overhead. 'Ah-ha! See that creeper above us, Molineaux?'

'Yur, but I don't think I can reach it from here,' the seaman replied sourly.

'The musket, man!' Killigrew handed it back to him. 'You're always boasting about how good a shot you are. Let's see what you can do, Dan'l Boone.'

Molineaux aimed the musket, and hesitated. 'If them savages are still around, you know the sound of the shot will bring them running?'

'We'll worry about that when the time comes.'

Molineaux squinted along the barrel, and fired. The bullet tore a piece out of the creeper, but not enough to break it in two. The recoil drove him a couple of inches deeper into the morass, and he had to tilt his head back to keep his nose and mouth out of the filth.

Killigrew fumbled for the cartouche box and took out a cartridge. 'The last one, Molineaux.'

'You'd better tear it open for me, sir.'

Killigrew complied and handed the cartridge carefully to Molineaux. Holding the musket above his head, Molineaux tipped the powder into the muzzle. He hissed.

'What's the matter?'

'Got gunpowder in my eyes, sir. Hang on . . .' Holding the musket by the stock, he raised it upright so the powder would fall to the breech. 'Ball?'

Killigrew took out a bullet and wrapped a piece of wadding around it, before handing it to Molineaux. The seaman thumbed it into the muzzle, then took out the ramrod and tried to ram the bullet home.

Molineaux spat out a mouthful of mud. 'It's no good, sir. I can't get any purchase, holding it like this.'

'Rest the stock against my back.'

Molineaux did so. 'Thanks . . . that's got it. Percussion cap?'

Killigrew handed him a cap and the seaman primed the musket. He took aim once more.

'Don't miss,' Killigrew told him.

Molineaux glared. 'Do you mind?'

'Sorry?'

The seaman took a couple of deep breaths, and squeezed the trigger. The recoil forced him under so that only his forehead showed above the morass. The creeper parted, and one end of it fell on to the surface of the quagmire.

297

Where the creeper lay closest to Killigrew, it was still two or three feet away. He reached for it, but his grasping fingers came up inches too short. Painfully conscious that Molineaux was suffocating now, Killigrew took the musket from his flailing arms and used the muzzle-sight to hook the creeper. He dragged it towards him and threw the musket aside when he could grasp it. He hauled on the creeper until it was taut. One of the branches it rested on bent under the strain, and then snapped, leaving Killigrew with several feet of useless slack to haul on.

The morass was over his mouth, now. He hauled on the creeper again, and this time it held.

All that was visible of Molineaux was his hands, groping weakly above the surface. Killigrew seized him by the wrist, and pressed the creeper into his palm. Molineaux's fingers closed over it, and then he had the creeper in both hands and was hauling on it. At first it looked as though he were losing the tug-o'-war to the quagmire; then there was an obscene sucking noise, and he came up all at once, his face covered in mud. Coughing and spluttering, he started to haul himself to solid ground.

By now the ooze was over Killigrew's nose and mouth even with his head tilted back, but he waited until Molineaux was safe before pulling on the creeper himself, for fear that their combined weight would be enough to tear it from whatever purchase it had at the other end.

It took all of his strength to pull him free of the quagmire's vile embrace. Holding on to the branch of a tree with one hand, Molineaux leaned out as far over the morass as he could, reaching out for him. Killigrew clasped his hand, and the seaman dragged him to safety.

The two of them collapsed on dry ground, sobbing for breath, the dead leaves clinging to their filthy clothes.

'Good shooting,' Killigrew gasped at last.

'Yur. Not a bad shot, though I say so myself. Am I good, or am I just lucky?'

'You're good,' acknowledged the lieutenant. 'There's only one problem now . . .'

'Huh?'

Killigrew pointed to where a dozen natives had emerged from the trees to surround them in a semi-circle, spears poised to thrust. The necklaces they wore were unmistakably made from human fingerbones.

'Out of the frying pan . . .' said Killigrew.

'And into the cooking pot,' Molineaux concluded for him gloomily.

Mrs Cafferty awoke with a splitting headache. *One glass of wine too many*, she told herself. But at least she did not have to get up for anything that she could think of. Besides, apart from the headache, it was nice to be able to luxuriate between the clean sheets of a huge bed after four nights sleeping in one of the cramped bunks on board the *Wanderer* . . .

She sat up abruptly, staring about in confusion. She lay in a huge, four-poster bed, in an unfamiliar bedroom decorated *à la chinoise*. Some small bottles stood on a lace doily on the bedside cabinet. She picked up one and glanced at the label: Rowlands' Kalydor. 'Gentlemen after shaving will appreciate its softening and ameliorating properties,' the label assured her. A man's room, then. A portrait of Thorpe himself hung on the opposite wall: hardly what she would have chosen to wake up to, but at least it gave her some idea of who the room belonged to.

She had no recollection of how she had come there. The last thing she could remember, she had been drinking coffee in the saloon of the *Wanderer*, listening politely while Thorpe had bored her with grandiose schemes of civilising the natives of Éfaté and setting up his own state on the island.

She threw back the covers. Beneath, she was still fully dressed, but for the boots she had been wearing. Whoever had put her to bed had been too delicate to undress her; either that, or they had simply not bothered. She swung her legs off the bed and found the boots neatly placed on the floor beside it. Feeling disorientated, she padded across the bare wooden floorboards to the window and threw open the shutters.

She gasped.

The window looked out from the first floor of a house. Immediately in front of the building, a long flight of broad stone steps led down to a square with deserted-looking buildings on either side and a wharf overlooking the lagoon opposite. The *Wanderer* was tied up at a wooden jetty that ran out from the wharf, and the only signs of life she could see were a couple of sailors coiling ropes on the deck of the yacht. The lagoon was about half a mile wide; on the far side she could see lush jungle stretching for about three or four miles, and beyond that the wide ocean. Either it was dawn or dusk, the sun halfway over the horizon to her right casting a golden glow over the exotic scene.

Now she was too intrigued to care about her headache or how disorientated she was. She sat down on the edge of the bed and hurriedly laced on the boots. She looked in the wardrobe in one corner to see if she could find a shawl, but only discovered some blankets. She threw one over her shoulders anyway, and crossed to the door. For some reason she could not fully explain to herself, she half expected to find it locked, but the handle turned to her touch and she stepped out into the corridor beyond.

She could hear a voice raised in anger, and followed it to the top of a stone staircase running down a wall on one side, with a wrought-iron banister on the other. A few steps down she found herself overlooking a hallway where Thorpe was berating a grubby-looking man who flinched at the trader's tirade.

'I gave you specific instructions to keep the *Avon* here, Mr Underwood! Don't you realise there's a ship coming in tomorrow with a consignment of sandalwood for Shanghai? How am I to get it there? I'm ruined, you fool! Ruined!'

'You didn't say anything to me about any consignment of sandalwood, sir,' whined the grubby little man. 'What was I supposed to say to Captain Hawkes? He asked me why you wanted him here, and I couldn't give him a reason. He left. I tried to stop him—'

'Obviously you didn't try hard enough!'

They were too busy arguing to notice Mrs Cafferty's arrival, so she coughed into her fist to draw their attention to her presence. 'Mr Thorpe? Is everything all right?'

The scowl was gone from Thorpe's jowly face in an instant, to be replaced by a broad beam as he tried to put a friendly arm around Underwood's shoulders, but the man shied away. 'Everything's fine, Mrs Cafferty. How are you this evening?'

'I must confess I'm a little confused, Mr Thorpe. Where am I?'

'Thorpetown, m'dear. And this is my home: Thorpe Hall.' He gestured proudly around him, although the rather bare hallway did not seem to boast much to be proud of. 'You fainted. Perhaps you don't remember. Hardly surprising. You've been through a terrible ordeal, and you lost a good deal of blood from that wound in your arm.'

She raised a hand to her shoulder. The wound had been healing nicely, and after a couple of days living in the luxury the *Wanderer* had to offer, she had soon recovered her strength. If she had been going to faint, surely she would have done so shortly after she had come on board the yacht, not four days later?

'Is the *Tisiphone* here?' she asked.

'Alas, no,' replied Thorpe. 'Mr Underwood here tells me the *Tisiphone* sailed for Aneiteium several hours before our arrival . . .'

Underwood lowered his eyes guiltily to the flagstone floor.

'. . . but I believe she will return in a couple of days,' concluded Thorpe. 'In the meantime, you are more than welcome to share whatever comforts my humble abode has to offer.'

'It would seem I have little choice in the matter,' she replied drily, descending the last few steps to the floor.

A bell jangled noisily close by, making Underwood start visibly. The three of them stood there, staring at one another, until Thorpe rounded irritably on Underwood. 'Well, don't just stand there, you nincompoop! Go and see who it is.'

'Yes, Mr Thorpe, sir. Right away.' Underwood hurried across to the front door.

'Just now you said I was welcome to share whatever comforts your humble abode has to offer,' Mrs Cafferty reminded Thorpe, pressing the back of her hand to her forehead. 'I wonder if those include Dr James's Powders?'

'You are feeling a little unwell? I'll have some brought as soon as possible. It seems we're suffering from a little servant problem at the moment.'

'Are there any?' she asked sceptically.

'I employ natives from some of the neighbouring villages as my servants,' explained Thorpe. 'Naturally I gave them permission to visit their families in my absence. It will take time for them to return. However, until then I'm sure Mr Underwood and my cook and steward from the *Wanderer* will be able to attend to our needs very nicely.'

Underwood returned from the front door with one of the hands from the *Wanderer*. 'Begging your pardon, sir, but there's a ship entering the lagoon – a whaler. Mr Irwin says it looks like the *Acushnet*. He said you'd want to know.'

'The *Acushnet*?' echoed Thorpe, rubbing his podgy hands together. 'Splendid, splendid! This could be the solution to all our problems.'

Molineaux was humming a tune. Killigrew recognised it as 'The World Turned Upside Down'. In view of the fact that the pair of them were hanging upside down from rough bamboo tripods, bound like pigs for the slaughter along with Moltata and his warriors, Killigrew found Molineaux's sense of humour anything but hilarious.

Kowiowi's people were performing a war dance. Somehow Killigrew had a feeling it wasn't for the entertainment of himself and the other captives. Wearing grotesque masks and feathered headdresses, the Erromangans leaped about and cavorted by the light of fires and flambeaux, performing intricate patterns that Killigrew did not doubt had some deep significance that was lost on him. And all the time the tam-tams beat out a wild, savage rhythm that matched the fearful pounding in his heart.

Kowiowi sat on a mat on the opposite side of the dancing ground, surrounded by his wives and guzzling *kava* from a coconut shell. One of the younger men had been appointed to act as guard over the captives. He did not seem to be taking his duties too seriously, but then he did not have to: Killigrew, Molineaux and the twelve Tannese were all quite helpless.

The Tannese warriors seemed to have accepted their fate with stoicism; but then, Killigrew was trying to give the same impression himself, while secretly (and futilely) working at the bonds of creeper which bound him; if it was untrue for him it might be equally untrue for them. He had already noticed Moltata and his son talking to one another in low voices out of the corners of their mouths. Perhaps they were planning something. But what? Their hands were tied, and even if they could break loose, they were in an enemy village, trapped on an island where they could expect to find no help.

But Killigrew had not survived countless encounters with slavers and pirates to die at the hands of savages. He would not go down without a fight. What was it Cusack had said? *Sometimes it's the fights we cannot win that are most in need of fighting.* He would see about that.

Periodically, one of the Erromangoans engaged in the dance would break off from the intricate figures and leap about in front of the captives, waving a spear or a club threateningly at them, to the approval of the other villagers. It was frightening at first, but after a while it just became wearisome. They were showing off in front of their women, like sailors flexing their muscles in a Portsmouth tavern.

'You wouldn't be so brave if my hands were free,' Molineaux sneered at one of them, although his voice was drowned out by the general clamour of drums and chanting. Their posturing might put the fear of whatever gods they worshipped in these islands into the Tannese, but this time they were picking a fight with a couple of British tars.

Killigrew gave up trying to tear or wear away his bonds: he was just chafing the flesh on his wrists. 'Hey!' he whispered. 'Molineaux!'

'Sir?'

'You know your friend Lissak escaped from the prison hulk in Gallions' Reach before he was transported to the colonies?'

'Yur?'

'And from Port Arthur. Twice.'

'Yur.'

'And now from Norfolk Island.'

'Uh-huh.'

'You know you said he taught you everything he knew . . .?'

'Forget it, sir. If we was on a prison hulk, or at Port Arthur, or on Norfolk Island, I might be able to come up with a notion or two. But my education never got as far as how to escape from being tied upside down at a cannibal feast. I don't suppose you've got any ideas?'

302

'I'm applying myself to the problem in hand, yes.'

'Well, if you're going to come up with a plan, you'd better do it *pronto*,' warned Molineaux. 'Any moment now they're going to haul out a big old iron cooking pot and give us the hottest bath we've ever known.'

'These people belong to a stone-age culture, Molineaux. They don't have the skills for metal working.'

'No cooking pots?'

'No. They'll probably just burn us alive.'

'Plummy,' sighed Molineaux. 'Funnily enough, Foxy once told me a story about a missionary who got captured by cannibals. The chief of the cannibals told him they couldn't make up their minds whether to fry him or boil him, so they wanted him to say one thing: if it was true, they would boil him, and if it was a lie they would fry him. So he said: "You are going to fry me".'

'So?' asked Killigrew.

'So they couldn't do either,' Molineaux explained patiently. 'If they'd fried him, what he said would have been truth, so they'd've had to have boiled him; but then what he'd said would've been a lie, so they'd've had to fry him.'

'So they let him go?'

'No, they roasted him instead, for being a clever Dick.'

'If that's your notion of trying to keep our spirits up, I can't say I think much of it.'

The younger children were having an argument. One boy, perhaps six years of age, was crying. As far as Killigrew could work out, the children were playing 'Warriors and White Men', and the boy had been told he would have to be one of the white men. He walked away from the game, and the others were happy to let him go. They returned to their game without him, and he wandered over to stare curiously at the captives, picking his nose.

Killigrew glanced towards the guard and saw that he was sleeping, presumably overwhelmed by an overgenerous draught of *kava*. 'Hullo there, young shaver,' Killigrew whispered to the boy. 'Can you understand me?'

From the blank expression on the boy's face, there was no indication that he could, but Killigrew pressed on anyway. 'Cut us down and we'll give you some sweets. Would you like that? Of course you would. All boys like sweets.'

The boy took his tiny penis in both hands and piddled in Killigrew's face until his mother came along and chased him away, scolding.

Molineaux laughed. 'Prob'ly telling him not to widdle on his dinner, sir.'

'Bunch of savages in this town,' muttered Killigrew.

303

The drums fell silent, and the dancers ran into the bushes on either side. Kowiowi rose to his feet and spread his arms wide. '*Eranu!*'

'*Uvavu!*' the other Erromangoans responded with one voice.

Kowiowi indicated Moltata. '*Klaatu barada nikto!*'

Four of his warriors ran forward and hoisted Moltata to his feet. The chief went passively, but behind him his son struggled furiously – futilely – against his chains as his father was dragged towards the largest bonfire. Everyone's eyes were on Moltata and his captors.

Except Killigrew's. He caught sight of a movement out of the corner of his eye, and saw that Molineaux had got his hands free. Now the seaman started to work on the creeper that bound his legs. Working before him now instead of fumbling behind his back, it was much easier.

But Moltata was only a few feet from the fire.

'*Abo abome!*' One of the guards had seen that Molineaux had got his hands free and was trying to free his legs. He ran across the dance ground, hefting a spear.

Molineaux got his legs free and, gripping the wooden tripod, lowered his feet to the ground. He rolled out of the way of the spear-thrust and snatched up one of the legs of the tripod. Pulling it free of the creeper which tied it to the other poles, he used it to parry the native's next spear-thrust, then slipped it between the native's ankles and tripped him up. The warrior landed on his back and Molineaux was on him in an instant, the two of them struggling for possession of the spear.

Killigrew was not sure if the seaman actually had a plan, or was just determined to take as many of them with him as possible before he died. He watched helplessly as more warriors ran across to aid Molineaux's opponent.

Molineaux managed to get a knee into the man's poorly protected groin, and forced the spear down against his throat, throttling him. The other natives were standing around him now, belabouring him across the back with their clubs; the only thing that stopped him from being beaten to a bloody pulp was the fact that there were too many of them crowded around him, all trying to get a blow in and only getting in one another's way.

Molineaux pulled the spear from the lifeless fingers of the native below him, and thrust the point into a thigh. The wounded native went down with a scream, but then a blow landed on the back of Molineaux's head and he slumped. Seeing him at their mercy, the natives backed off a little, and as he rolled on to his back in a daze, one of them aimed a spear thrust at his heart.

'*Abo!*'

The warrior froze. The warning had come from Kowiowi. He

waddled across to where the warrior stood and took the spear from him. He clearly wanted to kill Molineaux for himself.

Get up! Every nerve of Killigrew's fibre tried to will the seaman on to his feet, but Molineaux still lay in a daze, like an upturned turtle.

Kowiowi drew back the spear.

At that moment the bonfire flared up with a roar, throwing flames almost as high as the tops of the trees surrounding the dance ground. Smoke billowed, and a hideous, half-human creature came flying through the smoke and flames holding a gourd in one hand and a burning flambeau in the other.

The warriors surrounding Molineaux turned to stare at it; the seaman had a perfect opportunity to grab a spear from one of them, except that he too was staring in horror at the grotesque apparition. It was vaguely human in shape, but it lurched about like something out of a nightmare, its skin a ghastly pale grey, its face a demonic mask. Hideous, guttural sounds issued threateningly from the hole where its mouth was.

One of the warriors plucked up enough courage to run at the demon, swinging a club. Before he got close, Killigrew heard something which might have been a rifle shot, and the native was thrown down with a small hole in his forehead, the back of his skull missing. The demon raised the gourd to its lips, then passed the flambeau in front of its face and breathed fire at the natives.

Screaming, they dropped their weapons and turned and fled, disappearing into the bush.

Molineaux remained transfixed to the spot as the demon performed some kind of victory dance, cavorting about, turning its back in the direction in which the Erromangoans had run, bending over and waggling its buttocks in an unmistakable gesture of contempt.

'You all right, Moltata?' asked a voice. Killigrew twisted to see a second apparition emerge from the trees carrying a rifle: a tall, rangy figure with a bronzed face and sun-bleached hair beneath a pilot cap, he was either a rumpled thirty or a fit-looking forty; it was impossible to be sure. He embraced Moltata.

'*Ale*, old-feller Jimmy!' exclaimed the *yeremanu*. 'I good now! You no *makas*.'

The white man turned to Molineaux. 'What name b'long you?'

The seaman shook his head. 'I'm sorry, I don't understand.'

The white man's eyebrows shot up. 'Strewth! This feller speaks better English than I do!' His eyes took in the filthy, ragged remains of Molineaux's pusser's slops, and he shifted the cigar-stub he was chewing from one corner of his mouth to the other. 'You Royal Navy?'

'Able Seaman Wes Molineaux, at your service . . . and very, very grateful.'

The white man nodded as if to say that thanks were worse than unnecessary, it was a waste of precious time. He crossed to where Killigrew and the rest of the captives still dangled. Pulling a bush-knife from a sheath on his belt, he cut the Tannese down one by one, working his way along to Killigrew. When he got to the lieutenant, instead of cutting him down, he turned away and then bent double, so that he was facing him upside down from between his legs.

'G'day! You look like you're in a fix.'

'Yes. I'd be much obliged if you could cut me down.'

'I'll bet you would. If I help you escape, you ain't going to come back here with a navy sloop to bombard the place, are you?'

'I have neither the time, the inclination, nor the authority, I assure you.'

'Good.' Without a word of warning, the white man straightened and with a single blow of his bush-knife sliced through the creepers suspending Killigrew. The lieutenant landed painfully on his head and sprawled on the ground. He picked himself up, dusted himself down, and found himself facing the stranger once more.

'Jimmy Paddon,' he introduced himself, and jerked his head at the 'demon', who pulled off his carved wooden mask to reveal a human face beneath. 'I believe you've already met Sharky.'

XXII

Out Of The Frying Pan . . .

'Shall we get moving?' suggested Paddon. 'The Erromanga men may be superstitious, but they ain't stupid, and they sure as hell ain't cowards. Won't be long before they start wondering if that really was a demon that interrupted their supper, and start creeping back to check.'

Sharky led the way out of the clearing and the others followed at a jog trot through the bush. 'I thought you said Quested shot Sharky last night?' Killigrew hissed at Molineaux as they hurried along behind Paddon.

'He did,' insisted the seaman.

'Well, he looks remarkably agile for a man in his condition,' snorted Killigrew. It was obvious the seaman had seen some other albino get shot on board the *Lucy Ann* the previous night. Still, it was unlike Molineaux to make a mistake: perhaps Sharky had only pretended that Quested's bullet had hit him, and Molineaux had been fooled along with everyone else on deck.

Killigrew dismissed the matter from his mind: he had more pressing things to worry about. He speeded up until he was level with Paddon. 'Is that your cutter I saw anchored in the next bay?'

'The *Rover's Bride*? Yeah.'

'I'm indebted to you, Captain Paddon. It's fortunate for us you came by when you did.'

'Luck had nothing to do with it, mate. Sharky told me you'd been captured by that bastard Quested. When I heard the tam-tams tonight, I realised that you must've wound up in Kowiowi's larder.'

The more Killigrew tried to get an explanation out of Paddon, the more questions the trader's answers raised, so he gave up and they hurried on in silence. Sharky led the way through the trees and undergrowth as if it were broad daylight, and his pale body was easy to follow from the occasional splashes of moonlight which dropped through the leaves above.

The jungle was alive with strange sounds all around them. 'Those bird calls . . .' Killigrew began tentatively.

'Ain't made by birds,' confirmed Paddon. 'We'd best keep moving. Sounds like Kowiowi's people have rallied.'

Killigrew was relieved when they emerged on to a beach after a mile or two. A jolly boat was drawn up on the sand, and in the light of the crescent moon Killigrew could see a small but handsome sailing cutter rode at anchor out in the bay beyond.

'Thank Christ!' muttered Paddon. 'She's still here. I had to take a big risk leaving her out there, but it was either that or let you fourteen wind up as cannibal turds.'

'Is there room for all of us in that boat?' Molineaux asked dubiously.

Before Paddon could reply, Sharky ran down to the water and splashed out through the surf until the water was deep enough for him to dive into it and swim out in the direction of the cutter. 'I guess there is now,' said Paddon.

'Isn't he afraid of sharks?' asked Killigrew.

Paddon laughed. 'Sharky? Afraid of sharks? That's a good one!'

As they were carrying the jolly boat back to the water, they heard war-whoops from the trees behind them. A spear came whistling out of the undergrowth to bury itself in the sand close to Moltata's feet.

'Didn't I tell you they'd be back?' Paddon left the others to carry the boat, stepping aside and drawing a brace of revolvers from his belt. He fired a dozen shots in quick succession in the direction of the trees. The war whoops were silenced at once. 'That should discourage them long enough for us to get clear.'

'Aiming kind of high, weren't you?' asked Molineaux.

'Apart from the fact I had no chance of hitting them anyhow, I don't bear them any particular ill will. It ain't their fault they're cannibals; they just don't know any better. The Tanna and Aneiteium men were cannibals too, once, not so long ago. If they can be civilised, so can the Erromanga men. Just so long as they ain't civilised too much: I kind of like them the way they are. The only reason it's taking longer for the Erromanga men to accept white men as their friends is because so far their contact with us ain't endeared us to them. And fellers like Quested ain't exactly a good influence on them. He's the real savage in these islands.'

'I wouldn't argue with that,' Killigrew said with some feeling.

They rowed out to the *Rover's Bride* and found Sharky waiting for them, plucking on a jew's-harp. Molineaux stared at the *nakai-mo*'s midriff, and following his gaze Killigrew saw a small, star-shaped scar there. Molineaux gave Killigrew a significant look, as if to say: *I told you so.* But the scar was obviously an old one, and given the profusion of cicatrices and tattoos that decorated Sharky's body, it was hardly surprising neither of them had noticed it before.

'How did you get here, Sharky?' Killigrew asked him.

The *nakaimo* took his jew's-harp from his mouth, and grinned, showing his pointed teeth in the moonlight. 'Me swim.'

'Thirty-odd miles?'

'Me swim good.' Sharky thrust the jew's-harp back in his mouth and started playing 'Oh, Susannah!' again.

Killigrew sighed. The *nakaimo* must have taken a canoe from a village on the north coast of the island. The natives of the New Hebrides often travelled between the islands in their outrigger canoes; many of them had sails for that very purpose. Sailing from Tanna to Erromanga, he would have had the wind behind him . . . yes, it was perfectly possible. All the talk about swimming across: another trick of his, a pathetic yet endearing attempt to convince Killigrew he had magic powers.

'Sharky and Quested are old sparring partners,' explained Paddon, unfurling the cutter's fore-and-aft sails. 'Quested's left hand? Got it bit off by a great white off Tanna two years ago. He's convinced that was Sharky's doing.'

'He's quite mad, isn't he?' said Killigrew.

'Which one?' asked Paddon, hauling up the anchor. 'Quested? Or Sharky?'

'Both,' Killigrew said heavily. 'Does Sharky get the blame for every shark attack in these islands?'

'No.' His teeth showing whitely in the moonlight as he grinned, Paddon took the helm. 'But he claims responsibility for quite a few.' Realising the stub of the cigar he had been chewing had gone out, he took it from his mouth, glanced at it, and tossed it over the side. He reached into the breast pocket of his shirt and dug out another cigar stub; as far as Killigrew could tell, that one had already been smoked down to a length not much longer than the one he had just discarded.

Steering out of the bay, Paddon glanced astern, but the sea behind them was empty. 'They're not coming after us in their canoes. Looks like we made it; this time. Where to, Killigrew? Port Resolution?'

'Thorpetown.'

'Thorpetown's eighty miles in the wrong direction. Any particular reason why you want to go there?'

'That's where Quested's headed with the *Lucy Ann*.'

Paddon nodded thoughtfully. 'He exchanged you fellers for sandalwood logs, didn't he?'

'That's more or less the long and the short of it. You knew it was going on?'

'I'd suspected. I'm a sandalwood trader too, but I'm not a

monster like Quested. It's buggers like him get the rest of us a bad
name. What say you, Moltata? You wantem go long Éfaté, catchem
Quested?'

'*Ale!*' growled the *yeremanu*, and his warriors nodded their
assent. '*Oa!*'

Paddon grinned at Killigrew. 'Looks like we're going to Thorpetown, then. You two look like you could do with a drink,' he added
to Killigrew and Molineaux.

The two Britons exchanged glances. 'Don't mind if we do,' said
Killigrew.

'Take the wheel, Sharky.'

'*Ale!*' The *nakaimo* took the helm from Paddon.

'You trust him at the wheel?' Killigrew asked as he and Molineaux followed Paddon down the booby hatch to the cabin below.

'Listen, mate, I ain't a married man, but if I were you'd be
welcome to share my wife's bed for the night in return for a good
cigar. But the *Rover's Bride*? That's a horse of another colour. And
that's how much I trust Sharky. Can't say I know any white fellers I
trust that much.'

The cabin was in sore need of the attentions of a housekeeper:
charts and dirty crockery with cigar-butts stubbed out in the
leftovers were jumbled on the small table, and potted orchids took
up much of the rest of the available space. Paddon found a
half-empty bottle of whisky, and three dirty mugs. He poured them
each a generous measure and passed out the mugs.

Reluctant to drink from such a filthy vessel, Killigrew used the
mug to gesture at the flowers. 'Is this what you were doing on
Erromanga? Collecting orchids?'

'Yeah. Hey, don't go getting any ideas about stealing them, mate.
They're my orchids. I found 'em.'

'Believe me, Captain Paddon, I'm an officer of the Royal Navy.
The last thing I have on my mind right now is stealing your orchids.'

'I've heard that one before,' snorted Paddon. He moved a couple
of plant pots from a seat, sat down, and pushed some charts off the
table to clear a space for his feet. 'So, Quested's back, is he? And
working for Thorpe.'

'So it would seem. What do you know about it?'

'Nothing I can prove, but I've had my suspicions for years now.
Quested met Thorpe in Sydney about five years ago, when he was a
whaling captain – and a damned good one, by all accounts – and
Thorpe owned one of the largest fleets of whaling ships under
Capricorn. I say Thorpe owned a whaling fleet: he bought up a lot
of ships when there was a slump in the whaling trade. What he
couldn't get for them was crews. That's why he approached Quested.
Quested's got a hell of a reputation in New Bedford as a whaling

skipper, and in whaling terms that's an international reputation. Thorpe figured if he could get Quested to join his fleet, others would soon follow. But the whole thing fell through thanks to Thorpe's financial mismanagement, and he started losing interest in whaling, the same as he lost interest in agriculture within a couple of years of buying up half of New South Wales . . . the half that turned out to be nothing but desert, that is.

'After the whaling venture went up the spout, Thorpe took a look at how much money I was making in the sandalwood trade and decided to try to move in on my territory. Well, it's a free ocean . . . hell, that's the main reason *I* came out here. Thorpe's the one that can't handle a little competition. He's been ingratiating himself with the missionaries ever since he started trying to build that crazy white elephant he calls Thorpetown. The missionaries can't stand me because I've got more influence over the natives than they have. It never occurs to blokes like the Reverend Mr Geddie that might not be entirely unconnected with the fact that I treat the natives with respect. I don't go round telling them that all their customs are sinful, demand that they give up drinking and dancing, or force them to wear second-hand clothes which turn out to be lousy with smallpox. But that's another story.

'Quested left off whaling for a couple of years and took to sandalwooding instead. There was no obvious connection between him and Thorpe, but if he wasn't working for Thorpe, who was he working for? For a time people thought maybe he was working for me, but I soon straightened them out on that account! About that time natives started disappearing from Tanna. The finger of suspicion was immediately pointed at Thorpe because a couple of natives turned up as indentured labourers on his estates in New South Wales, complaining that they'd been lied to about the working conditions they could expect. Well, Thorpe had the paperwork to prove it was all nice and legal. He'd cheated those poor bastards, right enough, saying they were the ones who'd misunderstood the terms and conditions, which had clearly been set out in plain English.'

'A language they can't read.'

'Exactly. The courts said it was the natives' fault they hadn't made sure they'd understood the terms and conditions before making their mark. It left a pretty sour taste in the mouths of Sydney society, but no one could prove Thorpe had acted illegally. That was when HMS *Dido* was sent out here to the New Hebrides to investigate things. Must've been a couple of years ago. Cap'n Maxwell didn't investigate any more than he had to. He was terrified of being eaten by cannibals, so he didn't even land at half the islands he should have visited. I tried speaking to him, but after

Geddie got at him, Maxwell wasn't going to listen to *me*. The natives were still disappearing from Tanna, but since they weren't turning up on any of Thorpe's estates everyone assumed they were just getting killed in wars between the tribes, and they were trying to put the blame on the white man in the hope of getting some kind of compensation.

'It took me a while to put two and two together and realise that Quested was kidnapping Tannese warriors and selling them to the Erromanga men in exchange for sandalwood. But I didn't have any proof, and by then Quested must've decided that things were getting a little too dangerous, what with the Royal Navy starting to show an interest in these islands. So he went back to whaling. I couldn't tell you what brought him back now, after two years.'

'I can,' said Killigrew. 'Devin Cusack.'

'Who's he?'

'An Irish rebel.'

Paddon frowned, and then his brow cleared and he nodded. 'Oh, yeah, I think I remember reading something about that somewhere. Young Ireland. Where does he fit into all this?'

'It's a long story; the essence of it is that some of Cusack's friends in the United States hired Quested to rescue Cusack from Norfolk Island. My ship – HMS *Tisiphone* – was there at the time, and we've been on their trail ever since.'

Paddon raised his eyebrows. 'Quested freed Devin Cusack from Norfolk Island? That's something to be said in his favour. Don't get me wrong, but from what I've heard about the way you British have been treating the Irish these past few years, then fellers like Cusack have every right to have a grievance.'

'And what are you, if not British?'

Paddon raised his mug in a toast. 'Citizen of the world, mate.'

'Hm. Well, it's not as simple as that. When Cusack escaped from Norfolk Island on board the *Lucy Ann* ten days ago, he took six of the most ruthless convicts in the British penal system with him. Incorrigibles, Captain Paddon.'

'Convicts, eh? I remember we had half a dozen convicts escape from Norfolk Island about six years ago. They got as far as the Loyalty Islands, I seem to recall.' He grinned savagely in the light of the oil-lamp that swung overhead. 'Cannibals et 'em.'

'They also took a woman hostage.'

The smile faded from Paddon's face. 'A shaler? That ain't right,' he growled, in a tone of voice which boded ill for anyone who harmed a woman when he was around. 'She's on board the *Lucy Ann*?'

'From what we can make out, she managed to escape from the *Lucy Ann* at the Isle of Pines, and she was picked up by the *Wanderer*.'

'Thorpe's yacht? He'll have taken her to Thorpetown, then.'

'Which is exactly where the *Lucy Ann*'s bound now. There's only one thing I can't understand: the last time we saw our ship, the *Tisiphone*, she was bound for Thorpetown. Why would Thorpe arrange to meet Quested at Thorpetown when he knew the *Tisiphone* would be there?'

'Does your captain know Quested and Thorpe are friends?'

'I don't believe so.'

Paddon grunted. 'Then I wouldn't put it past that slimy bastard Thorpe to find some way to get rid of the *Tisiphone* long enough for him and Quested to conclude whatever business it is they have together at Thorpetown.'

'That means we haven't got much time,' said Killigrew. 'Quested's going to be in a hurry to sail from Thorpetown before the *Tisiphone* gets back.'

'Well, the way I see it . . . either we're overestimating Thorpe's intelligence, and the *Lucy Ann*'s on its way to a harbour where your ship is waiting for them; in which case it'll be all done and dusted long before we get there . . .'

'Or?'

Paddon grinned. 'Or it's all down to us to save the day, mate.'

Mrs Cafferty made her way to where the *Acushnet* was moored alongside the jetty opposite the try-works the following morning after breakfast. The whaler had arrived with a whale carcass chained to each side, and her master – a burly, bearded, barrel-chested bear of a man named Captain Valentine Pease – had regaled Thorpe and Mrs Cafferty with the story of how he had caught and killed them both a few hours earlier using the new Allen bomb-guns. Being so close to Éfaté at the time, he had decided to try-out the blubber at the Thorpetown try-works rather than do it at sea, before resuming his voyage.

'By all means,' Thorpe had said. 'Things are a little quiet here at the moment – I expect most of the whaling fleets are at the whaling grounds off the Japans at present – and we'll welcome your company.' But for some reason the trader had not aired the possibility of the *Acushnet* taking Mrs Cafferty back to civilisation: just one more thing out of many which had started to puzzle her over the last few hours. His silence on the subject had made her feel it would be wise to hold her own peace . . . for the time being.

The whale carcasses had been winched up on to the slipway beside the jetty, and it was from there that the *Acushnet*'s crew were busily engaged in slicing off the blubber, chopping it up, mincing it and melting it down in the try-pots. The process had started late last night and now, nearly twelve hours later, they seemed no nearer completion, even though they had been working through the night. The stench seemed to have permeated the whole of Thorpetown. Gagging at the stink, Mrs Cafferty approached one of the *Acushnet*'s boatsteerers, who was cutting off the blubber with a long-handled cutting-in spade with a flat-edged, razor-sharp head.

'Excuse me? Sir? Could you tell me where I might find Captain Pease?'

Like two of the boatsteerers on the *Lucy Ann*, the man she addressed obviously hailed from one of the Polynesian islands, but he spoke English with the nasal twang of a New Englander. 'Well, you *might* find him in his cabin, missy.' He jerked his head at the ship.

'May I go on board?'

'Surely.'

She climbed the gangplank. The upper deck was deserted – nearly all the crew were working ashore – and there was no one to challenge her as she made her way down the after hatch. She knocked on the door to Pease's cabin.

'Come in!' he boomed from inside.

She entered. He looked up in surprise, not unmixed with delight. 'Why, the lovely Mrs Cafferty! What can I do for you, ma'am?'

'I'll come straight to the point, Captain Pease. I was wondering if I could impose upon you to provide me with transport from this place?'

'I'd be delighted to, but . . . I haven't told you where I'm headed yet. To tell the truth, I ain't sure as I've made up my own mind on that account.'

'It's of no consequence, Captain Pease. Just as long as you take me away from here.'

'Why? Whatever is the matter? I thought you were waiting for the *Tisiphone* to return?'

'If she ever does. Captain Pease, may I confide in you?'

'Why, surely, little lady. I should consider it an honour.'

'How well do you know Mr Thorpe?'

'Not at all. Why, I never clapped eyes on the man before yesterday evening.'

'Captain Pease, it is my suspicion that Mr Thorpe has not been entirely honest with me. You recall last night I told you over dinner how it was that, when I first went aboard the *Wanderer* at the Isle of Pines, Mr Thorpe went on board the *Lucy Ann* and confronted Captain Quested?'

'Indeed. I thought that was a mighty brave thing to do, too.'

'Really? I considered it foolhardy . . . at the time. Since then, I've started to suspect that it was neither. Mr Thorpe was never in any danger for the simple reason that he and Captain Quested are in league with one another.'

Pease arched his bushy eyebrows. 'You think so?'

'I'm sure of it. But the devil of it is that I cannot prove it.'

'What makes you think—'

'Yesterday, as we approached this island, Mr Thorpe invited me into the saloon on board the *Wanderer* for a cup of coffee. It struck me as odd at the time, because until then he had never served any hot beverage on board other than tea. Shortly after that, I passed out, and by the time I had regained consciousness we had arrived here in Thorpetown and I had been put to bed in Mr Thorpe's house. In retrospect, I believe the reason he chose coffee that day was because it has a strong, bitter taste which covers a multitude of sins.'

'You think he drugged you?'

'I'm quite certain of it.'

'But to what end?'

'I'm not sure, but I would guess that the *Tisiphone* was actually here when we arrived . . . as Thorpe knew it would be. He drugged me so I would not see it, and then told Commander Robertson some invented story that would require the *Tisiphone* to steam from here at once. Commander Robertson is an intelligent man, but he had no reason to suspect that Mr Thorpe might be lying to him, or that I might be an unwitting prisoner, drugged on board the *Wanderer*.'

'I guess it's possible,' Pease said dubiously. 'But if Thorpe's in cahoots with Quested, why in tarnation didn't he just hand you over to Quested at the Isle of Pines?'

'And risk exposing the fact that they were in league? Besides, Quested needed me as a hostage. What better way of keeping me captive somewhere where no one would ever think to look? Somewhere I would not try to escape from again, because Mr Thorpe thought he could fool me into thinking I wasn't even a prisoner.'

'I'm astounded, ma'am. To think that one man could be capable of such monstrous duplicity . . .'

'I thought it was rather clever of me, personally,' said Thorpe, coming through the door with Mr Irwin. The chief mate of the *Wanderer* had a pistol in his hand and he pointed it at Mrs Cafferty. 'But it seems I made the error of underestimating your intelligence, m'dear. Whatever am I going to do with you now?'

'My advice to you would be to give yourself up,' Mrs Cafferty said calmly. 'Whatever wild-goose chase you managed to send the *Tisiphone* on, I don't imagine it will keep her away for more than a couple of days.'

'As a matter of fact, I expect her to return at dawn tomorrow,

315

whereupon I shall be forced to apologise most profusely to Commander Robertson for having sent him on a fool's errand. As an experienced seaman, I'm sure he'll appreciate how wild rumours can arise from nothing in the far-off corners of the empire, where any news is seized at as gospel truth. But by then the *Lucy Ann* will have been and gone, and there will be nothing left to connect me with Captain Quested. Including you, m'dear, I'm sorry to say.'

'If you are indeed in league with Quested, then I don't doubt you are capable of cold-bloodedly murdering a defenceless woman,' she retorted coldly. 'Although I expect you'll leave your dirty work to Quested himself; not for the first time, I suspect. However, I doubt you have the ability to murder Captain Pease here along with all the crew of this vessel.'

'True. Fortunately for me, I am not the only one in this room guilty of what the good captain refers to as "monstrous duplicity".'

Pease shrugged. 'Sorry, ma'am. I've been working for Mr Thorpe for five years now.'

She felt utterly defeated: outmanoeuvred and betrayed on all sides.

'You've only yourself to blame,' said Thorpe. 'Had you not been so suspicious, I could have arranged it so that you did not see the *Lucy Ann* arrive, and then handed you safely over to Commander Robertson on his return here tomorrow. He left so precipitously yesterday, even he cannot argue that he hardly gave me time to mention that you were asleep in a cabin on board the *Wanderer*. Once the *Lucy Ann* had left here tonight, we would no longer have had any need of you for a hostage.' He glanced over his shoulder at Irwin. 'Take her up to the house.'

Irwin gestured with the pistol. 'Come on.'

She meekly went out of the door first . . . and then whirled, slamming it shut on Irwin's forearm as he followed her out with the pistol. He cried out in agony and the pistol fell to the floor. She snatched it up and levelled it at Irwin as he emerged, crimson-faced, from the cabin. He froze.

'Put the gun down, m'dear,' Thorpe called over Irwin's shoulder. 'There's nowhere you can run.'

'No? What about the trade house at Havannah Harbour, on the north side of the island?'

'Please don't be foolish. It's fourteen miles over rough country.'

She was grinning with desperation now. 'The same kind of rough country I crossed on the Isle of Pines?' she asked, backing towards the companion ladder that led up on deck.

Thorpe's gaze flicked past her shoulder and his expression turned to one of relief. She whirled and found Quested standing immediately behind her. He caught her right hand by the wrist, twisting her

316

arm until she dropped the pistol, and laid his hook against her throat.

As the *Tisiphone* steamed into Anelghowhat anchorage between Aneiteium and Inyeug, Yelverton levelled a telescope over the gunwale to where some figures played cricket on the beach to the right of the trading station. 'For a man who was grievously wounded, sir, his lordship seems to have staged a remarkable recovery,' the master commented drily.

Robertson snatched the telescope from him to see for himself, and raised it to his eye in time to see Lord Hartcliffe field the ball at silly mid-off. The staff of the trading station were at the bat, Hartcliffe and ten of his men fielding, and the Reverend Mr Geddie seemed to be umpiring. The lieutenant held the ball aloft, and Robertson saw his lips frame the word: 'Howzat!' Then as if guessing that his commanding officer's eyes were upon him, he turned to the *Tisiphone* and waved and grinned like an idiot.

'Tell Mr Muir to stop her,' Robertson instructed one of the midshipmen.

'Aye, aye, sir.'

'Shall I pass the order to drop anchor, sir?' asked the boatswain.

'Belay that, Mr Darrow. Lower my gig to have Lord Hartcliffe brought back on board, and then the pinnace to start ferrying his men back on board.'

Ten minutes later, Lord Hartcliffe was clambering up through the entry port. 'You caught them, sir?'

'What makes you say that, First?'

'I thought you were going to stay at Thorpetown for two weeks?'

'I was informed that *you* had caught them, First; but that you had been badly wounded in the process.'

'I, sir? Never felt better. Who told you—'

'Thorpe,' Robertson said heavily.

'Then he must have been mistaken, sir. We've seen neither hide nor hair of the *Lucy Ann*.'

'Mistaken,' agreed Robertson. 'Or lying in his teeth. Get your men back on board like one o'clock, First. We're going back to Thorpetown. How long will it take us to get there, Mr Yelverton?'

'With sail and steam, and a following wind? About sixteen hours. Maybe fifteen, if Mr Muir pushes his engines.'

'Then see to it he pushes his engines, Mr Yelverton. I only pray we're not too late already.'

The sun was setting over the island of Éfaté by the time Paddon ran the *Rover's Bride* into a secluded cove on the south coast of the

317

island. Killigrew took in the jungle that pressed close on all sides. There was no sign of any settlement.

'Don't tell me *this* is Thorpetown!'

Paddon shook his head. 'The entrance to the harbour is about five miles further along the coast. There's a lower lagoon, and an upper lagoon, with a narrow channel linking the two. But if I know Quested, he'll have posted lookouts. By the time I could sail the *Rover's Bride* to Thorpetown, Thorpe will have his yacht broadside on to the entrance to the upper lagoon. If you've been on board the *Wanderer*, you'll have seen what kind of an arsenal he's got on board. It might not be a match for the *Tisiphone*'s carronades, but she could blow the *Rover's Bride* out of the water.'

He pointed through the jungles ashore. 'The upper lagoon is about two and a half miles that way. I can lead you straight there. If we go overland, we can skirt the lagoon to the east and approach the settlement unseen. Oh-kay?'

'Oh-kay,' said Killigrew. 'Let's go.'

Even as Paddon and Molineaux lowered the jolly boat from the davits over the stern, Moltata and his men dived overboard, their bodies creating hardly a ripple where they cleaved the water. Sharky made to follow him, but Paddon caught him by the arm.

'Not you, Sharky! I need someone to stay here and keep an eye on the *Rover's Bride*.'

'M'be Sharky killim Quested,' the *nakaimo* protested truculently.

'Maybe,' agreed Paddon. 'But not tonight, old feller. We're just going to take a look, see what's going on there. Could be we'll find the *Tisiphone* there, having done our job for us. Stay here, oh-kay?'

Sharky scowled at being excluded, but nodded his assent. '*Ale.*'

Killigrew, Paddon and Molineaux climbed down into the jolly boat and rowed ashore, where they found Moltata and his people waiting for them. They dragged the boat ashore, and Paddon cut down some foliage with his bush knife and covered it over.

'It looks like you've done this kind of thing before,' remarked Killigrew.

'More times than I care to remember. Normally I'd be searching for untapped sandalwood groves, though, or hunting orchids. The natives of these islands will kill for a good clinker-built boat – I mean that literally – and they don't understand the notion of property, so they've no concept of stealing. They find something, they take it. Sharky will keep the *Rover's Bride* safe, but if Quested has patrols out, I don't want them robbing us of our only means to get back to the *Rover's Bride* if we have to leave in a hurry.'

As dusk fell, Paddon led the way inland. The Tannese moved silently through the jungle; Killigrew was almost as stealthy, having had some experience of this kind of work; but no one moved more silently than Molineaux.

They smelled the settlement before they saw it.

'Jesus!' muttered Molineaux. 'What's that stink?'

'Trying-out,' said Paddon. 'That's bad. There must be another whaler at Thorpetown, using the try-works there.'

'Potential allies?' suggested Killigrew.

'Unlikely. These days the only vessels that bother to visit this place are Thorpe's. I reckon we can safely assume the odds have just been increased in their favour.'

The next indication that they were drawing near was an intermittent high-pitched whine, the unmistakable sound of a steam-powered sawmill in action. Killigrew spotted bright lights through the trees ahead, and before long they were peering out through the foliage, across the lagoon to the settlement.

The area on the wharf, brightly illuminated with limelights, was a hive of activity. Men were hoisting blanket pieces of blubber up on the hoist in front of the try-works. The *Lucy Ann* and the *Acushnet* were moored on either side of the jetty, while the *Wanderer* was anchored a short distance out into the lagoon. On the deck of the *Lucy Ann*, men were constructing a deckhouse aft while others sat in boatswain's chairs to repaint the sides. One man was working on a new name on her escutcheon. Killigrew took out his miniature telescope to take a closer look, and saw him painting the name *Themis* there.

Surveying the scene, he recognised Gog (or was it Magog?) on the deck of the *Lucy Ann*, tossing slender sandalwood logs down to his brother on the jetty below. Magog (or Gog) caught them as easily as if they had been bamboo canes. Wyatt and Vickers stacked the logs on a truck which they pushed along the tracks to the sawmill.

'I can see Wyatt and Vickers,' he told the others. 'No sign of Thorpe or Quested.'

'What's the name of that whaler?' asked Paddon.

'The *Acushnet*.'

'Just as I'd feared. Captain Pease: one of Thorpe's men.'

'How big's her crew?'

'Twenty-seven, usually.'

'Add about ten from the *Wanderer*, another ten left on board the *Lucy Ann* when she sailed from Erromanga yesterday, and six incorrigibles,' Killigrew said grimly. 'That's . . . um . . . more than fifty.'

'And fifteen of us,' said Molineaux. 'What do you want to do, sir?'

Killigrew swore. 'We'll have to let them go. We can't tackle them head on, not against those kind of odds. At least now we know the

319

new name Quested's ship is sailing under: the *Themis*.'

'That's dandy,' Paddon said sarcastically. 'Who knows? Maybe one day he'll make the mistake of sailing her into British waters. Your navy can put a notice out to keep a weather eye open for him. Of course, by the time you ever do catch up with him, he'll have landed the convicts in California long ago; and probably have given the *Lucy Ann* a new name and another change of appearance.'

Killigrew rounded on him furiously. 'What else can we do?' he hissed. 'They've got muskets, pistols, whaling craft. We've got a rifle, a shotgun, two revolvers, a bush-knife and Molineaux's Bowie knife.' He wanted to say it was hopeless, but that would have been 'Quit' Killigrew speaking. He racked his brains – there *had* to be a way. 'At least we can drag Thorpe to Sydney in chains, put a stop to his nasty little trade in sandalwood.'

'Sir?' Molineaux pointed to the *Acushnet*, where a couple of figures were emerging from the after hatch. 'Is that who I think it is?'

Killigrew raised the telescope to his eye once more in time to see Silas Jarrett shepherding a woman to the entry port. 'Mrs Cafferty. At least she's still alive, thank God.'

'Not for much longer,' said Paddon. 'She knows too much about Thorpe and Quested. Take my word for it, she'll be marked for death.'

'We've got to get her out of there, sir.'

'I'm aware of that, Molineaux,' Killigrew replied tersely, following Jarrett and Mrs Cafferty with his eyes as the swindler led her across the plaza and up the broad flight of steps to the house above. They went inside.

Killigrew returned the telescope to his pocket. 'All right, Captain Paddon. You've played your part, and I'm grateful, but from now on this is a Royal Naval operation. Take Moltata and his people back to the *Rover's Bride*. If Molineaux and I aren't back by dawn, you can assume we're not coming. If you can't find the *Tisiphone*, sail to Hobart Town. You'll find HMS *Havannah* there. Tell everything you know about this business to Captain Erskine. He'll know what to do.'

'You're kidding, aren't you? You mean to tell me you and Wes here are going to tackle them all? Just the two of you?'

'We're just going to try to rescue Mrs Cafferty; it doesn't take fifteen of us to do that.'

Paddon looked inclined to argue, but finally nodded his assent. 'Oh-kay, mate, you want to get yourself killed, that's fine by me. You'd better take these.' He handed his rifle to Molineaux, his shotgun to Killigrew, took the revolvers from the holsters at his hip and handed them one each. 'You're going to need them.'

'Thank you. But I hope we can pull this off without a shot being fired. Silence and stealth, that's more my speed.'

Molineaux rolled his eyes. 'Whatever you say, sir.'

The lieutenant and the able seaman left Paddon with the twelve Tannese in the bushes on the south side of the lagoon, and worked their way around to the eastern end, approaching the settlement from that direction. They could hear sawing and hammering from the *Lucy Ann*, the intermittent whine of the saw-blade, and the clank and hiss of the machinery that drove it.

'What's the plan, sir?' asked Molineaux.

Killigrew glanced up to where Thorpe's house loomed over the settlement. 'Come to think of it, creeping stealthily is more your speciality than it is mine. Think you can get up there without anyone seeing you, and get Mrs Cafferty out?' It went without saying that Molineaux would probably have to deal with Jarrett, but the lieutenant had every faith in the seaman's ability to do so.

'Getting up there will be easy as caz, sir. The difficulty is going to be getting Mrs Cafferty out again.'

'Supposing I supply a diversion of some sort?'

'Like a fire, perhaps?' suggested Molineaux. He nodded to where the crew of the *Acushnet* were rolling casks of whale oil into the godown adjoining the try-works to cool. 'All that oil's going to burn a treat.'

Killigrew grinned. 'Let's do it.'

'Did Mr Thorpe say what he wanted?' Mrs Cafferty asked Jarrett as she followed him into the house.

'I'm afraid he didn't see fit to confide in me, ma'am.' He gestured up the stairs. 'This way.'

She knew he was lying. Even if she had not known he was a swindler, she fancied that his oily, urbane manner would have made her distrustful of him anyway. But the only way to find out what was going on was to comply. She suspected she did not have much choice, anyway: Jarrett had a pistol tucked in the waistband of his trousers.

She followed him upstairs, and he gestured to the door of the room where she had slept the previous night. 'In there?' she asked sceptically.

He nodded, and motioned for her to go in.

She hesitated on the threshold. It was dark outside, and the shutters were closed: the only light came from the oil-lamp that stood on the bedside cabinet, and the wick had been turned down low.

'Mr Thorpe?' She stepped inside. It took her less than a second to realise that Thorpe was not in the room: there was nowhere to conceal a man of his bulk. She started to turn back to the door. 'I think you must be mistaken, Mr Ja—'

That was when Mangal Griddha stepped out from behind the door and looped a strip of cloth over her head. Before she had realised what was going on, he had pushed her across the room and face-down on the bed. With one knee in the small of her back, he commenced to garrotte her expertly.

'Do not be afraid, memsahib,' he murmured almost tenderly in her ear. 'It is a great honour to die in Kali's name.'

XXIII

. . . Into The Fire

There was no need for silence. As Killigrew and Molineaux crept through the shadows beneath the sawmill, the clank of the steam engine and the whine of the blade cutting through wood precluded the danger of their being heard by Lissak or Noah Pilcher who were stacking up the sawn planks a few yards to their left.

Hunched over – there was barely four feet between the floor of the mill above them and the ground below – they made their way to the far end and crouched behind the steps leading up to the door of the mill. The try-works was directly opposite, another building with a light showing in the window to their right. Molineaux wasted no more time, but slithered off and disappeared round the back of the building to their right, keeping his head down below the level of the windows.

Killigrew glanced across to where a couple of dozen barrels were stacked in front of the try-works and patted his pockets down for matches. The box he had been carrying had got soaked when he had swum out to the *Lucy Ann* the night before last. Gog and Magog came from the direction of the jetty, pushing a truckload of sandalwood logs along the rails. Killigrew waited until the twins had disappeared in front of the sawmill before he crossed to the building off to his right, and peered cautiously through the grimy window. An oil lamp illuminated what appeared to be an office, with ledgers and papers spread out on a desk. There was no one in sight. Feeling exposed against the wall of the building, Killigrew tried the handle of the door. It was not locked. He slipped inside, at once drawing the faded, mildewed curtain over the window.

A second door led into another room, and he could hear voices. 'Splendid work, Mr Greeley.' Thorpe's plummy tones were unmistakable. 'You really are an artist.'

'Not the kind of masterpiece I had in mind when I agreed to come to work for you, Mr Thorpe,' Greeley replied huffily. 'What

323

the devil's going on, sir? What does Captain Quested need with forged papers, anyhow? And why are they disguising the *Lucy Ann*?'

'You mean you don't know?' asked a third voice Killigrew did not recognise. 'Quested's been a naughty boy. Rescuing convicts from Norfolk Island, feeding natives to the cannibals on Erromanga—'

'All right, Mr Underwood, that will do,' Thorpe snapped pettishly.

Killigrew tiptoed across to the desk and opened the drawer. He found papers, a bottle of ink and some pencils, a ball of twine, a few loose percussion caps, but no matches.

'What's he talking about, Mr Thorpe?' demanded Greeley. 'Rescuing convicts from Norfolk Island? You mean . . . Wyatt and those others? They're escaped convicts?'

'Ask no questions, hear no lies, Mr Greeley,' said Thorpe. 'Now you get on with that master's certificate while I give these papers to Captain Quested.'

A moment later the door opened and Thorpe stepped into the outer office. He froze when he saw Killigrew, and the lieutenant levelled Paddon's shotgun at him.

'Mr Killigrew!' exclaimed Thorpe. 'Thank the Lord above you're here! Captain Quested – he's a pirate, sir, nothing but a pirate! He forced me to—'

'Spare me your lies,' sighed Killigrew. 'Raise your hands above your head.'

'But surely you cannot conceive that I—'

Killigrew prodded him in the stomach with the barrels of the shotgun. 'Hands up, I said. It's all up with you, Thorpe. We're on to your nasty little trade, and I'm here to close you down. Permanently. Now, get back in there.' The lieutenant gestured with the shotgun and Thorpe backed into the inner room. Killigrew took the ball of twine from the drawer before following him.

The inner room was some kind of printing works. Greeley and the other man – Underwood – had heard them talking and were waiting for them when they entered. The artist looked bewildered, the other man resigned. 'Mr Killigrew?' Greeley asked in astonishment. 'What the devil's going on?'

'I'm arresting Thorpe for conspiracy to mass murder,' explained Killigrew. He tossed the ball of twine to Greeley. 'Tie him up. We'll see if you're as much of an artist with knots as you are with printer's ink. Sit in that chair, Thorpe.'

Ashen-faced, Thorpe complied. Greeley approached him hesitantly, an apologetic expression on his face as he started to tie up the shipowner.

'But this is intolerable!' protested Thorpe, glowering at Killigrew. 'Do you have any idea who you're dealing with, young man?'

'A fat tub of lard who's going to hang,' Killigrew told him cheerfully, before swinging the shotgun towards Underwood, who had been slinking towards the door. 'And where do you think you're going?'

'I didn't want any part of this!' whined Underwood, and gestured at Thorpe. 'He forced me into all this!'

'Tell it to the judge in Hobart Town,' said Killigrew, and turned to Greeley. 'When you've finished with Thorpe, you can tie up this fellow, too.'

'What's going to happen to me?' asked Greeley.

'I overheard you talking just now. Turn Queen's evidence and you might just walk away from this whole affair a free man.'

'Turn Queen's evidence!' snorted Thorpe. 'Untie me now, Greeley, or you won't live long enough to see the inside of a court-house!'

Killigrew rammed the muzzle of the shotgun into his stomach. 'Pipe down!' He turned to Greeley, who had started to bind Underwood into the other chair. 'When you've finished tying him up, my advice to you is to get away from here as quickly as possible. Make your way to the east end of the lagoon and then cut due south across the jungle. There's a trail there that leads to the coast. You'll find a cutter tied up in the cove there, the *Rover's Bride* . . .'

'Paddon!' spat Thorpe. 'So, that's how you got off Erromanga!'

'I think we've had enough out of you, Mr Thorpe.' Killigrew found a couple of inky rags and used one to gag Thorpe, tossing the other to Greeley who did likewise with Underwood.

Killigrew checked that both Thorpe and Underwood were securely bound and gagged, and then reached into the pocket of Thorpe's coat. 'Don't mind if I trouble you for a light, do you?'

Thorpe looked as if he *did* mind, very much, and made a strangled sound of rage behind his gag.

Killigrew gestured for Greeley to follow him into the outer office. 'Where are the rest of your men?' asked the artist.

'Able Seaman Molineaux's getting Mrs Cafferty from the big house at the back of the square even as we speak,' said Killigrew, extinguishing the oil-lamp so that no light would show when he opened the door.

'And the others?'

'I'm afraid that's it.'

'Dear God!'

Killigrew opened the outer door a couple of inches and looked out. Gog and Magog were pushing another truckload of lumber to the sawmill. 'As soon as those two are out of sight, make your way round the back of the mill and head for the coast. Now . . . go!' He opened the door and gave the artist a shove in the back.

Greeley took a few lumbering steps across the open space

between the offices and the sawmill. He stumbled and for a moment it looked as though he might fall. He righted himself, and to Killigrew's chagrin he stopped and looked around stupidly. Then he remembered where he was going and covered the last few yards to the shadows behind the sawmill.

Killigrew slipped out after him. He made his way into the dark alley behind the try-works, which formed a dogleg where it met the side of the adjoining godown. The far end of the alley opened out on the square. There was more light there, and he would be exposed as soon as he stepped out of the alley, but there was no one in sight. He cast a glance at the house; there was no sign of Molineaux or Mrs Cafferty. He wondered if the seaman had succeeded in getting her. He was tempted to go to help, but knew he had to put his trust in Molineaux; the seaman would be putting his trust in him, and was doubtless waiting for him to start the diversion that would enable him and Mrs Cafferty to get away from Thorpetown.

Gripping the shotgun tightly, Killigrew edged down the side of the godown and peered around the corner. Pushing a truckload of sawn sandalwood towards the jetty, Gog and Magog had been intercepted by five spouters Killigrew did not recognise; men from the *Acushnet*, presumably, since they did not wear the white uniforms of the *Wanderer*'s crew. The seven of them argued over whose turn it was to use the truck. For a moment it looked as though a fight might break out. Killigrew's money was on the twins, but then Quested arrived and ordered Gog and Magog to let the spouters take the truck as soon as they unloaded the sandalwood on the jetty, and then load the wood into the hold of the *Acushnet*.

The twins pushed the truck on to the jetty and unloaded the timber, allowing the men from the *Acushnet* to load the truck with the last blanket pieces of blubber from the whales they had caught. They pushed it up the ramp into the half-loft of the try-works, and as soon as they were out of sight Killigrew took his chance and broke cover, dashing across twenty yards of open ground to duck down behind a stack of barrels on the wharf.

He peered over the barrels. He could see no one looking in his direction, so he pulled one of the barrels at the back of the stack on its side and broached it, the sound of the steam-engine in the sawmill covering the noise of the planks breaking. As the liquid within splashed across the ground, he stepped back quickly. He tucked the shotgun under his arm, took the box of matches from his pocket, struck one, and tossed it into the puddle.

The match went out as soon as it landed in the liquid.

Someone touched him behind the ear with the muzzle of a pistol. 'Brine,' Jarrett explained smoothly. 'The barrels containing whale oil are stacked in the godown.'

'I'll bear that in mind,' Killigrew said ruefully, slipping the box of matches into his pocket.

'Hands above your head,' said Jarrett. 'Now turn and face me. Nice and slowly, if you please. No sudden moves.'

Killigrew did as he was bidden. The shotgun fell from under his arm. He turned, and Jarrett promptly smashed the grip of his pistol against his forehead. Lightning flashed inside Killigrew's skull and his legs crumpled beneath him.

Jarrett stood over him. 'I owed you that one.' He plucked the revolver from Killigrew's belt and tucked his own pistol in his belt before picking up the shotgun. 'Now, on your feet. I expect Captain Quested would like a word with you.'

Mrs Cafferty could feel herself blacking out as Mangal pulled the garrotte ever tighter about her throat. Clawing at the strip of cloth, she struggled desperately to cling on to consciousness. There was no point hoping for a rescue at the eleventh hour: the only person who could save her now was herself.

Through the red mist that swam before her eyes, she could just make out the bottles on the bedside cabinet. She reached out for them, but her fingers came just a few inches too short. She tried clawing at the bedclothes to drag herself nearer, but they only came untucked from beneath the mattress.

Mangal pulled tighter, his knee pressing hard against her throat. With a supreme effort, she managed to lift both him and herself a couple of inches off the mattress. Then she slumped forwards. She reached out again, but her fingers only brushed against the bottle of kalydor and knocked it over.

It started to roll towards the edge of the cabinet, and dropped off. She managed to catch it on the way down. She smashed the neck against the edge of the cabinet, and dashed the contents over her shoulder into Mangal's face.

He screamed in agony.

She pushed him off and rolled off the bed. Wiping his streaming eyes with his sleeve, he leaped off the bed and blocked her path to the door before she could reach it. He drew a dagger from his belt and held it out towards her, slashing at her throat.

She dodged back behind the bed. He started to follow her round, then realised she was going to try to climb over the bed to get to the door. He doubled back and jumped on the bed, advancing. She snatched the oil-lamp from the bedside cabinet and hurled it at his head. He dashed it aside with a grunt of annoyance, and the lamp smashed against the wall to the right of the door.

For a moment they were plunged into darkness. Mangal lunged at her with the knife, leaping from the bed, but she had already moved. The pool of oil abruptly burst aflame, setting ablaze the carpet and the drapes on the bed. In its eerie, flickering light, she saw Mangal silhouetted with his back to the flames, advancing again. She backed away until she bumped into something: the chair in front of the desk. She snatched it up and held it before her, thrusting its legs at his face. He backed away, less sure of himself now, realising that for once one of his victims would be no easy kill.

She tried to squeeze past him to the door, but he moved to block her. He thrust again with the knife. She swung the chair and caught him a glancing blow on the arm which dashed the knife from his hand. As he went to retrieve it, she dropped the chair and made a dash for the door. But now that corner of the room was an inferno, the heat of the flames driving her back.

She glanced over her shoulder and saw that Mangal had got his knife again. She turned to face him and snatched up the chair once more. The room was beginning to fill with smoke that stung her eyes and clawed at her throat. Realising she had to act fast, she charged. Mangal was caught between the legs of the chair and smashed back against the wardrobe. The doors broke under his weight and he became entangled in the splintered planks, his fat body wedged inside the wardrobe.

She looked around frantically while he tried to break free. There was no way past the fire to the door; that only left the windows. She threw up the sash of the nearest and thrust her head out. The flagstone terrace at the side of the house was about ten feet below her. She tried to tell herself she could make it, but that was neither here nor there. She had no choice but to try.

She squeezed out. It was awkward – the window was narrow – but she managed to twist and by gripping on to the stone coping she was able to pull herself up and get her feet on the window ledge. She took a deep breath, bracing herself to jump . . .

Mangal grabbed her by the ankles and tried to pull her back inside. She overbalanced and pitched forwards. The world spun around her, and in her mind's eye she saw herself hitting those flagstones headfirst, splitting her skull.

Molineaux reached the rear of the big house and tried the back door. It was locked. He suspected it would only take a minute or two to pick the lock, but some time had already passed since he had seen Jarrett bring Mrs Cafferty to the house; more than enough time to kill her. Fearing he was already too late, he backed away from the house and looked for a swifter means of entry. The door at the front was too exposed. He tried one of the windows, but it was locked. If one was locked, they would all be locked.

On the ground floor, at any rate.

He made his way around the side of the house. A drainpipe ran down from the gutter to a rain barrel. It passed tolerably close to a window on the first floor behind which a light flickered, like a log fire in a hearth. He would be able to look through the window to see if anyone was waiting for him inside, while all they would be able to see was their own reflection against the black night sky.

He tested the pipe: it felt more than strong enough. He braced his feet against the stonework behind it and shinned up as nimbly as a monkey. When he was level with the window he stretched out an arm to see if he could reach it, when someone threw up the sash from within.

He froze. A head was thrust out, and a moment later a figure started to climb out. To his astonishment he recognised it as Mrs Cafferty. She had not noticed him clinging to the drainpipe only a couple of feet to her left, and he wondered how best to draw her attention to his presence without startling her into losing her footing.

A moment later a pair of hands reached out from the window behind her and grabbed her ankles. She toppled forwards.

Molineaux grabbed for her instinctively and caught her by the arm. She cried out in shock, and as the hands holding her ankles let go, the seaman's arm was almost wrenched from its socket as it bore her full weight. Then he lost his grip on the drainpipe, and the two of them fell.

Molineaux landed heavily on his side and lay there for a moment, the wind knocked out of him. He felt someone drag the rifle from his shoulder and rolled on his back to see Mrs Cafferty standing over him, levelling the rifle at his head.

'Don't shoot, ma'am!' he hissed. 'I ain't one of them!'

'You're that black seaman from the *Tisiphone*, aren't you?' she asked in astonishment.

'Able Seaman Wes Molineaux, at your service.'

She lowered the rifle and reached out a hand to help him to his feet. 'What the devil were you doing, clinging to the side of the house like that?'

'Mr Killigrew sent me to rescue you—'

'Help!' screamed a voice above them.

They looked up. Mangal Griddha had tried to climb out of the window after her, but his fat body had got wedged in the narrow frame. Now he could neither climb out nor climb back into the blazing room behind him.

'I'm burning!' he screamed. 'Help! Help! I'm burning! Oh, Kali! The fire! It burns.' Sobbing, he started to jabber away in Hindi.

'Oh, dear God!' gasped Mrs Cafferty. 'Can't you do something, Mr Molineaux?'

'Only put him out of his misery,' Molineaux said grimly. 'And I ain't sure he deserves—'

'Then do it, for heaven's sake!'

The seaman glanced down the steps towards the wharf below. 'The sound of the shot . . .'

'Don't you think he's making quite enough noise as it is?' she asked. Mangal was shrieking in agony now.

Molineaux sighed, raised the stock of the rifle to his shoulder, took aim, and fired. Mangal's body jerked as a black hole appeared in the centre of his forehead, and he slumped.

She gazed down to the lagoon. 'Where's the *Tisiphone*?'

'Not here. Come on, ma'am. We've got a cutter waiting off the south coast.' Taking her right hand in his left, he set off down the steps.

The spouters from the *Acushnet* had seen the fire now, and were crossing the plaza. As Molineaux and Mrs Cafferty headed for the alley behind the godown adjoining the try-works, the spouters tried to cut them off. Molineaux pulled the revolver from the waistband of his trousers and discouraged them with a couple of shots. As they scattered, Mrs Cafferty caught him by the arm and dragged him into the dark alley behind the godown adjoining the try-works.

They were running down the alley when a huge, dark shape stepped out from the far side of the try-works and crashed into Molineaux. Still holding the seaman's hand, Mrs Cafferty was jerked off her feet and the three of them tumbled in the shadows. Molineaux lost his grip on the revolver and heard it skitter across the ground, but could not see where it fell. He grappled with the dark figure – from the sheer weight of him, it could only be one of the Lawless twins. Molineaux was no match for his gigantic opponent, and the spouter rolled on top, pummelling the seaman's face with his massive fists.

Then Mrs Cafferty rose to her feet and kicked the twin in the head. It was enough to enable Molineaux to crawl out from under the dazed spouter, but the twin was on his feet again in an instant. Molineaux stood up and interposed himself between the spouter and Mrs Cafferty.

'Keep on going until you get to the far end of the lagoon, then make your way around it and head south until you come to the coast,' the seaman said to her. 'You'll be able to see our ship from there: there are friends aboard, they'll look after you.'

'What about you?'

'Don't worry about me: I can handle this bastard. Whatever happens, just keep going!'

She looked hesitant.

'Go!' he hissed.

She turned and ran. Before she had gone a few yards, however, Jemmy Fingers stepped out in front of her, grabbed her and slammed her against the wall at the back of the try-works. Pinioning her to the weatherboards, he leered. 'Alone at last.'

'Get your greasy hands off her!' roared Molineaux.

Gog caught him from behind and dragged him to the ground. Molineaux tried to get up and saw Fingers drag Mrs Cafferty out of sight round the back of the building behind the try-works. Gog stood up and Molineaux tried to crawl after her, but the giant caught him by the belt, hauled him to his feet, and threw him against the side of the building.

Molineaux picked himself up and turned to face Gog. For a moment he thought he was facing both Lawless Twins; then he realised he was seeing double. He shook his head muzzily to clear it.

Gog hit him again. Molineaux was hurled against one of the barrels stacked against the rear wall of the try-works, and it splintered under the impact. The twin tried to stamp on his head, but he rolled out of the way.

Something hard and cold was digging into his back. He reached behind him and his fingers closed on the revolver. He pushed himself to his feet and levelled the revolver at Gog. 'Hold it!'

The twin froze.

'No, you hold it, *amigo!*'

Molineaux twisted and saw Forgan standing in the mouth of the alley. He had some kind of harpoon gun cradled in his arms, levelled at Molineaux. Gog moved away from the seaman quickly.

'Know what this is?' demanded Forgan.

'A harpoon gun?'

'An Allen bomb-gun, *amigo*. If it can kill a whale, imagine what it's going to do to you. So drop the pistol *pronto*, unless you want me to blow your stinking black hide clean back to Africa.'

Molineaux threw the revolver away. 'I'm from Seven Dials, actually.'

'Whatever.' Forgan gestured with the bomb-gun. 'Get the pistol, Gog.' He gestured with the bomb-gun. 'Start walking, *amigo*.'

'I suppose you're wondering why I haven't just killed you out of hand,' Quested told Killigrew, leaning back against the rear hand-rail of the platform over the try-pots.

'I dare say you'll get around to it sooner or later,' gasped Killigrew, dripping with sweat. 'Although I must confess, the suspense is killing me.'

He dangled over one of the simmering try-pots, the cord that bound his wrists looped over the hook of a chain-hoist that hung from an overhead beam. Jarrett stood next to Quested on the platform, while Wyatt sat on the edge of the half-loft, grinning. Magog stood with his hands on the chain that controlled the pulley, and Utumate sat on a barrel, calmly sharpening the blade of his tomahawk with a whetstone.

Quested chuckled drily. 'Trying to hide your fear behind bad jokes, Mr Killigrew? Punning won't save your life.'

'If you're going to kill me, why the devil don't you get on with it?'

'You really are in a hurry to die, aren't you? Patience, patience! All in good time. You see, a couple of pulls on that chain Magog's holding, and you get lowered, inch by inch, into the try-pot. How far do you think you'll get before your heart gives out from the excruciating agony? Crotch deep? Chest deep? Maybe we'll get you all the way up to your face, and you'll burn and drown at the same time as the boiling blubber fills your mouth and nostrils and chokes you.'

'Yes, I think I get the point.'

Quested drew his revolver from its holster. 'Alternatively, I could just shoot you in the head. A relatively quick and painless way to die. All you have to do is tell me how you got here.'

'I already told you. I made a pair of wings, like Dædalus, and flew here.'

Quested nodded to Magog, who ran the chain through his hands, lowering Killigrew down towards the bubbling blubber beneath him. The heat was terrific, the stench almost overpowering.

When Killigrew's feet were only a couple of inches above the try-pot, Quested signalled for Magog to stop lowering him.

'We're wasting our time,' snarled Wyatt. 'He won't talk. Let's just croak him and get out of here.'

Quested rounded on him. 'And find the *Tisiphone* waiting to blow us out of the water as soon as we sail out of the lagoon? I'm damned if I'll take that chance. The only way he could have gotten away from Erromanga and got here is on a ship. Maybe the *Tisiphone*. Whichever ship she was, he didn't sail her here on his own. I want to know who came with him. All it needs is for a friend of his to see us disguising the *Lucy Ann*, and all the work that Mr Irwin's men are doing will be for nothing.'

The door to the try-works opened, and Molineaux staggered through the door, propelled by a shove from Gog behind him. They were followed in by Forgan, carrying a bomb-gun. 'Look at what we found, *amigos!*'

'What did I tell you?' Quested crowed triumphantly. 'Where there's one rat, there's another. Looks like we've got ourselves a regular infestation here.'

Molineaux glanced up at Killigrew. 'Sorry, sir. Looks like I made a mess of things again.'

'Is that what you were holding out for?' Quested asked the lieutenant. 'Counting on this nigger to rescue you? Think again. There's no one coming. Now tell me: how did you get off Erromanga?'

'We hitched a ride on the back of a passing whale,' Killigrew told him glibly. There was no bravado left in him; from the relish with which Quested had described his impending fate, Killigrew had a feeling he was going to be lowered into the try-pot whether he talked or not.

'Joke all you like,' said Jarrett. 'You won't find it so amusing when you're up to your waist in boiling blubber.'

'At least I can look down my nose at a bastard like you.'

Jarrett smiled. 'Trying to make me angry so I'll make a mistake? You're wasting your time. Ned's the hot-tempered one. Or did you think you were the only one around here with a stiff upper lip?'

'What should we do with this one?' asked Forgan, indicating Molineaux with the bomb-gun.

Wyatt gestured dismissively. 'Shoot him. We don't need him.'

'Oh-kay.' Forgan levelled the bomb-gun at Molineaux's back.

'Not with that!' snapped Quested. 'This place is full of whale oil, you half-wit! You want the whole place to go up in flames?'

'Besides, you'll make a terrible mess, and this shirt is clean on today,' added Jarrett.

'Use a regular gun.' Quested reached under the rail around the platform to take the bomb-gun from Forgan and was about to hand his revolver down when he hesitated. 'No, wait. I've got a better idea. Take him to the sawmill. Perhaps with the right kind of persuasion Mr Henson will prove more talkative than the lieutenant here.'

Forgan grinned. 'I get the idea, Cap'n. Come on,' he told Molineaux. 'You know the way.'

'See you later, sir!' Molineaux called over his shoulder.

'Not in this life, *amigo*,' sneered Forgan.

'Gog, Magog: go with him,' ordered Quested, balancing the bomb-gun across the angle of the rail on one corner of the platform. The twins nodded and followed Forgan and Molineaux out of the try-works. A moment after they had left, Solomon Lissak entered. He glanced up at where Killigrew hung, and then averted his gaze hurriedly, as if he preferred to pretend the lieutenant was not there. 'Thorpe's house is on fire, Ned,' he told Wyatt.

'Let it burn.'

'Did you find Thorpe yet?' demanded Quested.

Lissak shook his head. 'He wasn't at the house. Piggy was, though. He's dead.'

'Your handiwork, I suppose?' Jarrett asked Killigrew.

The lieutenant shook his head. 'I wish I could claim the credit for it, but—'

Quested laid his hand against Jarrett's chest. 'Piggy's that heathen you sent to kill Mrs Cafferty, wasn't he? So where is she now?'

'No sign of her up at the house,' said Lissak.

'Find her,' snapped Quested. 'We can't afford to leave any witnesses, do you understand me?'

Lissak nodded. He was halfway back to the door when he stopped and turned. 'Where were Mr Forgan and the twins taking Wes just now?'

'No need for you to concern yourself, Mr Lissak. They were just going to have a little chat with him.'

'He means torture him,' Killigrew explained helpfully.

Jarrett rammed the haft of a cutting-in spade into the lieutenant's stomach, making him gasp in winded agony. 'Shut up!'

'That's rum,' said Killigrew. 'A moment ago you said you were going to lower me into the blubber if I didn't talk. Now you want me to shut up?'

Jarrett hit him with the spade again.

Quested chuckled. 'You just don't know when to keep your mouth shut, do you?' He turned to Lissak. 'Go and find Mrs Cafferty, and bring her to me. Now!'

'Do as he says, Solly,' ordered Wyatt.

Lissak nodded and hurried out of the try-works.

'You think we can trust him?' Quested asked Wyatt.

'He hasn't got the guts to defy me.'

Quested rubbed his jaw with the curve of his hook. 'Go after him, Utumate,' he decided at last. 'Make sure he doesn't get any foolish notions about switching sides at the eleventh hour.'

Utumate hopped down from his barrel and left the try-works, swinging his tomahawk casually.

'Now, where were we?' mused Quested. 'Oh! Now I remember. Torturing Mr Killigrew here. Mr Wyatt, be so good as to lower Mr Killigrew's feet into the try-pot.'

'My pleasure.' Wyatt jumped down from the half-loft and crossed to the chain that controlled the pulley.

'Last chance, Mr Killigrew.'

'Go to the devil.'

Jarrett chuckled. 'After you, I thi—'

A shot sounded outside. Quested, Wyatt and Jarrett exchanged glances. 'What was that?' asked Jarrett.

'Another goddamned interruption,' sighed Quested. 'Hold it, Mr Wyatt. I'd better go see what that was.' He descended the steps from the platform, drawing his revolver from its holster once more, and headed for the door. On the threshold, he paused and turned back

334

briefly to address Killigrew with a grin. 'Hang around, Mr Killigrew. I haven't finished with you yet.'

Vickers pressed his mouth against Mrs Cafferty's and forced his tongue between her lips. She bit down with all her might. He gave a muffled scream, and pushed her away. She fell against the side of the try-works. He raised a hand to his mouth, and it came away covered in blood.

She got up and tried to run, but he caught her by the shoulder, spun her around and threw a punch at her jaw. She felt her teeth crack in her mouth as she fell. He crouched over her, unfastening the buckle of the belt that held up her trousers. She raked her nails across his cheeks, until he caught her by the wrist and pinioned her arm to the ground. 'Lie still!'

She rolled over and sank her teeth into his wrist. He screamed, and then slapped her across the cheek. She kicked him in the face with both feet. He was thrown back, and she got up to run, but he was on his feet in an instant. He caught her round the waist and dragged her to the ground. With one hand on her throat, he tore off the buttons of her trousers and tried to drag them away from her hips.

She saw the revolver thrust down the front of his trousers. She grabbed the butt and tried to pull it clear, but the hammer got caught in his shirt and she inadvertently pulled the trigger. There was a muffled bang, and his whole body jerked spasmodically. Wide-eyed with horror, he glanced down at the bloody stain that spread across his crotch.

Mrs Cafferty stared in horror at what she had done. 'Oh my God!' she sobbed. 'I'm so sorry!' Then she realised what she was saying and, more pertinently, to whom she was saying it. 'No, on second thoughts, I'm not sorry at all.' She stood up, cocked the revolver, and levelled it at his head.

He fainted.

She decided against shooting him, partly because she could not shoot a defenceless man, but mostly because a quick death from a bullet was too good for his kind: he deserved to bleed to death. Still holding the revolver, she staggered to the mouth of the alley, hurting in a dozen different places.

A figure appeared in front of her, silhouetted by the light from the wharf. It was Utumate, drawn by the sound of the shot. When he saw her, he swung his tomahawk back across his shoulder. She levelled the revolver at his chest, but before she could fire he had knocked the gun from her hand with the flat of the tomahawk. He aimed a second, killing-stroke at her head, and Lissak stepped up behind him and hit him on the back of the head with a plank of

335

sandalwood. The plank broke in two, and Utumate measured his length on the ground.

Mrs Cafferty scrambled for the revolver, but by the time she had retrieved it and whirled to face Lissak, he had dropped the four-by-two and thrown up his hands. 'Whoa! Careful where you point that thing, missy. I'm on your side. I may be a cracksman, but I ain't no croaksman.'

'How do I know I can trust you?'

'Well, if I wasn't on your side, why didn't I let that heathen bastard croak you just now?'

'Your logic is impeccable, Mr Lissak. Where's Mr Killigrew?'

'They got him in the try-works. They're torturing him.'

'Then there's not a moment to lose!'

'Yur, but they're also torturing my Wes in the sawmill!'

'All right. You help Wes, and I'll help Mr Killigrew.'

'I haven't got a gun!' he whined.

'Surely you can't expect me to tackle them unarmed? I'm only a woman, for heaven's sake!'

'Yur, but I'm old!'

She ignored him. He seemed like a cunning fellow; he would work something out. She hurried across the wharf to the try-works, praying she would not be too late. She was about to pass under the ramp leading up to the loft of the try-works when Quested stepped out from behind a stack of barrels and held the muzzle of his revolver to her neck.

'Going somewhere, missy?' He pulled back the hammer of the revolver with his hook. 'Any last words?'

'Quested!'

Both Quested and Mrs Cafferty turned to see Thorpe striding towards them with Utumate, Underwood and Noah Pilcher. 'What the deuce do you think you're doing, Quested?' demanded Thorpe.

'Putting this bitch out of her misery.'

'Don't be a fool! We need her as a hostage.'

'No we don't,' Quested snapped back. 'She's brought me enough bad luck as it is. Got those forged papers, Mr Underwood?'

Ashen-faced and sweating, Thorpe's secretary nodded and patted the leather wallet-folder under his arm.

'Put them in my cabin on board the *Lucy Ann*.' Quested pushed Mrs Cafferty towards Utumate, who promptly held a knife to her throat. 'Kill me this bitch. Then meet me on board the *Lucy Ann*. We're leaving. Now.' He turned his back on them and set off walking across to the try-works.

'Where are you going?' demanded Thorpe.

'To make sure Killigrew's dead.' Quested strode off and left Mrs Cafferty with Thorpe, Utumate and Underwood.

'Turn away,' Utumate told Mrs Cafferty. 'You feel nothing, I promise.'

She shook her head. 'If you're going to murder me, Mr Utumate, at least have the courage to look into my eyes.'

He smiled. 'As you wish . . .'

She squeezed her eyes shut, waiting to feel the icy touch of the blade as it sliced her throat, but it never came. Instead she heard a click, and Underwood's tremulous voice. 'Put the knife down, Utumate.'

She opened her eyes. Underwood had pulled a small pistol out from behind the wallet and now he levelled it at the Polynesian.

'Mr Underwood?' spluttered Thorpe. 'Put that gun away, before someone gets hurt!'

'Before someone gets hurt!' echoed the secretary, laughing bitterly. 'So this kanaka here can murder the woman, you mean? Enough people have been hurt already, thanks to you.'

'Enough of this foolishness, Underwood. Put the gun down. That's an order.'

Underwood turned the pistol on Thorpe. 'I've taken enough orders from you, you lunatic. Don't you realise? Don't you understand? It's *over*.'

'Only for you.' Utumate punched the blade of his knife deep into Underwood's side, right up to the hilt. The secretary gasped as his blood pumped over Utumate's fingers, and as he crumpled the Polynesian prised the pistol from his limp fingers. Underwood slipped to the ground, and Utumate turned the pistol on Mrs Cafferty.

XXIV

Judgement

'Not so talkative now, *amigo?*' asked Forgan, propping his musket up in one corner of the sawmill. He had to shout to make himself heard above the clamour of the steam-engine.

'You pick a topic,' suggested Molineaux.

'All right. Why don't you start by telling us how the hell you vamoosed from Erromanga?'

'Why, it's just like Mr Killigrew said: we hitched a ride on a passing whale.'

'You know something? I'm glad you're not in a mood to co-operate.' Forgan nodded to Gog, who pulled a lever to set the sawblade, six feet in diameter, spinning. Another level engaged the ratchet that pulled the saw carriage Molineaux was tied to towards the blade. He looked at it fearfully between his feet, which were less than six feet from the cutting edge.

'You know, I don't care if you do talk,' shouted Forgan. 'I'm going to enjoy watching you get sawn in half. Any last requests, *amigo?*'

'Yur. You couldn't put me the other way around, could you? I'm kind of tender down there.'

'But that's the fun of it.'

The door opened and Lissak entered, carrying Utumate's tomahawk, the Polynesian's rifle over one shoulder. 'Gog, Magog?' he shouted hoarsely. 'Cap'n Quested wants a word with you two.'

The twins glanced at Forgan. 'Better go see what he wants,' the mate told them. They nodded and made for the door. Magog went straight out, but Gog paused and turned on the threshold. 'You gonna wait until we get back?' he asked, nodding to where Molineaux was tied.

'Sure. Go on. You know Cap'n Quested don't like to be kept waiting.'

Gog hurried out after his brother. Forgan turned to Lissak.

'Sometimes they're like a couple of big kids.'

'Some kids!' said Lissak. 'Er . . . aren't you going to turn the saw off?'

'That depends.' Forgan turned to Molineaux. 'Are you gonna tell me how you got away from Erromanga?'

Molineaux shook his head.

'Then I ain't gonna turn this machine off.'

'You'd better tell him what he wants to know,' Lissak told Molineaux. 'Otherwise I might have to do something drastic.'

Molineaux eyed the blade which spun less than three feet from his boots. 'Right now, Solly, whether or not you do something drastic is the least of my worries.'

Lissak nudged Forgan. 'I thought you said you were going to wait for Gog and Magog to get back?'

'I lied.'

Lissak nodded thoughtfully, and hit Forgan on the back of the head with the tomahawk. The mate crumpled. Lissak grinned at Molineaux. 'Not bad for an old man, eh?'

'Plummy,' agreed Molineaux. 'If you'd used the edge of the tomahawk, you might really have done some damage.'

'Hey! I'm a cracksman, not a croaksman. I save your life, and all you can do is complain?'

Molineaux was now less than a foot from the blade. 'You've come to save my life?'

'Well, sure I have, Wes. What, you think I hit him for the fun of it?'

'Then would you mind *switching this bloody thing off?*'

'Sorry!' Lissak looked at the machinery. 'How do I do that, then?'

'Pull the lever!'

'Which one?'

'How do I know which one? Pull them all!'

Lissak grabbed a lever and pulled it. Released from the ratchet, the carriage started to glide forwards under its own momentum.

'The other lever, you chucklehead!'

'You told me to pull them all!'

'Push it back and pull the other one!'

The saw sliced effortlessly through the ropes binding Molineaux's ankles together and his legs moved down on either side of it. He managed to brace the soles of his feet against the stanchions that held the axle on which the blade rotated.

'That was a close shave!' said Lissak, mopping his brow with a grubby handkerchief.

Molineaux glanced down to where the saw-teeth blurred barely two inches from his crotch. 'They don't come much closer,' he agreed. He pushed off the stanchions with his legs, propelling the

340

carriage back along the rails until he was clear of the blade. 'Now cut me loose!'

Lissak produced a pocketknife and sawed through the bonds on Molineaux's left hand.

'Behind you!' yelled Molineaux.

Lissak ducked instinctively and the tomahawk that Forgan swung at his neck passed harmlessly over his head. The old lag thrust at his stomach with the knife, slashing through his guernsey. Forgan dropped the tomahawk and clutched at the wound. 'You old sonuvabitch!'

Lissak tried to stab him again, but Forgan caught him by the wrist and forced his arm towards the spinning flywheel. With his free hand, Molineaux clawed frantically at the bonds on the other. Lissak could fight dirty with the best of them: he had taught Molineaux every trick he knew, but the most important lesson he had ever taught the black about fighting was that it was best avoided if at all possible.

But Forgan knew a few dirty tricks of his own, and he was much younger and stronger than the old lag. He forced Lissak's hand back until the blade of the knife struck the spokes of the flywheel and closed over the old lag's fingers. Lissak cried out and dropped the knife, blood dripping from his fingers. Forgan punched him in the stomach and started to force his head towards the flywheel.

At last the knot came untied and Molineaux swung himself down from the carriage. He tapped Forgan on the shoulder. 'Try picking on someone your own age.'

Forgan threw Lissak to one side and rounded on Molineaux. The seaman punched him on the jaw, but Forgan rode the blow easily and drove a fist into the seaman's stomach. Molineaux doubled up, raising his hands to protect his head while the mate relentlessly landed punch after punch against his ribs, driving him steadily back. Molineaux tripped over the tomahawk and sprawled on the floor beside the machinery. Forgan kicked him in the side.

'Get up, *amigo*! I'm going to do to your uppity hide what someone should've done a long time ago.'

Molineaux reached for the tomahawk, but Forgan kicked it under the machinery. Then he grabbed the seaman by his guernsey and threw him across the carriage. 'I'll cut you to the quick, boy!' he snarled, pushing the carriage towards the still-spinning blade.

'Let him go!' snarled Lissak. He had finally unslung the rifle he had brought with him, and levelled it at Forgan's head.

Forgan looked up. 'Put the gun down, you old fool, or I'll kill your pal here!'

'But you were going to do that anyhow!'

Molineaux saw Lissak's finger whiten where it gripped the trigger. 'No!' he screamed.

Lissak fired. The window behind Forgan's head shattered, and the mate laughed. 'You missed!'

'*I* won't.' Molineaux butted Forgan on the bridge of the nose, broke free, and did a backwards roll off the carriage to come down on the far side of the machinery. Forgan tried to grab him, but Molineaux caught him by the collar and dragged him across the carriage. With his free hand, he looped the still-hanging rope around Forgan's neck and tied it down.

'No!' screamed Forgan.

'*Adiós amigo!*' Molineaux gave the carriage a kick and sent it shooting along the rails to the blade. Blood fountained against the ceiling and Forgan dropped to the floor on either side of the machinery. Lissak winced.

'Are you oh-kay?' Molineaux asked him. 'Let me look at your fam.'

'My fam's plummy,' Lissak snapped pettishly, wrapping his handkerchief over his cut fingers. 'Why didn't you want me to shoot him?'

Ponderous footsteps sounded on the wooden stairs leading up to the mill. The door opened and the Lawless Twins entered, drawn back to the mill by the sound of the shot.

'That's why,' Molineaux said grimly.

'That *is* a nice shirt,' acknowledged Killigrew.

On the platform above the try-pots, Jarrett glanced up to where the lieutenant hung. 'Irish linen,' he said absently.

'Let's see now,' mused Killigrew. 'It can't be convict-issue, and somehow I doubt you found it amongst the pusser's slops on the *Lucy Ann*. Steal it from Cusack, did you? I expect Fallon arranged for some clothes to be brought on board the *Lucy Ann* for him.'

'If I were you,' said Wyatt, 'I'd be talking about how you got here from Erromanga. As soon as Quested gets back, we're going to start lowering you by inches into that blubber.' He opened the door to the furnace and scooped some fritters in to keep the fire roaring.

'Fortunate for you that the style is for loose-fitting shirts these days,' Killigrew continued, ignoring Wyatt. 'Cusack's a bigger man than you, Jarrett. But then, he's a gentleman. An aristocrat, even. Born on the right side of the blanket.'

'You're not getting to me, Killigrew,' sneered Jarrett.

'My shirt's tailor-made,' said the lieutenant. 'On Jermyn Street.'

Something snapped inside Jarrett. He lunged for Killigrew, but the lieutenant braced his feet against the rail of the platform and pushed himself beyond the reach of Jarrett's grasping hands. The swindler almost overbalanced and caught himself on the rail. Killigrew swung back and kicked him in the chest with both feet. Jarrett was thrown back against the rail behind him. Killigrew locked his ankles behind the swindler's head, and as he swung back over the try-pots once more he dragged Jarrett after him. Jarrett toppled over the rail and landed head-first in the try-pot without so much as a scream.

Boiling blubber splashed into the shallow cistern of water, narrowly missing Wyatt. He glanced up and saw Jarrett's legs sticking out of the pot. With a snarl, he snatched up a flensing knife and charged towards the stairs leading to the platform.

Killigrew managed to get his feet on the handrail. He teetered for a moment, struggling to get his balance. He leaped from the edge of the rail moments before Wyatt ran him through with the flensing knife, and swung across to the half-loft. He managed to hook his ankles over the edge of the loft and hung there for a moment, trying to get his centre of balance above his feet.

Wyatt threw the flensing knife like a spear. It whistled across the try-works, and missed Killigrew by inches to bury itself in the far wall. Wyatt snatched up the bomb-gun and took aim. Killigrew was helpless, hanging almost horizontal with his ankles on the half-loft and his bound hands still looped over the hook at the end of the pulley. At that range Wyatt could not miss.

He pulled the trigger. The hammer fell with a snap.

The percussion cap failed to go off. With a grimace of annoyance, Wyatt recocked the weapon, took aim again, and pulled the trigger. Again the hammer fell with nothing more than a snap.

Pulling himself up against the pulley, jerking his whole body, Killigrew managed to get upright. He teetered, and for a moment he thought he was going to fall back into his earlier, helpless position, but he managed to steady himself.

Wyatt threw the bomb-gun down to the platform and ran back down the steps, heading across the floor of the try-works to the ladder that led up to the half-loft.

Killigrew unhooked his bound wrists from the pulley, letting the chain swing back across until it hung over the try-pots once more, and crossed to where the flensing knife was embedded in the wall. As he used the two-foot blade to saw at the cord binding his wrists, Wyatt hauled himself up the ladder to the half-loft.

The cord snapped. Killigrew pulled the flensing knife from the wall and turned as Wyatt charged at him. The lieutenant jabbed the weapon at his face, holding him at bay until Wyatt slipped his guard and managed to grab the shaft of the flensing knife. The two of them grappled, chest-to-chest. Wyatt slammed Killigrew back against the wall behind him, pressing the shaft of the

343

flensing knife against the lieutenant's throat. Killigrew choked and felt himself blacking out as he struggled for breath. As his vision faded into a red mist, the last thing he saw was Wyatt's face grinning demonically.

'Don't worry, Wes,' Lissak told his young protégé. 'The bigger they are, the harder they fall.'

The two of them backed across the sawmill as the Lawless Twins advanced on them.

'Oh yur?' Molineaux snatched the rifle from Lissak. 'I seem to recall you always teaching me, "The bigger they are, the harder they hit you back".'

The Lawless Twins saw Molineaux trying to reload the rifle and charged. Lissak snatched a plank of sandalwood from a stack of timber and smashed it over Magog's head with such force that it snapped in two. Realising he did not have time to reload, Molineaux swung the stock of the rifle at Gog's head. The stock broke off, leaving the seaman clutching the breech and the barrel.

Now it was Gog and Magog's turn.

Gog picked up Lissak, raised him effortlessly above his head, and threw him against the wall. A section of the flimsy weatherboarding fell away, carrying Lissak with it, and the old lag dropped out of sight beneath the level of the floor.

Magog closed one of his huge hands over what was left of the rifle Molineaux held and snatched it from his grip. He bent the barrel into a U-shape and tossed it aside. Gog grabbed Molineaux by the shoulder and thrust him across the sawmill so that his head banged against the copper casing of the steam-engine's boiler.

His head throbbing, Molineaux sank to the sawdust-strewn floor feeling nauseous. It seemed to him that the sawmill was shaking. He looked up and saw the twins charging towards him. Molineaux scooped up a fistful of sawdust and dashed it in Magog's face. As the giant turned away, trying to rub the dust from his streaming eyes, Molineaux picked up two more pieces of timber and whacked them together on either side of Gog's head. Apparently unhurt, Gog grabbed a fistful of Molineaux's guernsey and lifted him up, tossing him back across the stack of timber behind him. The stack collapsed and Molineaux was thrown sideways across the floor in an avalanche of timber. He glanced across the room and saw Forgan's musket propped up in one corner, presumably still loaded. If only he could get to it, he could at least take care of one of the twins; then he might stand a chance of beating the other . . .

Magog stepped in front of him, blocking his view of the rifle. Molineaux rammed a piece of timber into the giant's crotch, with no discernible effect. Then Gog caught him by the scruff of the neck and hauled him on to his feet. He locked Molineaux in a full nelson, holding him fast while Magog rained blow after agonising blow into the seaman's stomach.

Molineaux's insides felt as if they had been pulped to liquid, but at last Magog paused for breath. Sobbing, Molineaux raised his head and found himself staring into the giant's hate-filled eyes.

'Give it to him, Magog!' said Gog. 'In the face!'

Magog drew back his fist, aiming a blow at Molineaux's head. The seaman jerked his head aside at the last moment, and Magog's fist crashed into his brother's nose. As Gog staggered back, Molineaux wriggled free of his grasp, but before he took two steps Magog caught him by the shoulder, spun him around, and punched him on the jaw.

Molineaux was thrown into the corner. Half-dead with the pain, he fumbled for the musket and levelled it at Gog and Magog as they advanced.

They stopped, backed up, and then moved apart, forcing him to swing the muzzle from one to the other and back again to keep them both covered. Gog grinned. 'One shot.'

Molineaux braced the stock of the musket against his shoulder and took careful aim. 'One is all I need.' He fired.

The bullet passed between Gog and Magog without touching either.

The pistol Utumate had taken from Underwood was tiny, but the muzzle looked huge as Mrs Cafferty stared into its stygian depths. Thorpe turned away; he might be able to order people to be killed, but he did not have the stomach to watch, let alone do his dirty work himself.

Utumate's finger tightened on the trigger. The sound of the shot was deafening. Mrs Cafferty gave a sob as blood flew in all directions. Her blood, she thought, and if she felt no pain it was because she was dead, she knew . . .

Except that she was not.

She looked at Utumate. His face had been turned to a mask of blood and mangled flesh by the blast of a shotgun at close range.

Thorpe turned and stared. 'Paddon!' he spat, in shock and hatred.

Mrs Cafferty twisted. A tall, lean man stood there with a shotgun in his hands, smoke curling from one of the barrels. Behind him stood a couple of dark-skinned natives, one armed with a harpoon, the other with a boat hook.

'Surprised to see me, Thorpe?' asked Paddon. 'Surely you didn't think you could go murdering natives all over these islands and putting the blame on me, without having to answer to me for it, did you? I've got bad news for you, fat man: it ends here.'

Paddon looked as though he was going to shoot Thorpe in cold blood – and Mrs Cafferty would not have condemned him if he had – but at that moment one of the natives with Paddon cried out a warning. 'Look out, Cap'n Jimmy!'

One of the *Lucy Ann*'s harpooners, Noah Pilcher, had appeared on top of the stack of barrels to one side of them, a musket levelled at Paddon. The trader fired first, and Pilcher dropped out of sight behind the barrels without so much as a cry.

Thorpe turned and ran. Paddon swore, and broke open his shotgun, loading both barrels with a couple of cartridges that he took from his pockets. 'I head him off, Cap'n Jimmy!' said the elder of the two natives. Hefting his harpoon, he ducked down the alley behind the try-works.

'Leave a piece of him for me, Moltata!' Paddon called after him.

Mrs Cafferty snatched the pistol from Utumate's dead fingers and turned it on Paddon. He glanced at her with amusement. 'You must be Mrs Cafferty?'

'And you are . . .?'

Before he could reply, a couple of shots sounded across the wharf, and the other native clapped a hand to his stomach and fell. Armed with muskets and pistols, the crew of the *Acushnet* charged towards them. Paddon picked off two with his shotgun, and then he and Mrs Cafferty ducked down behind the barrels. 'This ain't the time or the place for formal introductions, lady!' he hissed, struggling to reload his shotgun. 'Let's just say I'm a friend of Killigrew's.'

Before he could snap the breech closed, two white-uniformed sailors from the *Wanderer* – Owens and Appleby, the two men who had found Mrs Cafferty on the Isle of Pines – stepped around the barrels and covered them with muskets. Before they could fire, two more muscular natives materialised from the shadows behind them and dropped empty barrels over their heads, before picking up their muskets and using them to bring down two more of the charging spouters from the *Acushnet*. Paddon snapped his shotgun shut, stood up, and killed another two men. Suddenly there were nearly a dozen natives with Paddon. Realising it was time to rethink their strategy, the spouters started to withdraw to their ship.

'These bastards don't care for it so much when the natives start to fight back,' Paddon chuckled to himself, reloading his shotgun. 'Guevu, see if you and a couple of your lads can't work your way round that stack of barrels and retrieve those muskets they dropped. We'll try to keep their heads down,' he added, indicating the two natives who had helped themselves to Owens and Appleby's guns.

346

Guevu nodded and spoke urgently to two of the other natives before the three of them dashed out of sight.

'Where're Killigrew and Molineaux, ma'am?' asked Paddon.

'Molineaux's in the sawmill. Mr Lissak went to help him . . .'

A crash sounded from the sawmill. A section of weatherboarding fell away from the side, Lissak on top of it. Sprawled across the board, he slid down the planks that formed a makeshift ramp at the far end and lay still at the bottom.

'Butu!' Paddon called to one of the natives. 'You go helpim Molineaux!'

'*Ale!*' Butu started to sprint across the wharf, but before he reached the cover of the stacks of wood in front of the sawmill, a shot from the *Lucy Ann* took him between the shoulder blades and laid him low.

'Sonuvabitch!' Paddon whirled and shot the man who had killed the native. He shot another of the men on the *Lucy Ann* for good measure before ducking down behind the barrels next to Mrs Cafferty. He started to reload his shotgun once again; his pockets, which had bulged not long before, were starting to look decidedly limp. 'Looks like Molineaux's going to have to take care of himself for now. Still, he struck me as the kind of feller that knows how to handle himself in a scrap.'

Mrs Cafferty was not convinced. 'I saw Gog and Magog go in there a little while ago,' she said dubiously.

Paddon pursed his lips for a moment, and then snapped his shotgun shut. 'My money's on Molineaux. Where's Killigrew?'

'In the try-works.' She remembered that Quested had gone to kill him; and that she still had a pistol in her hand. 'I'm going to get him!' she told Paddon, and broke cover before the trader could argue.

'You crazy shaler!' Paddon shouted after her as she sprinted across the wharf with bullets flying all around her. 'Are you trying to get yourself killed? Come back here!'

Even as the bullet left the musket, Molineaux threw himself sideways, behind a stack of timber. He did not wait to see if his bullet had hit its target because he did not want to die. His ears told him everything he needed to know: a deafening clang as the bullet punctured the copper casing of the boiler, the brief hiss of steam escaping under pressure, and the godawful shriek of metal tearing as the casing of the boiler ruptured, hurling jagged shards of metal in all directions. He threw himself against the door and fell down the stairs on the outside as steam filled the sawmill. Red-hot pieces of metal riddled the wooden walls and rained down on all sides. Steam billowed from the opening at the far end of the building. The explosion had shaken the sawmill to its stilts, and the whole construction looked ready to fall down under the weight of the heavy machinery within.

Some kind of gunfight seemed to be taking place on the wharf, and Molineaux could see Paddon and the Tannese amongst the barrels stacked there, exchanging shots with the men on the two ships moored on either side of the jetty. Molineaux hoped they had the situation well in hand, because after his encounter with the Lawless Twins he did not feel up to being able to help. He crawled across to where Lissak lay, fearing his old mentor might be dead. But Lissak was only stunned. Molineaux patted him gently on the cheek until he started to show signs of life.

'You oh-kay?' the seaman asked him.

'Just plummy, thanks,' Lissak retorted sourly. 'What happened to the Lawless Twins?'

Molineaux grinned. 'They got all steamed up,' he could not resist saying.

'You sure they've croaked?'

Before the seaman could reply, the stilts on which the sawmill stood gave a creaking groan. The whole building started to move, the stilts giving way, the walls and roof falling in with a crash when the structure hit the ground. A cloud of dust filled the air.

Molineaux patted Lissak on the shoulder. 'I'm sure.'

As Wyatt throttled Killigrew with the shaft of the flensing knife, the lieutenant tried to knee him in the crotch. Wyatt merely twisted and caught the blow on his thigh.

He grinned. 'Think you can beat me like that, pretty boy? While you were learning which fork to use, I was learning how to stay alive on the back streets of London.' He tried to butt Killigrew on the bridge of the nose, but the lieutenant saw it coming and brought his own head forwards to meet it. It stopped the blow from gathering its full momentum, and Wyatt's forehead struck him on the brow rather than the bridge of the nose, but lights exploded in Killigrew's head and he felt sticky blood trickle down his face from a cut eyebrow.

He rammed a heel down against Wyatt's instep. Wyatt instinctively lifted the foot up with a yelp, throwing himself off balance, and Killigrew pushed him away. Wyatt managed to tear the flensing knife from the lieutenant's grip, however, and thrust it at his stomach.

Killigrew leaped from the half-loft and hit the floor below, rolling over. By the time he rose, Wyatt had jumped down after him and thrust at him with the flensing knife once more. Killigrew backed up and stumbled when his ankles tripped over the low stone wall

348

surrounding the cistern in which the try-pots stood. He landed on his back in the shallow pool of water, and Wyatt tried to bring the blade into his stomach. Killigrew rolled clear, and kicked Wyatt's legs out from beneath him. The incorrigible lost his grip on the flensing knife as he went down.

Quested appeared in the doorway. Seeing Wyatt and Killigrew wrestling in the shallow water, he levelled his revolver at the lieutenant.

Wyatt saw him. 'Don't you dare!' he snarled. He was on top of Killigrew now, trying to force his mouth under the surface, but the water was too shallow. 'This bastard's mine!'

'Get on with it, then!' Quested snapped back. 'We're leaving now, with or without—' He broke off at the sound of shots from the wharf, and alarm showed on his face. He pointed his revolver at someone outside and squeezed off half a dozen shots. Either he was a bad shot, or he was being attacked by several men; but Killigrew saw one Tannese warrior appear in the doorway and grapple Quested. The native was the stronger of the two, but Quested just buried his hook in his opponent's neck. Blood gouted, and the native slithered to the floor. Quested jerked his hook out, and tucked his revolver in its holster.

Wyatt sat astride Killigrew's chest, belabouring his face with his fists. Killigrew reached up until his left hand grasped the handle of the cast-iron door of the furnace beneath the try-pots. The metal was hot enough to burn him, but that was the least of his worries. He swung it open, smashing it into Wyatt's face.

Quested broached a barrel with his hook and kicked it over so that a tidal wave of whale oil washed across the floor of the try-works. Killigrew was about to charge across to grapple him when the captain lifted an oil-lamp from a nail driven into one wall.

'See you in hell, Killigrew!' He threw the lamp at the floor. The oil burst into flames at once, creating a wall of fire between Killigrew and the door. Quested waved mockingly at him through the flames, and then disappeared from sight.

Killigrew heard a sound behind him and turned to see that Wyatt had retrieved the flensing knife. The lieutenant nodded to where the burning oil continued to spread through the try-works, licking against the barrels in the adjoining godown. 'I'd say we've got about one minute to get out of here before this whole place goes up in flames!'

'One minute is all I need to kill you, pretty boy!' Wyatt thrust the flensing knife at Killigrew. The lieutenant side-stepped and caught Wyatt by the shoulder, slamming him against the side of the furnace. The shaft of the knife snapped. Killigrew tried to seize the incorrigible in an arm lock, but Wyatt rammed an elbow into his

349

stomach. Winded, the lieutenant stumbled back, and Wyatt turned to face him.

'I don't need a weapon to kill you!' he snarled, and showed Killigrew his fists. 'These are my weapons!' He punched Killigrew on the jaw, spinning him round. The lieutenant almost staggered into the puddle of blazing oil. He rallied and turned back, just in time for Wyatt to step up to him and punch him in the stomach.

Killigrew doubled up in agony. Wyatt linked his hands together and brought them down in a sledgehammer-like blow on the back of his neck. Killigrew felt his legs crumple, and he sprawled on the floor. Wyatt kicked him in the ribs.

He tried to stamp on Killigrew's neck, but the lieutenant rolled clear, swivelled on his back, and aimed a kick at Wyatt's kneecap. He missed, catching him on the calf instead, but it was enough to make the incorrigible reel.

'Still got some fight left in you, pretty boy?' Wyatt asked with a grin as Killigrew pushed himself to his feet. 'Well, that's good. I wouldn't want this to be too easy.'

Killigrew ran up the first few steps to the platform, and then turned to aim a kick at Wyatt. The incorrigible caught him by the ankle and twisted his leg. Killigrew sprawled on his back on the steps, and then kicked Wyatt in the face with his other leg. Wyatt teetered and almost fell back into the flames that had swamped the foot of the stairs, but he caught hold of the handrail and managed to steady himself. Killigrew turned and ran the rest of the way up to the platform, but Wyatt caught him again and drove a fist into one of his kidneys. Killigrew gasped in agony, and Wyatt seized him by the throat, driving him back against the handrail. The flames licked all around the platform now, and Wyatt tried to tumble Killigrew over into the inferno. He bent down to grab Killigrew by the ankles, and the lieutenant kneed him in the face. Wyatt was thrown against the handrail at the top of the steps.

Killigrew saw the bomb-gun lying on the boards at the far end of the platform and tried to make a dash for it, but Wyatt caught him by the shoulder and pulled him back. He spun him round, and started to belabour him with his fists. The incorrigible pounded Killigrew with all the precision of a prizefighter, taking him apart slowly and scientifically. Killigrew tried to protect his head with his hands, so Wyatt went to work on his stomach and ribs, pummelling away relentlessly.

'Some hero!' sneered the incorrigible. 'You ain't so tough. What does it feel like to lose, pretty boy?'

'You tell me,' gasped Killigrew, putting all his strength and concentration into one punch to Wyatt's face. The incorrigible's nose was flattened and blood gushed from his nostrils as he staggered back, but he was still on his feet and he stood between Killigrew and the bomb-gun. He raised an arm to his nose and then looked at the blood on his sleeve. 'You sonuvabitch!' he snarled. 'Now I'm really going to have to hurt you!'

Killigrew straightened painfully and braced himself for Wyatt's next onslaught. 'Somehow I doubt it. You fight like a girl, Wyatt. Four years on Gomorrah Isle hasn't toughened you – it's emasculated you!'

Wyatt roared in rage and charged. For a moment Killigrew thought he had miscalculated, but the incorrigible started to swing his fists wildly, with none of his earlier precision. When his blows landed, they were even more agonising than before, if such a thing were possible. But he was getting sloppy now, leaving more openings, and Killigrew took advantage of them, fibbing Wyatt on the ribs before landing a facer that stunned Wyatt long enough for the lieutenant to duck under his flailing arms and run to the far side of the platform.

Reaching into a pocket with one hand, he snatched up the bomb-gun with the other and levelled it at Wyatt.

The incorrigible laughed. 'Dud percussion cap, Killigrew, remember?'

With his left hand, Killigrew took the box of matches he had taken from Thorpe earlier out of his pocket. He managed to get one match out of its box, accidentally dropping the rest into the fire below in the process. That left him only one chance to get it right.

Wyatt stared at him in bewilderment, wondering what he was doing. Killigrew snicked the match with his thumbnail, but it refused to spark.

Realisation hit Wyatt, and he started to charge across the platform. Killigrew snicked the match again, and this time it fizzled into life.

He thrust the flame into the chamber of the bomb-gun.

'No!' screamed Wyatt.

The powder charge flared and the bomb shot from the muzzle, embedded itself in Wyatt's chest, and exploded, splattering pieces of the incorrigible all over the walls and ceiling.

The recoil slammed Killigrew back against the handrail behind him. The rail snapped and he almost fell through. He managed to catch hold of a piece of the rail that was still intact and saved himself from falling into the flames below.

He tried to climb down from the platform, but the flames blocked his path at the bottom of the steps and the heat drove him back. Through the fire and smoke he could see through the door to the adjoining godown where flames licked all around the barrels of oil stacked there. Standing in the cistern, the platform was an island in

351

a sea of burning oil; but now even the wooden beams which supported the platform were starting to burn. There was no way out across the floor, which only left one possible chance.

He looked up. The block and tackle overhead hung from a joist that ran to the half-loft over the door where the mincing tubs stood. Killigrew grabbed the chain, hauled on it . . . and the partially burned rope tied to a hook at the far end snapped. The chain ran out of the block to gather in his arms.

He swore, and then swung the chain like a leadsman sounding a lead line. The chain shot over the joist on the first try, and rattled back down to the platform on the other side. Killigrew made one end of the chain fast to the handrail, gripped the other . . . and then the platform finally collapsed. As it crashed into the flames below, Killigrew was dragged up to the roof. For a second or two he thought his fists would be smashed against the joist, but then the platform had hit the floor. He stopped only inches from the joist, and then dropped back a couple of inches as the section of handrail to which the chain was made fast started to break away.

Killigrew hauled himself up the last foot with less than a second to spare. He wrapped his arms around the joist just as the chain dropped back down again.

The smoke was much thicker immediately below the ceiling, stinging his eyes and clawing at his lungs. He managed to pull himself up until his feet were on the beam, then picked his way carefully across until he could drop down on to the half-loft.

Mrs Cafferty ran towards the blazing try-works. She was almost there when Quested stepped out of the smoke that drifted across the wharf. He caught her with his right hand, spun her round to face Paddon, who was running up behind her, and held his hook to her throat.

Paddon raised the stock of his shotgun to his shoulder. 'Let her go, Quested!'

'Shoot me with that thing, you'll kill the girl too.' Using her as a human shield, Quested backed across the wharf towards the jetty. Paddon followed, keeping his shotgun levelled at Quested's face, but there was nothing he could do.

Dragging Mrs Cafferty after him as he backed towards the jetty, Quested picked his way across the wooden tracks that led to the try-works. 'Shoot him!' Quested told the handful of men who lined the *Lucy Ann*'s gunwale, a mixture of sailors from the *Acushnet*, the *Wanderer*, and the *Lucy Ann* itself.

Paddon dived for cover behind a stack of barrels that was instantly riddled by a fusillade of shots from the *Lucy Ann*. Mrs Cafferty pushed the hook away from her throat and tried to break free, but Quested caught her by the wrist.

'Gangway for a naval officer!'

Silhouetted by the inferno behind him, Killigrew emerged from the first-floor hatch of the try-works, pushing the truck before him. As it started to gather momentum on the inclined ramp, he jumped into it.

The heavy wheels rumbled on the wooden tracks as the truck hurtled down towards the jetty. Realising he was standing right in its path, Quested let go of Mrs Cafferty and tried to throw himself aside. But now she caught him by the wrist, and dragged him back on to the tracks.

Hurtling towards them, Killigrew clambered over the truck until he was able to perch on the front of it. When he was only a few feet away, he launched himself from the truck and caught Mrs Cafferty around the waist, knocking her clear.

The truck slammed into Quested. It lifted him off his feet and he clutched at it instinctively, burying his hook in its side. Then he remembered the buffers waiting for him at the end of the jetty and tried to throw himself clear, but his hook was caught fast. The truck slammed him against the buffers, which smashed under the impact. Quested, truck and pieces of wood all flew off the end of the jetty to sail out over the lagoon and the truck hit the water with a tremendous splash.

A dull thump sounded a moment later as a barrel of oil exploded in the godown, which now burned as fiercely as the try-works. A heartbeat later two more barrels burst in rapid succession, and then they all went up with a huge roar. Fire blossomed in all directions, and burning barrels were thrown high into the sky, trailing flames. The ground seemed to shudder, and the walls of the try-works and godown burst outwards as the inferno sought to escape in all directions. It roared over the rooftops of Thorpetown like a towering afreet, billowing, twisting and turning as it faded into smoke and spiralled up towards the night sky. Killigrew and Mrs Cafferty flinched as pieces of burning debris rained down all around them.

When they straightened, nothing but burning ruins was left of the try-works, the godown, or indeed any of the buildings which had stood within fifty yards of them.

After the deafening thunder of the explosion, the silence which followed was broken only by the sound of hammers being cocked on pistols and muskets. The men on the deck of the *Lucy Ann* levelled their weapons at Killigrew and Mrs Cafferty.

'Kill them!' snarled Thorpe, stepping on to the jetty. 'Kill them both!'

XXV

Redemption

Killigrew held up a hand. 'Are you sure you want to do that? I mean, in front of all these witnesses?'

Thorpe thought he was referring to the sailors on the *Lucy Ann*, and chuckled. 'Oh, I think I can rely on these fellows to maintain silence on the matter of what really happened here tonight.'

Captain Pease cocked the hammer of his revolver.

'I think you should look behind you,' said Killigrew.

Pease grinned. 'No more tricks, Killigrew. This is where it ends.' He levelled the gun at the lieutenant's forehead.

As the *Vanguard* silently glided in astern of the *Lucy Ann*, Midshipman Cavan swung from a brace, swooping across the quarterdeck and hitting Pease in the back with both feet. Pease staggered against the rail and went over, landing heavily on his face on the jetty, the revolver skittering from his hand.

Then the bluejackets were swarming over the *Lucy Ann*'s taffrail. Ågård grabbed two of the *Wanderer*'s white-uniformed sailors by the throats, lifted one off the deck in each hand, and then banged their heads together. As the rest of the bluejackets levelled their muskets, the *Wanderer*'s chief mate – the supercilious Mr Irwin – threw down his pistol, and the rest of the men took their lead from him.

Killigrew disguised the feeling of relief that swamped over him with a show of dusting himself down and adjusting his cuffs. 'Your timing is impeccable, Mr Cavan.'

'Didn't think we'd let you have all the fun, did you, sir?' the midshipman replied with a grin, as Paddon appeared behind Thorpe and prodded him in the back with the barrels of his shotgun.

'Fun, he calls it!' groaned Molineaux, staggering on to the jetty with Solomon Lissak.

At the top of the *Lucy Ann*'s gangplank, Ordinary Seaman

Endicott levelled his musket at Lissak. 'Not another step, matey!'

'It's all right, Seth,' Molineaux said wearily. 'He's a friend. Foxy, this is Seth, one of my shipmates. Seth, meet Foxy Lissak, my old partner in crime.'

'He'll still have to go back to Hobart Town for trial,' Killigrew said firmly.

'Oh, come on, sir!' protested Molineaux. 'He saved our bacon back on Erromanga; and if he hadn't rescued me at the sawmill just now, I'd be half the man I am now.'

'I'll see to it that's taken into account, Molineaux,' said Killigrew. 'I'll act as a character witness myself at his trial, if necessary. I'm sure we can arrange for the lieutenant-governor to have Mr Lissak pardoned.'

'You mean, he'll go free?' asked Molineaux, his face lighting up.

'Pardoned for the crime of trying to escape from one of Her Majesty's penal settlements, I mean. You're forgetting he's still a convicted criminal. He'll go back to Norfolk Island to serve out the rest of his term.'

'But, sir! He's an old man. He won't live another year in a hellhole like Norfolk Island . . .'

'Calm down, Wes!' said Lissak. 'Your Mr Killigrew's right. I'm an incorrigible; I've got to be punished for my sins. Don't blame yourself for what happened. If I really hadn't wanted to do that one last job, neither you nor anyone else could've persuaded me to; not even Sammy the Swell. I made the one mistake I always warned you against. Got greedy, didn't I?'

He walked across to stand in front of Killigrew, looking him up and down contemptuously. 'And don't blame the lieutenant here, either. He's got his duty to do. And he'll carry it out without question, come hell or high water; even if it means sending a feeble old cove like me to an early grave. Take a good look at him, Wes. This is one of your new friends. You sure you want to go on being a lagger? You don't want to go back to the old life?'

Molineaux hung his head. 'I'm sorry, Foxy. But I made my mind up a long time ago.'

'Then I reckon I've got no choice.' With a swiftness surprising in one so old, Lissak managed to snatch up Pease's revolver and moved behind Killigrew, pressing the muzzle to his forehead. 'Tell your men to put down their weapons!' he snarled in Killigrew's ear.

'Sorry, Lissak. You know I can't do that.'

'Wes!' From the deck of the *Lucy Ann*, Endicott threw a musket to the able seaman.

Molineaux caught it, adjusted his grip and levelled it past Killigrew's shoulder at Lissak's face. 'Put the barker down, Foxy.'

'So you can drag me back to the Isle of Mis'ry? No, thank you, Wes.'

356

'It doesn't have to be Norfolk Island,' pleaded Molineaux. 'We can have you transferred to Port Arthur for the rest of your bird-lime, maybe even get you a soft job in Hobart Town as a . . . as a . . . I dunno, as a locksmith or something. Ain't that right, sir?'

'It's not up to me, Molineaux,' said Killigrew. 'But I can promise to put a good word in for him.'

'Oh, *sure*.' Lissak rammed the muzzle of the revolver harder against the lieutenant's head. 'He says that *now*, when he's got a barker to his noddle. But you can't trust anyone these days, can you?'

'He wouldn't say it if he didn't mean it,' said Molineaux. 'For God's sake, Foxy! If you don't trust him, at least trust me!'

'Didn't I always teach you? Never trust anyone! Least of all when they've got a barker in your face! Drop the musket, Wes. Maybe then we can talk.'

'I can't do that, Foxy. Put the gun down. It's over.'

'I ain't going back to Norfolk Island, Wes. I'd rather die first.'

'If you don't drop that barker by the time I count to five, it might just come to that.'

'Then start counting, damn you! Maybe the lieutenant here could put in a good word for me. Maybe it might get me transferred. But it's going to take time for the paperwork to go through. And all that time I'll be back on the Isle of Mis'ry. You think that bastard John Price is going to let me live long enough to get transferred? So you pull that trigger, damn you! Better a quick death from a bullet than a slow, painful one on Norfolk Island.'

Molineaux's face glistened with tears in the firelight. 'Please, Foxy! Don't make me do it.'

'Yes, Wes. You. I can take it from you, but not from that bastard Price! If I'm to die, let me die here and now: a free man.'

'Please, Foxy! I'm begging you! Anything but this!'

'Yes, Wes! Do it! Pull the trigger, damn you!'

'No!'

'Or I'll blow this bastard's brains right out, I swear!'

'Don't do it, Foxy! Didn't you teach me that cramping coves was a lay for flats?'

Lissak sighed. 'If that's the way you want it . . .'

Killigrew flinched at the sound of the shot, sure his hour had come. Then the gun was gone from his temple, and Lissak's body crashed to the planks of the jetty. Killigrew glanced down at him. Molineaux had drilled the old lag right through the centre of the forehead.

The seaman turned away and threw the musket into the lagoon with a gesture of disgust. Killigrew took a step towards him, to thank him, but Mrs Cafferty stopped him. 'Leave him.'

He saw the sense of that, and nodded.

357

Everyone else breathed again. Cavan started rounding up the prisoners on the deck of the *Lucy Ann*. 'Wait a minute, where's Thorpe?' demanded the midshipman.

'Ran off while you lot were watching what was going on on the jetty,' said Paddon. 'Don't worry, Moltata's gone after him.' He pointed to where Thorpe's rotund figure was climbing the steps to the blazing house. Moltata ran across the plaza after him, carrying a harpoon.

Thorpe had reached the top of the steps and was about to run into the jungles behind the house when Moltata threw the harpoon. The barbed iron flew true, and Thorpe's figure jerked as it was skewered. He stood motionless at the top of the steps, and then pitched over. The wooden shaft snapped off the iron at once, and Thorpe rolled over and over, tumbling down the steps until he bounced past where Moltata stood and pitched up at the foot of the plinth on which his own statue stood. The *yeremanu* crossed to where he lay, checked the trader was dead, and straightened and began walking back to the jetty, seemingly satisfied.

'What about the rest of the incorrigibles, sir?' asked Cavan.

'Wyatt did our job for us as far as Blake was concerned,' said Killigrew. 'I got Jarrett and Wyatt. That's three.'

'I got Griddha and . . . Lissak . . .' said Molineaux, in control of himself once more. 'What about Vickers?'

'I got him,' said Mrs Cafferty, without looking up from where she sat on a barrel, staring down at the planks of the jetty.

'*You* killed him?' asked Cavan. 'Good God!'

'I shot him,' she said wearily. 'I don't know if he's dead. You'll find him in the alley beside the sawmill . . . what's left of it.'

'Better go check,' Cavan told Ågård.

'Aye, aye, sir.' The petty officer hurried off to investigate.

'That's still only six,' said Molineaux. 'Who've we forgotten?'

'Cusack,' said Killigrew.

'My God!' exclaimed Cavan. 'The most important of them all! Endicott, check below decks. See if you can find him in any of the cabins.'

'Aye, aye, sir.' The Liverpudlian descended the after hatch.

Strachan climbed down to the jetty from the *Vanguard*. 'Everything under control?' he asked. 'Good. Anything I can do? Anyone hurt?' He looked at Killigrew's face, one half of it covered in blood from the cut behind his eyebrow. 'You're bleeding,' he observed, taking out a handkerchief and wadding it.

'I'll live.' Killigrew took the handkerchief from him and pressed it to his brow. 'But you might look to some of Moltata's people.' He nodded to where Moltata's son Guevu stood, clutching a wounded shoulder.

'Of course, of course!'

Ågård returned from the sawmill. 'I found him,' he assured them. 'Vickers, I mean. He's dead. Poor bastard bled to death.' He gave Mrs Cafferty a wary look.

'Don't waste your time praying for his soul,' said Killigrew, putting a comforting arm around Mrs Cafferty's shoulder. 'He was a rapist. He got what he deserved, and he's burning in hell for it now.'

'If you believe in that heaven and hell nonsense,' snorted Strachan, binding Guevu's wound.

A thud ran the length of the jetty as someone leaped from the forecastle of the *Acushnet* on to the planks. Without pausing, the figure turned and sprinted across the wharf.

'Who was that?' asked Cavan. 'Hi! You! Come back here!'

Endicott appeared at the rail above them, a massive bruise swelling around his left eye. 'Sir! Sir! That's was him!'

'Who?'

'The Paddy, sir! Cusack! I found him tied up in one of the cabins. I started untying him, and he planted one on me!'

'He won't get far,' snorted Cavan. 'Mr Cusack seems to have forgotten we're on an island!'

'What about the trading station at Havannah Harbour?' asked Mrs Cafferty. 'What if there's a ship there?'

'Want me to go after him, sir?' asked Ågård.

'No!' Killigrew stood up, and then stooped to take the revolver from Lissak's dead hand. 'Cusack's mine!'

'Leave him, sir,' said Endicott. 'He ain't worth it.'

But Killigrew was already running down the jetty after Cusack.

The Young Irelander ran through the back streets of Thorpetown and plunged into the jungles beyond. He knew about the trading station at Havannah Harbour, but first he had to shake off his pursuer. It was not long before the fires that raged in Thorpetown were far behind him, and he had only the light of the waning crescent moon and the stars to guide his way. He stumbled blindly through the foliage, following the slope upwards. The further inland he went, the further he was from Thorpetown; and he hoped that the steeper path would discourage Killigrew, who must have been exhausted as it was.

But nothing would shake off the lieutenant. Just as he had chased the carriage across Norfolk Island, just as he had chased the *Lucy Ann* across the Pacific Ocean, now he pursued Cusack on foot every bit as relentlessly. In that moment, Cusack understood what made Killigrew the man he was. He might not be the most intelligent officer in the Royal Navy; he might not be the strongest, or the

359

toughest, or the most skilled with pistol or cutlass. But he was a man who would never, ever give up; not until his final, dying breath rattled in his throat. That single fact alone made him more frightening than the hate-filled Wyatt or the deranged Captain Quested.

Cusack ran on and on as the darkness faded, giving way to dawn. He was tiring now, but still fresher than Killigrew. Nevertheless, the lieutenant stayed close behind him, neither gaining nor falling behind. Cusack crested a rise and stumbled down a slope until his feet splashed into a stream. He followed the stream, wading ankle-deep, the absence of foliage in mid-stream giving him a clear path. The walls of the gully suddenly grew steep on either side, until suddenly Cusack found himself standing on a precipice. The water cascaded out over the rocks to plunge into a pool nearly sixty feet below, gleaming like spun silver in the early morning light.

A dead end.

He turned back, and saw Killigrew standing ten yards behind him, levelling a revolver at his head. 'Halt! Halt, or I'll fire!'

Cusack felt utterly defeated. 'I had a feeling you'd come after me, Admiral,' he sighed. 'I'd hoped you wouldn't, but I knew you would. I think even when I first met you that night on Norfolk Island, when I realised Fallon had come to rescue me, I knew you to be the kind of man who'd chase me to the ends of the earth.'

'Sorry, Cusack. It's nothing personal. I'm just doing my duty.'

The Irishman nodded. 'Well, I'm not going back to Norfolk Island alive, so I guess you'll just have to shoot.'

'One last chance, Cusack! What's it to be?'

'You can give me a hundred chances if you like. This is the way it has to be. I've made my choice: now you make yours.'

'So be it.' Killigrew took careful aim, and fired.

There were twenty-eight prisoners in all by the time the *Tisiphone* steamed into the lagoon at first light: two men from the *Lucy Ann*, including the cook; Captain Pease and fifteen of his men from the *Acushnet*; and nine from the *Wanderer*. They would all be taken back to Hobart Town to stand trial for their part in the whole business. It would take months to unravel the mess, and the lawyers would get fat, so at least someone would benefit.

While Robertson was interviewing Cavan in his day room until Killigrew came back, Molineaux stood on the upper deck and cast a glance at the smoking ruins of Thorpetown. If anyone had told him when he had first met Solomon Lissak twenty-two years ago that their relationship would come to an end on an island in the South Seas, he would have laughed at them; he did not feel like laughing now.

Had Foxy deserved to die? Plenty would have said 'yes' to that,

360

but perhaps no one who had known him. Some said you shouldn't judge a man, that was up to God and Saint Peter. But Molineaux was not a religious man, and if he did not believe in God, then who was left to sit in judgement on men? Senile old fogies in ridiculous wigs? Twelve good men and true? Whatever people said about the rights and wrongs of sitting in judgement, the fact was that people judged each other's actions every day of the week, no matter how much they denied it; that was human nature; and only a fool failed to act on his own judgement.

He wondered briefly how someone might have judged himself: then he realised that he did not much care, one way or another. He was Wes Molineaux, able seaman, and that was good enough for him.

He caught sight of something in the water out of the corner of his eye and saw a figure swimming for the side ladder below the entry port. The man swam awkwardly, as if he had injured his left hand and was unable to use it.

'Foxy?' Molineaux muttered it to himself, hardly daring to hope. Even though he knew he had killed Lissak, part of him still could not believe the old lag was dead: he had escaped from so many tight spots in the course of his life, it was impossible to believe that he could not somehow escape death; even if he were in Hell, he was probably digging a tunnel to Heaven.

Then Molineaux saw the shark's fin cleaving through the water behind the swimmer at an almost leisurely pace. 'Shark!' he yelled. 'It's a shark! Swim for your life!'

Strachan joined him at the entry port. 'Jings! It's a *Carcharodon carcharias*!' he exclaimed.

'No, sir,' said Molineaux. 'It's definitely a shark.'

The swimmer reached the side ladder and got his right hand on the lowest rung. Molineaux hung down from the entry port to take his left, but when the man took it from the water he saw it was a hook. Grinning savagely, Captain Barzillai Quested caught it over the next rung, and used his right hand to take the pistol from his mouth. He levelled it at the seaman. Molineaux gasped and made to reach for his Bowie knife, but Quested had him cold.

Then something slammed the captain violently against the side of the hull. He gasped and dropped the pistol, grabbing for one of the rungs, but he was pulled down until he was chest-deep in the waves. Only his hook, implacably caught on the rung of the side ladder, held him above water. He screamed in agony as he was swirled about, now being pulled away from the side of the ship, now being smashed against its side.

Robertson, Strachan and Mrs Cafferty emerged from the after

361

hatch and joined the crowd at the bulwark. 'Dear Lord!' gasped Mrs Cafferty. 'Who is it?'

'Quested,' said Molineaux.

'Isn't anyone going to help him?' asked Strachan.

'I'll kill the first man who tries!' snarled Paddon.

Then Quested was gone, pulled under the water, leaving only a trail of bubbles and a cloud of vermilion in the water beneath the side ladder.

Molineaux dashed across the deck and peered over the far bulwark into the water between the hull and the jetty. 'Watch both sides!' he yelled. 'He might have swum under the keel!'

'Molineaux!' snapped Strachan. 'The poor devil's just been attacked by a great white!'

'If he has, then that shark's going to get a nasty case of indigestion,' said Molineaux. 'On the other hand, maybe that's just what he wants us to think.'

'Well, I can't see him,' said Robertson.

'Wait!' said Mrs Cafferty. 'There's something caught on the side ladder.'

'Can you see what it is, ma'am?' asked Robertson.

'No, it's too far down.'

'Molineaux!'

'Yes, sir?'

'Climb down there and see what that is.'

'Down there, sir? You must be joking! Begging your pardon, sir, but I ain't climbing down a ladder hanging over water where I've just seen a man eaten by a bloody great shark!'

Strachan sighed. 'I'll get it,' he said, easing himself backwards through the entry port.

'Be careful, sir,' said Molineaux. 'That was a man-eater.'

'No such thing,' snorted Strachan. 'Human beings aren't sharks' natural food; if we were, they'd've died out long ago. A shark might bite a man to see what it tastes like, but they rarely come back for a second helping.' His feet on the bottom rung of the side ladder, he squatted down to reach for the strange object that hung there. 'Jings!'

'What is it?'

'Quested's hook.' Strachan held it up for them to see.

'Eurgh!' said Mrs Cafferty. 'Throw it away!'

'Doesn't anyone want it as a keepsake?'

'Spare us your anatomy-school humour, Strachan,' growled Robertson. 'And get back up here, before—'

A great white shape surfaced with a spray of water immediately beneath the assistant surgeon. He lost his grip on the side ladder and fell into the water with a cry.

It was Sharky. The *nakaimo* climbed up the side ladder and strolled casually across the deck. Strachan swam back to the side and followed him up.

Molineaux exchanged glances with Strachan. 'Sir, you don't suppose that shark—'

'No,' Strachan said firmly. 'I don't.'

'But you have to admit, it looked rum . . .'

'Mere coincidence,' sniffed Strachan. 'There's a perfectly rational explanation for everything. Quested swam out to the ship; the shark attacked him; the shark swam away; Sharky climbed on board. That's all we saw, because that's all that happened. Now, if you'll excuse me, gentlemen, I'm going down to the gunroom to change into some dry clothes.'

'He's right, of course,' said Robertson. 'Our imagination's running wild, that's all. We're all overwrought and overtired; it's a miracle we're not seeing pink spiders.'

'I suppose you're right,' Mrs Cafferty agreed dubiously.

Molineaux glanced up to where Sharky sat in the rigging. The *nakaimo* took his jew's-harp from his mouth to grin at the seaman. It was probably just a trick of the light, but Molineaux could have sworn there was blood on Sharky's teeth.

A few minutes later, they heard the sound of a distant shot from somewhere inland.

'Killigrew,' said Molineaux.

'Or Cusack,' Mrs Cafferty replied, pale-faced.

Cusack flinched, and stared down at his body in the half-light as if searching for a bullet wound. When he did not find one, he raised his eyes to meet Killigrew's with an expression of bewilderment.

'You're dead,' Killigrew told him. 'Do you understand me? I'm going back to Thorpetown now; I'll be telling Commander Robertson I killed you. So if Devin Cusack turns up in the United States a few months from now on a lecture tour, inciting rebellion in Ireland against the Crown, my career will be over. That means I'll have a lot of time on my hands, and believe me I'll use every last minute of it to hunt you to the ends of the earth and finish what we started back on Norfolk Island.'

Cusack had only one question: 'Why?'

'Why?' echoed Killigrew. 'I don't know. Perhaps some of the things you said to me on board the *Lucy Ann* the day before yesterday made a lot of sense. Or perhaps I just think there's been enough slaughter and bloodshed for one day.'

Cusack grinned with relief. 'God bless you, Admiral. You're a darlin' feller!' He started to turn away, but Killigrew called after him again.

'Cusack! I'm giving you a second chance. Not many of us are lucky enough to get one, so use it well if not wisely.'

'And you do the same, Admiral!' Cusack turned back to the precipice, and before Killigrew could stop him or even say another word, the Irishman had stepped out into space and dropped out of sight.

Killigrew ran to the precipice, and then took a step back instinctively from the dizzying drop. The stream gushed over the edge and fell in a long, silvery cataract that plunged down into the pool far below, and even as Killigrew peered cautiously over he saw a white splash blossom outwards where Cusack had hit the water close to the foot of the waterfall. He did not expect to see the Irishman surface, but he did, swimming back to the shore and pulling himself out on to the rocks.

Killigrew found himself smiling. 'And it's "lieutenant", you sonuvagun!'

He walked back to Thorpetown, heading for the pall of smoke that hung over the south side of the island. He started whistling 'Oh, Susannah' to himself.

'Please, do take a seat, Commander Robertson.' In the superintendent's office on Norfolk Island, John Price pulled a chair out for the commander.

'It's all right; I don't intend to stay any longer than necessary. I have to get back to Hobart Town to make my report to Sir William Denison and Captain Erskine.'

'Surely you can stay for dinner?'

Robertson shook his head. 'Thank you, Mr Price, but I've had just about as much of this island as I can stomach.' He threw the seven manila folders on to the desk. 'You can close these now.'

'Wyatt?'

'Dead.'

'Jarrett?'

'Dead.'

'Blake? Lissak? Vickers and Griddha?'

'Dead, dead, dead and dead.'

Price hesitated before asking his next question, as if hardly daring to hope. 'Cusack?'

'Dead.'

The news of Cusack's death would create an uproar in Irish communities across the globe. There would be accusations of excessive brutality by the Royal Navy; some would even claim that the escape had been a set up, designed to rid the British authorities of the problem of Devin Cusack. But from the broad smile on Price's face, he clearly did not consider that his problem.

'What about the men who helped them to escape? Captain Quested and the crew of the *Lucy Ann*?'

'Quested's dead. So are most of his men; the rest I've got secured on board the *Tisiphone*. They'll stand trial in Hobart Town.'

Price chuckled. 'I've got to hand it to you, Robertson. You certainly don't pull your punches, do you?'

'Don't thank me,' the commander retorted drily. 'If it had been up to me, I'd've taken them all back to Hobart Town to stand trial. But things didn't work out that way. Lieutenant Killigrew . . . well, perhaps if I'd been through the ordeal he had, found himself in the situation he did, I'd've acted no differently. It's not my place to judge him. And as Captain Keppel warned me when he recommended Killigrew as my second lieutenant, he's no worse than God made him.'

'What about Mrs Cafferty?'

'I'm taking her back to Hobart Town. It seems she doesn't want to work as governess to your children after all.'

'Damn the governess position! That bitch tried to kill me!'

'That's not the way she tells it. She tells me she threatened to kill you – a serious offence, I'll grant you, but there are mitigating circumstances – but that she did not have the desire to carry it out.'

'Attempted murder, Robertson! That's a capital felony! She must be made to stand trial.'

'A trial could be embarrassing for you, Mr Price. I've seen the way you like to parade up and down right in front of your convicts with your pepperboxes tucked in your belt, taunting them to try drawing one.'

Price drew himself up to his full height. 'It's strength of will that runs this island, Robertson, not guns and whips. I know those dogs are too cowardly ever to try it.'

'Of course, if word got out that a mere chit of a girl could get the better of you with a pistol, don't you think that one or two of your charges might get the same idea?'

Price blanched at the thought.

'Your time's running out, Price,' Robertson said contemptuously. 'You can't get away with the kind of brutality you've been using to run this place for ever. Sir William and Dr Hampton might be prepared to turn a blind eye to your conduct, but when I get back to Hobart Town I intend to raise such a stink the public will demand your dismissal. If you're lucky, perhaps you'll be allowed to resign and live the rest of your days on a comfortable pension. If you're unlucky, one of these days you're going to push one of your charges too far, and he'll put a stop to your brutality before anyone else does. But one way or another, you're going to get your comeuppance. I met some wild savages in the New Hebrides; but none of them was as savage as you are.'

Price snorted contemptuously. 'You don't frighten me, Commander Robertson. My position here is secure. Have you quite finished, or is there anything else?'

'Just one other thing.' Robertson smashed his fist into Price's face. The monocle flew from the commandant's eye, and he crashed to the floor. 'Get up! I haven't finished with you yet.'

White-faced with fear and anger, Price shook his head.

'Just as I suspected. You're nothing but a bully, Price. A loathsome bully who takes pleasure in the suffering of others. Not so pleasant when someone gives you a taste of your own medicine, is it? Consider that a down payment on your eventual comeuppance. Good day to you, sir!'

The *Tisiphone* steamed back into the Derwent Estuary one week later. She anchored in Sullivan's Cove and, within the hour, Killigrew was escorting Mrs Cafferty ashore in the second cutter. The two of them sat in the stern sheets while the crew pulled on the oars.

'You know, you handled yourself quite well back there at Thorpetown,' said Killigrew.

She arched her eyebrow. 'For a woman, you mean?'

'For anyone. If I was the marrying kind—'

'No, thank you! I like my independence too much. And so, I suspect, do you.'

'What will you do now?'

'I don't know. I stopped living after my brother died and my husband was killed in Afghanistan. I'm starting to think it's time I started living again. How about you?'

'The same. You know, I expect the *Tisiphone* will be tied up here in Hobart Town for a couple of weeks. I don't know when the next ship departs for England, but it could be several days . . .'

'I'm not in any hurry to go anywhere.'

'Capital! Perhaps I could have the honour of calling on you at your hotel?'

'I think I should like that very much.'

He moved to kiss her, but then became aware of the grins of Molineaux, Endicott, and the other men pulling at the oars. 'Look to your oars, lads,' he growled. Taking his cap from his head, he held it up to hide his and Mrs Cafferty's face from them as he kissed her.

'Oh! Mr Killigrew!' she protested. 'Well! At least now I know what the "I" stands for.'

He grinned. 'Irresistible?'

'Incorrigible!'

Historical Notes

The south-west Pacific certainly seems to have been a lively place in the mid-nineteenth century. The Royal Navy had a negligible presence in the South Seas at the best of times during these years, and between 1843 and 1846 most of this was concentrated in New Zealand, where shore parties from HMS *Hazard* and other vessels were helping the army in the First Maori War. Certainly the navy was too busy to send any vessels to New Caledonia or the New Hebrides to protect British traders against attacks from natives – or vice versa. But all that changed in 1848, when HMS *Dido* was dispatched to New Caledonia as part of a cruise of the South Seas to investigate incidents relating to Benjamin Boyd's trade in island labour and accusations of slavery.

The inspiration behind Thaddeus Thorpe, Boyd was a man who cropped up again and again in some of the diverse sources I read while researching this novel, including a book on whaling in the South Seas, the biography of an admiral of the fleet, an account of the sandalwood trade in the New Hebrides, a history of the Royal Yacht Squadron and even a dictionary of surnames! Boyd sailed his yacht the *Wanderer* into Sydney Harbour in 1842 and over the next nine years tried his hand at a variety of money-making schemes: sheep-farming, whaling, sandalwood, and shipping indentured labour.

He built his own settlement, Boydtown, at Twofold Bay on the south-east coast of Australia, setting up his own magistrates and printing his own currency. He employed the artist Oswald Brierly – later Sir Oswald – to manage his whaling station there. Brierly was a fine artist but a poor manager, and the station did not last long. The lighthouse built there was never lit because Boyd forgot to get permission to light it, and before long it was known as 'Ben Boyd's folly'.

Captain Maxwell of the *Dido* failed to find any proof against

Boyd, perhaps because he was, it is said, too afraid to land at the Isle of Pines, even though Captain James Paddon had established a trading station on the island the previous year. Boyd sailed to California to take part in the gold rush at the end of 1849, but like all his other schemes that too proved to be pie in the sky. He was killed in 1851 – either on Guadalcanal or Guam, depending on which source you read – but all agree he was killed by the natives while trying to establish his own private empire.

The Royal Navy paid another visit to these waters in 1849, this time in the shape of HMS *Havannah*, which visited the New Hebrides to investigate a clash between Samoan sailors on an American sandalwood ship and the natives of Éfaté: the Samoans had chased the natives into caves, and there lit fires outside to suffocate them with smoke. Although a later generation of naval officers would respond to such difficulties by bombarding native villages, Captain J. E. Erskine of HMS *Havannah* – a member of the Aborigines Protection Society – seems to have been more tolerant, and made a real effort to investigate the matter fully. But since he did not arrive in the New Hebrides until seven years after the event, and the white population of the islands was mobile in the extreme, his chances of bringing anyone to justice were negligible.

Barzillai Quested was inspired by Captain Edward Rodd, an alcoholic, one-eyed, one-handed, blunderbuss-wielding sandalwood trader, who had sustained his injuries in a fight with natives in New Caledonia. Rodd was accused of seizing the natives from Tanna and selling them to the Erromangoans in exchange for sandalwood (a trade which seems to have been two way) in the late 1840s. Whether or not the accusation was true was never satisfactorily established, but one has to wonder about any man who chose to call his trading ship the *Terror*. Another source of inspiration was Captain White, 'the vindictive man who would wait in the bush for days to shoot an islander against whom he had a grudge . . . probably the same White who, when master of the *Deborah* late in 1851, shot a young chief on board his ship at Tana [*sic*] after some high words had passed between them.'*

Whether or not there is any truth in the stories of traders kidnapping natives to sell them for sandalwood we will probably never know; but if they are true one trader who can be absolved was Captain James Paddon. He established his trading station on Inyeug in 1844, having purchased the island from the natives of neighbouring Aneiteium in return for an axe-head and some

---

* Dorothy Shineberg, *They Came for Sandalwood: A History of the Sandalwood Trade in the South-West Pacific 1830–1865*, Melbourne University Press, 1967, pp. 91–2.

blankets (the natives had no use for it, believing it to be haunted). Paddon purchased a steamship and cannibalised it for parts to build his steam-powered sawmill, and did a roaring trade in sandalwood, whale oil, ship's provisions, and *bêche-de-mer*, as well as meeting a demand amongst the natives for jew's-harps. Today he would be condemned for having cheated them with worthless baubles, but they do not seem to have complained at the time. While many missionaries perished at the hands of the natives of these islands (not Geddie: by learning the natives' language, he succeeded in converting three thousand natives on Aneiteium to Christianity over the course of thirteen years), Paddon seems to have enjoyed good relations with the natives, and eventually married one.

Although Paddon helped Geddie set up his mission at Aneiteium in 1848 by providing the frame for the mission building, the two of them soon clashed. Geddie's protests strongly hinted that Paddon and the other traders on Inyeug were enjoying carnal relations with native girls, and he abhorred Inyeug as a den of every kind of vice. If the Presbyterian Geddie seems to have been excessively puritanical, forbidding his flock from dancing, smoking, drinking *kava* and taking part in traditional ceremonies, he should be given credit for discouraging the local custom of strangling wives on the death of their husbands; although, as with *suttee* in India, the wives seemed to resent this interference.

Paddon, meanwhile, expanded his operations to include a second trading station on the Isle of Pines in 1847. He helped to set up a Roman Catholic mission on the island two years later, perhaps as a way of getting back at the Presbyterian Geddie. Eventually – inevitably – the sandal trees were logged out in the New Hebrides, and Paddon moved to Grande Terre in New Caledonia and took up cattle farming.

The *Naghol*, or 'land-dive,' was peculiar to the natives in the south end of the island of Pentecost for many years. It is still carried out by the natives, but has recently become a more widespread practice, with an elastic cord known as 'bungee' substituting for yam vines.

Devin Cusack is a fictional character, although inspired by William Smith O'Brien and Thomas Meagher. Despite the desultory nature of their uprising at Ballingarry in 1848, O'Brien and his associates became heroes of the Irish people, perhaps because of the martyrdom of their transportation to the colonies of Australia. There can be no doubt that their original sentences of death by hanging, drawing and quartering were excessively harsh, even by the standards of the age, and one can only suspect the British authorities ordered these penalties so that they might appear merciful when these sentences were later commuted to transportation for life.

Although the Young Irelanders defied Daniel O'Connell's objection to the use of force in the cause of Irish freedom, their hearts do not seem to have been set on it if the low body count of the rebellion is any indication. Only two men were killed outside the Widow McCormack's house on Boulagh Common near Ballingarry, both of them rebels. O'Brien always professed loyalty to Queen Victoria to the end of his days, and only ever argued for repeal of the Act of Union. He was horrified by the activities of the more hard-line Fenian Society that emerged in the 1860s, which unhesitatingly used assassination as a means to put pressure on the British Government; what the Young Irelanders would have made of the atrocities committed by both sides in Ireland during the twentieth century can only be guessed at.

Of the Young Irelanders transported to Van Diemen's Land (renamed Tasmania in 1856), O'Brien was the first to be the subject of a rescue attempt. The only one of them who refused to give his parole, O'Brien was incarcerated on Maria Island. If his living conditions were not what he had been accustomed to as an aristocratic gentleman in Ireland, as a political prisoner and something of a celebrity he enjoyed better conditions than the ordinary convicts transported to Australia, and certainly nothing like as bad as propagandists in Ireland and the United States suggested. He had a small cottage to himself within the prison grounds, and became good friends with his gaoler, a Kildare Irish Protestant named Lapham, and even better friends, it was scandalously alleged, with Lapham's young daughter Susan.

O'Brien was permitted to go for walks on the island, as long as he was accompanied by a convict constable. It was on one such occasion, on 12 August 1850, that the master of the *Victoria*, a small vessel that sometimes supplied Maria Island, with the encouragement of the Irish Directory in New York, sent a boat ashore to rescue him. O'Brien had been told to expect such an attempt, word having been passed to him from Thomas Meagher, then on parole on mainland Van Diemen's Land, who had helped to organise the escape.

As soon as the boat drew near to the shore, O'Brien dashed in the sea and tried to swim out to meet it, but being weighed down by his clothes he got into difficulties and almost drowned. A second constable appeared, armed with a gun, and ordered the crew of the boat ashore. They complied, and O'Brien had to be dragged out of the surf. Once back on shore, he promptly sat down in the beached boat and refused to be moved; so the constables ordered the boat's crew to carry him back to the prison, and O'Brien suffered the ignominy of being dragged back to his gaol by the very men who had come to rescue him. The master of the *Victoria*, Captain William Ellis, turned out to be a ticket-of-leave man who had served fourteen years for piracy. He and his chief mate were fined £60 each.

The first of the Young Irelanders to escape successfully was Terence Bellew MacManus, who did so with the aid of a lookalike who substituted for him, enabling him to be smuggled on board a ship bound for San Francisco in February 1851. Thomas Meagher escaped in January 1852. While waiting to be picked up by the *Elizabeth Thompson* – the same ship that had rescued MacManus – from a deserted island off the coast of Van Diemen's Land, he saw an eight-oared boat approaching. At first he thought it was the police, come to drag him back, but when the eight men came ashore it soon became apparent they were escaped convicts. They kept him company until the *Elizabeth Thompson* arrived three days later. Meagher gave them all the money he had out of gratitude for their kindness to him before going aboard, while they continued their journey to the newly discovered goldfields of Australia.

Like MacManus, Meagher was welcomed as a hero in the United States: he went on to serve with distinction with the Union Army in the Civil War, rising to the rank of Brevet Major General. After the war, he was appointed acting governor of Montana, where he seems to have become involved in some kind of local feud reminiscent of the enmity between the Clantons and the Earps in Tombstone, finally dying in mysterious circumstances by falling (or being pushed?) from a paddle-steamer on the Missouri River in 1867.

One of my favourite accounts of an escape from the penal colonies of Australia is that of John Mitchel, who had been transported for 'sedition' some weeks before the Ballingarry uprising. His escape in 1853 was aided by another Young Irelander, Pat 'Nicaragua' Smyth, who had been involved in the uprising but had evaded arrest and escaped to the United States. All the Young Irelanders were gentlemen who took their word of honour very seriously, so Mitchel marched into the police station at Bothwell, and handed a note retracting his parole to the local magistrate (a copy of which he had also forwarded to Sir William Denison). It was tantamount to announcing his intention to escape, except that in the time it took the magistrate to finish reading the note, Mitchel calmly walked out of the police station, jumped on to a horse and rode off with 'Nicaragua' Smyth. Smith O'Brien himself did not escape, however: 'Nicaragua' Smyth was planning to spirit him away also when news arrived that Lord Palmerston, then Home

371

Secretary, had granted him a pardon conditional only on his never returning to Britain.*

Norfolk Island was (and is, of course) a real place. It was first settled as a penal colony in 1790, and abandoned in 1814; it was re-established ten years later as the *ne plus ultra*, the final sanction against irredeemable convicts – the 'incorrigibles' – short of the death penalty. When reading about the sufferings of the criminals transported in the late eighteenth and early to mid-nineteenth centuries, it is worth remembering that the worst criminals were still executed – those who were transported tended to be petty thieves, prostitutes, and con men, with an admixture of Chartists and trade unionists such as the Tolpuddle Martyrs for good measure.

Having read about both Norfolk Island and the more infamous Devil's Island in some depth, I can assure the reader that life on Devil's Island was a tea party at the vicarage compared to life on 'the Isle of Mis'ry'. The spread-eagle, the scavenger's daughter, the water pit, the frame and the tube gag: all these instruments of torture were in use on the island at one time or another during the first half of the nineteenth century. The colony suffered from a succession of vicious and sadistic commandants (and one or two good ones, including Major Maconochie, who was years ahead of his time as a penal reformer, and thus dismissed for being too 'soft').

One reads of punishments of thirty-six lashes of the cat-o'-nine-tails being handed out for 'having a tame bird', 'pushing a lot with his foot' or 'being at the latrine when the supper bell rang'. Punishments of 200 lashes and upwards were not uncommon; a death sentence to ordinary men, but few of the men who made it through the British penal system of the early nineteenth century to end up on Norfolk Island could be called 'ordinary'. Yet despite the island having been chosen because its geographic remoteness rendered it escape-proof, some convicts *did* escape, including one party of seven who drifted as far as Maré, one of the Loyalty Islands, in an open boat in 1844: five of them were promptly eaten by cannibals.

The rescue of Cusack from Norfolk Island by a whaler was inspired by an event that actually took place much later, in 1876. An American whaler, the *Catalpa*, was purchased outright by the Clan Na Gael, the successor organisation to the Irish Directory. The captain of *Catalpa*, George B. Anthony, succeeded in rescuing six Fenians from Fremantle Prison and carrying them to California,

* For the full, true story of the Irish rebels transported to Australia, their various escapes, and their subsequent adventures – at times as exciting as any adventure novel – I can heartily recommend Thomas Keneally's *The Great Shame: A Story of the Irish in the Old World and the New*, Chatto & Windus, 1998.

even stopping to hunt whales on the way to offset the cost of the voyage. Anthony was not an Irishman, but neither was he a mercenary, and he seems to have been motivated out of genuine sympathy for the Irish cause. It need hardly be pointed out that Quested was in no way based on him.

I cannot close without a mention of John Giles Price. The last commandant of Norfolk Island, he was probably the worst. I hope my portrait of him is a faithful one, right down to the two pepperboxes tucked in his six-inch wide leather belt, his monocle and his beribboned straw boater. He believed his skill at handling convicts lay in his ability to understand how their minds worked and to speak their cant; and he certainly instilled the fear of God in them with his savage punishments. To be fair to him, he seems a man of many contradictions, alternately referring to his charges as 'desperadoes' and his 'children'. He had a similar ambivalence to his work, proud of his skill as a penal colony commandant but at the same time wanting to raise his family in a more congenial atmosphere.

In 1852, the Roman Catholic Bishop of Hobart Town, the Right Reverend Dr Robert William Willson, paid a third visit to Norfolk Island to inspect conditions there. Either Price had grown worse in the three years since the bishop's last inspection, or this time he made less of an effort to cover up his atrocities: Willson's thirty-page report to Lieutenant-Governor Denison pulled no punches. When Price saw it, he apparently burst into tears and begged the bishop to suppress it, but to no avail. By now the system of transportation was in its long-overdue death throes – Norfolk Island was to be closed down as a penal settlement, and Price was happy to leave. The Secretary of State for the Colonies read the bishop's report, but decided that no censure should be passed on Price: the whole business was swept under the carpet.

And there it might have ended: yet another case of one of history's great villains getting away with it, and spending the rest of his days in comfortable retirement. Price became a gentleman farmer in Van Diemen's Land for a while, but within a year he had accepted a new post as inspector-general of penal establishments in Victoria. There, where his responsibilities included running five prison hulks moored in the port of Melbourne, he resorted once more to the most sadistic excesses of Norfolk Island.

The historian Robert Hughes tells us what happened next far more eloquently than I could ever hope to:

On March 26, 1857, Price paid an official visit to the quarry at Williamstown where gangs of hulk convicts were labouring. He had come, as his office demanded, to hear their grievances;

and with his usual bravado, he walked straight into the midst of them, escorted only by a small party of guards. A hundred prisoners watched him marching up the tramway that bore the quarried stone from the cutting-face to the jetty. Quietly they surrounded Price, and their circle began to close. There was a hubbub of hoarse voices, a clatter of chains, a scraping of hobnails on stone. Rocks began to fly. The guards fled; Price turned and began to run down the tramway when a stone flung from the top of the quarry-face caught him between the shoulder blades and pitched him forward on his face. Then, nothing could be seen except a mass of struggling men, a frenetic scrum of arms and bodies in piebald cloth, and the irregular flailing of stone-hammers and crowbars.*

To end on a lighter note, and included for no reason other than the fact I have been discussing escapes from the British penal colonies in Australia – and because a good anecdote always bears retelling – I should make mention of William Hunt, an actor who tried to escape from Port Arthur by disguising himself as a kangaroo. His costume was convincing enough to fool two guards, and he might well have made his escape had the guards in question not decided they had a hankering for 'roo stew for their supper. How they reacted when the kangaroo put its paws up and pleaded 'Don't shoot, I am only Billy Hunt!' is not, sadly, a matter of historical record.†

* Robert Hughes, *The Fatal Shore: A History of the Transportation of Convicts to Australia, 1787–1868*, The Harvill Press, 1987, pp. 550–1.
† *Ibidem*, p. 406.